Playing
St. Barbara

Playing
St. Barbara

A Novel by Marian Szczepanski

High Hill Press, USA

High Hill Press
www.highhillpress.com

First High Hill edition: 2013
10 9 8 7 6 5 4 3 2 1

Cover Art:
St. Barbara
Painted by Michele di Ridolfo del Ghirlandaio (1503-1577)
Vesta Mine No. 1, Jones & Laughlin Steel Corp. Photo Collection
Reproduced with permission from the Heinz History Center Library/Archives
Front cover image by Mo Ulicny, The Peach Tree Studio
Cover design by High Hill Press
ISBN: 978-1-60653-077-1
Library of Congress Number in publication data.

For Carolyn, Emily, and Hilary –

always a source of inspiration.

...one secret is liable to be revealed in the place of another that is harder to tell, and the substitute secret when nakedly revealed, is often the more appalling.

Eudora Welty
One Writer's Beginning

Chapter 1: Deirdre

Deirdre Sweeney saw him first.

She sat on the hillside above The Hive's baseball field, where the fans' silence further thickened the cinder-ridden air. It was the bottom of the ninth in the season's home opener, and The Hive, defending Frick League champions, trailed Buffington by two runs. Holding breath and tongues and a dwindling sense of hope, everyone surrounding Deirdre had eyes only for the batter's box. A peculiar glint, however, lured her gaze away from the field. Disbelieving her eyes, she blinked, stared, then blinked again. No miner had thrown a stone, much less walked off the job since the Big Strike's eighteen miserable months had ended last October. Still, there was no denying that a new policeman stood beneath a wizened crabapple tree ten yards or so behind the home team's bench. His badge shone as if placed in the path of a sunbeam. The sun, however, hid behind the smoke of three hundred beehive-shaped coke ovens that had given the patch its nickname. Surrounded by stinking haze, the shimmering badge seemed all the more unsettling.

A groan arose from the quilts that patchworked the grass. Deirdre glanced back at the field, where The Hive's lead-off batter had just struck out. She was dimly aware of her two sisters and Mutti, her mother, murmuring behind her. Of pit boss Big Bill Keating, the next batter, taking his stance. Of an exultant cicada-hum rising from the slope above left field, where revenge-bent Buffington fans hoped to upset the team that had deprived them of last year's trophy. At seventeen, Deirdre still took pride in the fact that she could recite the score of each championship game since the league began. Now, however, her meticulous box score slid, crumpled, into her pocket. More pressing than balls and strikes and even, unthinkably, a loss was the presence of the stranger slouched against the crabtree. He wore a military cap like that of the Coal and Iron Police, but his uniform was forest green instead of navy. She'd heard Pap say that the governor had recently changed the Cossacks' uniforms, not just their name. Irrelevant changes, since the new Industrial Police performed the same cruel duties: abusing strikers, evicting families, and dumping their furniture into the muddiest ditch at hand.

Deirdre heard Mutti gasp an instant before the bat's *crack!* Countless breaths caught, then released. A foul ball. A collective sigh. Mutti's chapped hand closed around Deirdre's shoulder and turned her around.

While the bosses' wives showed off permanent waves and crisp new dresses, Mutti's appearance confirmed her status as a downhiller missus—and an exceptionally deprived one at that. From her frayed straw hat to scuffed shoes, she appeared as faded as an old flour-sack towel. All but her cheeks, stained a hot red. "Do you see him?" she whispered. Releasing Deirdre, her fingers hovered, then closed into a fist. The hand nesting in her lap contracted, too, turning as compact as an egg, as hard as a stone. "*Gott bewahre, nicht wieder,*" she said, her tone no longer a wary church-murmur. God forbid, not again.

Under ordinary circumstances, Deirdre would have shushed Mutti, who'd carelessly broken Pap's rule against speaking what he called *Kaiser-talk*. Under ordinary circumstances, Mutti wouldn't risk a beating if Pap found out. But anyone with any sense knew that an Industrial Policeman appearing out of thin air meant that circumstances in The Hive had changed without warning from ordinary to God-knows-what.

Flanking Mutti, Deirdre's sisters Katie and Norah sat with parted lips and paling faces. Apple butter sandwiches lay, abandoned, in their laps. Their conversation dispersed like wind-blown ashes. They could not have appeared more shocked than if they watched a hundred Klansmen, led by the mine Superintendent, march down First Street in broad daylight.

Katie pressed against Mutti, gnawing a hank of auburn hair. "Did the Cossack come to arrest Pap on account of the union?" Her voice quavered as if she were two, not twelve, and about to graduate eighth grade.

"The union's dead," Norah replied, maddeningly matter-of-fact. A mere eleven months older than Deirdre, Norah acted as if a paltry year of employment at the Company store made her

2

privy to bosses' closed-door conversations, as well as the latest patch gossip. "Pap hasn't said a word about it since we left the tent camp. If he had, the white-hoods would be burning crosses again." She looked pointedly at Deirdre, inviting contradiction.

Deirdre longed to take the bait. *How do you know what Pap does or doesn't say? Do you hide under a table in the speakeasy every night and eavesdrop?* Instead, she jabbed a finger at the policeman. "Then what's *he* doing here?"

Predictably, Norah ignored the unanswerable question, preferring to scold Katie, whose knees had churned the quilt and upset a jar of lemonade. Deirdre turned back to the field, clamping her lips like the mangle through which Mutti fed each Monday's dripping wash. She stared at the officer's cap-shadowed face until pain flickered between her eyebrows. Perhaps his expression would hint at his purpose—though never had a Cossack been accused of good intentions. As if sensing her scrutiny, he nonchalantly removed his cap, revealing hair even redder than Katie's. Again, Deirdre blinked. Nineteen, maybe. Twenty, at most. Her surprise at his youth dissolved when, in quick succession, he wiped his brow, replaced the cap, and pulled a long, dark club from his belt.

She was startled when The Hive's bench whooped and hollered. Big Bill had made it safely to first. The tallest player off the bench slapped his glove against the metal fence, and the links reverberated with a jittery clang. That player was her pap—Finbar "Steamshovel" Sweeney, arguably Fayette County's best first baseman. The workhorse of a miner every boss in the Frick League dreamed of adding to his ball team. And the tireless union agitator who became a thorn in the side of every boss who did.

For the first time that afternoon, The Hive's half of the hillside rang with cheers. Spicy breath warmed Deirdre's cheek. A whisper tickled her ear. "Where are you looking?"

The whisperer was her best friend Rosie, who'd absconded with her lunch from the Tonelli family's quilts spread further uphill. Discreetly, Deirdre pointed, then caught the bread and sausage that slipped from Rosie's hand. Her shoulder trembled against Deirdre's. The Coal and Iron Police had beaten Rosie's brother and reduced her family's backyard bake-oven to rubble during last year's strike. "His uniform is different," Deirdre said, handing back Rosie's sandwich, "but he's a Cossack, just the same."

Rosie batted away the food. "*Madre Maria*, he is going right to your papa."

Katie crawled between Deirdre and Rosie. "Can the Cossack hit Pap if he's not on strike?"

The Cossack will do whatever the bosses say. Before the words escaped, Deirdre caught Mutti's eye, wide with worry—and warning. If the wrong person overheard her bad-mouthing the bosses, Pap could be reassigned to the mule barn or lose his baseball bonus.

By now, everyone on the hill gaped at the Cossack and the billy club slapping his palm. The same question passed from quilt to quilt. *Where on earth is Deputy Harrison?* The Hive's longtime security guard knew better than to brandish a weapon for no good reason.

Incredibly, no one on the field seemed to notice the Cossack slowly approaching the home team's bench. The Hive's pitcher Stan "Shorty" Dvorsk, who occupied the batter's box, relentlessly hit his opponent's curves and sliders into foul-ball territory. Mr. Donovan, the weigh boss, warmed up on the first baseline. He and Big Bill were the only ball-playing upperhillers, and, like Big Bill, he swung his bat with a boss' authority.

Putting her arm around Mutti, Norah grimly predicted the obvious. "When Pap sees that club, all hell's going to break loose."

Deirdre found herself on her feet, hauling Rosie up with her. If she managed to distract the Cossack, maybe, just maybe, Pap wouldn't slap her the next time she missed a spot when scrubbing the front porch. Before Norah could grab or Mutti could forbid, she ran downhill with Rosie, muttering nervously in Italian, close behind.

Zigzagging around baskets and blankets, she took in a low-flying turkey buzzard's view of the patch, whose official name—Heath—was used only on maps. To the north: The Clean Hill, dotted with spacious, single-family boss houses. To the south: No. 2's mine yard, surrounded by smoking beehives that fried coal into coke to fuel Pittsburgh steel mills. Towering above the ovens were the slate dump and The Dirty Hill, its stunted foliage withered by half a century of incessant smoke. Between the hills: rows of diamond-shingled double houses separated by rutted alleys and streets made of packed-down mine waste called red dog. A glaring misnomer, since the streets, like the downhillers' houses and all that surrounded them, couldn't claim any color but that of soot.

In vivid contrast, the policeman's green jacket stood out like a Christmas tree planted directly behind Pap. Stone-faced, he ignored his teammates, who cast wary glances at the Cossack and each other. His gaze fixed on the field, where the catcher called time and jogged to the mound to confer with the pitcher.

Deirdre longed to dash, screeching like a banshee to startle the Cossack into dropping his club, but her pace slowed halfway down the hill. Though lacking demarcation by so much as a bush, boundaries of the boss families' viewing area were scrupulously observed, even by greenhorns fresh off boats from the Old Country. Shortcutting through this sector required a cautious tread, an obsequious smile, and oh-so-polite greetings to each boss, his missus, and children, whose everyday clothes were far nicer than what Deirdre wore to church. Rosie followed on Deirdre's heels, echoing *hello* like a well-trained parrot. Rosie had good enough English to be counting the days, like Deirdre, till high school graduation, but she turned hopelessly tongue-tied in the presence of even one upperhiller *signora*.

They smiled and nodded at Assistant Superintendent Phelan and his family, who ignored them. Mary Margaret Donovan, however, actually responded to Deirdre's greeting, obliging her to stop and pay extra homage to the weigh boss' daughter. "Is Steamshovel going to win us another trophy this year?" asked Mary Margaret, her tone oozing syrup. She ran a careless hand through sunny, Marcel-waved hair, the latest concession from a doting mother. Her Norma Shearer body, enviably curvaceous, shifted restlessly on the crazy quilt. The aroma of her condescension nearly overwhelmed the cloying florals of Mrs. Donovan's Arpege cologne.

Deirdre glanced at the officer, who pointed his club at the back of Pap's head. "How can he think about baseball when a goddamn Cossack is trying to scare the daylights out of him?"

Mrs. Donovan's plump jaw sagged. In the ensuing beat of silence, Deirdre realized that she'd committed two mortal sins: cursing, and in front of an upperhiller. Mary Margaret, too refined to comment on, much less react to the faux pas, directed her attention to the ovens' murky billows. A mix of outrage and humiliation enveloped Deirdre. She needed to sally forth, to sound an alarm, but her feet, two wretched traitors, balked.

Mrs. Donovan stopped sputtering long enough to warn, "Deirdre Sweeney, when your mother hears about this, she'll march you straight to the confessional."

"That's Billy McKenna, the new patrolman," said Mary Margaret. She pointed a languid finger, its pink-lacquered nail unacquainted with a washboard or garden soil. "He'd be awfully close to handsome if his hair wasn't as red as a stop sign."

The club appeared to graze Pap's head. Rosie squeaked like a rusty hinge when it lifted, then dropped into the Cossack's open palm. When it rose again, Deirdre realized that the sound had come, not from Rosie, but her own constricted throat.

"The superintendent thought Deputy Harrison needed an assistant," Mary Margaret went on. Even on the brink of a donnybrook, Mary Margaret would make sure to remind Deirdre that the Donovans lived high enough on The Clean Hill to know what the Big Boss was thinking.

Again, the club lifted. Unable to restrain herself, Deirdre shouted, "Pap! *Run!*"

Snickers rose around them. Every upperhiller eyed the shrieking banshee who'd used her tongue to cut her throat. Sweat gathered in the small of Deirdre's back. Which was worse—the Cossack striking Pap, or Pap hearing his own daughter publicly advocate cowardice?

Pap's chin jerked. He'd heard. Rosie's arm crept around Deirdre's waist. If not for that support, she'd have dropped to the ground like a brittle brown leaf.

6

Mary Margaret persisted, her tone implacably patient. "Mr. Phelan hired Billy last week. Didn't you know?"

Of course, Deirdre didn't. Such knowledge was the privilege of upperhillers. Deirdre knew only the ugly and obvious—how the paint was peeling on the three wooden crosses marking her brothers' graves; how the Klan's horses sounded at night, galloping down First Street to scare the Negroes and Catholics; how shabby her made-over missionary-box frock appeared, much less the skinny body it clothed, compared to that of Mary Margaret.

The catcher rose and signaled the pitcher, who aborted his wind-up. One by one, everyone on the field turned and stared at The Hive's bench, where Pap and his teammates sat, rigid as statues. Just behind them, the Cossack's club quickened the pace of its dance.

"Play ball!" someone hollered from the hillside. The sound struck Deirdre's chest like a wild pitch. Rosie's arm tightened around her.

Pap's thick brows lowered, reducing his eyes to shadows. His mouth tightened until his lips all but disappeared. This was the face that prompted Mutti to step in front of Deirdre and her sisters before he removed his belt. The face he wore when he staggered home from the speakeasy, swearing and insensible to the damage his coal-blackened hands and heavy boots were doing, and to whom.

Deirdre gasped when Pap leaped from the bench, spun, and snatched the club. The surprised Cossack teetered, but held onto his weapon. He squared himself to face Pap as Big Bill and Mr. Donovan stalked toward the fence. The crowd rumbled like a wagonload of slate emptied onto the dump. The sound died when Pap abruptly released the club. The Cossack stumbled backward. Dust billowed around his boots. When he regained his balance, he returned the club to his belt and, with exaggerated slowness, began to walk away.

Pap slipped his mitt onto his left hand and punched it with his right. Though his stance was typical of a first baseman, gooseflesh crept up Deirdre's back. Pap's fist thumped the leather as if determined to hurt it. She stifled a cry when the

Cossack half-turned, resting his hand on the butt of his tethered pistol. He and Pap regarded each other for a long moment, then—as if arriving at a silent, unsavory understanding—simultaneously turned away.

An exhortation echoed across the hillside. *"Play ball!"*

With a warning glance at Pap, Big Bill returned to first base. After a brief warm-up, the pitcher hurled a fast ball that Shorty chased without success. He trudged back to the bench as the Buffington fans gleefully chanted. *Two down, one to go!*

"The outfield fence," Deirdre whispered to Rosie. She needed to hide, and quickly, before Pap recalled her shameful outburst and directed his attention to the hill.

Ever a stickler for good manners, Mary Margaret graced them with a lilting *bye-bye* that Deirdre took pleasure in ignoring. Almost as shocking as her careless *goddamn*, this etiquette breach would be discussed over every pristine picket fence dividing the bosses' backyards, eventually making its way downhill. If, on that particular day, Pap were of the rare but occasional opinion that his pay envelope would fatten if his daughters slavishly kowtowed to those of his superiors, Deirdre's face would endure at least one hard slap. She beckoned to Rosie, who tarried, stammering, beside Mary Margaret. Fortunately, Mr. Donovan hit a line drive past the shortstop. In the ensuing upperhiller uproar, they made their escape.

Boys milled around the fence in hopes of catching a homer. Threading her way through them, Deirdre risked a glance at Pap, taking his place in the batter's box. The degree of punishment she'd suffer for her vocal transgressions hinged on the next three strikes. Beside her, Rosie stared unabashedly at middle fielder Mike Zoshak, warming up on-deck.

Warily, the base runners led off. The pitcher commenced his wind-up. Deirdre nudged Rosie and warned, "Your mother will have a fit if you take up with a hunkie."

Rosie blushed and sighed, but didn't look away. "Mike isn't even knowing my name."

The pitcher's shoulder whipped sideways as he threw to first, forcing Mr. Donovan back to the sandbag. The first baseman then appeared to throw the ball back. What he threw, however, was a peeled potato hidden in his shirt. When Mr. Donovan led off again, the first baseman tried to tag him with the ball, tucked in his glove. The trick, known from Brownsville to Uniontown as The Sweeney Switch, had been created by Pap to beat Buffington the previous year. Mr. Donovan had watched Pap practice The Switch too often to be fooled. He dove for the bag and, to the delight of The Hive's fans, knocked the first baseman off his feet.

Two down, one to go! Though as loud as before, the Buffington chant had lost its bluster. Emboldened by Pap's ferocious practice swings, The Hive's crowd countered, *Sween-ey, Sween-ey!* As Deirdre chimed in, she imagined the word changing to *Sa-vior, Sa-vior!* Along the fence and on the hill, those who had English stood shoulder-to-shoulder with those who did not. All shouted themselves into a frenzy to forget the ovens' smoke, the chest-crushing miner's asthma, the store debt, and unavoidable truth that their next shift—or their husband's or father's, brother's or son's—might well be the last.

The pitcher released. Big Bill hightailed it to third base; Mr. Donovan, to second. Pap's bat connected with a *crack!* that quelled the chants. The ball soared like a tiny white angel over the left field fence and dropped into an ecstatic tangle of boys. On the hillside, an eruption of shouts and airborne caps signaled yet another victory for The Hive.

Superintendent Finch appeared and made a show of shaking Pap's hand as he finished his home-run circuit. With forced courtesy, Pap tipped his cap at the Big Boss' wife—former Pittsburgh debutante Beatrice Heath—known to all downhillers as The Queen. Meanwhile, Old Smiley, the Company store manager, carried a megaphone to the mound that the Buffington pitcher seemed only too happy to vacate.

"Free ice cream for Heath fans, courtesy of the Superintendent!" Old Smiley shouted. "Line up outside the store! Mind you, keep it orderly!"

Deirdre and Rosie joined the exuberant procession blessed with three hundred ovens' gritty incense. Though St. Barbara's church bell chimed four, the low-hanging clouds evoked a

9

premature dusk. A breeze stirred the smoke into ghostly billows, hiding mothers from their children and husbands from their wives. It failed to obscure Mary Margaret, hurrying to catch up with the Cossack. In the time it took Deirdre to rid her streaming eye of a cinder, the hussy had feigned a stumble, then gracefully insinuated her arm around his forest green sleeve.

Rosie hissed like a cat when the Cossack transferred his cap to Mary Margaret's blond head. "I am hoping he gives her many small bugs to crawl through her hair."

"You mean *lice*," said Deirdre, ambushed by a pang of envy. Why couldn't she also have inherited the creamy Irish complexion and cinder-dark hair that had passed to Norah? Or be a striking redhead like Katie, lacking, of course, the freckles? A younger version of mouse-brown Mutti, Deirdre might as well have been a windowpane, so unremarkable as to be looked straight through—unless she happened to be dirty, which a certain blond upperhiller's appraisal unfailingly implied.

Swiftly she bent and scooped a fistful of cinders. Before she could fling them, Mutti's voice pierced the clamor. "Deirdre Sweeney, *don't you dare!*"

She glanced back at her mother, whose head inclined reluctantly toward that of sour-faced Mrs. Donovan. The upperhiller's fingers trapped Mutti's thin wrist as effectively as a handcuff. "Get a move on," Deirdre urged Rosie as a curtain of smoke unfurled before them. Somewhere beyond it strode the Cossack who'd prompted Deirdre to curse—and likely endure a licking on account of it. The cinders trickled uselessly between her fingers. Within the week, she resolved, she'd find a way to get even.

Chapter 2: Clare

May 9, 1929
Feast of St. Gregory Nazianzen, Bishop and Confessor

Limp as pulled weeds, Clare lay on the kitchen floor. Echoes of her furtive steps were embedded in the wood. But, unlike the dead, it wouldn't speak.

"Wo habe ich es versteckt?" Where did I hide it?

Beneath the flour sack?

Between the winter blankets?

Out of habit, her eyes, fearful, cut to the door. The back porch was vacant. Fin had left hours earlier, well before dawn, his lunch bucket in hand. His ears wouldn't be blistered by the *Kaiser-talk* he'd forbidden her to speak. She lowered her head, wincing as cinders ground into her brow. Her eyes closed, too spent from searching to weep.

For eight years, she'd taken such care. Three days here. Five days there. Two more days somewhere else. Eight years of clandestine nooks and crannies. Not once had she forgotten. Until today.

Through the patched window screen, she heard a baby begin to cry. It was a balmy spring morning, yet the sound might as well have been carried on a frigid winter wind. A chill passed through her as she turned her head. Pressed a desperate ear against wood as mute as her boys' graves.

Under a couch cushion? Buried in a bag of beans?

The baby's wails grew louder, overwhelming her whispered litany of empty places.

"Wo ist mein Korb? Wo sind meine Samen?" Where is my basket? Where are my seeds?

How long would her womb remain empty without them? She slid a hand beneath her belly, imagining it swollen, the skin rippling as a baby kicked inside. Without the seeds, how could she possibly prevent the conception of Finbar Sweeney's fourth son?

A splinter stabbed her scalp. She raised her face, level with the scarred legs of his chair. And there it was—the buckled board.

Scrambling to her feet, she pinched eager fingers beneath the creaking plank. Freed the tiny basket. Turned like a top until she thought of the pantry, its half-light and highest shelf. She climbed and stowed and dragged his chair out again, placing it just so.

"Please, St. Gregory and all the saints and angels," she prayed, gripping the chair, "don't let him notice if it's off by half an inch."

Hands trembling, she tore a strip from an old newspaper in the tinder pail. Her memory had failed and would surely fail again. With a pencil stub no longer than her thumb, she printed *P-A-N-T*. She stopped herself from adding *R-Y*. *P-A-N-T* was all she could risk. *P-A-N-T* had to be enough to pry the basket's latest hiding place from the dark corner of her mind.

She ran upstairs to their bedroom and wrenched open the dresser's warped bottom drawer. Carefully, she slid the paper into the pile of folded rags. These—though bleached and bearing but a rusty shadow of their monthly stains—he would never touch.

She closed the drawer and began wiping cinders from her face. Then her hands froze. Despite her frantic pulse, she nearly smiled.

He'd once torn her library card to pieces. Thrown the borrowed books into the stove. She'd suffered his kicks and slaps, her punishment for wasting time on words. Since then, she'd cultivated the precarious art of concealment. And today, heaven had graced a sinful woman with a miracle. She'd discovered something in plain sight, something that belonged to her that he would not disturb.

The butcher line stretched the length of the Company store—past flour sacks and canned-goods shelves, candy case and post office counter. Outside, women studied neatly typed notices tacked on each side of the door. The notices were identical, but everyone read them both, those with English translating for those without, passing words and gestures up and down the line. An oddity, this line, since every woman had enough sock-darning, soup-simmering, and garden-weeding waiting at home to keep her on her weary feet till long past sundown. The order clerk peered down the steps, her freckled nose wrinkled with puzzlement. Old Smiley summoned her back to her desk. His hoarse voice rose above the first floor's commotion. "The word's out about the festival."

Clare stood behind Kamila Zekula and in front of Concetta Tonelli and her mother, linked together like the spicy sausages on their Sunday dinner platter. She savored the cozy chatter particular to women, who somehow manage to communicate, even if the only word held in common is *hello*. Today, however, the tone differed from that at a christening party. Nobody shared her new trick to stretch a pork shoulder and fill ten hungry bellies. Nobody enviously recalled the chiffon dress worn by The Queen at Saturday's ball game. Instead, they quietly debated, predicted, and hoped against hope, caught up in news that had passed like a fairy-bubble through the ovens' smoke to hover before their disbelieving eyes.

Polish, Croatian, and accented English words of amazement moved from one to the next. A festival for their church, arranged by The Queen. The *Presbyterian*. A pageant, an essay contest, and fireworks, to boot—all paid for by the Company.

Each woman's posture had subtly changed. Faces, some framed by faded *babushkas*, glowed like dogwood blossoms. The announcement had elevated the morning to holiday status. The produce crates and pickle barrel, even the pulley-wires to the clerks' office, might have been draped with vivid bunting. Everyone had at least one unwashed pot encrusted with oatmeal or polenta, a back porch layered with bug dust. Still, they lingered, their heady anticipation briefly freeing them from the tedium of yet another smoky Thursday.

A lányomat.
Mia figlia.
Măj dcéra.
My daughter.

In Magyar and Italian and Slovak, each told herself, *my daughter will take the best part in The Queen's pageant. Unlike me and my worked-like-a-dog, paid-like-a-slave husband, my daughter will be somebody important, if only for one weekend. I will be the mother of the girl who plays St. Barbara.*

Kamila crossed herself. "Thanks be to God," she declared. "He got us through the strike in those leaky tents. Now He gives us something nice to look forward to."

Clare hid the skepticism she'd learned from Fin. He'd grumbled since Saturday about the new Cossack's eagerness to pick a fight. "Who do you think The Queen will choose?" she asked Kamila. "Your Helena made a lovely picture at Mass, crowning the Blessed Mother."

Kamila smiled broadly, revealing two missing front teeth. "Your Katie—"

"Too young. The paper says the players should be at least thirteen. She can enter the essay contest. Deirdre will audition, but I don't know about Norah. She's never been one to call attention to herself."

"My Anton heard that the baseball team might get new uniforms. The Big Boss must be a decent man, after all. Think of it—new uniforms *and* a pageant less than a year after a strike." Kamila crossed herself again, eyeing Clare until she crossed, too. "May God keep trouble away." Kamila lowered her voice. "I haven't heard the white-hoods' horses in I don't know how long."

Clare nodded warily. Anton had apparently missed Big Bill's warning to Fin about what the bosses call *Bolshevik-talk*. If Fin didn't pipe down about the union, the Company would get word to the white-hoods, and they'd all watch a cross burn on The Dirty Hill that very night. Eager to change the subject, she motioned to a crowded shelf. "Those can't hold a candle to your sauerkraut. I've used your recipe a dozen times, but it never tastes as good."

Kamila's broad face beamed. Nothing pleased her more than to be complimented on her cooking. Or her daughters, six broad-hipped stair-steps, who, like their parents, could talk the teeth out of a saw. Anton, Fin's pit buddy, drove him to distraction with accounts of his darling girls' accomplishments.

Just ahead of Kamila, Roza Sestak told the butcher's assistant, "Pork chops, three pounds." Roza's work-worn hand tucked a strand of hair behind her ear's pale curve, then flicked the gold circlet threading the lobe. She smiled, awaiting a fancy cut of meat Clare knew better than to ask for. Lovely Tereza, Roza's eldest, wouldn't need so much as a powder puff's stroke to convince every miner and missus that she was beautiful, tragic St. Barbara.

Kamila rolled her eyes. "The month's first envelope and Roza buys chops. She'll be filling Frank's bucket with bacon grease sandwiches by the tenth, or I'm a monkey's uncle."

Clare shrugged, hoping Kamila would say no more about envelopes. On washdays, she occasionally found Fin's crumpled in a pocket. His wage was written at the top, followed by deductions for rent, the store, blacksmith, and doctor. More often than not, the *Balance Due* box was marked with a snake, the wavy black line that indicated an empty envelope. He'd never told her the amount of his baseball bonus, paid under the table, but it didn't matter. He spent every penny at the speakeasy, setting nothing aside for the store.

Already, she heard the pulley's derisive rasp, hoisting the yellow ticket with her modest bacon order. She saw a clerk's brisk finger slide down a ledger's column to *Sweeney, Finbar, Miner #20,* and the meager figure of their allotted credit. If Fin were a different kind of man, she could have shared her fears. *Listen to Big Bill and keep your voice down. And steer clear of that new Cossack.* The instant Fin raised a fist in the policeman's direction, he'd be off the payroll. They'd be thrown out of their house, and, well before the dust settled, Dan Phelan, the assistant superintendent, would be dancing a jig.

Then again, if Fin were a different kind of man, she'd have so much less to fear.

Down the steps, smart navy shoe-heels tapping, came Big Bill's wife. Pretty, freckled Maeve, still slim as a bride after bearing six boys, each the spitting image of their pap, and a girl, who'd just turned three. Maeve held bundles of snowy eyelet, yellow seersucker, and polka-dotted organdy—yards and yards of it—all for one woman and a toddler. Clare gladly would have given a tooth for just enough to sew a blouse for Norah, who'd never had so much as a sock someone else hadn't worn hard first. When Maeve caught her eye, she realized that she'd stared her way into a conversation she couldn't avoid.

Roza left the counter, her basket packed with the pricey chops. A private smile lit the plump white moon of her face. "Good morning, Maeve," she said. One finger reverently stroked the eyelet. "Soon be sewing?"

"That I will. Congratulations on your Frank passing the fire boss exam. My Bill says he had the top score in the county." Maeve shifted her bundles and patted Roza's shoulder.

Kamila greeted Maeve in a sugary tone, then shot Clare a look as she moved to the butcher counter. Clare turned toward the shelves, but it was too late.

"How are you, Clare?" asked Maeve, so close that their sleeves brushed. So close that Clare couldn't pretend to be studying tomato cans with such intensity that she didn't hear.

"No complaints," she replied. "And yourself, Maeve?"

Before the H. C. Frick Coke Company had bought and renamed the patch after the Superintendent's wife, Maeve's husband had been a pick-and-shovel miner just like Fin. Like Clare, she'd waited out the '22 strike in a flimsy tent provided by the union—the same union Big Bill was now paid handsomely to hate. Since Big Bill had become pit boss and moved his family uphill to Furnace Street, Clare—unlike her husband—chose her words with care.

Each word was yet another step away from the woman she'd once been. If that woman's reflection somehow appeared in her mirror, she doubted that she'd recognize it. She couldn't imagine the miracle of moving uphill, but if she had, would time have eased its relentless etching of her face? Would she look closer to her age—thirty-seven, same as Maeve—instead of ten years older?

Maeve walked on, smiling as if she knew. Time's damage was inconsequential, compared to the damage Clare had done herself.

She ignored Kamila's incredulous whisper—*Frank Sestak?*—while the butcher's assistant wrote her ticket. No need for further speculation about who'd replace The Hive's longtime fire boss, who was moving to West Virginia. As the wire labored up to the clerks' office, she imagined Kamila's whisper rushing like intemperate wind the length of First Street. It crossed the mine yard and plummeted down the hoist shaft, swept through the haulageways and into a cramped, dust-choked room, where Fin swung his pick.

When the whisper pierced Fin's ear—*Frank Ssssestak*—he threw down the pick. Motioned to Anton to stop loading the wagon. Shouted without regard for who might hear. *Now we've got to trust the likes of that dumb hunkie to track down the black damp? Jesus, Mary, and Joseph, in a mine as gassy as No. 2, 'twill surely be the death of us all.*

For the very first time, a Slovak family would move uphill. And Dan Phelan's new Cossack prowled The Hive, primed to light any match that would ignite Fin's smoldering discontent. Jesus, Mary, and Joseph, indeed.

She walked past the remaining wives, who greeted the woman they knew as Clare Finnegan Sweeney. Clare, the home-run hero's missus, brought to The Hive to pack his bucket and scrub his back, raise his daughters and bury his sons. She returned their greetings until she stepped onto the store's front porch. There, her glance fell upon the barn-owl eyes of Essie Hunt, the wiry-haired Negro woman at the end of the line.

They pretended, as always, that they didn't know each other's names. That they'd never seen each other before.

Chapter 3: Deirdre

"Walk faster," Rosie whispered.

She gripped Deirdre's arm and attempted to cross First Street, but Deirdre held firm. "I need to stop at the store," she lied. "Go on ahead and save me a seat."

Rosie risked a backward glance. "What if the green soldier comes after me? Or you?"

Deirdre's neck ached from resisting the urge to glance back, too. "He's keeping an eye out for troublemakers. I'm not planning to cause trouble. Are you?" When Rosie emphatically shook her head, Deirdre pulled away. "Then there's nothing to worry about, is there? Go on now. I'll just be a minute."

Rosie's face puckered. She stepped off the sidewalk, glanced back again. "What if you are not coming? I don't want to be all by myself with The Queen."

Exasperated, Deirdre motioned to the new Community Hall, built next to St. Barbara's at the foot of The Clean Hill. Painted pale blue, it was the patch's only downhill building whose color hadn't gone gray from the ovens' smoke. Its impressive double doors swung open and shut, admitting a steady stream of animated girls, and the occasional boy. "It looks like you and The Queen will have lots of company. Go *on*, will you? No sense in us both being late."

Rosie stepped into the street, then spun around. "You can't be late! The Queen—"

Deirde threw up her hands and headed purposefully toward the store until Rosie joined Tereza Sestak and three pairs of Zekula sisters on the opposite sidewalk. Deirdre's pace slowed as the sidewalk planks thrummed in rhythm with the Cossack's boots. When she sensed him directly behind her, she stopped short, squatted, and pretended to tie her shoe. As she'd hoped, the boots' cadence abruptly lost its rhythm. The Cossack shuffled frantically to avoid tripping over her.

"Having trouble, miss?" His tone, more boyishly curious than officially gruff, caught her off guard. Cossacks shouted: orders, insults, curses. Hadn't Mr. Phelan told her so?

Her eyes lifted to Billy McKenna's, as green as his fitted jacket. A strand of stop-sign hair curved beneath his cap's stiff brim. His left hand rested on the belt-tethered club. His right extended. A pink seam marred one of its scrubbed knuckles. She rose, careful not to tread on her skirt, and pointedly ignored his proffered hand. She caught sight of Rosie, wringing hers beside The Hall's entrance. "I'm Deirdre Sweeney," she said, then interrupted his attempted introduction. "I know who you are."

His lips thinned. She celebrated silently, having gotten precisely the reaction she'd hoped for. He, with the amply armed belt, had been led into uncharted territory—off-balance, on the defensive—by a downhiller. And a girl. She thrust her hands into her pockets and appraised his. Aside from the scar, they appeared oddly soft, more like Mary Margaret's than her own, much less a hardened miner's. What sort of work had those hands done, or avoided, before he'd donned his uniform? "My pap is Steamshovel Sweeney. The ballplayer you tried to hit at Saturday's game."

Ashes flurried around them. His grin, so perfectly white, drew her eye the way lamplight lured incautious moths. "What if I did?" he said.

"He wasn't causing trouble. Nobody was, except you and your stupid club." Her eyes flicked to his belt. "Mind your own business, or next time he'll knock the daylights out of you."

"I'd like to see him try." Billy tapped the club with his fingertip. "I take my orders from Deputy Harrison, not you." He said *you* the way Mary Margaret would say it, the way any upperhiller would. As if the word were a bug beneath his heel.

"If you have any sense, you'll leave Pap alone. You'll leave all of us alone." Over Billy's shoulder, Deirdre glimpsed the formidable bulk of Mrs. Zekula, parting the smoke with the determination of a mine mule straining at its harness toward the feeding trough. Luckily, her attention appeared fixed on her shopping list. Deirdre darted across the street before Mrs. Zekula—or anyone else—noticed that she was conversing with a Cossack.

As The Hall's heavy door swung shut behind her, she pressed her calloused palm against the wood and recalled the Cossack's soft, scarred knuckle. It occurred to her that maybe, just maybe, the coat and cap and heavy belt offered Billy McKenna what the coveted part of St. Barbara might offer her. Perhaps they were simply a costume. A role dramatically different from the one his birth had dictated.

A disguise.

Fortunately, The Queen was also late.

Deirdre dropped into the seat beside Rosie just in time to hear Tereza announce, "Mary Margaret brought the invitation herself." Seated in the row just ahead, Tereza held up a pale yellow card. Regarding the rapt faces surrounding her, she allowed their dull downhiller brains to grasp the full import of her announcement. Satisfied that she'd sufficiently impressed her audience, Tereza continued, "Mrs. Donovan had a printer make them up special."

Tereza cleared her throat and proceeded to read, raising her voice so that everyone in the auditorium could hear. She'd been invited to an upperhiller's eighteenth birthday party the following Saturday. And not just a cake-at-the-kitchen-table gathering, but a garden party to be enjoyed in the Donovans' hydrangea-bordered backyard.

Rosie's older sister Majella hung over her seat back to inspect the invitation. "You're soooo lucky. What will you give her as a present?"

"Mama said I can take the streetcar to Uniontown and buy something very nice," Tereza replied. She glanced back at Deirdre and held up the card. "Would you like to see?"

Deirdre, seated behind Tereza, realized that she'd leaned sharply forward, making almost as big a spectacle of herself as Majella. "No, thanks." Deirdre hunched over and swept her fingers across the dusty floor. "My button fell off. I'm trying to find it."

Rosie bent, too. "I will help you," she whispered. "Then I will go home."

"You will not," Deirdre whispered back. They'd been through this half a dozen times already—Rosie protesting that her accent was too strong, Deirdre vehemently disagreeing. "Tell The Queen you want to be the angel. I bet she hardly says anything."

"I am afraid of The Queen. She doesn't like greenhorns."

"You're not a greenhorn anymore." Deirdre tilted an ear toward Tereza, asked by Majella about the Sestaks' impending change in circumstances. A change so incredible that Pap had slapped Mutti and accused her of lying when she'd repeated what she'd overheard at the store. *How can a hunkie have enough English to pass such a complicated exam? Didn't I earn an International Miner's Certificate working the Welsh pits? Wasn't I shooting cuts while Frank Sestak was still growing potatoes in the Old Country? Dan Phelan may think he can make a racehorse out of a donkey, but sure as I'm an Irishman, nothing good will come of this.*

Tereza raised her voice again. "When we move up the hill, we'll have wallpaper in *every* room. And lights you turn on with *switches*. *Tatko* says he will buy Mama an electric washing machine. And—"

Tereza's perfectly timed pause prompted Majella to plead, "What?"

Gott in Himmel! Deirdre bit back the epithet just in time. She imagined Mutti's face, aghast at such carelessness with the language she and her sisters had pledged to keep secret.

"We'll have a toilet *and* a bathtub *inside* the house," Tereza concluded triumphantly.

Rosie gasped and straightened up. Reluctantly, Deirdre joined her. Every girl, slack-jawed with amazement, regarded the improbable upperhiller. Deirdre had often speculated that, given the glaring absence of outhouses on The Clean Hill, the bosses' families enjoyed such a personal convenience. The subject of toilets, however, was hardly one to bring up in polite conversation. Tereza's brazen eagerness to do so seemed yet another reason why her family's imminent ascent was shockingly misguided.

A deep, dramatic sigh from Majella. "You are soooo lucky."

Though Deirdre would sooner climb onstage and undress than echo Majella's envy, she couldn't deny sharing it. Tereza caught her eye. "Did you find your button?" Tereza asked with poorly manufactured concern. Sparing Deirdre the need to offer a patently false reply, she smiled and turned away.

"Here comes The Queen!" hissed one of the boys.

Rosie paled and slid down in her seat.

The Queen emerged from the wings and, clipboard in hand, strode briskly across the stage. She positioned herself just inside the footlights, affording every would-be St. Barbara the opportunity to admire her ruffled ivory shift and rosette-trimmed cloche, bathed in the glow of a hundred incandescent bulbs. "Good afternoon. I'm delighted to see such a fine turn-out." She held up the clipboard. "Each of you must print your name, age, and the part you would most like to play. The cast list is typed at the top of the first page."

Rosie attempted to sneak into the aisle. Deirdre's knee shot forward to stop her. "She is looking at me already," Rosie whispered, miserably dropping back into her seat.

"Do you need to be excused, young lady?" The Queen called.

"False alarm," Deirdre called back. Everyone laughed, except Rosie and The Queen.

The Queen pursed lips tinted the color of a wild rose, the same shade as the ribbon adorning her hat. Her gaze fixed on Deirdre. "You there," she said, holding out the clipboard. "Come up here and take this. I have an engagement later this afternoon, so we must get started."

Rosie's expression might have been that of the peril-prone film heroine Pauline, trapped on a railroad trestle with an oncoming locomotive. "Stay put!" Deirdre hissed. Masking sudden, profound reluctance, she approached the stage.

"And you are—" The Queen prompted when Deirdre reached for the clipboard.

"Deirdre Ann Barbara Sweeney," Deirdre replied. The place between her shoulders tingled, assaulted by thirty hard stares.

A soft dent appeared between The Queen's perfectly arched brows. The unease overtaking Deirdre as she'd left her seat dissolved. Elation surged in its place. With four words, she—who shit in an outhouse and turned on her home's lone indoor light by standing on a kitchen chair and twisting the bulb—had managed to provoke The Queen. Was this how Pap felt when he said *union*, and Mr. Phelan's lips curled inward as if he'd suddenly lost all his teeth?

"Are you related to Steamshovel Sweeney?" The Queen hesitated just a beat before pronouncing Pap's nickname, making it clear that she referred to the notorious striker her husband deplored, rather than the home-run hero downhillers idolized.

"His middle daughter." Deirdre realized that the clipboard had risen out of reach and lowered her hand. She'd be damned if she'd behave like a begging dog, teetering on tiptoe.

The Queen's eyes cut to the seats, then returned to Deirdre. "And are your sisters auditioning?"

Deirdre's hands clasped behind her back. A whiff of rose perfume drifted from the stage. "My younger sister is writing an essay. My older sister is too shy."

The corners of The Queen's lips twitched, as if fending off a smile. Her pale blue eyes remained mirthless. "But you, Deirdre Ann Barbara Sweeney, most assuredly, are not."

Gasps sounded behind Deirdre, who pretended not to hear. "I wouldn't be here if I was," she declared. Desire inflated her chest. "I want to play St. Barbara."

The Queen regarded the seats. "Who else wants to be the pageant's leading lady?"

Deirdre turned to find a dozen raised hands, the most prominent of which belonged to Tereza. Rosie's seat, as she'd feared, was now empty. *Verdammt!* What excuse would allow Deirdre to leave The Hall long enough to find Rosie and bring her back—and not compromise an audition already tainted by the inescapable fact that she was Steamshovel's daughter?

"It appears you have a great deal of competition, Deirdre Ann Barbara Sweeney," said The Queen, her tone decidedly, despicably amused. She handed Deirdre the clipboard.

Giggles followed Deirdre back to her seat. Hastily she printed the required information and passed the clipboard to a new arrival. Even in the gloom, the boy's ruddy face glowed as if sunburned. He'd apparently come straight from his coke-drawing shift, eight hard hours spent emptying the hellishly hot ovens. The rank odor of his sweat wafted over the assembly, prompting Tereza to employ the party invitation as a fan.

"While the list makes its rounds, I'll explain how I adapted Barbara's story for theatrical presentation. I've had extensive dramatic training, so I wrote the script myself," said The Queen.

As she launched into a description of the first scene, the auditorium door opened. Four more coke drawers entered, led by Mike Zoshak, wiping his flushed face with a rag. Their ripe aromas preceded them down the aisle. Tereza's improvised fan fluttered like a hummingbird's wing. In the first row, Helena Zekula turned and coyly pointed to the empty seat beside her. Mike's fiancée had run off with a Buffington boy on Palm Sunday. Since then, Helena had fixed come-hither eyes on him, undaunted by the fact that he continued to keep his distance.

Mike and his companions chose seats in the row behind Deirdre. Fighting the urge to hold her nose, she turned and asked, "When you were coming in, did you see Rosie?"

Mike stuffed the rag into his shirt pocket and peered at her as if she'd spoken Italian.

Gott in Himmel! Had the ovens' heat fried his brain, as well as the coal? "You know, Rosie. Rosie Tonelli. She lives right across the street from you."

Mike shrugged as he was offered the clipboard. Deirdre hunched down in her seat to avoid the new arrivals' stink. She took a small, perverse satisfaction in the fact that Rosie's spineless bail-out had not only cost her the chance to play angel to Deirdre's saint, but also to encounter Mike and employ her own come-hither glance.

Concluding her scene-by-scene summary, The Queen bent gracefully to accept the clipboard from Tereza. As she straightened up, the door opened again. Deirdre crossed her fingers, hoping that Rosie had come to her senses, but the face that peeked inside the auditorium belonged to Willie Hunt, whom Mike had trained as a coke drawer. The cavernous space turned perfectly silent. Not an eye looked away as Willie headed down the center aisle, scanning the rows until he noticed Mike. Unlike those of the other coke yard workers, Willie's smooth black face displayed no reaction to the ovens' heat.

He seated himself behind Mike, who whispered something that prompted him to rise. "I guess I need to write my name on your list, ma'am. I'm real sorry I'm late. Boss had me take some scrapers needed fixing on over to the blacksmith."

The Queen's eyes moved from Willie to her clipboard. "I believe I have more than enough audition candidates for today."

Willie shifted his weight from one side to another. "That's all right, ma'am. I don't mind coming back tomorrow. I got the whole day off, so just tell me when—"

"You misunderstand me, boy. Auditions are today and today only. I will finalize the cast list tomorrow when I return home from church. It will be posted on the door of the Company store around noon. Costume fittings will take place immediately after. Those players working in the coke yard tomorrow will be fitted Monday evening at seven. Rehearsal starts promptly at seven-fifteen." With each syllable, The Queen's voice sharpened. The words fairly whistled as they left her painted mouth to slice the air. When she finished, Deirdre imagined the space around her, shredded like a threadbare rag.

"People say, if you get a part, then you get a little extra in your envelope." Willie edged into the aisle, shaking his head at Mike, who whispered something Deirdre couldn't hear.

"Those are rumors, boy. If you want to know something, ask your boss. He doesn't pass on hearsay." The Queen stared at Willie until he turned and hurried up the aisle.

When the door closed behind him, Deirdre let out a shaky breath. Though she knew as well as anyone that Willie was as likely as the Zekulas' nanny goat to perform in the pageant, she felt an odd spark of kinship. Upon learning Deirdre's surname, hadn't The Queen regarded her with the same narrowed eyes she'd turned on Willie?

"Can you imagine—a *nigger* in the pageant?" Tereza whispered to no one in particular.

It wasn't much of a stretch to imagine Tereza—or any upperhiller—rolling eyes and saying as much about a Sweeney. No matter which way the wind blew when the cast list was posted, Deirdre resolved to deliver an audition that made Tereza's efforts look like a fresh-off-the-boat greenhorn's attempt to recite the Pledge of Allegiance.

Mike surprised Deirdre by getting to his feet. "Excuse me, Mrs. Finch. I changed my mind about the audition. With work and baseball, I guess I'll be too busy."

The Queen's eyebrows rose until they hid behind her hat brim. Mike walked up the aisle and out the door, followed by the boys who'd accompanied him. Another boy rose, but, unable to withstand the weighty stares, sank back into his seat.

Deirdre couldn't decide if Mike and his pals were brave or foolish. The Queen wasn't likely to take the trouble to find out their names in order to have them fired. Then again, with coke yards closing left and right throughout Fayette County, why would Mike and the others risk their jobs—and for Willie, who, after all, should have known better?

"If anyone else has changed his or her mind, come up here at once and cross out your name. We've wasted far too much time already." The Queen surveyed the group and her eyebrows lowered. She lifted a gloved hand, extended a finger, and began to count.

Deirdre had already counted. Only eight boys remained to audition for ten male roles. She felt her hand rise.

"Deirdre Ann Barbara Sweeney, am I correct in assuming you're also withdrawing from the audition?" The Queen asked. "Stand up, so I can see you."

A grinning Tereza twisted around in her seat. *Go on, Deirdre Sweeney, make a complete fool of yourself, just like Willie. She'll never give you the best part, or any part, now.*

Deirdre forced herself upright. "I just thought—I mean, we learned in English class that, a long time ago, girls—well, women—weren't allowed onstage. Boys played the girls' parts. Maybe we could do the opposite. Have some girls play boys."

The Queen's mouth twitched. "Are you telling me how to cast my pageant, Miss Sweeney?"

"No, no, of course not!" Deirdre's hands retreated to her pockets, forestalling the overwhelming urge to slap Tereza's giddy face. "It just—occurred to me, that's all." It also occurred to her that The Queen had done her the courtesy of calling her *miss*.

"Would you be willing to play a boy's part, Miss Sweeney?"

A snicker escaped from Tereza, who covered her mouth with the invitation.

Deirdre's pocketed hands clenched until a knuckle cracked. "As I said before, Mrs. Finch, I want to play St. Barbara."

The Queen shocked Deirdre—and, no doubt, everyone else—by laughing. Not a genteel titter or lilting giggle, but full-out laughter than rose from her belly to rock her shoulders and nearly dislodge her hat. She laughed until her rouged cheeks glittered, forcing her to search her handbag for a hankie. Dabbing her eyes, she motioned toward the wings. "Well, Miss Sweeney, let's see if your dramatic ability supports your ambition. You'll find scripts stacked on a table just offstage. Take five minutes to study Barbara's speech on page fifty-two. Then come out here and deliver those lines as if your life depended on it. You—" The Queen's eyes cut to Majella and Helena. "Go backstage with Miss Sweeney and bring out the rest of the scripts."

Feeling utterly weightless, Deirdre found herself onstage. Laden with booklets, Majella careened around the proscenium and nearly knocked her over. Helena followed, whispering, "We left one for you. Good luck."

Deirdre ducked behind the stage curtain, rippling in their wake, and found the script on a table. She opened it, releasing a faint scent of roses, then rubbed clammy palms down the front of her dress. Her heart pumped so swiftly that she feared she would keel over and die—until she recalled Tereza's cat-got-the-canary grin. Planting a hand on either side of the script, she bent over it and silently read the speech. Then, starting over, read in a whisper, *"I have spent the five and twenty days of my imprisonment in prayer and meditation. Over and over, I asked God, my heavenly Father, to grant you, my father here on earth, a change of heart."*

The response of Dioscorus, Barbara's father, followed, then directions in parentheses for Barbara to inspect her surroundings. Deirdre regarded the spotlights mounted overhead, the dusty planks beneath her shoes. *Look at them,* she told herself, *like they're rooms in a boss house, and you're about to move in.* Her fingers brushed the curtain, which turned yellow and ruffled, covering the window of a wallpapered bedroom that was hers alone. She breathed in the scent of roses that lined her new home's front fence.

Was this acting, pretending to shed her dress, her skin, her very name? Could such a transformation occur simply by reading a script?

"How lovely once again to be surrounded by God's creation. Yet, though all these natural wonders delight me, how they must pale before the glories of heav—"

"Miss Sweeney? Are you sufficiently prepared to bring down the house?"

Five minutes had never passed so quickly. Deirdre made her way to the front of the stage. Blinking against the fiery lights, she scanned the faces arrayed before her until she found Tereza's, stiff and unsmiling.

From the balcony, The Queen's command swooped down like the voice of God. "That's far enough, Miss Sweeney. Please proceed."

Deirdre drew a deep, bracing breath and began the speech that she had determined would change her life.

Chapter 4: Clare

May 12, 1929
Feast of Saints Nereus, Achilleus, Domitilla, and Pancras,
Martyrs

They genuflected and filed into the pew: Clare first, then Katie, Deirdre, Norah, and Fin. Same order, same pew, every Sunday and holy day, funeral and wedding. Sestaks behind, Visockys in front, Kukoces across the aisle.

Today, however, the order had changed.

The Sestaks moved across the aisle to enlarge the upperhillers' section. They arranged themselves like royalty behind the Donovans as a new Polish family filled their former pew. The new arrangement displaced the late-arriving Kukoces, whom the Sestaks ignored. The Kukoces huddled in the aisle, conferring quietly in Croatian, until Maggie Phelan glanced back from the front pew. Some wordless communication passed between the woman in the crinoline-brimmed cloche and the one in the *babushka*. Mirta Kukoc took her aged mother's elbow and directed her to a pew at the rear of the church. Katie's friend Tina Kukoc lingered to stick out her tongue at the Sestaks until her older brother Jack pulled her away. Clamped lips prevented his tongue from imitating his sister's.

The Kukoces had no sooner seated themselves than the door groaned, admitting a gust of smoky air and the young, red-haired policeman.

A Cossack. In church.

Every head turned to watch him slowly progress down the center aisle, glancing left and right in search of a seat. His badge glittered in the candlelight. The black belt, studded with the grim tools of his trade, was noticeably absent.

Fin muttered and glared at the crucifix, as if reproaching Christ for admitting a Cossack to His house. Katie and Norah looked at the officer, then quickly looked away. Deirdre appeared to do likewise, but her body canted ever so slightly backward, preserving her view of the aisle.

The policeman paused beside their pew. He stood so close to Fin that Clare was sure she heard him breathing. Katie shrank against her. Deirdre sat, silent and still, yet somehow drew Fin's attention. Before Clare could intervene, he'd knocked aside Norah's rosary-threaded fingers and seized Deirdre's knee. Her head snapped forward. Beneath the embedded bug dust, Fin's knuckles blanched around the bunched organdy of her skirt.

Brows lowered, the Cossack watched.

Los! Clare longed to shout. *Go away! Any harsh business you have in store for Fin can't happen inside a church.*

The wheezing organ urged everyone to rise. Dan Phelan turned and gestured. The Cossack's boots squeaked as he quickly genuflected, then squeezed in beside the Phelans' youngest son.

Fin released Deirdre, who'd surely been daydreaming about the pageant and allowed her gaze to stray. When she rose, Clare opened a hymnal and offered it to her, but Deirdre's hands remained at her sides. Norah took it to share with Fin, who'd resumed scowling at the crucifix.

Fr. Kovacs processed down the aisle. Behind him, carrying candles, walked Peja and Duje, the hell-raising Lubicic twins, uncommonly docile in starched white surplices. It was the second Sunday in May, so the organist played a hymn to the Virgin Mary. The perfect mother, who, unlike Clare, had reared a son.

Clare sang, head bowed, all too aware of the severe scrutiny of three painted plaster faces. Crucified Christ, hanging above the altar. To the right, in a niche massed with lilacs and peonies, His Blessed Mother. St. Barbara, grasping her chalice and sword, in a flowery niche to the left. Their eyes registered grim pleasure that Clare had returned to writhe inwardly before them.

Fr. Kovacs intoned, "*Mea culpa, mea culpa, mea maxima culpa.*"

Dropping her gaze, she repeated the chant. With each phrase, a beat of the fist between her breasts, the motions of rote repentance.

For my fault, for my fault, for my most grievous fault.

Her body spoke and sang in unison with the rest, but her will remained defiantly separate.

Each time she entered the plaster trinity's sanctuary, their hard eyes challenged her, as Fin did almost nightly, to be dutiful. To yield to him and, through him, to the suffocating embrace of the Almighty Father. Both would use Clare to enlarge the Church with fresh, new, corruptible souls. But, thanks to Essie, she—no pious, compliant virgin—wouldn't cooperate.

Fr. Kovacs began the *Gloria*, which she echoed. Her heart, however, couldn't move beyond *mea culpa*.

Durch meine Schuld, durch meine Schuld, durch meine große Schuld.

The words thudded in her chest through the Gospel and the sermon, preached in English, Polish, Slovak, and Croatian. Through the intonation of the *Credo*. All for nothing—this prayer and any other, offered in desperation to any given saint—because she knew she was damned. The thought greeted her when she woke before sunrise to cook Fin's breakfast and pack his bucket. It dogged her through each moment of every smoky day until she was briefly redeemed by dreamless sleep. It gnawed most keenly whenever she occupied the prison of this pew, separated from Fin by three precious daughters and too many ghosts to number.

Sünderin, the statues whispered. *Sinner.* They knew she'd never risk the spectacle of covering her ears. *Sssssssinner.*

Over and over, she asked forgiveness, but she didn't regret her most grievous transgressions. She mourned her dead sons, but didn't waste on foolish wishes the energy needed to bake bread, pick coal, mend clothes, scrub floors, and endure the regular humiliation of a trip to the store. Her soul might as well have been a decrepit mine mule, stabled so long underground that its eyes no longer comprehended daylight. She'd lived too long in this smoke-hole, and the one before it, and the one before that, to believe things could ever be different.

Sssssssssssssinner. The relentless statues hissed until overpowered by the organ's chords.

Fin's hands clasped. His eyes closed. His lips moved in a silent plea for a son who wouldn't stop breathing while asleep. He appeared to have forgotten, at least momentarily, about the Cossack. Clare's gaze, however, was inexorably drawn to the young officer's broad green back. His presence unsettled her as much as the statues' scrutiny. In the pew just ahead, the Visocky boys huddled and pointed at the officer till their father's elbow persuaded them to resume postures of prayer. Whispers filled pauses in the organ's meditative drone. In the boss pews—and the Sweeneys'—pious order reigned, while everyone else leaned and muttered.

Bells jangled as Fr. Kovacs lifted the consecrated host. Fin got to his feet and allowed Norah to enter the aisle, then yanked Deirdre off the kneeler. It happened so quickly that Clare was unable to slide between them, to quietly remind Fin that the pageant's cast list would be posted in a few hours. Wouldn't he be proud to be the father of The Hive's first St. Barbara?

Fin motioned to her. His face was stern, but his eyes revealed the guttering fire of his spirit. He should have been a soldier like his broken brother, instead of laboring to line the pockets of Pittsburgh millionaires. He was dying by inches on the inside, but not from miner's asthma. Not like his blistered, wheezing brother Seamus, who'd ultimately suffocated from his exposure to mustard gas during the Great War.

A part of Fin died each time the Company broke yet another strike. Another part, each time Clare's pregnancy ended too soon. When he looked at her like this, it was almost possible to forget how quickly he could change. How easily he became someone alien and hateful, able to relieve his daily torment only by tormenting another. Standing beside the pew, his expression bordered on prayer, beseeching Clare to stay.

How could a worn-out woman with no skills beyond housework possibly do otherwise?

Her cousin Trudy, who wrote monthly from Pittsburgh, disagreed. *Pack up your girls and come.* She called her North Side neighborhood Deutschtown and claimed German was spoken openly on the street. *Hier kannst du wieder frei sein,*

32

she insisted. *Here you can be free again. Nobody will beat you for being who you are.*

Freiheit. Freedom. It might have been possible twenty years ago, when Clare was a different woman. She couldn't bring herself to tell Trudy that the woman she'd made herself into had incurred heavy debts that could only be discharged here.

Though she needed no reminders, the statues persisted. *Ssssinner.*

She caught her breath when Fin leaned into the pew and seized her arm. "For the love of Christ, stand up and come to Communion. Will you be having people think you're kneeling here and not in a state of grace?"

The altar candles' flames quivered like those in Clare's stove, greedily eating the letters Fin must never see—letters written in the language he must never hear—reducing Trudy's promises to ashes. Obediently, she went to the rail, kneeling beside the prideful man who believed that trouble following death is preferable to trouble following shame.

The Communion wafer trembled between Fr. Kovacs' thick fingers. *Corpus Domini nostri Jesu Christi custodiat animam tuam in vitam aeternam.* May the body of Our Lord Jesus Christ preserve your soul into life everlasting.

Her whispered lie. *Amen.* So be it.

Each time she faced that quivering wafer, she expected God to fill the priest with outrage. She expected to be refused and reproached. Unmasked as polluted and unworthy before the whole congregation.

Ssssssssssssssinner.

She returned to the pew, unable to push away the memory of the Sunday when the disintegration of her soul had commenced. That rainy November morning, she had trudged through sodden red dog and wept for her fourth child, the first Finbar, killed by influenza like so many others in 1918. Weak from her own bout, she'd clung to Fin's arm, passing doors marked with quarantine notices and fluttering black crepe. The small procession, thinned by the epidemic, left a trail of footprints that slowly filled with blood-colored water. A gauze mask from the Red Cross nurse covered each face.

In St. Barbara's, four in five pews were empty. The priest raced through the Latin, cramming the rite into the Public Health Department's fifteen-minute limit for church services. She no sooner knelt at the Communion rail than a shocking realization overtook her, and she fainted dead away. Coming to in the vestibule, her head in Kamila's pillowy lap, she tried to confess a sin whose recognition had struck her temporarily unconscious.

A week earlier, she'd buried her infant son, and, *mea culpa, mea culpa*, she was no longer sorry. He would never grow up to be like his father, driven by obligation into the black hell that broke the spirits of mules and men. Her son had escaped his father's fate, and, God forgive her, she was glad. Oh, had she had the strength she would have danced for joy.

Freiheit. Freedom. Such was the state of her tiny Finbar, released from The Hive's smoke and sorrow. Never to follow his father's harsh example.

When laughter bubbled beneath Clare's mask, Kamila's forehead pleated with concern. She stroked Clare's brow, checking for fever, fearing her strange elation hinted at a relapse. In that dim vestibule, Clare did not yet understand that succumbing to such dire mirth would endanger her salvation. How could she have known, then, how far she could fall from grace?

How did it feel to possess grace? She only felt its dearth—a hole inside her, dark as the mine, deepened by each small, bloody interment beneath the front porch.

The clang of a paten drew her back to the present. Fr. Kovacs and the twins were clearing the altar. Katie's and Norah's heads bowed over folded hands. Deirdre's face, however, angled toward the aisle. When Clare touched her hand, Fin noticed and growled a warning.

Not ten feet away, the Cossack knelt in prayer.

Brazenly, urgently, Clare prayed, too. *Please, holy martyrs, keep this reverent, handsome, dangerous young man away from my family.*

Heaven surely laughed at this request, coming from a willful woman who repeatedly broke the laws of Holy Mother

Church. Still, she persisted. The words sounding in her mind covered up the voices of her dead children, who whispered whenever she was silent for too long.

Sssssssssssssinner.

Fr. Kovacs intoned, "May the prayers of Thy blessed martyrs Nereus, Achilleus, Domitilla, and Pancras obtain for us, we beseech Thee, O Lord, that the holy sacraments—"

Martyrdom was accomplished in ways other than spectacular slaughter.

Earning a living—or what had to suffice for it—in the deep, dangerous bowels of the earth.

Or living amid the dead.

The priest and twins began their exit. Everyone rose to sing. *O God, our help in ages past, our hope for years to come, our shelter from the stormy blast...* Clare turned toward the window so Katie wouldn't notice her brimming eyes.

Es gibt mir keine Hoffnung. Kein Schutz.

For me, there is no hope. No shelter.

Chapter 5: Deirdre

Mutti pulled Deirdre behind her as Pap unbuckled his belt. "She's done nothing wrong, Fin. It was such a surprise. Have *you* ever seen a Cossack attend Mass?"

"'Tis God's business who comes to Mass. 'Tis a father's business to correct a disobedient daughter." Pap freed the belt from his pants and slapped it against the kitchen floor. "Leave her be, Clare, or I'll be taking the strap to the both of you."

Katie, who'd gone upstairs to change, peered around the kitchen doorway. Her face paled until each freckle stood out like a pinprick. When Pap's belt met the floor a second time, she disappeared. Deirdre heard her frantic retreat up the steps. Behind Deirdre, the back door squeaked, telling her Norah had returned from the outhouse.

"I looked at the Cossack, too, Pap," said Norah. "Everybody did. Didn't you hear the whispering? I thought Fr. Kovacs would stop Communion until—"

"'Tis a great difference between looking and staring." The belt slapped the floor again. "Much less looking and talking."

Mutti's arms tightly encircled Deirdre, but she wrenched free. She no longer craved the shield of her mother's body. "I told the Cossack to stay away from you!" she cried.

Pap shoved Mutti aside and forced Deirdre, face down, across the table. Sinking her teeth into the soft, scarred wood, she resolved to deny Pap the satisfaction of hearing her so much as wince. If only the table were Mrs. Zekula's tongue! Without question, the old busybody had seen Deirdre confront Billy McKenna, then described it to others as a lurid tryst. Deirdre gripped the edge of the table as if it were Mrs. Zekula's neck. *Not a sound out of you. Not even a peep.* She chanted through the mouthful of wood—*not a peep, not a peep*—as Pap's belt buckle raked her shoulders.

A draft blew across her legs, and Deirdre realized Pap had yanked up her skirt. Quickly, it was yanked down. Mutti flung herself over Deirdre's back. "Disobedient as your daughter, then?" said Pap. With a jerk, Mutti's body lifted. Deirdre tried to rise, but Pap pushed her head onto the table. She heard a thud, a muffled cry. As always, Mutti had tried to prevent a daughter's punishment, only to earn fresh bruises herself.

Deirdre's skirt flew up. She bit again into the table, and a splinter snagged her lip. Eyes clamped shut, she pictured The Queen, pretty and unperturbed, glowing beneath the stage lights.

"I don't need a lass to be fighting me battles with a goddamn yellow dog!" Pap cried.

The pink rosettes studding The Queen's hat swelled into full-blown flowers. A vast field of roses bloomed behind Deirdre's eyelids as the strap lashed the backs of her thighs. She set her teeth and breathed deeply, straining to detect the blossoms' fragrance.

Harsh blows punctuated Pap's warning. "You'll never—lay eyes—on that bastard—again!"

Despite Deirdre's determined silence, the kitchen rang with screams. Pap's hand lifted from the back of her head. The vision of roses vanished. Pain ran ragged paths from her ankles to her neck, then congealed into one enormous misery. With effort, she lifted her head. Mutti, red-faced, strained toward the table. Norah struggled to hold her back.

Pap's belt whistled again, cutting across their knees, knocking them both to the floor.

Despite pain attending all but the shallowest breath, how could Deirdre refrain from shrieking?

PAGEANT CAST LIST:
Miss Deirdre Sweeney..........................St. Barbara

Pressing a hand to her torn lip, she scanned the names beneath. Just as she'd suggested, The Queen had given almost every other girl both a female and male role. Two boys, who'd left school in fifth grade and could barely read, hadn't been cast at all. Deirdre smiled behind the screen of her palm when she reached the end of the list:

Miss Tereza Sestak....................Stage Manager/St. Barbara understudy

She noticed Tereza wriggling through the cluster of girls at the store's door. When Tereza read the list, her shoulders slumped. Deirdre steeled herself for a sharp remark, but Tereza surprised Deirdre by extending her hand. Deirdre allowed hers to be shaken, even more surprised by Tereza's admission, offered without a trace of sulkiness. "You gave the best audition of anybody. Maybe, if you want to, we can help each other learn the lines."

How had Tereza failed to notice the bloody seam on Deirdre's lip? Mary Margaret, no doubt, would soon school her to observe downhillers more critically. Deirdre nodded, still wary. "Won't you be too busy, packing up to move?"

Tereza shrugged. "Not until after the pageant. *Tatko* is still practicing how to use the special lamp to find bad gases. Mr. Phelan says he will make a very good fire boss."

Since Tereza had made an effort to be polite, Deirdre felt obliged to return the favor. Once the Sestaks were living on Church Street, Tereza might recall Deirdre's courtesy and someday walk downhill to deliver a party invitation of her own. "I heard your pap made the top score on the test. No. 2 will be the safest mine ever when he takes over," Deirdre replied.

Tereza beamed. Deirdre turned away, having curried sufficient favor with an understudy, who, after all, still lived in a double on Second Street. Though the pats on her back caused her to wince, she reveled in each *lucky you* and *congratulations* as she made her way out of the crowd.

Rosie, persuaded to volunteer as a backstage helper, waited on the sidewalk. "I knew you would be the best," she said, linking arms with Deirdre. "You will do in the pageant the way your papa does in the base ball. Everyone will be shouting your name at the end."

As they walked to The Hall and Deirdre's costume fitting, she saw herself onstage precisely where she'd given her audition. Before her, a packed auditorium, every miner and missus in The Hive out of their seats, applauding and cheering. *Deir-dre Sween-ey, Deir-dre Sween-ey!* At the very back, discreetly keeping to the shadows, stood a chastened Billy McKenna, nodding humbly as he clapped. She'd convinced him, as she had The Queen, that a Sweeney was capable of more than hitting baseballs, aggravating bosses, and instigating strikes.

A breeze stirred her skirt, skimming the welts hiding beneath it. She blinked hard to force back tears. After such a beating, how dare the goddamn Cossack infiltrate her daydream? A tear slipped down her cheek. She wiped it away, but not before Rosie noticed and asked, "You are crying because you are happy?" When Deirdre nodded, Rosie's finger moved toward Deirdre's splinter-snagged lip. Deirdre flinched, and Rosie's finger quickly retreated. "Your papa—" she began.

"The Cossack came to Mass. Pap got mad because he looked at me."

Deirdre reached for The Hall's front door, but Rosie stepped in front of her. "Yesterday, I am waiting here, and I see you talking to the green soldier."

"I told him to stay away from Pap. That's why he looked at us in church. At all of us, not just me. Pap got mad about that, too." Deirdre kicked the sidewalk, wincing as the impact set her body throbbing. "He never listens."

Rosie pressed herself against the door. "Promise me, you will go the other way when the green soldier comes again."

"I promise." Deirdre wiped away another tear. "I hope he shoots himself in the eye so he can't look at anybody."

In The Hall's spacious basement, The Queen's dressmaker clucked her tongue as she wrapped a measuring tape around Deirdre's chest. "Skinny as a rail," she said, draping the tape around her neck and scribbling in a tablet.

"Willowy," said The Queen, looking up from costume sketches laid out on a table. She appraised Deirdre, who gritted her teeth as the tape squeezed her bruised shoulders. "I, too, was quite slender as a girl. Today's fashions look best on slim figures, don't you agree?"

The dressmaker made a sound of assent around the pencil clamped between her teeth.

As she measured from neck to waist, Deirdre felt her cheeks flush. Surely The Queen mocked her. Who could say *fashion* without sarcasm while regarding Deirdre's dress—faded, patched, and flaunting a long skirt and pin-tucked waistband ten years out of date? Beneath lowered lashes, she studied The Queen's dress, its snow-white sailor collar and short, knife-pleated skirt, its stylish dropped waist. Pale curls peeked from beneath a bonnet-brimmed cloche with a lavish bow in back. Norah, who pored over old Sears catalogs the way she'd once studied schoolbooks, might well have overcome her shyness and auditioned in order to gain access to this one-woman fashion show. Much as Deirdre coveted The Queen's ensemble, she was grateful, at least today, for an overlong skirt that covered her damaged legs.

The Queen's fingers, tipped with rosy nails, lifted her drooping collar. "Did this dress belong to your mother?"

"No, Mrs. Finch. It came from a missionary relief box." Moving like a brush fire, heat claimed Deirdre's whole face. Relief happened only in the event of evictions and tent camps. She might as well have reminded The Queen that her pap had been the miner who'd started the Big Strike.

Oddly enough, The Queen failed to make that connection. Her fingers, to Deirdre's amazement, didn't flee from the hand-me-down as if from contagion, but continued their ruminative pleating. "Are all your dresses like this?"

All equaled four. Two, faded but unpatched, Deirdre wore to school. A beige organdy, equally outdated, was reserved for church. And this, by far the dowdiest, served for everything else: floor-scrubbing, garden-weeding, coal-picking, and now, to her embarrassment, a costume fitting. "I guess so," she admitted.

The Queen released her collar. "Doesn't your mother sew?"

Deirdre nodded. She glanced at Rosie, who fixed her gaze on the list of duties for the pageant's costume mistress. Rosie knew what Mutti sewed. Patches. Old flour sacks into underwear. Never had a Sweeney, mother or daughter, enjoyed the luxury of a new dress.

The Queen's gaze turned quizzical. Everyone in The Hive knew why the Sweeneys dressed little better than Masha, the leather-faced peddler who sharpened scissors and claimed to be a gypsy. The Queen, however, lived in a mansion in Beetown, a true town on the other side of The Dirty Hill. Beetown had many stores, not just one run by the Company. Its residents worked at jobs that didn't force them to risk their necks underground and get filthy—and, eventually, asthma—in the process. Even if Deirdre weren't too ashamed to say why, even on payday, the Sweeneys never had two cents to rub together, The Queen wouldn't understand. She lived a life so different it might as well have been on the moon.

"A girl your age should have at least one nice dress," The Queen declared.

The door opened, and in trooped the girls Deirdre and Rosie had left behind at the store. Tereza led the pack, clad in the new candy-striped percale frock she'd shown off that morning at Mass. Though it couldn't hold a candle to The Queen's attire, it certainly hadn't been scrounged from a musty-smelling relief box. Soon after Mr. Sestak was named fire boss-in-training, Mutti had seen Mrs. Sestak leave the store, her shopping basket packed with fabric.

Deirdre fixed her eyes on the floor, willing The Queen to walk away. Before she did, she said, so softly that Deirdre feared she'd imagined it, "There are probably half a dozen dresses in my closet that I don't wear anymore. I'll have my maid pack them up for you. Your mother can alter whatever doesn't fit."

"The Queen gives you dresses for nothing? She doesn't ask you to do first some special work?" asked Rosie, whose cousin had been hired by The Queen as a kitchen maid. Rosie halted, gaping at Deirdre. "The Queen likes you. Your papa makes big trouble every time for *Signore* Big Boss, and she still gives you dresses. *Straordinario.*"

Straordinario. Amazing. How else to describe such largesse? Deirdre took Rosie's hand and swung it as if they were little girls again. The prospect of a new wardrobe magically eased the ache in her shoulders. "If you hadn't been such a chicken about auditioning, you might be getting dresses, too."

Rosie shook her head mournfully. "Never. Not to a greenhorn."

"You're *not*—" Deirdre threw up her hands. "Tell you what. When the maid brings the dresses, you can come over and pick one for yourself. We'll wear them to school the same day." She dodged Rosie's hug and ran ahead, exultant. "I can't wait to see Mary Margaret's face!"

They tightrope-walked the railroad tracks, lunch pails swinging from their elbows. The afternoon stretched before them, hours to ramble in the woods and gather wild greens and flowers. Everyone but the Sunday-shift coke yard workers and pageant hopefuls had followed the baseball team to Edenborn. Deirdre had intended to follow, even if the fitting meant she'd arrive late. The sound of Pap's belt against the kitchen floor had changed her mind.

"I must be telling my cousin he is chosen for many parts," said Rosie.

They paused at the mine gate, flapping hands against the beehives' gritty smoke. Behind them, downwind of the ovens, rose The Dirty Hill. At its crest, nearly hidden by billowing cinders, stood Heath School, which challenged the tipple for the dubious distinction as The Hive's filthiest structure. Between the hill and the coke yard loomed the slate dump's dark, craggy mounds—eighty years' worth of rocks and other waste dug out with, then separated from the coal. Mysterious fires smoldered deep inside the dump, and the smoke mingled with that rising from the ovens.

Most days, the dump would be dotted with coal-pickers and children sledding down the rough slopes on their paps' shovels or raggedy pieces of cardboard. Until Deirdre had started high school (when Norah admonished her to *grow up* and *act like a lady*), she'd done plenty of sliding, whose thrills far outweighed Mutti's inevitable fury over her blackened clothes. Every missus in The Hive claimed the sooty heaps weren't as solid as they appeared, telling stories about runaway pigs and disobedient children swallowed by air pockets that opened and closed in the blink of an eye. Since the stories never named a child or pig owner, Deirdre was certain that mothers made them up to save on washing soap.

Even taller than the dump was the head frame, the towering metal grid attached to the wooden tipple directly above the entrance to Heath No. 2. Layered with cinders, both appeared to be covered with thick gray fur. On workdays, hoist cages moved inside the frame, carrying miners in and out of the shaft and loaded coal wagons up to the weigh boss landing. There, Mr. Donovan removed each wagon's check, the small brass circle stamped with the number of the miner who'd loaded it. To be paid for a load, the miner had to heap the wagon with what was derisively called *King Frick's hump* after the Company's founder Henry Clay Frick. If Mr. Donovan suspected the wagon was cribbed, he jabbed the hump with a metal pole. Pap wasn't the only miner who'd figured out how to prop big coal chunks to hold up the hump, leaving the wagon hollow in the center. It was the only way to subvert the Company's ironclad policy of paying by wagon instead of weight, but few miners got away with it.

Each morning at daybreak, the gated-off expanse hummed with activity. Before boarding the hoist cage, a miner paused to hang his check on a large board, a safety measure that told the bosses who was underground and needed rescuing in case of an accident. Yard men crisscrossed the area, carrying out their duties in the stable and carpenter shop, lamp house, blacksmith shed, and motor barn, where Norah's boyfriend Paul Visocky worked as a machinist.

Rising over the men's shouts and clanking equipment was the rattle of coal. It streamed down the chute that jutted from the tipple's side to fill waiting larry-cars. An electric locomotive pulled the hitched-together cars along tracks laid over the coke oven runs. Shaped more like an igloo than the brick beehive in which Rosie's mama baked bread, each oven had an opening at the top, the tunnel head or eye. A loaded larry-car parked above it to dump a seven-ton charge. A charger strode alongside the larry-cars, covering each eye with its metal damper before the cars moved on. Below him, a leveler hurried from one beehive to the next, thrusting his iron duckbill scraper inside the oven's arched jamb, or doorway, to even out each charge. The scraper, more than three times the height of a man, looked like an enormous spoon bent backwards. A dauber, like Rosie's cousin Pasquale, followed close behind, quickly sealing the jamb with bricks and mud to retain the heat from the previous burn. Daubers left a crescent-shaped air-chink at the top to keep the fire going, one that Pap claimed was hotter than hell. The charges fried for two to three days before a quencher broke open the door and hosed down what remained inside: a mass of pure carbon called coke. Mike Zoshak, Willie Hunt, or another drawer loosened the coke from the oven with a duckbill and loaded it into railroad hoppers parked on the siding. Freight trains arrived regularly to pick up the hoppers, then hauled the coke away to fire Pittsburgh steel mills.

The coke burner, who bossed the ovens, planned the charging so that, on Sundays, a skeleton crew kept an eye on beehives that wouldn't need opening till at least the next morning. The crew included Pasquale, who sat on a pile of bricks, eating his lunch with two other boys.

"You are a guard! And a miner!" Rosie shouted, but her cousin ignored her.

Deirdre suspected that the boys discussed the topic weighing heavily on all coke workers' minds. How long would The Hive's ovens stay in blast? The Company had installed new ovens at its steel mills, machine-drawn ovens that saved their smoke. Somehow, the Company turned the smoke into tar and other products that it sold along with steel. Coke yards had already closed at Footedale, Ralph, Buffington, and the Colonial mines around Grindstone and Smock. Nobody—not even know-it-all Mr. Phelan—was sure when The Hive's ovens would fry their last charges.

Shoulders flouncing, Rosie turned away from the gate. "*Stupido*! He will not hear me."

Deirdre pinched her nose against the rotten-egg smell of coke smoke. "They think we're bad luck," she reminded Rosie. It was common knowledge that a miner who encountered a woman on his way to work immediately turned around and went home before setting out again. Though most mines had women's names, no woman was ever allowed inside one. Some yard men and coke workers were equally superstitious, refusing to look at or speak to a girl or woman until they had finished their shifts. Deirdre regarded the plumes of smoke—ash-gray, mud-yellow, bug dust-black—stirring themselves into a thick, stinking canopy. It seemed glaringly obvious that yard workers were just as unlucky as Pap and the other miners—and girls had nothing to do with it. All were equally beholden to King Frick's successors, whom Pap habitually cursed as if both they and the long-dead millionaire could somehow hear him.

"When Pasquale is late coming tomorrow for the costume-missus to measure him, then he will have the bad luck," Rosie declared.

Before moving on, the girls paused out of habit to cross themselves and whisper a prayer. It was impossible not to notice two startlingly green seedlings behind the tipple. Planted last month, they memorialized Pap's former pit buddy and his son, killed in a roof fall shortly after Christmas. Before long, the pine seedlings would turn as gray as the surrounding trees. Each honored a pit worker accidentally killed in the nine years since the Lambert superintendent had started the custom.

"Let's go," said Deirdre, pulling Rosie away before she crossed herself again. The pines reminded Deirdre of the ugly rumors following the accident, whispers claiming that Steamshovel had come to work with whiskey on his breath and failed to brattice the part of the ceiling that had collapsed.

The girls followed the railroad tracks into the woods. Diligent Rosie moved at a snail's pace, parting clumps of grass and ducking under low-hanging branches, marking the discovery of each purple-stemmed poke sprout with a triumphant *aha*! Rosie professed to enjoy eating such gleanings, while Deirdre merely endured them. Dropping an occasional strand of chickweed into her bucket, Deirdre sought violets shaded by blackberry canes and umbrella plants. Rosie insisted that the flowers were tasty, too, but Deirdre's intent was adornment, not dinner. She assembled a nosegay and tucked it into her folded-over waistband, one of Mutti's many tricks to shorten relief-box dresses.

Despite Rosie's painstaking progress, they'd gone far enough for Deirdre to glimpse rust-colored water through a tunnel-like thicket of blooming mountain laurel. "I'm ready for lunch," she called to Rosie. "Let's eat by the creek."

Hunching tender shoulders, she made her way through the tunnel. A pocket opened in the smoky sky, freeing sunlight that traced a sparkling path across the creek. Deirdre scouted the muddy bank until she found a patch of flattened grass littered with old canning jars and a chipped milk bottle. No doubt Peja and Duje, The Hive's notorious truants, came here to play hooky. The bottle contained a grainy puddle of what looked like creek water. When Deirdre lifted it, however, the powerful odor of Mr. Lubicic's moonshine prompted her to throw the bottle and jars into a lush patch of poison ivy. By the time Rosie emerged from the pink-blossomed thicket, Deirdre had gingerly seated herself on the grass to eat her bread and jelly.

"Why is the river smelling so bad?" Rosie asked before tasting a portion of the Tonellis' homemade sausage.

"Creek, not river." Deirdre licked sticky fingers, which only made them stickier. She got up to rinse her hands in the water. "Peja and Duje left some of their pap's moonshine right where you're sitting." She laughed when Rosie, wide-eyed with alarm, scrambled to her feet. "Don't worry, I got rid of it. The revenue agents would never come snooping around way out here to look for a still."

Rosie settled back with her lunch. Flicking water from her hands, Deirdre shed her shoes and socks. When she turned, barefoot, to place them on a rock, she noticed Rosie's shocked expression. She turned in a swift circle, scanning the ground. "Did you see a snake?"

Rosie shook her head. "Your legs! *Madre Maria*, what is making so many *contusioni*?"

Deirdre hiked up her skirt. Purplish-red bruises striped the backs of her calves. Her thighs, similarly striped. Till now, she'd managed to distract herself from the pain. Violets fluttered to the ground as she stuffed handfuls of skirt into the folds of her waistband. She stepped into the creek and sighed, soothed by the cool ripples. "It's nothing," she told Rosie.

"Is not nothing! Promise, right now, you are never looking at the green soldier again."

"I already promised." Deirdre slid one foot forward, then another, nearly swooning with relief. Not even The Queen, standing on the bank with an armful of dresses, could have enticed her to exit the creek until every inch of submerged skin had puckered like a peach pit.

"*Madre Maria!*"

"*Now* what?" asked Deirdre, enjoying the sensation of silt slithering between her toes. When Rosie didn't respond, she glanced back. What she saw turned her completely around, so quickly that she nearly lost her balance.

Hands on hips, Rosie faced the woods as two fishing poles emerged from the mountain laurel. A furious barrage of Italian caused the boys who carried them to stop short.

"Jesus, Mary, and Joseph," Deirdre murmured. It was impossible to know in that moment who was more surprised—she, Rosie, or Billy McKenna and his pimply-faced, tow-headed companion. Had some stern Italian saint heard Rosie's ultimatum and promptly dispatched the green soldier, now clad in a brown work shirt and pants, to test Deirdre?

Rosie waved her arms and shouted in Italian, speaking so quickly that Deirdre made out just two words. *Deirdre*. And *gambe*. Legs.

"What's eating her?" Tow-head asked Billy McKenna, who shrugged.

Rosie turned toward the creek. "You promised! Tell him right now to go away!"

"Promised what?" Billy McKenna asked. Tow-head motioned with his pole to move downstream, but Billy McKenna held his ground. Repeated his question.

Before Deirdre could respond, Rosie shocked her by walking straight into the water, shoes and all. Rosie planted outraged hands on Deirdre's shoulders and turned her back toward Billy McKenna. "See her legs? Her papa is beating her because she looks at you!" A final shock: modest-to-a-fault Rosie lifted Deirdre's skirt, exposing her thighs. "Next time, he will kill her—and it will be your fault! A terrible sin upon your soul!"

Mortified, Deirdre pulled away from Rosie. Her skirt dropped back to a decent length. Her foot skidded on a slick mat of submerged leaves. Arms flailing, she teetered, then grimly conceded her body to gravity. She was vaguely aware of Rosie's fluttering hands and fiery blush, of Tow-head's snickers. Her primary focus was Billy McKenna, regarding her as if she were a complicated arithmetic problem on an important exam, a problem he hadn't the faintest idea how to solve. The fishing pole slipped from his hand an instant before she hit the water.

Rosie, weeping now, hauled her to her feet. "*Scusatemi!*" she wailed. "I am very, very sorry." She peeled a sodden leaf from Deirdre's dripping skirt and, turning, hurled it at Billy McKenna. "Why do you not hear me? Go!"

This time, he heard. Snatching up his pole, he turned and plunged back into the woods. Tow-head lingered long enough to twirl a finger beside his temple. "Crazy dago," he said, then followed Billy.

Chapter 6: Clare

May 17, 1929
Feast of St. Paschal Baylon, Confessor

Clare passed women crisscrossing the alley, their hands filled with strips torn from old clothes past mending. They were heading for Kamila's porch, where they'd thread the simple wooden loom the Slovaks call a *bardo* and weave rag rugs as they gossiped and nibbled cookies. Clare's old bushel basket scraped the dirt behind her, echoing Kamila's *pffft!* when she'd excused herself from the gathering.

"Let your girls pick coal. They've got the backs for it," Kamila had advised. As Clare had turned away, Kamila had called, "Would it kill you to have a little fun?"

Kamila would never believe that, despite the backache and dirtied dress, Clare enjoyed this task. It offered her the wide-openness of an hour or two, when her only observer was an occasional squirrel.

No need to line up the dishes just so on the shelf—or suffer Fin's slap for carelessness.

No need to occupy the smallest possible space, to pretend with all her strength that, when he came at her for whatever purpose, she wasn't there.

For amusement, she balanced the basket atop her head. As soot dusted her nose, she tried to imagine herself with coal-black hair and a creamy complexion garnished with freckles. She saw that Irishwoman in her mind's eye: Moira, clad in an identical maid's apron and cap, hanging out the wash and polishing silver alongside Clare in a Uniontown judge's house. Moira had her heart set on city life, not a coal-patch marriage to baseball star Fin Sweeney. Stung by Moira's rejection and wanting to hurt her back, he'd proposed a week later to Clare.

Where was Moira now? Lowering the basket, Clare hoped that she had gotten her wish, that she lived in a bustling town with a husband who had never lifted a hand against her. And never would.

When Clare emerged from the alley onto Railroad Street, the Boyles paced alongside the tracks. Old Widow held open a lumpy flour sack, rope-lashed to her waist. Her daughter-in-law Angela, known to everyone as Young Widow, dragged a basket as splintery as Clare's. She turned and urged Lizzie, her sixteen-year-old Mongoloid daughter, to follow. Slow of foot and speech, Lizzie lifted her face, flat as a plate and filled with wonderment at the swirling cinders. She watched the heavy air as if it were thick with rainbow-hued butterflies.

"Coal, Lizzie!" Angela brandished the chunk she'd just plucked from the weeds.

Like the miners' wagons, passing coal cars wore generous humps. As the trains rattled and swayed, coal tumbled to the ground. Each gleaned lump was one less to buy at the store.

Angela tossed the coal into her basket and inched it forward. Bending, she called again to Lizzie and exaggerated the act of patting the grass. Lizzie, however, spied Clare and waved extravagantly, employing every inch of her stocky, innocent body.

Clare greeted Lizzie and the widows, whom she simply couldn't bring herself to hate. After the fire in No. 2 that had killed her husband and father-in-law, Angela had turned to what had been her family's business back in Limerick and opened a pub, which literally went underground when the government outlawed liquor. Most patch women allowed the widows, at best, a nod—even Veronika Lubicic, whose husband tended his own strong brew in a cobbled-together still. Boss wives snubbed them altogether, referring to them as if they were whores, not hardworking, husbandless women.

How Angela stocked her speakeasy was the best-kept secret in The Hive. Clare had long suspected the two men Angela called cousins, decked out in natty, double-breasted suits, their black hair slick with brilliantine like Rudy Valentino's. They drove a Model T as glossy as their hair, its rear windows tightly curtained. Clare used to marvel that the car, conspicuous as a rosebush on a slate dump, had never caught the eye of Deputy Harrison. Then, last Sunday, the deputy had arrived at the Edenborn ball game in a Ford of his own. Whispers circulated that he'd purchased the car, smaller and older than the cousins', with Angela's hard-earned hush money.

Kamila and the other wives wondered at Clare's silence when backyard fence chats changed to judgmental whispers about so-and-so's husband losing a day's wage while sleeping off a late night in Angela's basement. Nobody knew, least of all Fin, that Angela and Clare had an unspoken agreement. Clare smiled as if they were sisters, pretending she didn't mind Fin handing Angela money better spent on shoes for the girls or a Sunday-supper rump roast. In return, Angela turned him away when his tab reached five dollars, the equivalent of a month's rent. Then it was up to Clare to deal with his raving and shakes. To bite her lip and bear it when he used her body as if it were a warped door that blocked his way to freedom.

That morning, however, he worked half a mile beneath her feet—and she was free to admire the shy violets and May apples clustered along the railroad tracks. She pushed away the dread that had swelled since Sunday, when the Cossack had eyed the Sweeneys as if they formed a one-family picket line. She'd warned the girls to avoid him, then heard from Kamila that he'd been assigned to night patrol.

After dark, the only Sweeney he'd encounter would be Fin, liquored-up and staggering home from the speakeasy. Fin, making up in strength for what he lacked in sense, snatching that dire black club and leveling the Cossack. His job, lost. Their house, lost. Their furniture thrown into a wagon, then onto the side of the road.

A cardinal chirped. Clare caught herself. Brooding neither prompted nor prevented abject destitution. She waved again to the Boyles and followed the bird into the woods.

The coke yard's smoky veil thinned, shredded by scaly white sycamore trunks and green-mitten sassafras leaves. Lowering her basket, she was immediately rewarded with a glimpse of a fist-sized chunk of coal. Glancing back, she saw only trees, so she began her cherished secret pastime. Touching the rim of her basket, she said, "*Der Korb.*"

Added another dark chunk. "*Die Kohle.*"

Stepped over the train track. "*Das Zuggeleise.*"

"Zug-ge-leis-e." Each crisp syllable, tripping off her tongue.

Kaiser-talk, as Fin derided it, could not blister his or any neighbor's ears the way the Huns' poison had eaten away at his brother's lungs in the Great War. The girls, as wary as they were fluent, shied away from the covert conversations they'd grown up with. Remarkably, they'd never called her *Mutti* in Fin's presence. They'd occasionally humor Clare if Fin wasn't at home, exchanging a whispered sentence or two, but no more.

Clare picked a bouquet of dandelion greens. Folded them into a clean rag. *"Die Löwenzahnblattgemüse."* Breathing deeply, she imagined that she smelled them cooking, just as she had eight years earlier.

Essie had been heating up home-canned greens that frigid February night when Clare had first tapped on her door. She'd trembled with dread that someone would notice a white woman entering The Hive's falling-down fringe known as Niggertown.

When Essie had opened the door, she'd looked Clare up and down. No surprise. "You be Masha's friend?"

Clare had nodded.

She wasn't Masha's friend.

That morning, the tinker had happened to push her cart past Clare's gate the instant she'd burst from the kitchen. Nearly felled by the icy stairs, she'd made it to the outhouse just in time to vomit her scanty breakfast. When she emerged, Masha was waiting, her cinnamon-colored face wrinkled like an apron in need of ironing. She glanced up and down the alley. Leaned over the gate. "I know who can help you."

Not a friend—an angel in disguise. But Clare didn't know that yet.

Instead, she stared, incredulous, at Masha. Fin expected her to pray, as he did, for heaven's help, not that of a gypsy. *Please, God, send us another boy. A sturdy boy. A survivor.*

"Go see Essie Hunt," the unlikely angel whispered. "She knows what to do."

Clare ran back into the kitchen, into an interminable day. Fear, mounting since the last birth, became unbearable. Minute by minute, it eroded her doubt that anything could be helped.

Now she gathered greens, grateful for the chance to give back to Essie, who'd taught her how to reclaim her body. Essie always dismissed Clare's feeble offers, insisting, "I reckon it be sinful to take payment for something growing wild and plentiful, right there for the picking."

Another sin. Was any human action free of it?

Greens, however, grew wild and plentiful, too. Eagerly, Clare picked, knowing Essie wouldn't turn them down. She needed to feed her husband Josiah, eighteen-year-old Willie, and twin daughters two years younger. Though Josiah had mined as long as Fin, he earned less than white men, even greenhorns fresh off the boat. The Negroes had stood shoulder-to-shoulder with Fin a year ago, but he still considered them scabs, brought north to break the strike of '22.

If he suspected Clare's secret dealings with Josiah's wife—or knew about the seeds—without question, Clare wouldn't survive his punishment.

She took her basket and moved into a copse of birches, drawing her hand across the peeling, papery bark. Essie wove it with wild grapevines into baskets she sold to Masha, who peddled them for a few cents more. Clare had bought one for shopping, ignoring the disapproving eyes of Ada, Old Smiley's spinster daughter, who clerked at the store. Buying too often or too obviously from Masha or the Jew-store just outside the patch boundary prompted a visit from Old Smiley. He'd remind the missus (as if anyone needed reminding) just who owned the roof over her head and employed her husband so she could stay under it.

Eight years ago, Essie had given Clare a different basket. Fashioned from pine needles, it was flat enough to hide in an apron pocket. The lid closed it as tightly as a metal cap sealed a pop bottle. "Be good for storing small things, like seeds," she'd said, then smiled warily, unaccustomed to eyes in a white face looking upon her or anything she created with appreciation.

Her grandmother, who lived in Mississippi, was a Seminole Indian. "My mama be dead getting me born, so Granny raised me up. She be teaching me Indian things, like weaving needles," Essie had explained. "And knowing which seeds be keeping a baby from starting." When Clare had clasped Essie's hand, her owl-eyes brimmed. "No white folk ever be touching this one before."

Clare would have kissed her feet, had she allowed it.

Clare returned home, shivering and queasy. In her pocket, she'd hidden the basket and a small bottle of the same tincture Essie had dosed her with before sending her away. Fin didn't bat an eye when she entered the kitchen. He'd believed her lie—that she'd gone to church to light a candle and pray a novena for a healthy son. She filled the kettle, watching him fold the newspaper, then go upstairs. His feet fell heavily, taking out the day's frustrations on the steps, instead of his pregnant wife. Clare filled a teacup, opened Essie's bottle, and carefully added ten precious drops. Gulped the bitter liquid. Noted the time.

She hadn't dared to set the clock's jangling alarm, for fear of waking Fin. Instead, some dark angel nudged her awake at two-hour intervals, when she forced down another cupful. At four, the cramps started as she fried Fin's eggs and potatoes, brewed coffee, packed bacon and bread in his bucket, all the while praying. *Mea culpa, mea culpa.*

At five, when she watched the gate swing shut behind him, she swallowed what she sensed would be the final dose. A severe cramp bent her double. The rag she'd tucked between her legs turned warm and damp. "*Gott sei Dank,*" she said, then burst into tears. Thanking God was sacrilege. The appropriate thanks had already been tendered—in Essie's kitchen.

What she'd done, essentially, was spit in God's face. *Take back what You gave me. My husband wants this child, but I don't.* God had twice given and taken back between Deirdre's birth and Katie's, but not like this.

Durch meine große Schuld. Through my grievous fault.

God and every saint and angel heard her now and laughed. Professing guilt without regret had no more substance than a gaudy minstrel show. True remorse would send her scurrying to the confessional. Baring her soul to Fr. Kovacs. Meekly accepting the priest's chastisement, the heavy penance. Vowing, henceforth, to follow a blameless path.

Instead, during weekly confessions, she withheld these, her worst sins. Accepted as penance the leaden yoke of guilt. And chose a path that led her, again and again, into the woods. When summer waned, she'd crouch to forage for withered flowers. Replenish the seed-store in the pine-needle basket. Then profligately scatter more seeds, ensuring another flowery summer awash in wild white lace.

If only a desperate woman would cross her path—but no heavenly being would grant this request. Who could she pray to but the ground?

Let that desperate woman open a hand into which I can drop some seeds. Let her accept a bottle of the tincture Essie taught me to brew. If what I've learned can spare another, please, please, let me share it.

She'd never enjoy the bliss of absolution. But if she ever met that woman, she knew she'd feel some small ease.

She'd had none after that long-ago night of two-hour doses. Gritting her teeth through each cramp, she'd sent Norah and Deirdre off to school and taken Katie to Kamila's. *Miscarriage,* she'd whispered. Kamila had God-blessed her and promised to keep Katie as long as needed. Ignoring the basket of wrinkled laundry, Clare had returned to bed.

At noon, Masha, that unwashed angel, appeared in her doorway. "Essie told me to check on you." She reminded Clare what to watch for; when, if necessary, to send for the doctor.

By the time the girls returned from school, Clare was weak from bleeding, but emptied, utterly. Of that she was sure.

Norah heated water for Fin's bath, scrubbed his back, then served the goulash Kamila generously had provided for supper. When Fin came upstairs, his eyes moved from Clare to the slop jar, brimming with bloody rags. He made a harsh noise and lifted his hand as if he would strike her. She regarded him, too exhausted to flinch. "Another one gone, then," he said, his eyes begging for contradiction. She managed a nod. He departed with heavy footsteps that set the stairs keening for another lost child.

Had it been a son? There was no way to tell, but Fin surely believed it—as did Clare.

After he'd departed for Angela's, Norah brought Clare tea and toast. She pointed to the slop jar, which had begun to smell. "Should I take it to the outhouse?"

The toast turned to cinders in Clare's mouth. Who was she to decide what was sinful? Still, Norah's suggestion, practical as it might seem, struck her as wrong. She slid off the bed and reached for the wall, bracing herself against a rush of dizziness. "Get a towel."

Norah darted to the cupboard in the hallway.

Clare dropped to her knees beside the jar. Lifted one rag. Another. Tenderly, laid each aside. At last, she cupped bloody hands around the tiny, flaccid balloon. Tears dropped into her palms.

To God, a mockery. To her, baptism.

Norah stood in the doorway, her pale face pinched in horror. Slowly, the eleven-year-old crossed the room and knelt beside the jar. Not yet bleeding herself, and here was her mother, the one charged to protect her innocence, initiating her into a gory fact of her sex.

She obeyed Clare to the letter. But how she managed, with the frozen ground beneath the front porch as hard as coal, Clare would never know.

Chapter 7: Deirdre

"This—" The Queen swept a hand toward the seats—"is known as *the house*. The term also refers to the audience. The house is the reason you perform. Nevertheless, when onstage, you must behave as if the house doesn't exist. Your awareness must never cross the footlights."

Majella looked at Deirdre, who shrugged. Since The Queen had taken the stage and begun her sermon, every player had eyed Deirdre, as if the leading lady knew precisely what the director was talking about. Deirdre slid down in her seat and watched Tereza, taking notes as if her life depended on it. For the first time since hearing about Mr. Sestak's promotion, Deirdre pitied his oldest daughter. The Queen had introduced Tereza ahead of Deirdre, calling the stage manager *my right-hand man*. Tereza's smile was short-lived, however, as The Queen recited her duties. Not only was she required to learn St. Barbara's part, but also shadow The Queen and write down everything she said, supervise the backstage helpers, monitor cast members' entrances and exits, and cue anyone unfortunate enough to forget a line.

"Questions?" The Queen surveyed the silent, befuddled cast. Given the expressions on several faces, notably Pasquale's, Deirdre suspected that most, if not all, of the director's information seemed less intelligible than the Latin mumbled at Mass. She recalled Rosie's assessment: *The Queen doesn't like greenhorns*. It wasn't a question of like or dislike, Deirdre decided. In The Queen's world, greenhorns didn't exist—especially inside the footlights.

The Queen bent over the lights to hand Tereza a sheaf of papers. "Please pass out the schedule. Players, I expect you to write these dates in red ink on your calendars at home. The only acceptable excuses for missing practice are work, illness, or death in the *immediate* family."

Tereza took a single step, then turned a stricken face toward the stage. "Mrs. Finch, do we really have practice this Saturday afternoon?"

"Every weekend afternoon until the performance." The Queen's tone sharpened. "Does that compromise your personal schedule, Miss Sestak?"

Tereza's mouth trembled. She shook her head. "I—well, no, Mrs. Finch." Her crestfallen expression was as easy to read as The Queen's schedule. Saturday's rehearsal would force her to miss Mary Margaret's upperhiller birthday party.

Before Deirdre could smile, she realized that her personal schedule would be compromised. She'd miss every baseball game for a solid month. Pap, who'd taken a surprisingly dim view of the pageant in general and her choice role in particular, surely would consider it a personal affront that she wouldn't witness his ball field heroics. Though she needed no reminder to tread lightly when Pap nursed a grudge, her shoulder blades, still black and blue beneath her dress, pulsed painfully against the wooden seat back.

The papers made their way along the rows, ending with Deirdre, who folded hers and slipped it into her pocket. Eyeing it, even blandly, might draw The Queen's attention. *Does that compromise your personal schedule, Miss Sweeney?* She'd resolved to tread lightly around The Queen, too, until she received the promised dresses. When Deirdre rose from her seat, she caught her breath as The Queen beckoned from the stage. "Miss Sweeney," said The Queen, her ice blue dress shimmering beneath a spotlight, "you realize that I'm taking a substantial leap of faith by giving you the lead role. When I showed the list of players to my husband, he cautioned me against casting a member of your family."

The house's bustle changed, in a heartbeat, to humiliating silence. Players onstage froze in place. Players in their seats ceased whispering. Surely The Queen intended this conversation to be confidential. Why, then, hadn't she lowered her voice? Worse yet, why was Tereza standing not three feet away, industriously taking notes?

Deirdre opened her mouth to—what? Assure The Queen that her husband, the Big Boss—who, with a snap of his fingers, could fire Pap—was dead wrong?

"Although I respect my husband's opinion, I told him I'm quite sure you'll give me no reason to regret my decision." Standing above the brilliant bulbs, The Queen regarded Deirdre with eyes that no longer saw Miss Sweeney, whose audition had brought down the house, but the daughter of that goddamn Bolshevik.

"I'm going to be the best St. Barbara this patch will ever see," Deirdre declared. A glare at Tereza. "Did you write that down?"

"Every word," Tereza said grimly, concluding her notes with a pencil-stab. She followed Helena up the steps, calling, "Onstage, leading lady."

The Queen consulted her script and motioned to Paul Visocky, cast as Dioscorus, to stand center stage. Slowly, Deirdre mounted the steps. It no longer seemed prudent to bring up the promised dresses, at least, not today. Today, her task was delivering an Act One, Scene One that would delight The Queen to the point that she'd tell Tereza to put down her pencil in order to watch and learn. Then The Queen would return to her mansion and tell the Big Boss that, while he might know how to run a coal mine, he hadn't the foggiest notion how to cast a play.

A brisk draft nearly stole Deirdre's script as she opened The Hall's front door. Storm clouds swarmed above the wind-driven cinders. The sky flickered between the slate dump's peaks. Thunder rumbled like a hard-driven wagon down First Street, rattling windows as it passed over The Hall. Hooting, the boys galloped into the rain; the girls huddled in the entryway. A black car pulled up, and a young woman whom Deirdre decided must be The Queen's maid emerged and opened an umbrella. "Watch out," Tereza warned as Majella backed away from the door and nearly collided with the director.

The Queen gracefully inclined her head beneath the umbrella. Rain spattered the maid's back, but not a drop dampened The Queen's frock, which, Tereza took the opportunity of informing everyone, was made of pure China silk. The car pulled away, the sound of its engine lost to another wagon-roll of thunder.

Majella squealed and trod on Deirdre's toe. "Oh, for pity's sake, you won't melt," Deirdre said, pushing past Rosie's prissy sister. "And neither will I."

When Deirdre sprinted across Main Street, a brilliant burst of lightning directly overhead convinced her to take cover on the store's porch. She reached its steps just before the sky ignited again. As if succumbing to the wind's insistent breath, every light—on porches and street posts, uphill and down—went out. The store's porch steps disappeared, causing her to stumble. Her elbow collided painfully with a post. Her script dropped into a bush's black, scraggly shadow. Despite the explosive thunder, she heard the sound of tearing paper.

She dropped to her knees and thrust an arm into the bush, but gained only scratches for her effort. Fearful of foraging rats, she withdrew her hand, willing another lightning bolt to relieve the darkness. The storm obliged with a brilliant blade that knifed across the sky. For a long moment, everything gleamed like Fr. Kovacs' silver chalice: the shrub's sparse leaves, the script splayed against the steps, and two water-beaded boots jogging across the puddled grass.

Deirdre spied her script and lunged—but Billy McKenna moved faster. "Lose something?" he asked as everything again went dark. The one-two-three thump of his heels told her that he'd mounted the steps. Paper rustled. A deep breath was drawn, then released. "I'd give you your book if I could see you," he said.

Warily, she got to her feet. "Why are you out on a night like this?"

"If I'm not out, I don't get paid. Wish I got paid more for sloshing around in a storm." Another flash transformed the droplets to diamonds on Billy McKenna's jacket and cap. In his hand, the opened script revealed a ragged tear on one side, and a waterfall-shaped stain of bleeding ink on the other. "Will this get you in trouble?"

The lightning subsided. The porch reverted to shadow. The ruined pages glowed dully, taunting her. Each gust of wind echoed The Queen's challenge: *I'm sure you'll give me no reason to regret my decision.* "Everything gets me in trouble," Deirdre admitted.

"Including me."

"I just broke two promises. Only one is about you." Her vision finally had adjusted to the darkness. She watched him draw a handkerchief from his pocket and futilely blot the paper. "It's ruined, isn't it?" she asked, trying to sound nonchalant, even as tears stung her eyes. She blinked hard, determined not to cry in front of a Cossack. What heinous sin had she committed, prompting God to dispatch Billy McKenna to participate in this fiasco?

He turned the page. "This one's not much better."

"I should've stayed put till the storm passed." Deirdre motioned to The Hall, noticed with relief its closed doors. Terrified of lightning, Majella had probably insisted that the girls—sensible girls, unlike Deirdre—hunker down till she gave the all-clear. Deirdre reached for the book, but Billy stepped back. "Give it here," she said sharply. Why, oh, why had she told him off in front of Mrs. Zekula? He'd likely tear it up now out of spite. With effort, she softened her tone. "That script is really important. Please, give it back."

He flapped the damp pages. "What other promise did you break?"

"It's complicated." Again, she extended her hand.

Again, he ignored it. "What's complicated? Those marks on your legs?"

Her neck warmed, then her face. "That's none of your business."

"You shouldn't get beat up just for looking at somebody."

She laughed: a single harsh note. "If Pap saw me right now, I don't know what he'd do." She did, of course. He'd whip her straight into eternity.

"Your friend said he'd kill you."

"Rosie's Italian. It doesn't take much to get her all worked up."

"The other promise," Billy McKenna persisted. "Is it about your father, too?"

Thunder rumbled, distant and feeble. Deirdre glanced at The Hall's closed door, then scanned the dark streets. Mrs. Zekula would hardly venture out during a storm, but what if the

Lubicic twins were sneaking around, looking for trouble? "Please," she said, careful to keep her tone even. Only a heartless Cossack would make her beg for what was hers. Did it give him pleasure, exerting small, petty power over a girl? "I need to go home. The storm's letting up."

"No, it's not," he said. As if cued, the sky turned liquid. Rain lashed the sidewalk. Snapped branches whirled through the air like disoriented birds. A thick black bough thumped onto the steps. Before she could resist, he seized her arm and pulled her toward the building.

She cried out when her shoulder met the sharp edge of a window frame. Quickly, he released her. Despite the shadows, she saw his face contract. "He beat you there, too?"

He reached for her shoulder, but she stopped his hand. "Don't," she said, cringing as his fingers closed around hers. Like tangled branches, their hands hung in the air, swaying as she struggled to free herself. What if he pulled her off the porch? Though his hand was soft, its grip was strong. She shuddered, recalling tent camp rumors during the Big Strike. He could drag her behind the store and do something terrible and indecent. He could do anything he wanted to a downhiller and get away with it on account of his goddamn badge.

"What'll happen when Mrs. Finch finds out you spoiled your script?"

Their hands, at last, broke apart. Deirdre backed away, breathless and shaking. "I promised not to disappoint her, even though I'm a Sweeney."

He made a sound, both speculative and threatening, a sound uncannily similar to the one Pap made before he hurt someone. Her heart rose into her throat. If she snatched the script, jumped off the porch, and ran like a bat out of hell— Her hand tingled, inched forward, then, inexplicably, balked. "If I'm not home soon, Pap will come looking for me," she warned. If, indeed, that dire event happened, who would fare worse: the Cossack, for detaining her, or she, for allowing it?

"If you go out in this—" he nodded at the rain—"you'll ruin the whole book." Before she could stop him, he'd unbuttoned his jacket and tucked the script inside. "The lady I board with, her daughter works in an office in Beesomtown. She can type those pages over. Mrs. Finch won't know the difference."

A Cossack, offering help. Astonished, Deirdre felt her hand drop. All she could think to say in response was, "Everybody calls it Beetown since The Queen moved in."

His laughter was high-pitched, almost girlish. "Queen Bee. I like that." He buttoned his jacket. The shadows had deprived his badge of its shine. Now it looked no different than a patch on a shirt. "When do you need your book again?" he asked.

"Why are you doing this?" she returned. Out of nowhere came Rosie's voice, louder than thunder, more furious than the rain. *Why are you letting him?*

He studied his boots, intricately embossed with cinders. "I guess—to make up for those marks on your legs."

Her pulse throbbed in her ears. She could barely hear her own reply. "You don't have to make up for anything. It's just the way things are."

"Sometimes I like doing things I don't have to." He pointed. "They're coming out of The Hall."

She glanced back. Majella was crossing the street, followed by the others. Deirdre turned to face him. "I need the script tomorrow night. Rehearsal starts at seven. Sharp."

"Better start walking before somebody sees who you're talking to," he said. "Don't worry, I'll give it back. I keep my promises."

Wait! Had she shouted? Or was it the wind, as appalled as Rosie would be when she found out?

It didn't matter. He'd already leaped off the far end of the porch and disappeared.

The next evening, Deirdre slipped out the front door before Norah noticed her empty hands. Majella and Tereza were already crossing Main Street. The nosy Zekulas, *Gott sei Dank*, were nowhere to be seen. Unfortunately, neither was Billy McKenna. Despite the warm evening, Deirdre shivered as she walked down First Street. What if Pap had been right to beat her? What if, at this very moment, Billy McKenna smiled as he watched his boarding missus empty her stove of a large mound of ashes—the fine, feathery kind that came from burnt paper?

She lingered outside The Hall's double doors, ignoring the other players' quizzical glances. Paul Visocky pointed down Main Street at an approaching car. "Get a move on, leading lady. Here she comes."

Paul hurried inside, his script enviably tucked beneath his arm. The Queen's car rolled to a stop. The shivers returned, stronger than before, rattling Deirdre's teeth. Even simple Lizzie Boyle knew better than to trust a Cossack.

The car's driver, a gray-haired man wearing a black suit and cap, got out and opened the back door. Offered a hand. The Queen emerged, instructing, "Come back at nine-thirty." The driver touched his cap brim and returned to the car. As it pulled away, The Queen noticed Deirdre—and her empty hands. "Where's your script? Don't tell me you've lost it already."

It seemed impossible that Deirdre's ribs could contain such a furiously beating heart. Her mouth opened to answer, but no sound emerged. Lips pursed with annoyance, The Queen regarded Deirdre, then turned to behold something that apparently annoyed her even more. Over her banging pulse, Deirdre heard someone shout, "Mrs. Finch! I need to speak to you!"

Billy McKenna sprinted down the sidewalk as if he were a striker with a Cossack in hot pursuit. The script flapped rhythmically in his hand.

He stopped, panting, and thrust it at Deirdre. His face had turned almost as ruddy as his hair. "I need to—apologize—Mrs. Finch. To you—and especially—Miss Sweeney. I thought I'd—play a trick—and snitch—her play book. But my brother—said that—was a real low-down thing—and he'd tell Mr. Phelan if I didn't give it back." He concluded his speech with a gasp.

Deirdre's body felt as substantial as broth. She leaned against The Hall, longing to open the book and inspect the pages. But The Queen now regarded her as if she'd confessed to ruining it in the first place. "I expect you to be more careful. Setting that script down—"

"It wasn't like that at all, Mrs. Finch," said Billy McKenna, enduring The Queen's hard stare at his impertinent interruption. "I grabbed it right out of her hand. Last night, when it started raining? I was on patrol, and I saw her and the other girls leave The Hall, and—"

"I get the picture, Officer—what's your name again?"

"Billy McKenna." He removed his cap. "I hope you'll accept my apology, ma'am. I'd hate to lose my job on account of a stupid joke. I promise I'll never do any—"

"Apology accepted. Good evening, Officer McKenna. You've wasted quite enough of my time." The Queen opened the door and stalked inside, calling to Deirdre to hurry up.

"It's all fixed," Billy McKenna whispered as Deirdre pushed herself away from the wall. He caught her elbow as she swayed. "Are you all right? He didn't beat you up again, did he?"

"I was so scared. I didn't think you'd come." A deep breath restored her balance. His hand, with its tiny pink scar, withdrew. "Could you really lose your job?" she asked.

He fitted his cap back onto his head and grinned. "Your father sure hopes I do. He hates me more than the devil, doesn't he?"

"I'm not anything like my pap. And you're—" she hesitated as the hammering resumed in her chest—"you're not like the other Cossacks." She glanced down the sidewalk, found it vacant, then slowly extended a peace offering: her hand. "I wish I could pay you back. I'd bake you a cake, but Pap would ask questions. I'll say a prayer, at least, that your brother doesn't tattle to Mr. Phelan."

"I made that up about my brother." Billy McKenna's hand clasped hers. His thumb slid across her knuckles. "You could pay me back by taking a walk sometime." She stiffened. He relinquished her hand, adding, "I know we'd have to be really careful. But I'd sure like that."

Again, Deirdre felt herself sway. Again, his hand steadied her. It struck her that the hate she'd harbored since first seeing him had vanished. Fear had taken its place, but not the same fear that had gripped her on the store's porch the night before. This fear inflamed each bruise on her back and legs as if Pap's belt had done its damage all over again. She craned her neck to peer over Billy McKenna's shoulder. What if Mrs. Zekula stood, pop-eyed, on the corner?

"Saturday." The word slipped from Deirdre's mouth and floated in the air between them like a cinder fresh from the oven, its fluted edges glowing fiery red. "After rehearsal, everyone will go to Dearth for the ball game, or—" She caught herself before adding, *Mary Margaret's party*. Surely he was invited. She waited for the inevitable. *Sorry, I'm busy on Saturday.*

He, too, glanced over his shoulder. "We could meet by the creek."

She nodded, shocked to realize that, already, she missed the sensation of his hand—far too soft, surely, to wield a club, to cause harm.

"Don't bring Rosie with you," he added.

"Not a chance." She succumbed to a smile, inviting his, and was rewarded.

"A decent effort," The Queen pronounced at the rehearsal's conclusion. Her gaze moved from one player to the next as they lined up inside the footlights. "Until everyone learns his or her lines—" she looked pointedly at Deirdre—"it will take longer to block each scene. I want everybody off-book by Thursday. Off-book means no script when you step onstage."

A few players nodded. Most stood in shocked silence. Three days to memorize lines filled with words they could barely pronounce.

Tereza raised her hand. "Do I have to be off-book, too?"

The Queen tapped her chin reflectively. "Not till next week. You need a solid command of the entire script, not just Barbara's part, so I'll give you some extra time."

Majella whispered to Deirdre, "No fair. Tereza has to learn the whole thing, and she doesn't get a pretty costume."

"She gets a boss house," Deirdre whispered back. "I'd memorize the whole Bible for that."

After Tereza read the evening's notes, Majella beckoned to Deirdre to walk home. Quickly, she turned her back and pretended to tie her shoe. When every girl had departed, she made her way toward The Queen.

The Queen glanced at her watch. "My driver is waiting. Whatever it is, I'm sure it can wait till tomorrow."

Before The Queen could turn away, the question tumbled out. "Did you have a chance to pick out the dresses you said you don't need anymore?"

The Queen looked Deirdre up and down. "I haven't the slightest idea what you're talking about, Miss Sweeney. Please turn out the lights before you leave."

Deirdre watched The Queen's icy blue back move up the aisle and through the door. Had Deirdre's failure to be off-book caused The Queen to change her mind? Deirdre stared at the barren stage for a good five minutes before it dawned on her. The Queen truly had no recollection of her promise. She'd made the offer, and as soon as the words had left her mouth, they'd left her head. Perhaps, during the costume fitting, she had felt genuinely sorry for Deirdre and intended to help. But that moment had passed, and the feeling with it, and now Deirdre was once again nothing more than a troublemaker's daughter who didn't know her lines.

Her right foot flew out and kicked the stage. The lights flickered, then regained their impervious glare. Toes smarting, she headed for the door. The top of her shoe, rent from its sole, flapped loosely—just like her foolish tongue.

Chapter 8: Clare

May 25, 1929
Feast of St. Gregory VII, Pope

Clare awoke to rattling and banging downstairs in the kitchen. Fin had returned, his appetite fanned by a late-night binge. She burrowed like a rabbit beneath the quilt, but it was no use. Her pulse quickened, dispelling the sweet fog of sleep. His shoes began a stop-start cadence upstairs, a sign that he was too far gone to walk a straight line, much less a flight of steps.

Fin slapped the bedroom door until he found the knob. "Clare, are you asleep, then?" He bumped the bed, and his slurred voice swelled. "Clare, rouse yourself and light the lamp before I break me leg."

Pretending to wake, she obeyed. He'd shed his clothes, all but his whiskey-spotted shirt, tented where it hung between his legs. The drink drowns most husbands' lust, she'd been told, discreetly, by other women. But not Fin's. *Gott in Himmel*, why had she obeyed yet another trick up the sleeve of the famous first-base Sweeney? He'd forced her awake, so he'd not end his night with the pale pleasure of raping a rag-doll wife, limp and mute with sleep.

He was on her before she could extinguish the lamp. "Leave it be," said his sour mouth. He dragged her nightgown over her head, leaving it tangled around one shoulder. As his rough hands moved over her, she glimpsed over his shoulder the jagged crack that bisected the ceiling.

No, not a crack—a tree branch. She rose to meet it. Soared above it. Higher and higher until it seemed no more than a scratch upon the sky.

Had someone said this—*a scratch upon the sky*—when she'd listened that afternoon to the radio? *Describe for our audience, Miss Earhart, the view from your cockpit.*

Clare felt her legs forced apart and plummeted back to earth.

Fin's blackened hands pinned her shoulders to the bed. "For shame! 'Tis a sin to deny your husband."

Miss Earhart, how does it feel during take-off?

Like freedom? Like the ascent of your soul to heaven?

Fin seized Clare's chin. "You'll do your duty now, won't you?" Thrust with such force that she couldn't help but moan with pain.

Then she found it again, that scratch on the sky. Once more, she was Lady Lindy, secure in the silver angel of her airplane. She soared above the coke yard, piercing the smoke. Sunshine, benevolent and cleansing, poured over her.

Dimly, she was aware of Fin's furious rutting. He'd finish only when she voiced her submission. Through the drone of the engine, the rush of the wind, she heard his faint, but insistent question: "Won't you do your duty?"

Miss Earhart, how can you bear to land?

"Won't you?" Fin demanded, then dipped his head and bit Clare's lip.

Splayed beneath him, she shuddered. Blood loosened her tongue from its parched bed. The syllable slipped out before she could snare it. *"Ja."*

His face blanched as he thrust a final time, as if trying to break her bones, impale her heart. Then he pulled away and, with a cry of disgust, shoved her off the bed.

Her body breached the air. Her ears roared like an engine.

The middle of my month. My ripest time.

Her head struck wood, releasing her into perfect darkness that substituted for sleep.

In the chill of dawn, Clare opened her eyes. Her naked body sprawled beside the bed. Fin's juicy snores told her that nothing short of a blast-powder shot would rouse him. She pulled on her nightgown, wincing as the cloth grazed her forehead. Her lower lip throbbed from the effort of covering herself. She rose slowly, gripping the bed as the room spun. As quickly as possible, she had to crush seeds, drink them down, and keep them there, despite a stomach as unsteady as the floor beneath her feet.

Feeling her way downstairs, she chose her explanation. *I tripped when I got up to use the slop jar. I fell against the door.* The last time, it had been the bed frame. She never blamed the same innocent object twice in a row. The girls, though disbelieving, would accept this tale in accordance with the Fifth Commandment. *Honor thy father. And mother, too, even when thy father doesn't.*

In the kitchen, bread crusts littered the table. A greasy knife reclined in its center. The butter, reduced to a slim shingle, smelled rancid after sitting out all night. Ashes drifted across the floor, escapees from the stove, whose door hung ajar. Fin must've stoked the fire, perhaps intending to fry a piece of bacon in the skillet he'd left on a chair. *Gott sei Dank*, an ember hadn't tumbled onto the floor and set the house on fire.

In the pantry, she stood on tiptoe to reach the topmost shelf, but her probing fingers met only dust. She shoved Fin's chair through the narrow door and, with quaking hands, lit the lamp. Dizzy with disbelief, she stared at the shelf's empty corner.

She'd become complacent. In three weeks, she'd moved the pine-needle basket just four times. Pantry shelf to sewing basket to linen cupboard. Then back to the shelf.

Pushing the chair out of the pantry, she met Norah, who took one look at her and began to cry. "I've lost something," Clare said, too panicked by her loss to guard her tongue.

Norah wiped her face on her nightgown sleeve. "I'll help you look."

"*Mach' nichts.*" Clare's voice nearly broke. It doesn't matter. She didn't dare tell Norah—diligent novena-maker, scrupulous conscience-examiner—what she'd lost. Her strained smile tore the raw seam on her lip. "Get dressed," she told her daughter. "We've got baking to do before the ball game."

"*Gern*," said Norah and hurried upstairs.

No matter how tiring or tedious or distasteful the task—scrubbing Fin's work clothes, helping Deirdre learn her lines, burying Clare's miscarriages—Norah's response never varied. Gladly.

Katie and Deirdre entered the kitchen. "Pap snores like the Visockys' pig," said Katie, attempting an imitation. She stopped short, as did Deirdre, when they noticed Clare.

She offered the standard excuse. "*Ich bin hingefallen.*"

"Against the door?" Deirdre asked. Her eyes narrowed, studying Clare's bruises. For an unsettling moment, they reminded Clare of Fin's.

Unlike Norah, Deirdre kept her distance when Clare appeared so obviously damaged. Her mind worked the occasion of her mother's wrecked face like Clare washed a shirt: rubbing, stretching, turning inside out. Norah solved problems with her hands, while Deirdre pondered them till they were threadbare, hoping to open a peephole through which to glimpse the truth.

Katie's face labored to maintain her smile. She tugged Deirdre's sleeve, but Deirdre ignored her. Biting her lip, Katie hurried back upstairs.

Deirdre lingered. "Are you going to bake bread in your nightgown?"

"I'll change as soon as I sweep the floor." Clare reached for the broom, expecting Deirdre to follow Katie, but she didn't move.

Deirdre's breath came hard, as if she'd just run the length of the alley. Her enraged expression took Clare by surprise. "Pap has no right—" her whisper abraded like sandpaper—"but we put up with whatever he does. Then we make stupid excuses." She stood, trembling but defiant, just as she had before Fin had beaten her for speaking to the Cossack. When Clare touched her arm, she bristled at the contact. "He thinks he knows everything about everybody. He thinks he's just like God—but he's wrong." She ran from the room. The stove flue rattled as her feet pounded the stairs.

She'd never reacted with such outspokenness to Fin's actions before. Never dared. Had she secretly transgressed? Clare stared after her daughter until fear seized her heart. The Cossack. She was about to call Deirdre back when a different question overwhelmed her. *Where is my basket?*

She set the broom aside and resumed her search, lifting the washtub, the coal bucket, even the flour sack—forty pounds of wasted effort. Breathless, she clung to a chair, massaging a stitch in her side. As she straightened up, the Tonellis' raucous rooster crowed, greeting the day for which she was perilously unprepared. Not a single seed to counter Fin's.

When the girls came back downstairs, she sent Katie next door to gather the eggs Concetta had promised. Norah rolled up her sleeves and took the large mixing bowl from the shelf. Deirdre considered the floor, still adrift with ashes. She seized the broom and began sweeping, barely glancing at Fin when he entered the kitchen. "We're having eggs for breakfast, Pap." Her tone was just shy of civil.

Fin held two jars: one for slops, the other coated with the black phlegm he coughed up each night. "Me gut is knotted up with the cramp. 'Tis strong coffee I'm needing, not eggs." The door banged behind him as he headed to the outhouse.

Norah squatted beside the flour sack, counting cupfuls into the bowl. Deirdre finished sweeping and turned to the table. She sniffed the butter. Her lip curled. "It stinks."

"Throw it out," advised Norah, getting to her feet. She peered out the window, then nudged Clare toward the sink. "Fill the coffee pot. He's coming inside."

Fin apprehended Deirdre at the garbage pail just inside the door. His hand closed around her arm. "Are we as fine as the Finches, then, too good to eat butter scraped down a wee bit?"

"It smells, Pap." She lifted the dish. He swatted it. Incredibly, she managed to hold on.

Furiously, Clare worked the pump, raising her voice above the rushing water. "Set the table, Deirdre. The coffee will be ready in two shakes of a lamb's tail." Her hands quaked as she measured it into the pot. Dark grains peppered the floor.

Small. Black. Just like seeds.

Deirdre quickly swept them up. Shovel in hand, Clare knelt on trembling legs beside the stove. Odd dark threads were mixed with the cinders. They puzzled her until she drew out her basket's charred, crumbling lid from the back of the stove.

Fin stood at the mirror, guiding the razor along his lathered chin. Clare held up the blackened needles. Her voice thrummed with fury. "Did you do this?"

Deirdre froze, a plate pressed to her chest.

Fin looked over his shoulder and shrugged. "'Twas in the pantry, full of maggots. Next thing you know, they'd be in the bacon." He resumed shaving, his hand uncommonly steady after last night's bender.

Clare gripped the shovel with such rage that her knuckles cracked. *Gott in Himmel*, only a drunk would mistake seeds for maggots. When Deirdre caught her eye, she nearly toppled over. *He thinks he knows everything about everybody.* Had Fin searched the pantry, suspecting his wife's barrenness wasn't the will of God?

"A cold stove won't cook the coffee," said Fin.

Clare imagined rising with the shovel. Walking, only to stumble.

Ich bin hingefallen.

The shovel bumping his hand. The froth at his throat turning pink, then crimson. The razor and basin clattering to the floor. Sudsy water soaking her nightgown's hem. His knuckles thudding onto the planks, the last thing he'd ever strike.

The grisly images faded. Reason returned. She emptied her rage with the scorched needles, sliding with a puff of soot into the ash can. The aroma of coffee filled the kitchen. Her empty stomach contracted. She took quick, shallow breaths, willing herself not to gag.

The middle of her month. Her ripest time.

Just as she'd done eight years ago, she'd have to sneak into Niggertown.

Fin, fresh-shaven, wiped his chin with the towel. He rinsed the basin and hung it and the razor on the hook beside the sink. Wringing out the towel, he passed it to Clare. "Better see to that lip. You don't want to be receiving Communion tomorrow and bleeding all over the body of Christ."

Deirdre slammed the last plate onto the table and ran outside. She collided with Katie, mounting the steps. Deirdre barreled toward the outhouse, ignoring Katie's cry. Beside the dropped basket, a vivid mosaic of cracked shells and pooled yolks spread across the dusty porch.

Chapter 9: Deirdre

Crossing her arms on top of the fence, Rosie shook her head. "If you are not coming, I'm not either. I will wait for you to finish the practice, and then we can—"

"The Queen may keep us till suppertime." Over Rosie's shoulder, Deirdre watched Mrs. Tonelli bustle between the kitchen and the icebox on the back porch. She had ten minutes, at most, to change Rosie's mind, then make it to The Hall in time for rehearsal. "You'll waste your whole day, waiting on me. *And* you'll pass up a chance to talk to Mike Zoshak."

"Majella is not saying she will practice so long."

When Rosie got that look on her face, talking sense into her was as likely as convincing the Lubicic twins to enter the seminary. Thinking quickly, Deirdre said, "Majella doesn't have many lines. It's just me, Paul, and Tereza, who has to miss Mary Margaret's party." Deirdre glared at the sky, dark with cinders and thunderheads. Was God colluding with Pap, sending a storm to prevent her from meeting Billy McKenna? Or was He sending her a warning to play it safe and steer clear of the Cossack? She regarded Rosie—no longer Deirdre Sweeney, but a beseeching saint. "*Please* go to the game and keep a box score. Then, at least, I'll know who got hits, and when." She pressed Rosie's arm. "Won't you do that for me?"

Rosie wavered. "But you know I am not so good at making the box—"

Leaning over the fence, Deirdre whispered, "Ask Mike. I bet he'll ask you to sit beside him, so he can make sure you're doing it right." Hell would freeze over before the team allowed a girl on its bench, but Rosie didn't know that. "If you do me this favor—" Deirdre leaned closer—"when The Queen sends me the dresses, you can pick two."

"*Two* dresses?" Rosie pushed away from the fence and twirled like a wobbly top.

"You'll do it, then? You'll go to the game?" Deirdre ignored a twinge of guilt. It wasn't a lie, not really. The Queen hadn't said, straight out, that Deirdre would get no dresses.

Clinging dizzily to the fence, Rosie declared, "I will do anything for Queen-dresses."

"Bring the box score over as soon as you get home," Deirdre said. "I want to hear everything Mike says." She congratulated herself when Rosie blushed. Mrs. Tonelli shouted from the kitchen window for Rosie to come inside and help make the picnic. At last, Deirdre was off, weaving through families with babies and blankets, baskets and umbrellas, all heading in the opposite direction to the game.

Before entering The Hall, Deirdre paused to look uphill. Colorful streamers fluttered from the trees and the picket fence enclosing the Donovans' backyard. Forsythia, bridal wreath, and peonies bloomed in bright profusion. Cloth-covered tables dotted the lawn like enormous mushrooms. Not a single tomato stake or beanpole spoiled the property's perfect uselessness. Unlike downhillers, who employed every last inch of soil to raise chickens and grow vegetables they'd put up for the winter, boss families kept yards just for show. The maples shading the houses produced only leaves that downhiller boys got paid a nickel to rake. Downhillers mowed every lawn, weeded every flowerbed, whitewashed every fence, and trimmed every hedge on The Clean Hill, so girls like Mary Margaret could paint their fingernails, instead of scrape dirt out from under them.

The shiny black car pulled up to The Hall as Deirdre prayed fervently to St. Barbara to postpone the rain until the ball game ended. "And Mary Margaret's party, too," she added. It was no skin off her nose to be generous with this particular petition.

The car's back door opened. The Queen's maid leaned out and called, "Mrs. Finch can't come today. Her little boy's got a bad fever. Are you Tereza? No? Then tell Tereza she's in charge of rehearsal. Maybe tomorrow, too, if Hal doesn't get better."

The car departed. Deirdre entered The Hall a moment before the auditorium door flew open, banging the wall. "You're late," Tereza snapped, seizing Deirdre's sleeve.

"I was detained," Deirdre replied, in her best imitation of the director. "I just spoke with The Queen's maid. The Finch boy is sick, so you're in charge of rehearsal." Deirdre freed her sleeve from Tereza's grip. "Too bad you have to miss the party. The decorations are so pretty."

Tereza lowered her eyes and fingered the clipboard. Bit her lower lip. Finally, she regarded Deirdre. "If I cancel practice, will you tell The Queen?"

Deirdre smiled, guileless as a saint. "I'd just get in trouble for not taking it over myself."

Tereza swayed from side to side. *Go to the party. Get in trouble. Party. Trouble.* She glanced into the auditorium. "Somebody else might tattle."

"There isn't a single person here who wouldn't rather go to Dearth for the ball game. Anyway—" Deirdre smiled again—"we can practice extra long tomorrow to make up for it."

"But The Queen might be back tomorrow. She'll know we skipped out."

"The maid said she doubted The Queen would be back before Tuesday." Deirdre sighed and shook her head. The difference between a good performance and a convincing lie was truly negligible. "You know how mothers are. She won't leave her little boy till he's better."

A smile bloomed on Tereza's face. "There's nothing to do on Sunday except go to church. I wouldn't mind a long practice then, would you?"

"Not at all." Deirdre steered Tereza into the auditorium. "And neither would they."

In case Rosie had changed her mind, Deirdre chose a roundabout route home. After passing the store, she turned right onto Second Street. She walked backward for a stretch, solely for the entertainment of viewing Tereza's breakneck pace up The Clean Hill. Encircled by girls in spring frocks, the Donovans' backyard tables had changed from mushrooms to flowers with colorful petals surrounding their snowy centers.

When Deirdre reached Railroad Street, she paused and took in the dispirited cluster of Niggertown shanties at the street's dead end. Willie lived in the last one facing the tracks. The tumbledown structure, topped with a rusted metal roof, looked no bigger than the Tonellis' and Lubicices' chicken coops put together. Mutti had actually befriended Willie's mother, going so far as to enter the Hunts' shack to visit. Why Mutti bothered with a Negro woman mystified Deirdre, but she had decided not to ask. A secret, after all, was as good as money. You never knew how much it was worth till an opportunity arose to spend it.

Deirdre hurried up the alley and hid behind her family's outhouse, counting to one hundred as she scrutinized the Tonellis' house and backyard for any clue that someone had stayed home. It struck her that Majella and the other girls had set out for Dearth as soon as Tereza had cancelled practice. Rosie would surely wonder why Deirdre, the passionate fan, had failed to come along. A plausible explanation would require another stellar performance from the pageant's leading lady— but not for several hours. For now, the only performance worth considering was that of a downhiller meeting a Cossack by the creek. A quilt and some sort of picnic would serve as props. Deirdre hurried inside to find an appropriate costume.

Norah's dresses—hand-me-downs like Deirdre's—were, at least, different hand-me-downs. And, as luck and the missionary relief box would have it, decidedly more stylish. Deirdre chose the blue gingham that Norah wore to work at the store. Though faded, it had a fashionable dropped waist, just like The Queen's clothes. Katie's one-and-only white hair ribbon complemented it nicely. Sliding a hand beneath the mattress, Deirdre drew out Norah's compact and lipstick, bought on the sly from Masha, who didn't share Pap's opinion that girls with painted faces were going to hell in a hand basket. Deirdre thanked her absent sisters with a pat on each one's pillow before returning the contraband cosmetics to their hiding place.

From the linen cupboard, Deirdre took the worn-out quilt, which Mutti draped over the bed of anyone needing to sweat out a fever. Unfortunately, the quilt smelled like everything else in the cupboard—a medicinal scent that leaked from an old Sloan's Liniment bottle, half-full of brownish liquid. Mutti brewed the stuff from plants that, she claimed, kept moths away from the wool blankets and sweaters. Deirdre unfolded the quilt and flapped it vigorously as she went downstairs. A foolish economy—saving pennies by boiling weeds, instead of buying mothballs. Envelope after envelope, any saved pennies tippled into the Young Widow's till.

An apple in each pocket. A glance at the faded picture of The Sacred Heart, tacked on the wall beside a yellowed newspaper image of union leader John L. Lewis. An affirming thought about keeping company with a Cossack—hadn't Jesus said, *love thy enemies*?

"You're early," said Billy McKenna, rising from his seat on a rock. He pointed to his wristwatch. Its sturdy leather strap bisected a long pink scar.

Deirdre stared at his arm. "What happened?"

"Peja and Duje Lubicic threw a broken bottle." He shrugged. "Part of the job."

Boldly, she touched the faint seam on his right knuckle. "Also part of the job?"

His hand captured hers. He looked at her for a long moment before stroking her lower lip. The pink smudge on his fingertip prompted a smile. He lifted the finger. "Is this for me?"

The flush claiming her face surely surpassed the lipstick's rosy hue. "I guess so."

He wiped his finger on his pants, the same ones he'd worn the day Rosie had screamed at him. "I should've asked you to the movies."

"I couldn't. Somebody might—"

"See us. Yeah, I know." His hand rose again and cupped the back of her head. A strand of bright hair fell across his forehead as he bent toward her.

Instinctively, her throat tightened. The quilt dropped to the ground. Uniform or not, a Cossack was a Cossack. He'd saved her script and risked his badge to do it, but that badge marked him as a pussyfoot, a yellow dog. A sworn enemy to every miner and his family. "I've never—" she said as he straightened up. "I mean, I'm not used to—"

"I didn't come here to hurt you, I swear. Look at me." He stepped back, arms outspread. Anyone who didn't know better might take him for a downhiller, albeit one lucky enough to own pants lacking patches. "I'm not a policeman. I'm just me."

If you put a silk dress on a goat, it's still a goat. Pap might have been standing right behind Deirdre, intoning one of his tired Irish proverbs. So clear were the words that, holding her breath, she turned around. Of course, nobody stood there. If Pap had sneaked up on her, he'd hardly waste time or energy on speech.

When she turned back, Billy McKenna's arms dropped to his sides. Her eyes traveled from his soot-streaked shoes to the opened collar of his white shirt, then, hesitating, rose to meet his. His lips tightened, as if bidden by better judgment to let her speak next. Beneath drooping strands of stop-sign hair, furrows etched his high forehead.

She suppressed a smile. A Cossack, unnerved by a patch girl, who, clearly, had the upper hand. She could send him away and never risk another beating for encouraging this ill-advised friendship. Then she imagined seeing him after Mass, arm-in-arm with Mary Margaret. She didn't want him as a friend. Rosie would call her *stupido*, but even the prospect of Pap's harshest punishment didn't diminish her sudden, overwhelming desire to kiss Billy McKenna.

She closed her eyes just before their lips met, before his hand moved to her cheek. When she opened her eyes, his face remained level with hers. Steeling herself for the answer, she felt compelled to ask, "Are you kissing Mary Margaret, too?" When he looked blank, she prompted, "Mary Margaret Donovan? You shared her ice cream cone after the first baseball game. She's not one to share boys, though."

Billy rolled eyes as green as crocus leaves pushing through snow. "She just wanted to make this other fella jealous. Big Bill's son. As soon as he showed up, she told me to get lost."

Though Deirdre sensed Billy was telling the truth, the knot in her chest only tightened. "You and I, we're on opposite sides. If there's another strike—"

"There won't be." Gently, he lifted her chin and turned her head from side to side. His eyes narrowed. "Has your pap ever hit your face?"

She flinched. "Don't talk about him. It spoils everything." Her finger found the seam on Billy's right knuckle, reading it the way the milky-eyed lamp cleaner read the dots in his Braille Bible. The scar reassured. Billy, likewise, had been damaged—and healed.

His left hand closed around a drifting cinder. When he opened his fingers, soot lined the palm. His pale brows drew together. Like Masha, could he read the future in the dark fretwork of his skin? She started when he slapped the palm against his hip. "Things never turn out like you expect. Almost from the start, I knew I shouldn't've come here."

She picked up the quilt, its pattern blurred by tears. "I shouldn't've come here either."

"No! Jesus, Deirdre, that's not what I meant." He pulled the quilt from her grasp and threw it aside. His hands settled on her shoulders. "Listen to me. Joining up was Joe's idea. My older brother, the one who came fishing with me? He was flunking out at Pitt, and he thought being a soldier would be a big adventure. Our parents told him, no, absolutely not, he had to stay put and study harder. So he ran away—and talked me into coming with him."

"You left *college* to be a Cossack?"

Billy's face flushed. "Crazy, huh? No, worse than that. Just plain stupid. Joe's the crazy one, always getting himself into scrapes. I should've known better, but I thought, why not? Maybe I could do some good. Sitting in a classroom—how did that help anyone?"

Deirdre shook her head. College seemed as remote as Africa. Billy clearly expected an answer, so she ventured, "My sister Katie would give her right arm to go to college."

"Your sister's obviously smarter than me. Still, I have to hand it to Joe. He had a good argument. We'd join the National Guard, he said. We'd take care of people in trouble. Trouble is, the guard wouldn't take two college boys with no training. So we ended up in the Industrial Police, which was fine by Joe. He's stationed in Dearth and loving every minute of it. I got sent here, and the deputy spelled it out pretty plain. I don't take care of people. I spy on them." His hands rose to cradle her face. "I was about to call it quits. Then I nearly tripped over you."

She laughed, recalling the shoe that didn't need tying. "I did that on purpose."

A tiny cleft she hadn't noticed before dimpled his chin when he smiled. "You're not afraid of much, are you, Deirdre Sweeney?"

Her laughter was cut short when a huge hole opened inside her. "I'm afraid now—that you'll quit and go back to school." Backing away, she added, "And I'm afraid that, if you don't leave, my pap will figure things out and kill you."

She covered her face with her hands. If she pressed hard enough, perhaps the imprint of his mouth would be lost. He was right. It was a terrible mistake to have come here. To avail herself of a memory as indelible as it was heartbreaking. Blindly, she turned, catching her foot in the rumpled quilt.

He caught her waist as she pitched forward. "Don't be afraid," he said, drawing her to him. "Nobody's going to die over this."

"What is *this*?" she asked, her voice muffled by his shirt. Her mother and sisters and friends would call it madness. An act of such prodigious insanity that it made his decision to leave college for a coal patch seem almost sensible. She lifted her head, met his gaze. "Tell me, what is *this*, Billy McKenna?"

"I'm not sure yet." His lips caressed her hair. "But I'm not leaving till I find out."

Though the truth threatened to leap from Deirdre's mouth each time it opened, she told Rosie only, "I stayed home to study my lines. I'm way behind everyone else."

Sitting beside Deirdre on the Sweeneys' back porch, Rosie, unfailingly understanding, nodded. "You have so many words to remember." Smiling, she drew a crumpled paper from her pocket. "You are right, telling me to ask Mike about the box score. I was afraid to stay by the bench, but he is standing up every time and coming to where I am sitting with Majella."

Deirdre pretended to study the shaded boxes. Temptation rose in her throat, urging her to confide. If Billy were a ballplayer or a townie in their high school class, such fun they'd have, trading *he said*'s and *then I said*'s.

Rosie blushed. "Then Mike comes to me in the ice cream line, telling me he will help again make the box score at the next game. When I turned around, who do you think I see? Helena Zekula—and she is so jealous, her face is red like a tomato!"

Norah's shrill query interrupted their laughter. "Why are you wearing my dress?"

She opened the gate, set down Mutti's basket, and planted her hands on her hips. Beside her, Katie licked an ice cream cone. Mutti, holding a folded blanket, brought up the rear.

Deirdre's stomach turned over. How could she have been so careless? Imagining the next secret meeting with Billy, she'd completely forgotten to change her clothes.

Katie lowered her cone and frowned. "That's my ribbon. You're supposed to ask before borrowing other people's things."

Snatching up the basket, Norah stalked toward the house. She stopped at the porch steps and studied Deirdre's face. "You used my makeup, too. What on earth for? I know for a fact your rehearsal was cancelled. Every cast member except you showed up at the game."

Katie followed. "We won, five to two. Pap hit another homer. Why didn't you come to the store for ice cream?"

"She was studying her St. Barbara words," Rosie said. Her tone was matter-of-fact, but the corners of her eyes narrowed, so slightly that only a best friend would notice.

"You didn't need my dress to read your script," said Norah. She mounted the bottom step and crossed her arms. The basket dangled from her elbow, quivering with outrage. "What *did* you need it for?"

Katie joined Norah on the step and thrust out her hand. Deirdre pulled the ribbon from her hair and draped it over her sister's palm. Rosie said something about helping with supper and slipped away. As Deirdre watched Rosie leave the yard, her eyes met Mutti's. Except for the bruises, Mutti's face had turned the color of chalk. How, Deirdre couldn't guess, but, without question, Mutti knew.

Chapter 10: Clare
June 8, 1929
Feast of St. Barnabas, Apostle

"I be having no more," Essie said, her owl-eyes dark with regret. "The roof opened up itself a hole, and rain be dripping in, turning my basket moldy. Every seed gone bad."

Two weeks had passed since Fin had burned Clare's basket. Repeatedly, she'd tried and failed to visit Essie after dark. Finally, desperation had driven her there in broad daylight.

"I don't know what to do," she told Essie.

"You do be knowing," Essie said. "Your bottle burnt up, too?"

Clare drew a deep breath. "It's too hard, that way."

Essie smoothed her apron, revealing a gently rounded belly. "All ways be hard."

"Are you—" Clare swallowed the word before it could take root, like any insistent seed.

Essie nodded as if each chin-dip exhausted her. "I be fooled. Bleeding all along, so no worrying. Then I wake up and be vomiting, all day, next day, so hard my throat bleeding, too. Midwife say I be four months gone. Josiah say, this time we get a boy to help him load the wagon. He not be thinking how we feed another one." Her shoulders slumped. "Now I be praying, please, King Jesus, please, no twins. Boy or girl, just one this time."

Clare clasped Essie's hand, as chapped as her own. "Use the tansy."

Essie pulled away and opened the door. "Too late for me now. But not you."

Clare darted from the shadow of one shanty to the next. Faint cheers drifted from the ball field. Clare stayed in the shadows, fearing that someone might have felt sick and stayed home. What if that someone caught sight of her from a bedroom window? She'd claimed to be under the weather herself. As soon as the words had left her mouth, Fin's frown had changed to a face alight with expectation.

A phantom cramp knifed through her. She staggered into the questionable shelter of a rotting, abandoned shack. Everything she beheld—ovens, train tracks, red dog street—wavered like a landscape reflected in a rain-washed window. Tears were a luxury she had no time for, yet she couldn't stop crying.

The fans' cheers grew louder. Someone blew an exuberant fanfare on a trumpet.

Had fresh hope fueled Fin's bat? Had he, euphoric, hit the ball so hard that it had soared all the way to heaven, carrying his petition for a healthy son?

Clare breathed deeply, gathered herself. She wiped her eyes, and her gaze fell on the woods. Wishing was as useless as weeping. But she couldn't refrain. If only it were October, when seeds were in abundance.

An ember of absurd hope propelled her toward the trees. Though unlikely as snow in July, maybe, just maybe, somewhere between the mine yard and the creek, stood a stalwart, seeded stalk of last year's Queen Anne's Lace.

She plowed through brush until enveloped in a pink bower of crabapple trees, their vivid blossoms flecked with cinders. Lush green ferns and umbrella plant colonies filled each patch of shade. She paused beside a fallen tree to inspect the weeds snagged in its boughs. Her fingers trembled as they probed the brittle web of tangled stems, then dropped to her sides. Even if by some undeserved miracle she discovered some seeds, they would do her no good now.

Behind her, a twig snapped. She dropped to the ground. Another snap, and another. Slowly, she raised her head, peering through the weed-thatched branches.

Deirdre strode purposefully toward a tunnel of mountain laurel with Clare's oldest quilt folded beneath her arm.

Clare tried and failed to breathe. A hard blow of maternal intuition had knocked the wind out of her, and fear—raw and cold and paralyzing—had replaced it. She pressed a hand to her chest. It loosened just enough to let her gasp. Rise. Creep toward the laurel. She watched Deirdre spread the quilt, smiling up at the Cossack.

Branches raked Clare's arms and hair as she lunged into the tunnel. Her noisy progress interrupted their embrace. Panting, she emerged to find the Cossack brandishing the club with which he'd so emphatically introduced himself to Fin. Deirdre stood beside him, clasping his hand. A Cossack's hand.

"You told Pap you were sick," said Deirdre. Her tone, both accusation and rebuke.

"So did you." A fresh spasm gripped Clare's chest. Her voice nearly broke. "Have you forgotten when the Cossacks threw us out of our house? Have you no respect for your pap, risking his life on the picket line?"

Deirdre moved closer to the boy, who shoved his club through a belt loop. His arm encircled her shoulders.

A Cossack, touching Clare's daughter. And, clearly, not for the first time.

"How can *you* respect Pap?" Deirdre countered. "He hurts people and never acts sorry. He treats you like dirt, and you let him. Over and over, you just let him."

"Don't do this to our family," Clare implored.

Deirdre stared right through her.

Clare tried again. "Your pap will punish—"

"I swear to God, I won't let him hurt her again." The boy's eyes, young and defiant, met Clare's. "I love Deirdre. If you love her, too, you'll keep quiet about this."

Clare closed her eyes. She'd sensed that Deirdre had been hiding something, yet done nothing. From the day the Cossack had walked into church, she'd feared the worst, but failed to act. However this resolved, she'd lose her daughter. Yet another child, lost.

"Did you pretend to be sick, so you could spy on me?" Deirdre's eyes narrowed. "You went to see that Negro woman, didn't you?"

"Come home, Deirdre. The ball game will be over soon," Clare said wearily, then retreated into the woods. Strength ebbed with each step. When she reached the downed tree, she doubled over, retching.

It was then that she remembered why she'd gone there. What she'd failed to find.

Chapter 11: Clare
June 10, 1929
Feast of St. Margaret, Queen of Scots

On Monday evening, the entire patch turned out in The Hall for Heath School's graduation exercises. The Sweeneys filed into a back row amid a flurry of congratulations. Leading the way, Deirdre stared at her shoes. Clare's smile felt as false as the painted lips of a plaster statue. Behind her, Fin cursed under his breath as his tipsy body toppled into a seat.

The pianist began to play. Students processed from behind the side curtain, led by the school principal and eighth grade teacher. The Queen, arrayed in lilac chiffon, and Big Boss followed. The moment they appeared, Fin's whiskey-breath burned Clare's cheek. "If I could spare me shoes, I'd chuck them at the sonofabitch. Dresses his wife like royalty, but won't raise me wage by so much as a penny."

In the row just ahead, the Lubicices glanced uneasily over their shoulders. Fin's scowl quickly turned them back around. Norah watched the stage, awaiting Katie's entrance. Deirdre's gaze fixed on her lap. Though Norah sat between them, Clare felt tension rising from Deirdre like steam escaping a kettle. Since Saturday's confrontation, she had refused to look at Clare, confining her conversation to *yes* and *no*.

Norah elbowed Deirdre when Katie walked onstage. Deirdre grudgingly raised her eyes. When Norah, quizzical, turned to Clare, she shrugged and stared at the graduates.

She saw, instead, the Cossack's face. His eyes ablaze, just like Fin's.

Onstage, the graduates formed two rows. Those in back mounted a line of benches, so every eye could follow the teacher's hands as she directed the songs. Katie stood on the bench behind the fidgeting Lubicic twins and soldiered through the high notes of *America the Beautiful*. Katie couldn't carry a tune in a bucket, but nobody would have known by looking at her, radiant with anticipation at delivering the valedictory speech.

And deliver it she did, without a single stammer or mispronounced syllable. It took at least five minutes after she'd left the podium for the appreciative audience to stop clapping and sit down. Prideful tears washed Clare's cheeks until her hankie was wet enough to wring.

"Katie's way too smart to stay in this hell-hole," Deirdre whispered to Norah.

Fin rapped Deirdre's shoulder. She retaliated with a glare. Such boldness was surely due to the Cossack, egging her on. She gave Clare an equally defiant look.

He treats you like dirt, and you let him.

Clare stared at Fin's lap. His powerful hands—blackened and sinewy like root-choked soil—restlessly tapped his knees. The foolish boy had no idea how quickly and remorselessly Fin could break Deirdre's arm. Or worse.

Over and over. Over and over.

Clare's eyes returned to the stage, but she saw only a blur. A desperate scheme began to take shape.

Deirdre turned away before Clare could wordlessly reassure her. In flagrant disregard for everything Clare knew about Cossacks, she would believe the boy. She would count on his promise to protect her headstrong daughter. For once, Clare was grateful that Fin had tippled too much whiskey to look at her and grow suspicious. Her intentions were so flabbergasting that her face surely gave her away.

The presentation of certificates began. Fin's gaze turned positively murderous when The Queen pecked the cheek of Dan Phelan's daughter. "I'll wager she won't be dirtying her mouth on any downhiller's child," Fin said, no longer bothering to keep his voice down.

Gott sei Dank, he refrained from further comment—and The Queen, from additional kisses—while the rest of the certificates were distributed. Then The Queen stepped toward the footlights and announced, "Ladies and gentlemen, please remain in your seats."

"Ladies and gentlemen, me arse. Mules is more like it. Spineless greenhorn mules," Fin declared, flapping an irate hand as someone hushed him from across the aisle.

"Soon we'll celebrate the twenty-fifth anniversary of St. Barbara's Church with a picnic, pageant, and fireworks," said The Queen. "I'm sure you're looking forward to the festivities as much as I am. Tonight, I'm pleased to announce the results of the essay contest. I had a very difficult task choosing the winners, each written by one of our graduates. When I call your name—" she glanced back at the students—"please come forward." She took three envelopes from her handbag. "Third place, with a prize of one dollar, goes to Synan Keating."

"Sure, and 'tis a difficult task, deciding among the bosses' brats," Fin growled.

The twins' father twisted around in his seat and shook his head. "Steamshovel, not now."

Clare risked a hand on Fin's arm. *Sei still!* she urged silently. Be quiet! He shook her off as The Queen announced that second-place winner Bridget Phelan would receive two dollars.

"'Tis a mockery, this contest!" Fin shouted, swaying as he got to his feet.

The Queen regarded him for a long moment, then pretended to smile. "Mr. Sweeney, I'm not surprised that you'd be the first to applaud our top winner." She lifted the last envelope. "First place and five dollars is awarded to valedictorian Kathleen Sweeney."

Deirdre and Norah sprang to their feet. The entire audience followed their example as the teacher helped a dazed-looking Katie down from the bench. Clare clapped till she no longer felt her hands. Only then did she notice the empty seat beside her.

When she reached the stage, Katie fell into her arms. They peeked into the envelope, mute at the sight of a grass-green bill nearly equal to Fin's daily wage. Since Clare had left her job at the judge's house, she'd never held so much money at one time. They found Deirdre and Norah and made their way outside, where, oddly enough, someone was singing. Odder yet, the singer stomped atop the roof of the store's front porch. When he turned toward the streetlight, Clare caught her breath. How had Fin, three sheets to the wind, managed to climb up there?

Borne on a smoky draft crossing Main Street, his slurred lyrics hushed the crowd. *"We sometimes load six wagons, by working hard and late. If it wasn't for the cursed hump, we'd have coal enough for eight. Some men dig in the entries, while others have a stump. But, bless you, there is no one who don't put on the hump!"* He waved an arm, shouting, "Join in, lads, you know the words!"

"Jesus, Mary, and Joseph," said Deirdre. Norah simply stared, too distracted by her father's drunken antics to scold her sister for taking holy names in vain.

They reached the store as Fin launched into the chorus, *"Oh, the hump is on the wagon. The hump is on the wagon. The hump is on the wagon,* **and we're all dissatisfied!"** He roared that final line, punctuated with a juicy hiccup. Heads down, family after family crossed the street. All avoided the corner where Clare stood, begging Fin to hush and come down.

Katie tugged her sleeve and pointed. "Here comes Deputy Harrison."

Clare located the approaching figure, a swiftly moving shadow. It wasn't the deputy.

"No!" Deirdre screamed. Before she could take a single step toward the Cossack, Norah trapped her in a bear hug.

Oblivious, Fin kept singing. The moon sliced a hole in the coke cloud, revealing silver tear-tracks on Deirdre's cheeks. The Cossack halted beside the store and regarded Fin. "You're disturbing the peace, Steamshovel. Go home quietly now, or things might get ugly."

"You damn fool, things can't get any uglier!" Fin hiccupped again. "They throw us five lousy dollars, so I'll be kissing the Big Boss' arse. Give us fireworks and a pageant, so we'll forget we're earning less than before. Promote a hunkie to fire boss, so all the other hunkies will be running the other way when the union men come 'round."

Katie began to cry. "Will we have to move?"

Whispering about the union within earshot of the wrong people had gotten men fired. Shouting about it in a Cossack's presence could get the Sweeneys evicted and Fin blacklisted by every boss in the county.

Head tipped back, Fin addressed the moon. "Am I the only fucking slave with enough sense to know a pageant won't put scales in the tipple? Or pay down me store debt?"

Deirdre squirmed, but Clare managed to whisper in her ear. "Don't let on you know that boy. Don't say a single word, you hear? I promise I won't either."

The Cossack shook his fist at Fin. "You're a troublemaker without enough sense to know that whiskey isn't your friend. Or the difference between a baseball and your daughter. One, you hit. The other, you don't. Someone should've locked you up a long time ago."

Clare's legs nearly gave way. What had possessed the boy to mention Fin's daughter?

Deirdre struggled against Norah like a spooked mule bent on breaking its harness. "He's too far gone with the drink, Billy. He won't remember any of this tomorrow!"

Her voice was the equivalent of a bucket of ice water dumped over Fin. "How would a yellow dog like you be knowing anything about me daughter?" He spoke without slur, suddenly a stone-cold sober man who understood that the girl he'd punished for looking at a Cossack had done the unthinkable and befriended him.

Engine rattling, Deputy Harrison's car pulled up to the sidewalk. "That's enough singing for one night, Steamshovel," he called. He beckoned to the Cossack and, lowering his voice, said something that prompted the boy to get in the car.

Fin's finger jabbed the air. "That goddamn—"

"Pipe down, Steamshovel. Be glad Officer McKenna kept his head and didn't shoot you for abusing Company property." The deputy motioned to Clare. "Take him home, Mrs. Sweeney. Make some coffee and sober him up."

Clare nodded and, as was expected, thanked him. Fin climbed down the porch post. As soon as the car rounded the corner, Fin seized Deirdre by the hair and hauled her, stumbling and weeping, down the sidewalk toward their gate.

Clare sprang forward, but Norah corralled her. "Did you know about this?"

"I warned her," Clare said, wrenching free. "But I was too late."

Katie clutched her hand as they ran. "What will Deirdre do now?"

The word emerged from Clare's throat like a rock thrown through a window. "Leave." She flung open the gate. Inside the house, something crashed. Deirdre screamed. Clare let go of Katie's hand. "I'm sending her away. With that boy."

Before Clare could reach the porch, Norah grabbed her shoulders and shook her, as if doing so would return Clare to her senses. "You'll have her run off with a *Cossack*?"

Inside, more screams. Katie covered her ears. Cringing, Norah released Clare.

She took the front steps two at a time, calling over her shoulder, "He said he loves her. What else can we do now but believe him?"

Chapter 12: Deirdre

Katie dropped her side of the coal basket, forcing Deirdre to a halt beside a dented metal barrel. A stinking pool of moonshine spread out in the alley beside the Lubicices' fence, its slats cracked and sagging. The twins stood beside the damaged chicken coop. Peja held the broken boards while Duje nailed them back in place. The coop's door, torn from its hinges, lay like a splintery rug in front of the outhouse. Mrs. Lubicic knelt in the churned-up dirt that had been her garden, sifting torn green bits through her fingers. On the porch, four-year-old Jelena screamed and flapped tiny hands at squawking hens that ventured too near the steps.

Peja looked up and scowled. "It's your goddamn pap's fault!"

Duje stopped hammering long enough to add, "He brought the white-hoods back, singing his Bolshevik songs." His foot lashed the air, just missing the rooster. The bird screeched and took off across the ruined garden, scattering dirt as it ran. Mrs. Lubicic covered her face with her apron and began to cry.

"Your pap better lay low, 'cause the white-hoods hate Bolsheviks worse than niggers." Peja eyed Deirdre, who quickly turned away. "High school ain't let out yet. You playing hooky?"

Duje jeered, "Can't read the chalkboard, can you, with two black eyes?"

Katie grabbed the basket and pulled Deirdre away from the wrecked still. Mrs. Lubicic's sobs, hoarse as a dull saw chewing a tree stump, followed them down the alley.

They found Mutti in the kitchen, sweating over the ironing board. Deirdre paced beside the door and let Katie describe what had happened. The smell of burnt cloth surrounded them. Too late, Mutti lifted the iron. She'd scorched Pap's Sunday shirt, yet didn't seem to notice. "Put the coal in the bucket and bring the basket outside," she said, opening the door.

Deirdre followed Mutti out to the garden, where Mutti dropped to her knees and uprooted two tomato plants. Surely sound couldn't carry across four backyards, yet Deirdre was certain that she still heard Mrs. Lubicic, wailing from the deepest, saddest place inside her. Mutti set the tomatoes aside and pounded the dirt. *"Die Teufel! Mögen Sie in Hölle verfaulen!"* The devils! May they rot in hell!

Never had Deirdre seen Mutti so raw with rage, much less expressing it in German—and outside, where anyone might hear. "Is it Pap's fault, for singing that song?" she ventured.

Deirdre backed away from Mutti's fierce denial. A hinge squeaked. Katie hovered on the porch. Mutti rocked back on her heels and wiped her face, leaving brown smudges on her cheeks. "Take the basket to every house. Tell the missus what happened. Ask if she'll spare a few plants, so Mrs. Lubicic can make a new garden. Be polite, even if the answer is no."

Mutti crawled past feathery carrot fronds to the cucumber vines. The skirt of her patched housedress had turned as brown as her hands. "Don't go to Railroad Street," she added. "God knows, the Negroes have nothing to spare. Mind you, stay in the alleys. No telling who's in on this and not letting on." She flapped a grubby hand. *"Los! Schnell!"*

Deirdre's bruised face throbbed in time with her feet as Katie led the way into the alley. When Deirdre glanced back, Mutti still beat the earth with dirty fists. Was this the same meek woman so easily and often damaged? Deirdre turned away, at once reassured and unsettled by the revelation that, if pushed hard and often enough, Mutti would push back.

Sunrise revealed six freshly wrecked gardens, one of them Mutti's. Blood-red paint spattered St. Barbara's door. Cows and pigs had been killed; chicken coops, smashed; outhouses, tipped. Five Niggertown shanties, burned to the ground. Homeless Negro families trudged along the road to New Salem, pulling rickety carts piled with mattresses, tables, and stoves. Every man and boy gripped a pick or charred fence slat for protection.

Each downhiller missus with an undisturbed garden uprooted part of it and carried the plants to the neighbor who needed them most. Mrs. Tonelli and Mrs. Zekula helped Mutti hurry their donations into the churned-up dirt. Kneeling between Deirdre and Mutti, Mrs. Tonelli whispered that she'd heard the white-hoods had taken away, then deported an Italian family from Dearth. "Who can sleep?" she asked, wringing dirty hands. "Who is safe?"

Mutti just shook her head.

Later, Mrs. Zekula brought three more tomato plants and shocking news. A notice had been posted at the store. The Frick League had suspended The Hive's baseball team indefinitely. "On account of the Bolshevik trouble," said Mrs. Zekula.

"The white-hoods are doing all the damage," Deirdre protested. "Everyone knows that."

Mrs. Zekula passed the plants over the gate. "Fin better not raise another ruckus, or things will get even worse," she warned Mutti, whose face had drained of color.

Pap didn't come home for dinner.

By the next morning, downhillers had arrived at an unspoken conclusion: keep your heads down and stay off the streets. The alley became a playground, crowded with children rolling hoops and playing paddle and caddy. If someone shouted, the nearest backyard missus appeared at her gate to hush and scold. All activity ceased when the shiny black car driven by the Young Widow's cousins rolled past the garbage bins and outhouses. Masha and her peddler's cart were noticeably absent. Even the iceman made his deliveries with uncommon haste—hoisting the glistening fifty-pound block onto his broad back, huffing up the porch steps, then hurrying off to the next house.

Despite Rosie's entreaties, Deirdre refused to return to school. Bad enough to show her bruised face at rehearsal, where she'd told The Queen—from the stage, so everyone else would hear—that she'd fallen down the steps. Pap, who'd taken to drinking his dinner at the Young Widow's, had apparently forgotten about the other Sweeney graduate. Mutti said only, "Norah can take the streetcar to McClellandtown and pick up your diploma on her next day off."

Each night since his encounter with Pap, Billy was waiting on the shadowy store porch after rehearsal. Deirdre, fearful of what might happen if he saw her face, pretended not to notice.

On the third night, he called her name. Rosie, a self-appointed bodyguard, linked arms with Deirdre and walked faster. "Go away!" she shouted at Billy. "You make for her too much danger!"

Rosie forced Deirdre to cross the street, but Deirdre forgot herself and looked back. The Italian banshee, apparently, no longer deterred Billy, who now stood on the sidewalk. When his expression changed from perplexed to enraged, Deirdre realized, hurrying past the street light, that he'd seen her battered face.

"You will not break your promise again," Rosie said sternly, opening Deirdre's gate. When Deirdre failed to answer, she threw up her hands. "*Incredibile!* You are pretending too much to be *Santa* Barbara. Do you *want* your papa to kill you? To make you like your baby brothers, buried in the ground?"

She was still shouting as Deirdre ran inside.

When Norah and Katie went upstairs to bed, Mutti called Deirdre back. Putting a finger to her lips, Mutti closed and locked the back door. She drew Deirdre into the pantry and pressed a scrap of paper into her hand. Deirdre couldn't read the writing in the dim light.

"My cousin Trudy's address," whispered Mutti. "She lives in Pittsburgh. Have Billy take you there. I've already written and told her to expect you."

Deirdre clasped both hands around the paper. St. Barbara had never worked a miracle as astonishing as this. "I thought you hated him."

"I want you to be happy. And safe." Mutti's palm gently cradled Deirdre's swollen cheek. "Go to bed now. Don't let anyone, not even your sisters, see that paper."

Later, lying beside Norah on the thin mattress they shared, Deirdre whispered, "I'm leaving." Norah responded with a soft snore. On the cot beside them, Katie didn't stir. Shadows cast by the ovens' flames danced across the ceiling. "I'm leaving," Deirdre repeated.

By the time sleep overcame her, the declaration had become a litany, promising salvation.

***

The strain of alley-creeping and garden-replanting began to tell on Mutti, who turned quiet and pale. On Saturday morning, a sip of tea sent her running to the outhouse. Comb in hand, Norah stepped away from the mirror to watch her cross the yard. Before Deirdre or Katie could ask the question, Norah answered it. "She told me. She's pregnant."

Katie squealed and threw her arms around Deirdre. "Does Pap know?" Deirdre asked.

Norah shrugged and inspected her hair in the mirror. "Better get started on the baking. My shift ends at three, so I'll be back in time to make supper." She headed for the door, then turned back. "Don't let Mutti lift anything heavy. The less she does, the better."

Deirdre nodded, still wondering about Pap. Surely Mutti's news would distract him at least a little, improving her chances for escape.

She was kneading bread dough when Rosie appeared, sobbing, at the back door. Katie, scalding the breakfast dishes, dropped the steaming kettle into the sink. Mutti set down the sock she was darning. Her face was the color of flour. "Did the white-hoods come back?"

Rosie's voice was thick with tears. "Pasquale's boss is telling him to go home. They are closing the ovens."

"For good?" Mutti asked. When Rosie nodded, Mutti got to her feet and motioned Deirdre outside. "I'll do that," she said, rolling up her sleeves. When Deirdre hesitated, Mutti's tone sharpened. "For heaven's sake, go calm Rosie down. If women lost babies just by making bread, there'd be cobwebs all over the baptismal font."

Rosie backed away from the door and slumped against the icebox, muttering in Italian. Deirdre stroked her heaving back. "Mike will be all right. He'll hire on as a miner or—"

"No!" Rosie lifted a stricken face. "There is too much danger in the mine."

"There's danger for everyone," said Deirdre. She imagined the miraculous scrap of paper with Trudy's address, hidden in an old pillowcase that she'd stuffed under her mattress. Putting her arms around Rosie, she glanced at the sky. Already, the smoke was clearing. A ragged patch of blue appeared between the tallest peaks of the slate dump. In its center, the sun's bright, blithe eye stared back at her. *I dare you*, it taunted, *to take the next step.*

After supper, before Rosie arrived to escort Deirdre to rehearsal, she crept upstairs to the linen cupboard and removed her winter sweater. Her hand slid beneath the scratchy woolens to stroke the soft flannel of a blue receiving blanket. She noticed that Mutti's smelly brown bottle was gone and quickly closed the cupboard to keep out the moths. The sweater and two pairs of underpants went into the pillowcase containing Trudy's address. As she returned the bundle to its hiding place, she wondered, if Mutti finally had a son who didn't succumb to flu or crib death, would Pap change? Such a transformation would be yet another miracle, but one that Deirdre had lost all desire to witness.

Before concluding Sunday Mass, Fr. Kovacs announced that the Big Boss had granted permission for a Friday evening procession to open the festival. "The Company has donated wood, so I need volunteers to build a litter for the saint's statue. I also need women to sew a cover for the litter. Mrs. Finch has provided cloth left over from the pageant costumes. The Sons of Italy band will play, and the First Communion class will walk ahead of the saint, scattering flower petals. The three essay winners will walk behind. The Finches have also given a box of the highest quality beeswax candles for the altar boys to carry." He bowed his head and added, "May God richly bless Mr. and Mrs. Finch for their generosity to our congregation."

Everyone but Pap echoed the priest's *amen.*

After Mass, Mr. Zoshak and Mr. Lubicic nearly knocked over their wives in their haste to reach Fr. Kovacs. Mrs. Zekula elbowed her way after them, with Mrs. Visocky on her heels. "Flowers!" shouted Mrs. Tonelli over the chatter. "Who will bring?"

"They should be hanging a check on the pulpit," Pap said, ignoring Mutti's frantic *shhh!* "The priest may be wearing vestments, but he's a goddamn Company bastard, all the same."

Mike Zoshak broke away from the crowd and approached Pap. "Will you help carry St. Barbara's litter?"

"'Tis a statue, not a saint. Next thing you know, they'll be asking us to genuflect before The Queen," Pap replied.

"C'mon, Fin. We need to stand together, show the white-hoods we ain't afraid," Mike urged. "If we make a good showing, maybe the Big Boss will let us play ball again."

Pap's glance fell on Deirdre. His hand followed, hard against her back. "This doesn't concern the likes of you." He glanced at Mutti, and a trace of a smile crossed his face. "Take your mother home and make her a cup of tea."

Deirdre took Mutti's arm and steered her away from the men. Katie joined them, jubilant about her part in the procession. "Will you name this baby Finbar, too?" she asked. Mutti, who stared at the ground, didn't seem to hear, so Katie repeated the question.

Mutti kept her eyes on her shoes. "If that's what your pap wants."

Deirdre could barely conceal her glee. With a baby on the way, Pap would too excited to notice she was missing—until she was too far away to bring back.

That afternoon, the ball team—minus its upperhillers—crowded onto the Sweeneys' back porch. It took till suppertime, but the men finally convinced Pap to join the procession.

He stomped inside, grumbling. "A litter built by dumb hunkies. Shouldn't surprise me if the damn thing collapses in the middle of Main Street." One side of his mouth lifted. "Sure, and 'twill will be a fine thing for the Company priest, seeing his statue all broken to bits."

Norah's jaw dropped. Before she could say *sacrilege*, Mutti pushed a spoon into her hand and told her to stir the soup. Chuckling, Pap took his seat at the table. His amusement lasted until the *Figlii di Italia* band assembled to practice in the Tonellis' backyard. He shoved back his chair at the bass drum's first thump. "The deputy should arrest the lot of them for disturbing the peace." He grabbed his cap and stalked outside, glaring at the musicians before heading down the alley toward the speakeasy.

Mutti sighed. "Surely they won't ban baseball forever." She rose to clear the table, but Norah pressed her back into her chair.

"I'll do the dishes," said Norah. "Katie, make Mutti a cup of tea. Shake a leg, Deirdre, or you'll be late for rehearsal."

Deirdre stepped outside just as Mike Zoshak opened the Tonellis' gate. Circling the band members, he noticed Deirdre and waved. As Deirdre waved back, it struck her that she'd have no bodyguard that evening. Stunned at this stroke of luck, Deirdre raced across the yard. She looked up and down the alley, which—luck and more luck—was vacant. The church bell chimed the quarter-hour. She wavered for an instant, then ran toward the tipple. Let The Queen rant and rave. St. Barbara had given her another miracle, and she'd be a fool to waste it.

When she reached Railroad Street, the mine gate, burnished by the long-absent sun, caught her eye. The day after they'd closed the coke yard, Deputy Harrison had caught Peja and Duje prying bricks from the cooling beehives. Mr. Phelan had ordered the deputy to patrol the yard in case the persistent twins—or angry, laid-off coke workers—tried to help themselves to whatever they could carry off and sell.

She rattled the locked gate, scanning the soot-powdered yard. When something tapped her shoulder, she let out a scream, swiftly muffled from behind by a familiar hand. "Follow me," Billy whispered, taking a bulky ring of keys from his belt. "Quick, now, before somebody sees us." He glanced back at the street as the gate swung open. "Hide behind the larry-car." After locking the gate behind him, he ran to join her. His arms went around her, slowly and carefully, as if her bones were made of glass. For a long moment, he stared at her face. "I'll kill him, I swear to Jesus. I'll break every one of his goddamn—"

"Listen to me," she said, then told him about Mutti's astonishing change of heart. "As soon as I get money for train fare—"

He kissed her, so gently it felt like a feather-stroke. "You know what I've been doing, waiting at the store every night? Thinking up ways to talk you into leaving with me." He kissed her again, harder this time, and longer, as if making up for every lonely hour spent on the store's porch. "I'd ask you to marry me now, but my father would have a fit. I'll have to finish college first, so he'll forgive and forget."

"Is your brother leaving, too?"

Billy laughed. "Fat chance. Joe arrested a hobo last week, and you'd think he'd just gotten himself elected President. Compared to him, I'll look like the prodigal son in the Bible who wised up and came home. My parents can keep on being sore at Joe and start forgiving me." Another kiss. "And falling in love with you."

The sun slid behind the tipple, leaving her in shadow, all but blinded by the glorious assurance of Billy's smile.

On Friday evening, the only smoke left in The Hive was incense puffing from Fr. Kovacs' polished brass censer. The procession participants lined up in front of the church. Spectators jammed the First Street sidewalks. Deirdre and Norah stood behind Mutti, seated in the chair that Mrs. Zekula had made a show of carrying outside. Balancing Jelena on her hip, Mrs. Lubicic wormed her way through the crowd to offer Mutti a creased St. Barbara holy card. Mrs. Sestak followed with another card, newer and prettier than Mrs. Lubicic's. Norah stood behind Mutti's chair, discreetly holding the garbage pail, but Deirdre knew that Mutti would sooner die than vomit in front of the entire patch.

The *Figlii di Italia* drummers struck up a sedate cadence, and the procession commenced. St. Barbara's statue swayed gently on the litter carried by Pap, Mike, Shorty Dvorsk, and Shorty's cousin, who played shortstop. As the statue crossed Main Street, cheers rang out. Hands clapped. Shoes thumped the sidewalk planks in time with the thundering drums. The band director, marching backwards, waved his baton. Flutes and clarinets began to warble.

Without warning, the thick post of Mrs. Zekula rammed Deirdre's hip and sent her sprawling. Between Mrs. Zekula's ankles she saw a pool of blood beneath Mutti's chair. A trumpet blared, erasing Deirdre's scream.

All eyes had shifted to the statue. All the voices God-blessing Mutti minutes earlier now shouted petitions to St. Barbara. Pap's stony gaze was fixed straight ahead. He didn't notice the Tonelli boys carrying Mutti, chair and all, around the house. Mrs. Zekula barked, "The Young Widow," and Rosie took off like a runner stealing home. Grabbing Deirdre's hand, Mrs. Zekula followed Norah along a grisly red trail into the Sweeneys' backyard.

Mutti lay beside the garden, her skirt sodden with blood. Mrs. Tonelli brought a sheet and helped Norah wrap it around Mutti like a bulky diaper. Mrs. Zekula held Deirdre back, shaking her each time she sobbed.

As if leaking from a dream, the band's music continued. The shiny black miracle of an automobile rolled down the alley and stopped outside the gate. Rosie tumbled out of the curtained back door, and Norah took her place. Pasquale eased Mutti onto the seat, placing her head in Norah's lap. "Take her to Uniontown Hospital!" Mrs. Zekula shouted.

Deirdre felt her knees give way. Nobody but miners, crushed or burned, went to a hospital, and everyone who went—just like Pap's brother, Uncle Seamus—stayed there to die.

The car pulled away. Someone carried Deirdre into the kitchen. Someone else shut the door, leaving the sounds of drums and horns and happiness on the other side.

Pap, driven to Uniontown by The Hive's doctor, returned home the next morning. He entered the kitchen with sunken eyes and hunched shoulders. "Norah's still with your mother," he told Deirdre and Katie, as if that was the matter of most importance. He pushed past Deirdre, then paused in the living room doorway. "She'll live. They gave her an operation."

Katie breathed out a sound like paper tearing. Deirdre waited, hoping Pap would say more, then asked, because somebody had to, "Did the baby live, too?"

"There'll be no more babies," Pap said, his voice as rough as his unshaven face. He felt in his pockets and found a quarter, which he pressed into Katie's hand. "Get yourself some ice cream. Thanks be to God, you're not orphans."

They stood, motionless, until he started up the stairs. Katie regarded the coin in her hand as if it were a spider, then looked at Deirdre. "Do you want ice cream?"

Deirdre dropped into Mutti's chair and covered her face with her hands. In a few hours, she'd take her pillowcase— telling Pap, if he asked, that it held a petticoat to wear under her costume—and pretend to leave for The Hall. Instead, she'd hightail it to Railroad Street, take a short cut through the railroad tunnel, and emerge on the opposite side of The Dirty Hill in Beetown, where Billy would be waiting. Such was their plan—but how could she possibly follow through with it now?

Katie crouched beside her, stroking her knee. "So what if we don't have a brother? I'd rather have Mutti, alive and well, than ten brothers, wouldn't you?"

Deirdre lowered her hands. "I'm running away with Billy."

As if slapped, Katie toppled backward. "Today? How can you leave when—"

"I mean, I'm *supposed* to run away with Billy. But now, I don't know. I just—don't—know." Deirdre's fist thumped the table. Damn St. Barbara! Why had she worked a miracle, only to cruelly take it away?

"Are you head over heels in love with him?" Katie whispered. "Like they say in books?"

Despite herself, Deirdre laughed. "Yes. Absolutely. And he is with me."

Katie looked up as Pap's heavy footsteps sounded overhead. "You may not have another chance," she said slowly. She got to her feet and put her arms around Deirdre. "I'll tell Mutti and Norah goodbye for you. They'll understand why you couldn't wait."

The screen door rattled. Rosie's little brother Tommy stood outside. "F-f-fella in the alley g-g-gave me a ni-nickel to t-t-tell you—" he pointed at Deirdre—"to c-c-come outside."

Deirdre went to the window, clutching the sill when the sun glanced off Billy's bright hair. She held out her hand. "Katie, give me that quarter."

Katie joined her at the window. "It's him, isn't it?" she asked, but Deirdre was already out the door, handing an incredulous Tommy the most money he'd ever held in his life.

When she reached the alley, Billy drew her behind the outhouse. "I heard about your mother. Jesus, Deirdre, I'm so sorry. Don't worry, I'll stick around till she's out—"

"Hurry!" Deirdre opened the gate and pushed him into the yard. Mrs. Zekula had entered the alley, swinging her shopping basket as if it were a weapon. "Don't let her see you. We're leaving now, as soon as I get my things. Quick, go inside. I'll distract her." Deirdre stepped into the alley and waved her arms until the busybody noticed her. "My mother had an operation! She's still in the hospital, but Pap says she'll pull through!" she shouted, then ran after Billy. Hopefully, whatever saint smiled on gossips would escort Mrs. Zekula straight to the store and ensure an audience that she could impress with the latest news.

When Deirdre entered the kitchen, Katie crouched behind the table, fearfully eyeing Billy. "Are you kidnapping her?"

Billy grinned. "I'd say we're kidnapping each other."

Deirdre pounded upstairs to her room and pulled the pillowcase from beneath the mattress. When she straightened up, her heart flew into her throat. Pap stood in the doorway. "And what would you be doing with that?"

Mrs. Zekula's voice floated upstairs. "For the love of God, Kathleen Sweeney, why would you let a Cossack in the house? Wait till your poor, sick mother hears about this."

Pap spun as if shot and made for the stairs. Deirdre raced after him, screaming Billy's name. A colossal mistake, she realized, when Billy ran into the living room. Katie huddled in the doorway. Mrs. Zekula barreled past her. "What's going on,

Fin?" she demanded. "Clare goes off to the hospital, and all hell breaks loose here."

Pap stopped halfway down the stars. He regarded Billy as if viewing the rotting corpse of King Frick, risen from the grave. Two steps above Pap, Deirdre motioned frantically for Billy to leave. "Let your daughter pass, Mr. Sweeney," Billy said, his tone shockingly even.

"I'll not be taking orders from a Cossack in me own house." Pap turned to Deirdre. His finger jabbed the pillowcase. "Thinking you'll run off and shame your family? Well, think again." He drew back his hand.

Deirdre shrank against the wall. Katie screamed. Billy sprang toward the stairs.

Lacking the element of surprise, Billy would have had no chance of knocking over a man so much bigger and stronger. Had Pap not turned his back, it surely would have been Billy, lying on the floor, blood streaming from his forehead after it hit the bottom step. It would have been Pap who seized Deirdre's hand and pulled her down the stairs.

Instead, it was Billy, running just behind her out the front door.

They'd made it onto the sidewalk when Pap's voice overtook them. Without breaking stride, Deirdre glanced back. Pap stood on the front porch, a hand pressed to his bloodied brow. "You're dead now, you hear me? No one in this family will ever be speaking your name again!"

Chapter 13: Clare

June 22, 1929
Feast of St. Thomas More, Martyr

"The Queen is fit to be tied. Tereza was supposed to know the part, but whatever she knew wasn't good enough." Norah sat ramrod-straight in the wooden chair provided for visitors. Her expression hinted at sympathy for The Queen.

According to a notice posted at the store, *unforeseen circumstances* had necessitated the pageant's postponement until the second Saturday in July.

Norah rolled her eyes. "They didn't need a notice. Everybody knows what happened. It's the biggest scandal since—" She breathed deeply. A hot red flush stained her cheeks. Her lips pressed together until they were nearly as colorless as the curtains separating Clare from the patients on either side. She looked, for all the world, like her father. Shamed. And furious at the cause.

"Deirdre didn't intend to spoil the pageant," Clare said, then winced. Moving anything, even her lips, shot pain through her stitched-up belly.

At the mention of her sister's name, Norah, likewise, winced as if freshly wounded. She'd all but swallowed the syllables of that name, telling Clare, when she was lucid enough to understand, that Deirdre's escape had been accomplished.

A plan Norah clearly considered reprehensible.

"Deirdre's safe now," Clare said, setting her teeth against the slash of an invisible surgeon's knife. "That's all that matters."

"You might as well have killed her. We'll never see her again." A tear crept down Norah's flaming cheek. She wiped it away as if it were an affront.

Clare shifted her eyes to the curtain, pristine and inoffensive, until she was certain she wouldn't weep, too. Yet another child, lost. Safe. But still lost.

She longed to console Norah, to say whatever would rid her of the anger she'd caught from Fin, contagious in his fury. He'd have her and Katie believe they were irrevocably tainted. Have this belief eat away at their insides on account of something they had no part of.

Better the trouble following death than the trouble following shame. Clare could hear him saying it, plain as day.

Norah got to her feet. "I'd better go. I have to work tomorrow." She squared shoulders too thin to bear such unearned weight. She regarded the wall as if it were a penance. No doubt she was imagining the look she'd get from Ada Smiley when she walked through the store's front door. No matter how anyone looked at her, she'd feel the attention as a slap.

"You are not to blame," Clare whispered.

Norah had already turned away. Parting the curtain, she sent shivers through Clare's soft white shelter.

When Clare returned to The Hive, she'd be regarded with pity. Such terrible losses. Another unborn child. And the means by which to conceive again. Nobody would dare utter Deirdre's name in her presence. Not until she said it herself.

But not in front of Fin. Never, Norah had cautioned, in front of Fin.

The curtain rippled again, admitting the sweet-faced nurse, whose smile was as pearly as an angel's cheek. She took Clare's temperature and checked the bandage, begging her pardon, knowing the ministrations caused pain. "Was that your daughter who just left? Such a pretty girl," she said.

"I have three daughters." Despite the rent in her belly, Clare repeated it.

"Have you now?" The nurse prepared the injection. "What a fine family."

Clare barely felt the needle. "Norah, Kathleen, and Deirdre."

"Lovely names," said the nurse. She wrote on the chart that hung on the foot of the bed. Parted the curtain. "Sleep now. I'll check on you in a little while."

Clare closed her eyes, suffused with relief that she would never display. Deep beneath the bandage, no son of Fin's would ever grow. Already, she'd assumed an exquisite mask of resignation and regret. She'd wear it as religiously as a scapular.

106

As the medicine's thick veil descended, she whispered, "*Meine Tochter*. Deirdre, my daughter."

As long as Clare lived, she'd say the name—over and over and over—whenever Fin wasn't there to listen.

Deirdre.

Deirdre.

Deirdre.

Part Two
Crosses

(Katie, 1933)

Chapter 14: Clare
May 26, 1933
Feast of St. Dyfan, Missionary

Ada Smiley handed Clare the envelope. Her pinched spinster-face affected disinterest, but Clare knew better. She thanked Ada and folded the envelope in half. The coarse skin on her fingertips made a faint scratching sound against the fine cream-colored paper. As the envelope slid into her pocket, she turned to admire the dress worn by the mannequin in the front window. "I love dotted Swiss, don't you?" She could pretend, too.

They had both read every word on the envelope. Katie's name and address. That of the sender. Noted the small, shield-shaped escutcheon. Tiny palm fronds framing a lamb. A bold black cross.

Clare had taken it all in between breaths. Ada surely had pored over it at every opportunity since it had arrived. Kamila had caught her, squinting, holding the envelope up to the window. In the time it had taken Kamila, flushed and sputtering, to arrive at Clare's gate and for Clare to retrace Kamila's steps to the store, Ada could well have steamed the letter open, then read and resealed it.

Clare could tell by the clerk's eyes, narrowed and ravenous, that she hadn't. Ada's appetite for the contents of Katie's letter had been fanned, not satisfied. How fitting that she'd been found out by Kamila, who'd yet to hear a secret she deemed sacrosanct. Clare sensed words seeping between Ada's teeth. Her mouth watering, her tongue longing to pose the question that prim, pursed lips held back. *Why are the nuns writing to Katie?*

Clare's lips parted. Ada's eyes widened behind her rimless spectacles. She leaned, oh so slightly, into the counter. The cant of her reed-thin body was nearly imperceptible. Clare pretended not to notice. Pretended that she'd opened her mouth simply to share another trifle. "They're calling for storms tomorrow. Hopefully, not till after the ball game."

Ada rocked back on her heels. Her chagrin, quickly tamped. She shrugged, indifferent to tired topics like weather and baseball, and busied herself unpacking a carton. Her back, half-turned, implied similar indifference to the contents of Clare's pocket.

Clare's leisurely pace down the main aisle implied the same. A desultory shopper in an all-but-empty store. Upstairs, Old Smiley was the picture of solicitude as Maggie Phelan dithered over reels of lace. She hadn't troubled herself to so much as nod when Clare had entered. None of them, least of all Ada, suspected that Clare's heart had become an agitated bird, trapped at the back of her throat.

She forced herself to pause and appraise a crate brimming with oranges. Her hand hovered, then selected. She brought the orange to her nose, sniffed discerningly, and smiled. She smelled nothing. Heard only the echo of chapped skin scratching thick paper. She glanced back at Ada, whose spectacles caught the light and transformed to opaque circles. Her eyes, hiding. Her tongue, with its question, forced to bide its time.

Maggie, empty-handed, descended the stairs and regarded Clare, holding the leaden orange. "Clare," she said. A nod, but nothing more. The hard blue marbles of her eyes rolled as she passed. Nobody knew better than Maggie that Clare couldn't afford the fruit in her hand.

Ada bid Maggie a gracious goodbye. As soon as she'd crossed Main Street, Clare set the orange back in the crate. She stalked down the aisle and out the door. Ada called after her, but she pretended not to hear. Alone in the alley, she leaned against the back of an outhouse. Her frantic pulse, acknowledgement. Folded in her pocket was the harbinger of Katie's future.

Chapter 15: Katie

"Two hundred and fifty dollars."

The words seemed to come from someone else's mouth. Each syllable warily placed like an egg on a warped board. Katie's tongue barely dared the final *s*, the slender out-breath that could rock the board and crack her thin shell of hope. She scanned the convent's neatly typed list and bit her lip. Deirdre had carried only a pillowcase into her new life. If Katie arrived on the nuns' doorstep with empty pockets, would they, with times so hard, truly turn her away?

Mutti stood beside the stove, wringing an apron washed too often to claim a color. Her chin jerked, as if pushing aside the stunning sum requested by the Mother Superior. Clearly dreading the answer, she asked, "*Was noch?*" What else?

"A small trunk. Sturdy oxfords." Katie looked up from the list. Eyes narrowed, Mutti frowned. Surely she, like Katie, was estimating prices. Katie swallowed hard and returned to the list. "Two plain nightgowns, extra-large."

Mutti blinked. "For a girl as skinny as you?"

"You dress and undress underneath. For modesty. Betty told me." Katie's gaze returned to the letter, adding weight to the stationery. She wouldn't mention what else Betty Zekula had revealed about sparse meals and fitful sleep in the convent dorm. About shivering for fear that a careless word, failed test, or unchecked tear had caught the attention of Sr. St. John the Baptist. Never, Betty claimed, had she seen the Mistress of Novices smile.

Shaking her head, Mutti slid two browned loaves out of the oven; two more, spongy, in. Since the banks had closed and the Company had drastically cut back shifts, bread had become each meal's mainstay. With a thin smear of jam at breakfast, sandwiching baked beans for lunch, then accompanying more beans for supper. How could anyone, even nuns professing poverty, eat more meanly than this?

Your stomach growls all night. Sister doesn't use her cane to walk, just to whack postulants. Betty's bleak assessments filled Katie's ears as completely as the kitchen's yeasty fragrance filled her nose. *You'll never make it to final vows.*

"Betty only lasted nine months," Mutti said, "and she's a lot stronger than you."

"Everyone in The Hive is strong," Katie countered. "If not, they're dead."

A bread pan slipped from Mutti's grasp and hit the floor with a hollow, metallic reproach. She bent to retrieve it, back braced with one hand. Beneath fingers and fabric, a fresh bruise surely bloomed. The night before, Pap, home late and liquored-up, had kept Mutti downstairs for his slurred account of a secret union meeting in a farmer's field. Norah had begged to stay, claiming that working girls supported the union, too. Pap, however, had ordered her to bed. The brave sister, Norah had hurried back downstairs as talk gave way to thuds and cries that *Käthi-die-Memme*, Katie-the-Coward, muffled with her pillow.

Favoring her puffy left ankle, Mutti carried the pans to the sink. "Anything else?"

"Corsets. A robe. Towels." Eyes trained on the paper, Katie chanted the list with the same grim efficiency as Fr. Kovacs intoned The Litany of Saints. Under this roof, only the names of those departed could be spoken without consequence.

Mutti's floury fingers lifted Katie's chin. "Is it really the convent you want, or do you just want to leave?"

"I want to go to college. I want to be a teacher." Did Mutti notice Katie's blouse buttons, bouncing in swift rhythm with her heart? Hastily, she added, "I have a vocation."

Mutti crossed her arms, leveled a piercing gaze. "What about Jack? He hasn't looked at another girl since you started high school. And you certainly haven't discouraged him."

"Jack doesn't matter as much as God." Katie smiled just as The Queen had coached her: St. Barbara, joyfully embracing her holy fate. Her palm stilled the quivering buttons. If she prayed hard enough, surely God would convince Jack to let her go—but what about Pap?

Mutti held out her hand. Katie passed her the letter, which she folded and placed in her apron pocket. "I'll write to my cousin Trudy. She may be able to spare something, but—"

Mutti's voice trailed off. She lifted the flour-sack towels draping the remaining pans and inspected the pillowy dough. Brushing Katie's cheek, she added, "*Du muß geduldig sein.*"

Be patient. For as long as Katie could remember, someone (usually Norah) had offered this advice as if it were a coke cinder, easily flicked from one sleeve onto another. "Fr. Kovacs said the nuns will take a girl without the money if her family's hard up," Katie said.

"Your father won't accept charity. Mr. Zekula paid for Betty."

"Whatever Trudy sends will be charity," Katie persisted. "We can hardly tell Pap we found two hundred and fifty dollars under a bush."

Mutti's hands resumed punishing her apron. The stationery crackled inside the pocket. "No sense saying anything yet. Do as he says and look for work, so he won't ask questions."

Her eyes cut to the screen door. Katie's followed, fearful they'd behold Pap, home from whatever clandestine business he undertook each day the mine left him idle. She saw only Mrs. Tonelli, pulling round loaves from her backyard oven with a worn wooden paddle. Clouds like wisps of cattail floss drifted overhead. Smoke-shrouded no longer, the surrounding green hills rose above the rooftops across the alley.

As Katie watched, the hills seemed to swell against the belligerent blue sky, emblem of The Hive's swift slide from difficult to desperate straits. Somewhere beyond those hills, Deirdre might also be baking. Pausing, perhaps, by her city kitchen's window. Momentarily recalling the sorry place from which she'd managed, at great cost, to escape.

Mutti's arm crept around Katie's shoulders. "If you enter, you'll have to give up everything. Are you willing to make that sacrifice?"

Katie took in the whitewashed walls and sagging window screens. The dented washtub and sooty ash pail. The stoop-shouldered woman standing beside her. Mutti's limp brown hair was threaded with gray. A history of harsh blows and hard times was written on her thin face. Had she, at sixteen, ever imagined that her life would dwindle to this?

"Giving up The Hive isn't much of a sacrifice." As soon as Katie's thought became sound, the sound became something else, obdurate as Pap's hand, pushing Mutti away.

After dark, the coke ovens resembled abandoned tombs. When Katie shared this observation, Betty snorted. "Sometimes a good imagination is a bad thing."

Betty's convent trunk swayed between them, thumping Katie's hip each time a broken brick caused her gait to falter. A sliver of moon gleamed above the slate dump. A lone spotlight glowed on the tipple, edging the hoist cage bars and Betty's cropped blond bob with silver. Halfway across the yard, Katie's fingers cramped around the handle. She switched hands, forcing Betty, humming softly, to halt. "Why not here? The ovens are all the same."

"Too close to the road. We'll use one in the back, behind the tipple," Betty replied.

Katie's hip throbbed as Betty pulled her forward. "Why did you bring the trunk? You could've fit everything in a basket."

Betty shook her head. "Not the papers. I saved every essay, every test, every—"

"I'm starting to think this isn't such a good idea."

"You think too much. Don't you ever do anything without thinking it to death?"

"Like entering the convent?" Katie countered.

"Nobody told me it would be so hard." Tripping on the cast-off wheel of a larry-car, Betty cut that last word into two gulps. Righting herself, she added, "Mama thinks I'm helping you learn your lines. If I'm not back soon, she'll come looking. Then we're both sunk."

Katie leaned into the trunk, soon to be hers. It satisfactorily thumped Betty, whose hips had shed considerable padding during her nine-month absence. "Everyone knows I memorized my lines before graduation."

"Then use your damn smarts to find us an oven you can't see from the road," Betty retorted. "And keep an eye out for hoboes."

In just seven days, Betty had reverted from blessed to bossy, reminding Katie why she preferred the company of Tina Kukoc, Jack's sister. Dear Tina, to whom Katie confided everything except the plan that required this trunk. A profound sense of disloyalty dogged her steps. "Did Sister whack you for swearing?" Katie asked, trying to sound severe.

Betty laughed—a long, flagrant trill. "I may not be a valedictorian, but I'm no dumb Dora. She caught me dancing while I mopped the dining room floor. I was singing, too. Maybe she wouldn't've been so mad if it was a hymn, but you can't do the Lindy to *Ave Maria.*"

"You did the Lindy with a *mop?*"

Betty's shoulders flounced. "I didn't think I'd miss dancing so much. I thought God would erase all that once I entered."

"I think God's got bigger things to worry about than a postulant doing the Lindy."

"Now that I'm out—" Betty's tone turned silky—"can I dance with Jack? Once you're gone, I mean."

"Dance with whoever you want." A pebble worked its way through the hole in Katie's shoe, forcing a wince and spoiling her determined nonchalance.

The tipple's bright beacon was now behind them. Betty's shadow dissolved into the gloom. "You think God's calling you, huh? You think He'll watch you pack this trunk, ride the streetcar, then the train, then walk through the priory's big doors. You think He won't take His eyes off you for a second or let you do anything that will keep you from taking perpetual vows." Betty stopped short, and the trunk again gouged Katie's thigh. A deep breath, and Betty added, "But once you're inside, know what? God disappears. All you hear is Sr. St. John the Baptist complaining about your lazy, sinful soul morning, noon, and night. Believe me, brainy girls got thumped as much as the rest of us without the smarts. Don't expect Sister to go easy on you because you're only sixteen."

The handle slipped from Katie's slick fingers, raking her leg before the trunk hit the ground. Was it really as bad as all that? Never before had Betty, the only Zekula girl who struggled with schoolwork, spoken with a fervor bordering on eloquence. "You could still go back," Katie ventured. "Maybe you need a little more time to think—"

Betty snorted. "Not for all the tea in China."

"If things get any worse around here, maybe you'll change your mind."

"Horsefeathers." Betty dropped her end of the trunk: heavy, indisputable punctuation. "Pap says things are bound to get better with Roosevelt in the White House. When they do, he'll send me to study at Uniontown Hospital, or maybe even St. Francis in Pittsburgh. I don't have to be a nun to be a nurse."

Mr. Zekula paid for Betty. Mutti might have been standing beside Katie, restating the obvious. Betty's pap had never crossed the speakeasy's threshold. When The Hive's miners had worked five-day weeks, Mr. Zekula never lacked money for movie tickets, Shady Grove roller coaster rides, even a brand new Philco Lowboy with such crystal clear reception that patch children packed the Zekulas' living room for each installment of *Little Orphan Annie.*

"Did the convent give back your pap's money?" Katie asked.

"Some," said Betty, hoisting the trunk again. "Pap didn't want to take it, but Mama made him. She says things are bound to get worse before they get better, no matter who's President, and we'd better have something set aside in case they shut us down like Gates and Edenborn."

"Don't say that. It's bad luck."

"If you ask me," Betty declared, "everything about mining is bad luck."

They'd reached the back of the yard. Betty lowered the trunk and boldly entered the inky belly of an oven. Fearful of snakes, Katie lingered outside. "Make sure the roof's sound," she called, scanning the darkness for any sign of movement. In some patches, evicted families had set up housekeeping in the ovens, but Mr. Phelan had ordered Company deputies to arrest any outsider who set foot in The Hive. A rat darted past, and Katie stifled a shriek.

"Pipe down!" commanded Betty, lighting a match. Katie warily peered through the jamb. The oven, which had once baked seven-ton charges, now contained only brittle leaves and

118

animal droppings. Fissures crosshatched its soot-streaked dome. Betty, likewise, was studying the ceiling. "Seems safe enough. The bricks are all here, at least."

In the four years since the Company had closed the beehives, bricks had steadily vanished. Everyone suspected that the Lubicic twins sneaked into the yard after dark, pried them out, and sold them to scrap dealers. What wasn't stolen, winters treated harshly, and the coke works appeared more and more depleted, like a possum carcass picked at by turkey buzzards.

Betty yelped as the match singed her fingers. The flame dropped to the ground. The oven went dark. Katie backed out quickly, but Betty stayed put. "Betcha this is how Houdini felt when they buried him alive. It's not as creepy as you'd think."

Katie shuddered. "Come help me with the trunk."

"Or," Betty's voice reverberated in the darkness, "what it's like after a roof fall, when the power goes off, and your lamp burns out. If you're not dead, that is."

Katie crossed herself. "If you don't come out this minute, I'm going home." She eyed the yard's dark grottoes. If only God would dispatch an angel to an oven's blank niche! *If You want me, send a vision, a sign, anything that tells me, go, go, no matter what.*

Betty emerged from the oven. "Too bad they won't let girls work in the pit. I bet I could earn a heap of dough, and a darn sight quicker than stocking shelves at the Company store."

"Nobody's earning a heap of anything," Katie said as Betty picked up a splintered board and, with another match, set it alight. "You could sell your leftover convent things to Masha."

Betty gripped the trunk handle and motioned with her makeshift torch for Katie to lift the other end. "I'd rather burn Sister's cranky old voice out of my head forever."

They carried the trunk into the oven. Betty handed the torch to Katie, then crouched to lift the lid. Directly beneath the tunnel hole, Betty built a pyre of red-inked papers, topped with two corsets. A dozen black stockings followed, unfurling like snakes poised to strike. "It's wrong, burning perfectly good clothes," Katie said, though Betty's mouth, tight as a hyphen, hinted that Katie's tone had veered into the cranky territory of the Mistress of Novices. *Thou shalt not waste.* "Doesn't this seem—pagan?" Katie persisted, backing away from the pile.

"In the Bible, they burned things up all the time." Betty slammed the trunk's lid. "If you weren't so skinny, you could've had this stuff, too. Anyway, you thought it was a good idea this morning." She kicked withered leaves onto the pile and extended her hand for the torch. "For crying out loud, give it here," she said, pulling the board from Katie's grasp.

The leaves and paper caught easily, but the stockings smoldered. At Betty's insistence, Katie collected more leaves and fed the fire. A thin column of smoke rose through the oven's eye. Betty crouched: cheeks flushed, lips parted, eyes fixed on the flaming remains of her vocation. For a moment, her smile wavered, as if she, like Katie, recalled the moment, one week earlier, when the streetcar conductor had set the trunk on the Main Street sidewalk.

Katie, fresh from pageant rehearsal in The Hall, had been the first to witness Betty's unheralded homecoming. Tina, angel to Katie's saint, had stood beside her, Betty's name a shocked whisper behind her hand. The other players had lined the sidewalk, wide-eyed at Betty's transformation from a chubby, would-be nun to a sullen stranger too slender to possibly be a Zekula. "Mind your own damn business!" Betty had shouted, one hand fumbling the trunk's handle. Only Katie had seemed to notice the other hand, swiftly wiping Betty's face.

Glistening with sweat, that face now tipped toward Katie's. "Know what? I think God's tricking you, just like He tricked me. Once *you* get inside—"

A rustle turned both girls around. The new deputy stood at the oven's entrance. His expression wavered between an authority's glare and conspirator's grin.

"We aren't stealing bricks." A bead of sweat dropped from Betty's chin. Two more followed, polka-dotting her collar. "We just needed someplace to build a little fire."

Pistol thudding against his thigh, the deputy entered and eyed the blaze. A flaming corset, its hooks and eyes blackened, rolled off the pile. He sneered as Katie, shamed, kicked it back. "That's not Company property you're burning, is it?"

"It's my property," Betty snapped. "What I do with it is my business."

"And it's my business to keep out the riff-raff. You can't swing a cat around here without hitting a union organizer," the deputy replied.

"We're not with the union," Katie said. Quickly, she lowered her chin, but not before the deputy's grin widened. His pimpled cheeks appeared painfully inflamed in the firelight.

"You're Deirdre Sweeney's sister, ain't you? Steamshovel's girl?" he asked.

"That's none of your business either," said Betty.

He removed the handcuffs from his belt and dangled them inches from Betty's face. "I could arrest you. Company says the ovens are off-limits."

"Fine, arrest us," said Betty, ignoring Katie's gasp.

The deputy stared at Katie, who forced herself to stare back. "Go track down some real troublemakers and leave us alone," she said.

With exaggerated slowness, he returned the cuffs to his belt. "Speaking of troublemakers, you wouldn't happen to know where your pap is right now, would you?"

"If I did, I certainly wouldn't tell you," Katie returned. She allowed herself a quick, proud smile: Katie-the-Coward had stood up to a deputy.

As he headed out of the oven, he called back, "When your pap shows up, tell him Deirdre's expecting a kid any day now. If it's a boy, she sure won't be naming it after him."

"How would you know anything about Deirdre?" Betty demanded.

The deputy turned, smirking. "Her husband, Billy? He's my kid brother."

Katie's hand went to the sooty wall, a brace against the blow of this revelation, as harsh as it was sweet. As the deputy's navy jacket and cap dissolved into the dark yard, his whistling drifted back. *Who's afraid of the big bad wolf, big bad wolf, big bad wolf?*

Chapter 16: Clare

May 29, 1933
Feast of St. Mary Magdelen dei Pazzi, Virgin

Adamant footfalls up the porch steps prepared Clare for Kamila's entrance. She crossed her arms beneath her bosom's broad shelf, heaving from a hasty trek down the alley. "What's this I hear about Deirdre having a baby? Did you tell Fin?" She flapped a hand, dismissing this difficult question to make room for another. "You'll go see her now, won't you?"

Clare hesitated, anticipating Kamila's reaction. "I don't know where she lives."

"*Pffft!* The deputy with the pimply face, he's the brother, right? Why didn't Katie ask him when she had the chance?" Another hand-flap. "Never mind. Go ask him now."

"I'm writing to my cousin. Deirdre lived with Trudy till she got married, so Trudy—"

"A letter." Kamila scornfully appraised the stationery and three-cent stamp, purchased from Masha with eggs that Concetta had generously passed over the fence. "How long will that take?" She waved aside Clare's reply, as if it were of less consequence than the chicken feathers riding her wake inside. "Angela's cousins have a warehouse in Pittsburgh now. With Fin such a good customer, for sure she'll tell them to drive you straight to Deirdre's door."

In three days, Prohibition would end in Pennsylvania. The Hive's speakeasy would become Boyle's Beer Garden, a legitimate enterprise—but it didn't matter. Clare shook her head. Kamila's solid rump met the bench, sending a quiver across the floor and up Clare's spine. "If I got the address and went—" She looked Kamila in the eye. "I couldn't come back."

Kamila's cheek churned, as if chewing the *why?* she knew Clare wouldn't answer. Her chapped hand, blunt as a spade, covered Clare's. "Then Deirdre should bring the baby for a visit. Even if Fin's still mad at her, he'd never lift a finger against his own grandchild."

Clare pulled her hand away. "She won't come. She hasn't written once since she left."

Kamila calmed her jaw. Her hand retreated to her lap, the wide saddle that, on any given day, bounced at least one of her seven grandchildren. None lived more than four streetcar stops away.

"You're lucky with your girls," Clare said.

"*Pffft*! You Irish and your luck. Us hunkies thank God for good things and offer up the rest."

You Irish.

Clare tightened her lips over a rebellious tongue that longed to correct. When she was sure of its compliance, she said quietly, "I offer things up, too."

Kamila's hands crossed the table, palms up, penitent. "Of course you do. More than me, more than anyone. God doesn't expect you to give up another child."

"Then God needs to change Fin's mind about Deirdre. And Katie's convent money, too."

"Katie doesn't have to be a nun to go to college. She's smart enough to get a scholarship, just like my girls. Norah should apply, too. Then she could get a good teaching job, instead of working that switchboard." Kamila sat back, arms crossed. "Let me tell you, it's not healthy, cooped up in a little room full of wires and no fresh air. It's a wonder she's not sick—"

"Fin won't take relief unless it comes from the union."

Kamila's fist slammed the table. Clare's pencil bounced off and rolled beneath the stove. "For heaven's sake, Clare, a scholarship isn't relief. It's a prize! An honor! In times like these, I'd even call it a miracle. My girls—"

"Are not Fin's." Clare looked away. As far as she knew, Kamila had never endured a black eye. Nor had she ever commented on Clare's—though Clare had sensed, on more than one occasion, that it sorely taxed Kamila's modest store of tact to refrain.

"Let me finish my sentence," Kamila said.

"There's nothing to finish—" Clare reached beneath the stove—"except my letter."

123

Kamila rose, hands planted on hips. "I don't suppose you finished that book I lent you either. Betty keeps pestering me, asking when she can read it."

Clare set the pencil on the table and stepped around Kamila to look outside.

"He's not likely to sneak up the hoist shaft at ten o'clock in the morning," Kamila said behind her.

Clare turned on her heel. Brushing past Kamila, she hurried into the living room and thrust a hand deep beneath the couch's middle cushion.

"Oh, never mind. If Betty wants it that bad, she can go over to the Beetown library," Kamila called from the kitchen.

Clare pulled the book from its hiding place. *The Door*— Pittsburgh author Mary Roberts Rinehart's latest mystery. Before she could decide on a response, she heard the screen bang. For a long moment, she considered the tempting red-bound volume. Maybe, after she'd written and mailed Trudy's letter and weeded the garden and scrubbed the floor—

With a sigh, she slid the book back under the cushion. Getting to her feet, she consoled herself. At least she hadn't been forced to admit to Kamila that she'd yet to read a single page.

Clare went to the store solely to mail her letter. She went, praying that Ada would be home baking a pie for tomorrow's Decoration Day picnic. She paused on the porch until she noticed the new girl, a Visocky cousin, standing behind the post office counter. The girl didn't even glance at Trudy's address.

Clare had no intention of looking for the deputy, no matter what Kamila had said. But just before she turned into the alley, she saw him standing behind the store. His body curved around the cigarette he was lighting. A rifle rested against the delivery truck's front wheel. Any day now, he might encounter Fin in a lonely place and use that gun to rid the patch of its unyielding union agitator. He noticed Clare and smiled as if her presence had reminded him of that possibility.

His dropped match expired in the dirt. Butcher-counter conversations filtered through the store's screened window. He

124

sized Clare up. His chin and cheeks were ruddy with angry pustules. "You want to know where your girl's at."

Clare wanted to know so many things that her thoughts scattered like Concetta's chickens. *Ist sie... Hast du...* The tip of his cigarette glowed, darkened, then glowed again before she recovered sufficient composure—and English—to ask, "Is my grandchild born?"

Her grandchild. Lost child of a lost child.

His pursed lips released a quivering circlet of smoke. It floated between them, an ashy halo in search of a head. "Talked to my mother on Sunday. She said it could come any time."

"Is your mother with Deirdre?" Clare asked, struggling to mask her envy.

How could she not resent this unknown woman? At that very moment, she might have been holding Deirdre's hand, wiping her brow as she labored.

The chance to offer a mother's loving ministrations, lost. Yet another penance.

The deputy looked past Clare. His cigarette dropped. Its smoke spiraled around his dusty boots. He seized the gun. The barrel's dark eye dared her to ask another question.

Fin's steely voice slapped her between the shoulders. "Here's a fine kettle of fish. Me wife off visiting with a goddamn pussyfoot instead of filling the washtub for me bath."

Blackened with bug dust from head to toe, Fin stood on the sidewalk, awaiting an explanation. Nothing short of death excused Clare from preparing his bath. In three strides, he was beside her, gripping her arm as if it were his pick—or the deputy's neck. "Go march yourself down the street like a good little soldier," he snapped.

The deputy's face had turned a feverish scarlet. A milk-pale finger hovered at the rifle's trigger. Clare felt feverish, too, weightless and woozy. She heard herself speak, faintly, as if from a great distance. "Tell him. About Deirdre's baby. His first grandchild."

The deputy's chin rose from his chest. A button had imprinted a fleeting cleft beneath his lower lip. His taut stance thrummed with distrust.

125

Fin let go of her arm. His gaze turned vacant. He swayed as if caught in a roof fall that had stoned him just short of senseless. Had all the whiskey-years suddenly drowned his reason?

"My folks' first grandchild, too." The deputy's tone turned conversational. They might have been sitting around a table laid with teacups and cake.

How was it possible to tender such a comment across the barrel of a rifle?

"Daft, the both of you." Fin sounded just as dazed as he appeared. "I've got two good girls. Neither one with a husband, much less a baby."

The butcher appeared in, then departed from the store window. Inside, shoes thumped. Someone repeatedly shouted the name of Christ.

The noise roused Fin from whatever trance he'd entered. He glared at the deputy. Like a dog's growl, his voice rose from the back of the throat. "Who are you to be spreading slander about me family? Are they paying you to gossip while you're snooping around with that gun?" As he spit the last syllable, he flung out a hand. Knocked the rifle to the ground.

A single shot.

The bullet whistled into a clump of weeds.

Somewhere overhead, a woman's scream echoed Clare's.

The store's back door opened, banging the wall. Old Smiley emerged, pistol in hand. Behind him, ghoulish in a blood-smeared apron, the butcher gripped his cleaver.

"Hold still, goddamnit!" Old Smiley shouted as the deputy bent to retrieve the rifle.

The deputy's cap dropped onto the ground. Fin, defiant, crossed his arms. Old Smiley's pistol tracked the movement. Again, Clare found herself opposite a twitching trigger finger.

Bitte, bitte. Mercifully, her incoherent whisper emerged in English. "Please. Please."

Holding his pistol steady, Old Smiley eyed the deputy. "What's the trouble?"

"Ask Sweeney here," the deputy said. "He started it."

126

Old Smiley's chin jerked. "Get that gun the hell away from my store."

The deputy aimed a finger at Fin. "Keep your dirty hands to yourself, or somebody just might shoot them both off." He shouldered the rifle. Retrieved his cap. Dust motes sparkled as he fitted it onto his head, then stalked past Fin, taking with him whatever knowledge he had of Deirdre's whereabouts.

What did his mother look like? Did she have a gentle nature? Had she grown to love Deirdre? Did Deirdre wish, even for a moment, that Clare was with her instead?

Did she ever think of Clare at all?

"It's a sorry state of affairs when they pin a badge on any Tom, Dick, or Harry and hand him a gun," said Old Smiley, finally lowering his.

"'Tis a sorrow easily fixed if they'd let in the union," Fin countered.

Old Smiley's shoulders sagged as if suddenly burdened with a full sack of flour. "You were here in '27. If push comes to shove, it'll happen all over again. They'll close the mine and throw every last one of you out of your houses."

"Once Roosevelt signs the Recovery Act, we'll see some changes around here," said Fin.

He nudged Clare. A prompt. An obedient wife was expected to parrot her man's opinions. But she couldn't.

The millionaires controlling the steel mills and the captive mines that fueled them had broken every strike prior to Black Tuesday. Striking now, with shifts so scarce, seemed nothing short of lunacy. Deputies would dump their furniture in a field even as new men lined up at the tipple, eager to pledge allegiance to the Company in exchange for store credit.

Fin pinched her arm. Another prompt. An obedient wife would've answered by now.

She wasn't that wife. That wife would have been kneeling in the kitchen, scrubbing his filthy back. Nothing she said now would prevent the beating she'd earned through oversight. Finally, she ventured, "Recovery will surely be a blessing."

The only blessing she craved was to be with Deirdre, holding her hand, assuring her the pain would end. Watching Deirdre's face as she greeted her first child.

Fin frowned. He'd expected Clare to name the men he considered saviors. From the kitchen wall, their grainy newspaper portraits watched her cook and iron. Roosevelt. Union leader John L. Lewis. And the new addition, Grindstone miner Marty Ryan. Fin's equally outspoken friend, Ryan was hell-bent on ending the captives' open shop. It wouldn't have surprised Clare to see Fin genuflecting before this holy trinity. She'd genuflect, too, and gladly, if she believed any of them could mend the rift between Fin and Deirdre or pay Katie's way to a teacher's diploma.

"Let's go home, Fin," she said, steeling herself for the punishment that awaited her there.

"Listen to your wife, Steamshovel," Old Smiley said wearily, turning away. His hand, struck with a sudden palsy, bumped the pistol against his leg.

Chapter 17: Katie

Jack waited in the twilight beside The Hall's front door. He pushed up the sleeves of his work shirt, revealing forearms dotted with mosquito bites. Katie's careless hand stroked the welts, crosshatched with red fingernail tracks. "When you scratch, it only makes the itch worse."

"A kiss will make it better."

Katie snatched back her hand. Jack's arm slipped around her waist. Behind her, a cat call. Joey Dvorsk, his lisp more pronounced when he shouted, reminded the exiting pageant cast of the obvious. "Thaint Barbara'th got a boyfriend!"

"Kiss her, saint boyfriend!" shrieked simple Lizzie Boyle.

Katie walked faster, away from Joey and his pals. Away from Lizzie, to whom nothing was ever obvious. Away from Jack's inviting arm.

"Hold your horses," said Jack, catching Katie's waist.

Why had she touched him first? She'd lain awake the night before, doggedly begging heaven to erase her feelings for him. Why had God let her touch him?

"Let's take a walk," Jack said, his face dipping toward hers.

She turned her head away, but he held fast to the rest of her. How could God allow her to enjoy this—against her will, against every prayer she'd said since reading the Mother Superior's letter? *Home*, commanded her conscience. But her body, steered by Jack's, headed for the churchyard.

Lizzie kept hollering. "Kiss her, saint boyfriend!"

Jack led Katie around the church and behind the bristly screen of a towering spruce. His tongue, quick and moist, probed her ear, muting Lizzie's taunts. She backed into the church's ivy-laced wall and bumped her head. *Punishment for impure acts*, her conscience censured.

Jack's shadow enfolded hers. "What's wrong?" He breathed the words between her lips.

Desperately, she imagined herself onstage: faithful Barbara, unperturbed by her father's insults and the magistrate's heavy sentence. Jack's mouth, pressing hungrily, was just a fleeting temptation. God would keep her, like Barbara, safe from sin. Why, then, did her hands long to drop the wretched script and cling to Jack instead?

His lips retreated. He stepped back, planting a hand in the rustling ivy on each side of her head. The fine hairs on his skin grazed her cheeks. Even in the spruce-scented gloom, she could make out his expression, more quizzical than annoyed. "Do I taste bad?" he asked. "I brushed my teeth after supper."

She shook her head. "It's just not right, sneaking around like this."

His hands cupped her face. "Don't tease me, Katie, that's not right either. I've loved you my whole entire life. Sometimes I can't stand it, loving you so much, and wanting you to love me back, and not being able to do more than this." His mouth met hers with fresh fervor.

Her script fell to the ground. She could no longer recall how it felt to be a saint.

"I can't love you anymore," she whispered, even as her shameless hands lingered on his back. Betty's taunt supplanted Lizzie's. *God's tricking you...*

Jack drew her head to his chest. Her face rose and fell with his ribs, her ear a witness to the urgent rhythm within. "I'll try to back off, if that's what you want. Only it can't be for long, or I'll go crazy. I'd marry you tomorrow, but I guess you'll want to sew a wedding dress and—"

"No!" Just in time, God intervened. Her arms, a saint's once more, pushed away her playmate, her friend, her only love. Her future, if she kept listening. Ivy pricked the back of her neck. Beneath it, cold, stern stone, embedded with God's voice, commanded her to make clear her intentions. "I'm entering the convent."

Jack's laughter surprised her. "Oh, go on, Katie, you're not onstage."

"I'm not play-acting. I've decided to become a nun."

His hand, reaching for hers, hung in the air like a beggar's. "Go on," he repeated, no longer laughing.

She retrieved her script. Holding it, she felt stronger, infused with holy purpose. "I've said, lots of times, I want to go to college and be a schoolteacher."

"I thought you were just talking."

"I was. Weren't you listening?"

"I thought it was just *talk*. You know, pie in the sky." He lowered his hand. "I talk, too. Someday, I'll be the Big Boss. We'll live in that fancy house in Beetown. Just so much hot air."

She made her voice strong, the way The Queen had coached her. A voice that reached all the way to the balcony's top row. All the way to heaven. "I'm leaving as soon as my mother's cousin sends the money."

"Then you don't love me." Jack's voice turned flat with disbelief. "All this—" he flung out his arms—"*was* play-acting, and I believed it. One big, dumb, hunkie sucker."

"I *wasn't* pretending. And you're *not* dumb. I've loved you since I was a little girl."

His head sagged. He wasn't listening. *God, why wasn't he listening?*

He hunched over. His fists pounded his legs. "I was so proud of you, making that graduation speech. My girl, two years younger and still smarter than everyone else. But now, Jesus, I wish you weren't. Jesus, God, I wish you were as dumb as me. A dumb miner's dumb wife, scrubbing my back, packing my bucket, thinking about me every minute I'm in the pit." His fists stilled. His chin dropped onto his chest. Katie had to strain to hear him, and what she heard tore her heart. "No matter what happens down there, I'm never afraid. I know I'm safe because of you, because—" his voice broke—"you're thinking about me."

Jack doesn't matter. Dear God, had Katie really said that? Betty was right. God had tricked her into thinking this conversation would be painless.

Jack turned his back, trying to hide unmanly tears. "I should've known you'd want more than this. More—"

She heard what he couldn't bring himself to say. *More than me.*

He walked away, moving as slowly as *Baka*, his grandmother, crippled with rheumatism. Something whined, grazing Katie's cheek like a phantom kiss. Then she felt the sting. When she brought her hand away, her palm was marked with a mock stigmata. The dark scar of a dead bug. A bright smear of blood.

"Don't climb too high!" Mutti called. Gripping her embroidery hoop, she repeated every warning Katie had heard since she could fit inside the blackened burlap sack trailing behind her.

"Tina's coming with me," Katie called back. She smiled and waved until Mutti, reassured, seated herself on the porch step and resumed the fancywork paid for by the Beetown mayor's wife. Katie's pulse, however, beat louder than the gate's squeak. By the time she reached the Kukoces' backyard, she could scarcely hear Jack's little brothers, squabbling over a ball made of old socks.

Jack's mother sat on a chair beside her garden, shelling peas into a bowl. Her grim expression hinted that she'd heard how hateful Katie Sweeney had rejected her eldest after leading him on for years. Katie paused at the gate, her throat too full of heartbeats to speak. She'd come to take Jack's sister coal-picking, but also to find Jack and somehow make things easier between them.

Mrs. Kukoc surprised Katie with a welcoming smile that creased her face, tucked like a ruddy apple inside the folds of a gray *babushka*. "Jack going very early, no eating. *Ta* working today, looking for Jack, maybe to be working, too. But no, not here, telling nobody." Her hands lifted from the bowl. "Telling, maybe, you?"

Before Katie could shake her head, Mrs. Kukoc turned to glare at a bulky, bearded man carrying a stool down the porch steps. Placing the stool beside her, the man settled himself on it as if it were a throne. He unbuttoned his shabby suit jacket to reveal a paunch that strained the buttons of a grease-spotted shirt. Katie recognized him as Drastovic, the tale-teller, who'd once lived in the same Croatian village as Jack's family.

Drastovic spent his days visiting the villagers who'd left after the Great War, gathering and relaying news about families scattered throughout coal country, as well as the Minnesota timber camps and Ohio rubber factory towns. Each year at the end of May, Drastovic's circuit brought him back to Pennsylvania. Making his way from house to house, he expounded on the year's births and deaths, weddings and funerals, windfalls, betrayals, and any other gossip worth repeating.

How long before the tale-teller got wind of Jack's jilting? He'd carry the news, luridly embellished, to Filbert, Ralph, and beyond, shaming the Kukoces in every house he entered. Drastovic looked Katie up and down as if she were for sale. Before he could pose a discomfiting question, Tina burst from the house. Her feet thumped the steps as if they deserved strenuous punishment. Her face, round as her mother's, was set in a similar scowl. The skirt of her patched, overlong shift flapped furiously around her long legs. Without a word to Katie, she snatched the sooty sack lying beside the garbage bin and stalked into the alley.

Katie jogged miserably after her, catching up just as Tina's fist apprehended a tear tracing her cheek. "I wish he'd drop dead," she said, "so we could talk about *him* for a change."

The knot in Katie's throat loosened. "Drastovic?"

"Last night, he told Mama that *Strina* Dora, her sister in Ohio, got married again. An Italian butcher with his own shop. Now she lives in a big brick house with a toilet and bathtub inside. Drastovic had photographs—of a toilet! After he went to bed, Mama hollered at *Tata* about how our house is so small, so ugly, with a smelly outhouse. *Tata* hollered back, *you want to shit inside? Then go to Akron and marry a goddamn dago.* They made so much noise that Branka and the boys woke up, and *Baka*'s heart started hurting. I had to run and get the doctor in the middle of the night."

"Is *Baka* all right?" Katie asked.

"She stayed in bed today. Branka's sitting with her to keep Drastovic away."

133

Katie expressed sympathy for *Baka*'s fragile heart as her own beat more easily. Drastovic had driven Jack away, and before he'd told Tina and Branka, their younger sister, the tale with Katie's name in it.

"At breakfast, Drastovic ate half the eggs and five pieces of toast. He talked the whole time, spitting little bits of food out of his mouth." Tina booted a stone against the back of the Zekulas' outhouse, provoking an aggrieved shout from within.

"Why doesn't your pap just tell him to leave?"

Tina's exasperated hand raked hair as dark and wavy as Jack's. "Because he's from Gujgco. Anyone from Gujgco is as good as family, even if he talks with his mouth full and makes people fight."

With studied nonchalance, Katie asked, "Did Drastovic make Jack mad, too?"

"Jack left even earlier than *Tata*. He could've had a shift today, too, the big dummy, but, no, he took off without saying where. Now Drastovic will tell everyone, *ah, Josip's son Janko, such a disappointment.*"

Ordinarily, Katie would have laughed at Tina's pitch-perfect impersonation of the tale-teller's frog-in-the-throat accent. All she heard now was the damning echo of Jack self-assessment. *Big dummy.* She tried to picture him, stalking through the woods, putting space between him and her and their unhappiness. The image that came and refused to leave was that of his shadow, huddled over the heartbreak she'd delivered in the churchyard.

Tina gripped Katie's arm. "Did you two have a fight?"

"No," said Katie-the-Coward. A fight was what Jack's parents had had over a toilet. She and Jack had had a difficult conversation that wasn't finished. "Maybe he's sick and tired of Drastovic, too," she offered. Tina shrugged, clearly unconvinced, so Katie puffed out her cheeks and turned her voice gravelly. "Janko, come, sit, I tell about your cousins, every one a genius, eating fresh Italian sausage morning, noon, and night."

"Stuffing themselves," Tina added, "so, morning, noon, and night, someone's bum is planted on that fancy toilet."

Laughing, they left the alley and headed for the slate dump. With shifts cut and store debts mounting, families turned out daily, seeking free-for-the-picking house coal. The boldest boys waited in the woods for slow-moving freights, climbing onto the hoppers and throwing coal down to pals waiting with wheelbarrows. After the lamp man's son had fallen from a hopper and broken his back, however, their numbers had dwindled. Early birds rose at dawn to search the tracks for cast-off coal. Everyone else scaled the dump, a century's worth of pit waste embedded with burnable black nuggets.

Dust smudged the bright sky like dirty fingerprints each time a scavenger dragged a foot or bag or basket. Women with babies tied to their backs chatted as they picked. Boys pelted each other with whatever didn't find its way into their sacks. Men worked alone, climbing the highest, picking the fastest. Strong men who'd drawn coke and blasted coal, heads bent with shame that, as hard times turned harder, their day's labor had been reduced to this. As pickers traversed the tall mounds like ants on a hill, a wagon lumbered from the tipple to dump a fresh load on the newest heap, just a year old and already half as high as the head frame.

Mutti's warnings revisited Katie as she teetered on a train rail, its deep vibrations warning of an approaching freight. As a child, Deirdre had climbed the most, enduring Mutti's fury when she'd return home, filthy as a miner, after riding a flattened cardboard box down the slopes. Deirdre had rolled her eyes at rumors that the heaps dimpled and shifted, stealthy as glaciers. Only when goaded by taunts of *scaredy-cat* had Katie climbed, too. She'd braked her descent with her heels from the moment she pushed off, hating the dust and fumes and oily taste in the back of her throat. How unfair that, with Deirdre gone, and Norah working the switchboard in a Uniontown department store, the cowardly sister was forced to climb again.

She dragged her sack along the stony base of the tallest heap as Tina resumed her rant about Drastovic. *If you enter, you'll have to give up everything.* Ambushed by Mutti's warning, Katie stopped short and watched her lanky friend hitch up her skirt.

"Hurry up, slowpoke," urged Tina as she began her ascent. "If there's a diamond buried up there, I'm going to find it and build myself a great big house with *ten* toilets."

Since the day Tihana and Janko Kukoc had moved to The Hive—well before they had enough English to call themselves Tina and Jack—Katie had been drawn to their easy laughter and sense of fun. Sharing a desk with Tina in second grade, Katie had whispered words and drawn crude pictures till her new friend caught on. When Katie took a test and moved up two grades, she knew Tina's big brother well enough to agree to the teacher's request to tutor him in arithmetic. In return, he showed her how to swim on her back, bait a fishing hook, and the summer after they started high school, to kiss.

I'm leaving. Katie forced a smile, suppressing the confession when Tina beckoned. Only when Jack had accepted her decision would she tell his sister, whom she'd have to give up, too.

Stones grating her shoes' thin soles, she followed Tina. Up, up a narrow, rust-brown ridge that marked the slope like a scar. Just ahead, Young Widow bent over her sack. Lizzie capered on the slope above her mother, her dirty bag left behind. The girls waved to the widow and traded *good morning*'s. Turning to Katie, Tina bowed and swept out an arm. "Welcome to Tina's mansion," she said, exaggerating the tale-teller's thick accent. To enhance the impersonation, she mashed her coal sack against her dress to form a large, sooty belly. "Such fine brick walls, much nicer than *Strina* Dora's." She indicated an abandoned bushel basket, its bottom slats rotted away. "And a bathtub!" Ignoring the black splinters spilling over her dress, she squeezed herself inside. "*Nedi Boje!* Oh no! I'm stuck!"

Katie laughed until her eyes overflowed. Soon she'd find herself in the convent dining room, wielding the mop that had served as Betty's dance partner, remembering Tina's coal-basket bathtub. Would Katie laugh, or would she have trained herself not to recall anything that might cause her to draw the Mistress of Novices' fierce attention?

A voice, shrill with fear, drew Katie back to the here-and-now she'd not yet sacrificed. "Lizzie, that's high enough!" shouted Young Widow, frantically motioning to her daughter.

Halfway up the slope, Lizzie noticed Katie and waved wildly. "St. Barbara, watch!" Her foot snagged the drooping hem of her skirt, and she pitched forward in an eruption of dust. Young Widow screamed and dropped her sack. Clumsily, Lizzie managed to get to her feet. With hands that glittered bloodily, she lifted her torn skirt and began to cry.

"I'll make you a pretty new dress!" her mother called. "Now come here to mammy!"

Lizzie sat down hard, legs splayed, flour-sack bloomers riding up her thick thighs. Keening and swaying, she pressed her shredded skirt to her chest as if cradling a child. Young Widow began to climb, promising Lizzie two new dresses and candy, to boot. Lizzie, however, shook her head. Digging in her heels, she scooted upward on her rump. A stone tore a window in her bloomers. Her shoes dislodged a waterfall of slate chips that forced her mother to retreat. "I show you, St. Barbara!" Lizzie bawled. "I can go to the top!"

By now, every coal-picker within earshot watched Lizzie's determined ascent. Boys, hooting at the spectacle of bloomers and bared thighs, egged her on. Women echoed Young Widow: "Come down, Lizzie! Come down right this minute!"

"Distract her," Tina told Katie. "I'll climb up behind and bring her down."

Katie whispered Tina's plan to Young Widow. Tina jogged down the ridge and out of sight. Lizzie surveyed her captivated audience on the surrounding slopes, and her tears gave way to a triumphant smile. "Watch!" she commanded. With renewed vigor, she scooted upward until she perched on the summit.

"I'm watching!" Katie shouted. Her eyes cut to Tina, nimbly ascending the stony knob behind Lizzie's perch.

"Look here, Lizzie! I'm taking your picture!" Young Widow pantomimed holding a camera.

As Lizzie preened and posed, Tina climbed, graceful as a cat. A hum rose from the spectators, who, one by one, caught on to the impending rescue. Katie clapped her hands, shouting at

137

Lizzie to hold still and say *cheese*. Finally, Tina reached the top. As she inched toward Lizzie, her foot dislodged a wedge of slate that rattled down the slope.

Lizzie's head whipped around. "Go away, you!" she shouted, hauling herself upright. "It's mine up here!"

"All done, Lizzie!" shouted her mother. "Come down now and see your pretty pictures!"

Tina seized Lizzie's hand. Young Widow let out a ragged sigh. The surrounding heaps rang with cheers that died the instant Lizzie lost her footing. Slipping from Tina's grasp, Lizzie commenced a long, punishing tumble. She screamed repeatedly as her body scoured a crooked trail down the slate. Every onlooker screamed with her. A freight train emerged from the woods, its whistle screaming loudest of all. Young Widow scrambled after the thrashing dust cloud that was her daughter. Every eye but Katie's followed the Boyles' descent. Only Katie, left alone on the slope's brown scar, was mute, paralyzed with disbelief as the slate overhead parted like hungry lips, then closed over Tina.

Katie flung herself at the dirty mountain and began to climb. "Hold on!" she screamed. She fixed streaming eyes on the summit. Somewhere just beneath, Tina swam through rippling stones. Tall, daredevil Tina was the strongest of swimmers, even better than Jack, who once dared her to jump off the railroad bridge into the deepest part of the creek. Seconds after her plunge, she bobbed to the surface, triumphantly displaying a fist slick with silt scooped from the bottom. Now, stroke after determined stroke, she was making her way back to the surface, one fist closed around the diamond she'd pledged to find. "Keep swimming!" Katie urged before a bitter paste of soot and saliva stopped her throat.

She forced her hands—throbbing, blackened, and sticky with blood—up and up. Up and up labored her knees, embedded with biting shards. She paused just long enough to cough and spit, then shouted again. *Tinatinatinatina*—the name flew ahead of her, each syllable woven into the next. The sound unfurled like a sturdy rope, the lifeline that would pull her friend to safety.

She heard her own name and, gasping, glanced back. Peja—puzzled, gesturing—stood beside her dropped sack. "Tina fell in a hole! Get the rescue team up here!" she shouted.

For the first time in her experience, a Lubicic twin immediately did as he was told.

She resumed her ascent, acutely aware of the placid, cloudless sky. The clatter of the tipple's coal chute. A hovering crow, its wings iridescent in the sunlight. The impervious world would crush her beneath an inexorable weight of brightness. "Peja!" she screamed, even as she prayed that he'd already reached the bottom and couldn't hear. "Tell them to hurry!"

As if in reply, the alarm whistle rose from the tipple like a fierce wind that swept her upward. Panting and sweating, she hauled herself onto the summit. A stony expanse spread out before her. A mound here, another there—but no trace of a hole. No telltale ripple pinpointing the site of Tina's tenacious struggle. Katie glared at the sky. "Help me!" she exhorted every benign holy being that had refrained from causing this. Then she fell upon the rubble and began to dig.

It seemed only moments before barking hounds and grim-faced men surrounded her. Someone seized her shoulders and pulled her away from her third urgent excavation. She screamed and kicked, but the hands held fast. Different hands, gentler, cupped her face. She recognized Paul Visocky, Norah's boyfriend, who worked in the motor barn and headed the Company's rescue squad. "Show me, as best you can, where it happened."

She pointed, fighting her captor's grip. "There, maybe. Or over there." Her straining shoulders threatened to snap. Her hands slashed the air, strewing drops of blood.

Paul motioned to his brother Jerry. "Quick, get out the gauze. She's all cut up."

Unleashed, the dogs hung back for a moment, pacing nervously. "Hup, hup!" someone shouted, slapping their tethers against the slate. The largest dog whimpered, then lurched forward. The others followed, their moist black noses gliding over the stones. Shouldering picks and shovels, the men fanned out. Some carried coils of rope that they unwound as they walked. Dividing into groups of five and six, each threaded the rope through a belt loop on his pants or overalls and knotted it, leaving several yards between himself and the next man.

Katie screamed when a man drove his pick into the slate. Glinting slivers erupted. Who knew where Tina might resurface? "Careful! You might hit her!"

"Lie down over here on the stretcher," said Paul, speaking as calmly as if Katie, having fasted for Communion, felt faint in the middle of Mass. "Jerry's going to clean off your—"

"She's drowning! I have to pull her out!" Katie thrust an elbow. Her captor grunted and let go.

She lunged toward the men, but Paul dragged her back. "Jerry! Get her outta here."

Twisting around, Katie beat Paul's chest. Each blow, an imprint of blood and ashes. "Her hands will hurt from swimming. I have to bandage her hands."

When Jerry scooped her up, her body went numb. Hoarse, meaningless sounds trickled from her mouth. A sooty cloud veiled the men and the hounds. Jerry laid her on the stretcher. Directly overhead, a ray of sunlight pierced the dust. The beam played across stones stippled with scarlet. As her eyes closed, she saw rose petals strewn across a rough black altar.

Chapter 18: Clare

May 31, 1933
Feast of St. Angela Merici, Virgin

The sun was setting when Clare encountered Fin in the alley. He eyed with suspicion the towel-draped bowl in her hands. "For the Kukoces," she said, trying to step around him. "Their daughter Tina, Katie's friend—"

How to describe what she couldn't comprehend?

Fin lifted a corner of the towel, damp with steam, then let it drop. The frown began with his forehead, pleating deeply. Before he could chide her for buying costly meat only to give it away, she found words he'd understand. "They've lost a child, Fin."

Fin's hands buried themselves in his pockets. His boot scuffed the dirt. He studied the dust, settling softly in the cracked leather tips of her shoes. "Sickness, then?"

"No. On the slate dump. A hole opened."

His head bowed. "Ah, no." A deep breath. A faint rattle in his chest. "Ah, Jesus."

When she'd poisoned, then lost her womb, his hope for a son was, likewise, lost. The fire left in him burned for the union, son and brother and father to him now. She had no doubt it would use him up and cast him off, another broken soldier like his brother Seamus. Now, standing with Fin in the twilight of another tragedy, she realized how alike they were. How small. How barren. A swollen river of regret washed through her. They'd never embraced outside the bedroom, whose threshold tenderness had yet to cross. Still, only the heavy bowl in her hands kept her from touching him.

Her voice forced its way into the gray space between them. "Katie watched it happen. She tried to dig her out." Again, Clare attempted to pass him. Again, Fin stepped in front of her. Their elongated shadows merged, then parted. "The rescue team has been up there for hours. Didn't you hear the whistle?"

He shook his head. "I was away."

She'd learned not to ask where.

"Did they bring in the dogs?" he asked.

She nodded. "Nothing. Not even a button." She lifted the bowl. "They'll be needing supper."

At last, he stepped aside. "Is Katie all right?"

"She's sleeping, thank God. The doctor gave her something for the shock."

They turned, heading in opposite directions. When Clare reached the Kukoces' gate, she saw that Fin had walked past theirs. On another day, acknowledging his destination would deepen the well of bitterness she drew from each time she patched a dress another woman would have torn into rags. Each time she meekly accepted the charity of a bacon rind or soup bone that wasn't recorded in the store's ledger. But on such a day as this, tears—Katie's and her own—had cleansed that well. All she felt, watching her unnaturally thirsty husband, was overwhelming fatigue.

"Angela closed the beer garden," she shouted. "Lizzie took a bad fall. She went to the hospital."

The Kukoces' back door opened.

Fin looked past her. Lifted a hand. "Jack," he called. "I'm so sorry, lad." Then he trudged to their gate, leaving her speechless in the face of Tina's approaching brother.

Jack's sweat-soaked shirt clung to his chest. Intricate webs of bloody scratches covered his hands and forearms. A deeper cut—long, jagged, darkly beaded—crossed his forehead. The sour smell of exhaustion preceded him, wrapping itself around Clare.

"It's not your fault," she told him. "You did your best to find her. Everyone did."

He stopped, regarding her with confusion. "Did something happen to Katie?"

They stared at each other until it dawned on Clare. Jack's hard-used body had labored somewhere other than the mountain that had swallowed his sister. He didn't know what had happened.

Ah, no. Ah, Jesus.

The bowl shifted. Broth slopped over the rim, burning Clare's hand. "Get the gate," she said. He obeyed, nostrils twitching at the dire aroma of beef.

She didn't need to tell him that food carried to another's house was a herald of disaster. She couldn't bring herself to tell him the rest.

A young woman—Jack's cousin, who lived across the alley— held open the back door. The sound of weeping rolled like an enormous stone out of the kitchen and down the steps, hurrying to crush perhaps the only person in The Hive still unaware of the day's shocking loss.

Jack ran ahead, taking the porch steps two at a time. As he entered the house, the weeping grew louder. Someone called his name. *Janko. Janko.* Chairs scraped. Something small—a spoon, perhaps—clattered onto the floor. These sounds, like smaller stones, rolled past Clare into the yard, slowly, steadily obscuring each plant, each patch of bared dirt beneath a hard, heavy layer of grief.

Clare mounted the steps, mindful of her brimming bowl. The cousin quietly instructed her to take the food inside. But Clare hung back.

What if the day had unfolded differently? What if it had been Tina, hands and knees encrusted with blood and cinders, carried home from the dump? What if the men with shovels and slavering hounds now searched the filthy heap that had entombed Katie? Would Clare, keening in her kitchen, be of any mind to see Mirta, whose daughter still lived?

"Tell them, please, how sorry I am." Clare pressed the bowl into the woman's hands. Her mouth remained open, but there was nothing more to say.

Ah, no. Ah, Jesus.

The woman nodded. She took the bowl, the only comfort Clare could offer, into the kitchen. Clare eased the door shut. From the edge of the porch, the top of the tallest slate heap was visible. A thin column of smoke rose behind it, lazily bleeding into the dimming sky.

***

An ambulance waited in the shadows near the mine gate. Its presence might have kindled a spark of hope if the girl for whom it was intended had been missing for five minutes, not nine hours.

Clare knew she had no business going up there. Stones crept into her shoes and chewed at her feet. High above her, light flickered. Muffled voices drifted down the slope. A dog howled—a sound eerily cut short.

If only she'd kept her coal sack...and the sack had snagged on a stable rock...and, despite her terror, she'd managed to hold on.... Clare began to count. "*Eins, zwei, drei.*" Step after step, number upon number. Busying her mind to keep gruesome speculations at bay.

A grayish glow bathed the summit. Kerosene lanterns dangled from poles planted in a ring around an area roughly the size of the baseball field. Dozens of sweating men bobbed like bulky scarecrows planted waist-deep in a maze of trenches. Some swung picks. Others hunched over shovels. Three sad-eyed hounds, their drooping jowls matted with soot, roamed the perimeter. The heavy air swirled with grit that made Clare's eyes water. She nearly tripped over a first aid trunk, opened to expose a small oxygen tank, rolls of gauze, and assorted brown bottles. Beside it lay a stretcher, its pale canvas peppered with chipped slate.

A man wearing a red-and-white rescue squad armband sprawled between a shovel and the stretcher. He noticed her and propped himself on an elbow. His dirty face was creased with fatigue. "Mrs. Sweeney, how's Katie?"

Clare knelt beside him. "How long have you been up here, Paul?"

"Since it started." He rubbed his eyes. "Katie scraped herself up pretty bad, huh?"

"Jerry left before I could thank him for bringing her home." Clare looked back at the trenches. Dust clouded her vision. "Is he here, too?"

"Everyone I know is here." Paul slowly got to his feet. "I'd better get back to work."

She caught his arm. "I saw an ambulance. Is there any chance—"

Gently, he lifted her hand from his grimy sleeve. "It would take a miracle." He bent to pick up the shovel, then surveyed the men. "I'm praying we don't lose anybody else. It could happen again tonight. Or tomorrow. Or never. We'll keep at it, though, till we find her."

"I'll send Fin up," Clare said, "if he's still at home."

Stones crunched beneath Paul's boots as he entered the ring of lanterns. He lowered himself into a trench, resuming a task that had no longer had anything to do with rescue.

Chapter 19: Clare

June 1, 1933
Feast of the Ascension of our Lord

After Mass, Norah stayed home from work to sit with Katie while Clare did the chores. She peeked in the bedroom and whispered, "I'm going to the store. I won't be long."

Norah looked up from the tiny yellow sweater she was knitting for Helen Zekula Novak's baby shower. She pointed at rust-colored patches on the gauze that enshrouded her sleeping sister's hands. "Should I change her bandages?"

Clare gazed at Katie, sedated with pills from the small white envelope on the nightstand. Her tangled red hair was flecked with slate. Gritty fists had abraded her freckled cheeks. Clare longed to lie down beside her, to hold her close. To convince herself that Katie wouldn't suddenly disappear. "The doctor's coming later. He'll show us what to do," Clare said.

She spoke with confidence she didn't feel, despite years of practice with mustard plasters and vinegar socks. The doctor had assured her that Katie's salved hands and knees would quickly cover themselves with fresh skin. "She's young," he'd said, packing up his bag. "And the young heal fast. She'll be herself again in no time."

On her way to the store, Clare decided that she didn't believe him. The Katie who awakened from this false sleep would be forever divided. Part of her would inhabit the graceful, slender body that the doctor had bandaged. The other part would keep constant vigil at the unmarked grave of the friend she'd failed to rescue. That part would be pierced with guilt at each breath, each hunger pang, and, eventually, inadvertent laughter.

Oddly enough, the store's porch was packed, and with more miners than wives. Fin was nowhere to be seen. Mike Zoshak and Shorty Dvorsk motioned to Clare from the edge of the crowd.

"The Company's starting its own union. There's notices up all over the yard. Somebody brought one of 'em here." Mike

146

pointed to the storefront. "Dan Phelan and Big Bill are down at the lamp house now, passing out the rule books."

"They're calling it a goddamn Brotherhood," Shorty said, then bobbed his head apologetically. "Beg your pardon, Clare." He took her arm and cleared a path through the murmuring crowd until they reached the display window and the notice tacked to its frame.

To Employees of H.C. Frick Coke Company:

It gives me pleasure to announce that the H.C. Frick Coke Company, adhering to the principles set forth in the National Industrial Recovery Act sponsored by the President of the United States, has inaugurated a plan of Employee Representation under the provisions of which the employees of our various plants and operations will have a voice in all matters pertaining to industrial relations.

A copy of the Plan may be obtained at the General Office of your Plant or from your Superintendent. It is hoped that you will secure a copy of the Plan, read it carefully, and give it your hearty support. Your Plant Officials will assist in every possible way in enabling you to properly nominate and elect your Representatives and otherwise perfect the workings...

The paper was signed by Thomas Moses, King Frick's current successor.

Gooseflesh crawled up Clare's back. She turned to Shorty. "Will you join this Brotherhood?"

He took off his cap and watched his hands twist it. "Don't seem like I have much choice. Before Big Bill gave me my book, he said he expects a good showing from the ball team."

"Will they put you off the team if you don't join?" When Shorty didn't reply, she recalled Old Smiley's warning. *You were here in '27. If push comes to shove—* She stared again at the notice. The last line seemed darker, as if typed with a heavier hand.

The whole-hearted support of the Plan by you and your fellow employees will hasten the end of the present emergency.

147

Kamila's voice rose above the commotion. "It says right here, only American citizens can be on the committee. I've told Anton a hundred times already he needs to get his papers."

"Whaddya think Steamshovel will do?" Mike asked.

"I don't know," Clare said.

But she did know. Fin would curse. Kick anything in range, including her. Then disappear to plot God-knows-what with Marty Ryan before Fin was arrested in Grindstone, or Marty was caught in The Hive. The Company's latest attempt to deal with *the present emergency*—a transparent reference to the renewed activity of United Mine Workers' organizers—meant that Old Smiley was right. Push had come to shove.

Kamila elbowed between Mike and Shorty, flapping what Clare assumed was the Brotherhood book. "I heard that, if you don't join and you're a greenhorn, you'll get deported. Fin's got his papers. What about you?"

Shorty and Mike nodded. Kamila pushed back into the crowd, asking each missus, "Do you have papers? Then get yourself to citizen class and take your man, too."

"Looks like Anton's going back to school," Mike said.

"Like it or not," Shorty added. The men eyed each other, as if for permission to laugh.

Clare excused herself, saying she needed to see the butcher. Behind her, someone shouted, "Steamshovel will join, won't he? The team don't stand a chance without him."

She forced herself to offer tepid reassurance. "He'd never desert the team." When the surrounding faces brightened, her stomach turned over. Would Fin interpret her response—sure to be spread throughout the patch—as evidence that she sided with Thomas Moses?

Inside the store, Ada sorted mail at the post office counter. "How's Katie holding up? I hear she took the Kukoc girl's accident pretty hard."

Clare looked at Ada. Just looked. Finally, she said, "How would *you* hold up if you watched *your* best friend get buried alive?" Teeth on edge, she turned on her heel and went back out the door. The Kukoces would get vegetable soup instead of pork and sauerkraut.

Outside, the crowd parted to let Maeve Keating and seven-year-old Emma onto the porch. Maeve wished Clare a good morning, echoed by Emma, twisting a tawny braid. Beneath the beribboned brim of her ivory cloche, Maeve's eyes moistened as she asked about Katie.

Again, Clare let her eyes reply. And she let them take their time.

Maeve's brows drew together, puckering the skin between them.

Despite the Brotherhood notice, and the loss of Tina, and the leaden sense that fresh calamity gestated just out of sight, Clare enjoyed the sight of that pucker. When Maeve's cheeks turned pink beneath her face powder, Clare said, "The doctor said Katie will be all right."

"I'll send Emma over with a little something." Maeve took a lace-edged hankie from her pocket and dabbed her eyes. "The other girl—Kozich?" she said, lowering her voice.

Clare raised hers. "Kukoc. Tina Kukoc. They still haven't found her body."

Maeve told Emma to go inside and pick out a nickel bag of candy. With palpable reluctance, she turned back to Clare. "Would they be needing anything? Visitors must be—"

"No visitors. The deputies won't let anyone who doesn't live here get off the streetcar."

Maeve's eyebrows shot up. Clare nearly laughed at such a poor pretense of ignorance. Everyone knew that deputies boarded each incoming streetcar. Everyone, even Emma, had watched the erection of barricades to block Main Street, east and west, at The Hive's boundaries. Everyone had seen cars stopped and searched.

"Women with babies have to unwrap their blankets to prove they're not carrying union pamphlets. Next thing you know, deputies will be looking inside the diapers," Clare added.

Maeve stared over Clare's shoulder, clearly wishing she could join Emma inside the store. When her eyes cut back to Clare's, her flush deepened. She dropped her gaze.

For an instant, Clare felt like a nightgown on the clothesline, billowing and inflated by a bracing wind. Was this how Fin felt when he spoke his mind, looking a boss dead in the eye?

Maeve crushed her hankie inside her fist. "I'm sorry, Clare," she said, so softly that Clare strained to hear her. "I wish things could be different, but it's not up to me." She drew a deep breath and slid the crumpled hankie into her purse. Squaring her shoulders, she met Clare's gaze. Raised her voice. "I'll bake the Kukoc family an angel food cake. I don't know anyone who doesn't like angel food."

Without saying goodbye, she entered the store.

Chapter 20: Katie

"The bosses were packing up," Jack said. "Then your pap showed up at the paymaster's window. *Don't tell me I missed the party, lads*, he said. Everyone laughed, even the bosses and deputies, but not him. He just wrote what they wanted on the Brotherhood paper. Big Bill told him about batting practice, and he said, *I don't need reminding about where I belong*."

Katie had already heard Pap tell this story—a longer, more sarcastic version about what he called the *Amos 'n Andy union*. She let Jack tell it again because she couldn't bear to sit in silence. Each time he paused, she asked about another miner. "Did Mike Zoshak join? And Mr. Visocky?"

Jack patiently recounted the name of everyone who'd stood in line, including the Negroes. "Only a couple fellas needed help filling out their papers. Pretty much everybody's got good enough English now." He lifted eyebrows so finely tapered they might have been a girl's. The long red scratch on his forehead peeked between dark strands of hair.

They sat on the Sweeneys' back steps, their knees angled toward each other, though not touching. Faint taps of forks against plates drifted over the Tonellis' fence. Majella, her husband, and their two-year-old daughter had come for a supper that Katie, who'd slept away three days, found hard to believe was happening on Sunday.

"Are you going to rehearsal tonight?" Jack asked. He'd asked the same thing soon after arriving, but she pretended to hear it for the first time.

In the hollow of her neck rested a small silver medal with an image of St. Barbara. Emma Keating had brought it, nestled in a blue velvet box, as a get-well present. Mutti said Katie didn't have to wear it if she didn't want to. Katie thought this was a strange comment until the cool oval touched her skin. Then she understood. The medal marked a division in her life— what had happened before her long sleep, what would happen after. For a moment, she'd considered taking off the medal, throwing it away, forgetting she'd ever received it. Yet one more thing to forget.

The only thing she'd forgotten were her lines. "Norah spent an hour cueing me last night, but it's hopeless. I'll have to memorize everything all over again," she told Jack.

"Do you still want to play the part?"

"It wouldn't be right to back out now." A second Sweeney giving up the coveted role would be unthinkable. "At least I don't have to do it right away." The Brotherhood was holding organizational meetings in The Hall, so the pageant had been postponed until the first of July.

"The Queen sent a note asking Branka to be a pilgrim. She's up at The Hall right now, trying on the costume." Color crept into Jack's face. He turned away, suddenly intent on the Tonellis' strutting rooster. Katie sensed that he hadn't meant to tell her this, though she'd have found out soon enough. They both knew whom Branka replaced, and why a thirteen-year-old had been given the part instead of some older girl who'd auditioned and failed to make the cast.

Katie silently weighed the name on her tongue. Yes, she believed she could say it now. Saying it quietly, like a prayer, might do some good. "Poor Lizzie."

Jack's tongue, likewise, hesitated. "Lizzie can be a pilgrim next year."

Neither commented on the angel, now played by Paul Visocky's sister Sobena, who also served as stage manager.

They started when Norah called through the screen. "I just took a pan of sand tarts out of the oven. I'll make up a plate for your family, Jack."

He thanked her, then looked back at Katie's hands, resting in her lap. Slowly, he reached across the step and gently touched the brown scabs and pink, shiny skin in between. He traced each knuckle's indention. "Does this hurt? If it hurts, I won't do it."

"It doesn't hurt." She watched his left hand carefully fit itself around her right.

"When are you leaving?" he asked, so softly she had to lean toward him to hear.

I just came back. She breathed in the warm-blanket scent of his hair, the faint tang of man-sweat escaping the collar of his white Sunday shirt. Defying every convention concerning boys and girls, Mutti had allowed him upstairs the day before. Groggy from the pills, Katie had seen him dimly, as if through rain. "I came every day," he'd said, "but you were asleep." The scent of him now was the first thing she'd noticed since rising that tempted her to stay awake.

Jack gently clasped her other hand. "Your ma said you're all right, but I didn't believe her till now, till I could touch you. I won't do any more than this, though, I promise."

Unbidden, the memory of the moonlit churchyard settled over her until her head grew heavy. She let it drop onto his shoulder; a single tear, onto his shirt.

"It's all right," he whispered against her hair. He slid across the step, closing the space between them. "Go ahead. Crying feels real bad at first, but then you feel better."

No more tears came. Sleep had drained her. His chest filled and emptied, lifting her, then easing her down. His breath stroked her forehead. His heart, deep beneath the warm white shirt, marked each moment as if it were just that, as precious as it was unremarkable. Everything had changed but this. *This,* assured his heart's steady meter, *will never change. This, if you want it, will gladly carry you, your medal, and your memories into whatever happens next.*

The screen door squeaked, but neither Katie nor Jack stirred. Footsteps lightly crossed the porch. Something was set on the planks behind them. The footsteps retreated, and the sweet scent of vanilla enfolded them like a blessing.

After five days of digging, the rescue squad gave up. Word spread quickly: there would be no wake. In essence, however, the wake had started the evening of the tragedy. Deputies still questioned streetcar passengers and stopped cars, but now anyone saying *Kukoc* received a nod and a gesture pointing the way. When Katie told Mutti about this turn of events, Mutti responded with a tight smile and puzzling comment. "I guess I underestimated Maeve." When Katie asked what she meant, Mutti just shook her head.

The Kukoces' relatives and friends came from as far away as Greensburg and Latrobe and didn't leave. Once quilts and borrowed pillows covered every inch of the the floor, new visitors spent the night with cousins in Buffington, as well as The Hive. Drastovic left for Pittsburgh to carry the sad news to Mr. Kukoc's mother and his brother, a steelworker. He promised to escort them back to The Hive for the funeral. He was the first and only person to speak that word.

Jack returned to the pit, working the occasional shift assigned to his father, and his own. When the rescue squad had given up, his exhausted father had come home and stayed there. Despite long hours underground and the ever-larger crowd assembling daily in his home, Jack faithfully appeared at the Sweeneys' back door each evening just as they finished supper. He sat with Pap on the porch, listening to Pap talk about William Feeney and Philip Murray, union men leading the charge to organize the county.

Pap's tone throbbed with excitement typically reserved for baseball. "Think of it, lad. The President himself is on our side. His recovery bill says that we've got the right to join any union we please. Soon John L. Lewis will win, and old King Frick will turn over in his grave."

After the dishes were done, Pap went off to find someone else to complain to about the Brotherhood. Jack helped Katie carry the dishpan outside. He sat in the grass as she watered the garden, his dark hair slicked back, his cheeks and neck pink from a hard scrubbing. When she finished, Jack carried the pan into the kitchen while she got her script. They walked down the alley, and Katie waited by his gate until he came out with Branka.

Dozens of people dressed in black filled the Kukoc house. Every window, alight and opened, leaked conversations across the yard. Holding her nose, Katie stood behind the outhouse, so nobody glancing out a window would ask who she was. With each shallow breath she wondered if Jack's mother could ever bear to look at her again. In the few minutes that it took Jack to bring Branka outside, thoughts of the convent, Betty's trunk, and the letter Mutti had sent to Trudy drifted into Katie's mind and then out again, distant and indistinct as birds crossing the sky.

Jack walked between her and Branka, but refused to enter The Hall. "I don't want to spoil the surprise," he said. He shook his head when Katie reminded him that not a word of The Queen's original script had ever been changed. "It's always different because the people in it are different," he insisted. He held the door for the girls, then headed back down the street. Katie assumed that he went home to sit with whatever newcomers had arrived that day.

He was always waiting outside when rehearsal ended.

After taking Branka home, Jack and Katie turned—always left, away from the dump—and walked until dusk surrendered to darkness. On most nights, the first star glittered before one of them spoke, usually Jack, recounting something that had occurred in the pit. A minor roof fall. A spooked mule that had kicked Mr. Tonelli. A jammed coal-cutter, the electric-powered machine that Jack called the Beast. He talked with studied nonchalance, as if mining weren't dangerous, just tedious and tiring like washing or weeding.

"I thought about you all day," she assured him. He walked with his chin down, his face cloaked in shadow, so she couldn't make out his expression. She hoped it came close to a smile.

When they returned to Katie's gate, Jack took her left hand in his. His right hand slowly worked its way from her wrist to the tip of her thumb, then slid back to her wrist and moved the length of her index finger. After reaching her little finger, he released her left hand and repeated his gentle inspection on her right. "Does it hurt?" he asked, lightly pressing here and there.

She assured him that it didn't.

When he finished, she pushed back the hair from his forehead. Her fingertip traced the scar inflicted by a tree branch the day he'd retreated to the woods and Tina had died. She could barely feel the seam of skin, but habit had trained her finger where to start, where to end. "Does it hurt?" she asked.

He shook his head, then caught her hand and held it to his lips before saying goodnight.

The following week, Drastovic returned on the streetcar with Jack's Pittsburgh relatives. The tale-teller's gravelly voice barreled down First Street and into the garden, where Katie knelt, pulling weeds. Hard as a baseball, the sound hit her square in the chest. She bent forward, gasping for breath, as Tina's voice spilled from the rustling cornstalks.

I wish he'd drop dead, so we could talk about him for a change.

Footsteps beat the back steps. Mutti knelt beside Katie. "*Was ist los?*" What's the matter?

Katie stared at the garden's neat green rows. It seemed impossible that anything, even a weed, still managed to grow. "I want to forget everything, but I don't know how."

Mutti stroked Katie's back. "You don't want to forget the good things."

"I don't know what I want anymore. Everything I thought I wanted—" Katie bowed her head, ashamed. Like the garden, she was alive. She had no right to complain.

"You don't have to make any decisions right now." Mutti rocked back on her heels, her lower lip caught between her teeth. "There needs to be a funeral. Mirta's mother is too old to live with a houseful of noisy guests. She needs peace and quiet. They all do."

"How can there be a funeral without—" The corn rustled again. Katie listened intently. Perhaps Tina would tell her what the rescue squad had overlooked. Such a thought surely bordered on insanity, but Katie didn't care. If a funeral would send Drastovic and the other guests packing, Katie owed it to Tina to help make it happen.

The Queen had cancelled that evening's rehearsal to attend a family function, but Jack arrived, as always, when supper ended. "You go on. I'll do the dishes," Norah told Katie, who went upstairs to change into her oldest dress. When she hurried back to the kitchen and into the pantry, Norah called from the sink, "You'd never catch me walking with Paul dressed like a tinker."

Katie emerged from the pantry with a folded tea towel hidden in her pocket. "Paul wouldn't care if you took a walk in your nightgown."

Norah rolled her eyes. "That wouldn't be decent."

Mutti, out on the porch with Jack, frowned when Katie opened the door. Before she could comment on Katie's attire, Katie grabbed Jack's hand and pulled him across the yard.

"What's your hurry?" he asked as the gate snapped shut behind them. When Katie turned a hard right, he forced her to a stop. "Where do you think you're going?"

"*We're* going to look for Tina. She wants us to find her." Katie closed her mouth, hard, so she wouldn't add, *Tina told me so.*

"If she was there to be found, don't you think it would've happened by now?" Jack drew Katie to his chest. His face tightened with what she thought was anger. When it moved closer to hers, she realized that his expression meant something altogether different.

She'd forgotten how his mouth felt, hard and soft at the same time. How the tiny bristles in his chin scraped hers until it stung. How the place between her legs turned heavy, almost hurtful, as his hands moved against her back.

"I'm sorry. I can't help it." His mouth retreated just long enough to say this, then returned to hers, giving her no chance to repeat what she'd said in the churchyard.

It occurred to her that nothing, not even twilight, shielded them from the scrutiny and disapproval of the neighbors—and Norah. Mutti, Katie suspected, wouldn't disapprove. If Mutti noticed, she'd discreetly turn away, relieved that Katie had finally woken up.

Jack's mouth lifted again. "I love you more than anything," he said fiercely. "Loving you is the only way through this. If you'd died up there with her, I would've died, too."

"Maybe that's why I'm still here. To find her." She laid a finger against his lips, stopping his protest. "If you love me, you'll come with me."

His forehead lowered to meet hers. "I'd never let you go back up there alone."

The path to the summit had become a wide gangway, pounded by the soles of countless boots. The evening sun's slanting light caught the edges of a million shards of coal, glittering like dark jewels. Their unexpected beauty brought tears to Katie's eyes. Beside her, Jack walked without comment, pausing when she paused at the place where Tina had climbed inside the broken basket. Katie nearly pointed to the spot, then changed her mind. For now, this memory belonged only to her, a small, priceless treasure she wasn't ready to share.

When they reached the summit, she stared in disbelief at the checkerboard of trenches. "It looks—so different."

"What did you expect?" Jack's tone was profoundly weary. "We tore this place apart."

Like mining, digging for a buried girl was clearly man's work. Had Katie really expected to march up the slope, thrust her hand into the stones, and clasp Tina's? She felt in her pocket for the towel with which she'd intended to clean her friend's face. She'd imagined it soot-streaked, but otherwise unchanged. With the rough evidence of determined shovels spread out before her, she let the towel drop.

Rays of the sinking sun poured into the trenches, gilding every stone. *Welcome to Tina's mansion...*

"There should be a marker here. A cross," said Katie, bending to pick up the towel. Her voice caught. "An angel."

Jack turned her away. "Let's go. I have nightmares that it happens to you."

They picked their way down the slope as the sun slid behind a hill. The sparkling jewels turned back into coal. When they reached the bottom, the slate, sky, and air shared the same shade of purplish gray. "Promise me," Jack said, "you'll never go up there again."

"Just once more," she said. "We'll go together to place a cross. Branka, too, and your parents, whoever wants to come. Big Bill will give you wood if you ask. We'll whitewash it, and I'll write her name. Everything will be done then, except the funeral." She turned toward him, her chest racked with sobs. His arms slid beneath her, and her feet left the ground.

His voice filled her ear. "It feels better now, doesn't it?"

"No." She struggled to breathe, to speak. "Not the least bit."

She wept into his shirtfront until it stuck to his skin. Finally, spent, she lifted her face to tell him, yes, she did feel better, but the words stalled on her tongue. He had carried her to the back of the coke yard. Before them stretched the run whose centermost oven had housed Betty's bonfire. To the left, the empty niches where Katie had sought a vision. A freight had picked up that day's loaded hoppers, so no deputy patrolled with a rifle on his shoulder.

"I come here every night while you're rehearsing," Jack said. He paused to kiss her, then resumed walking. "There's so much noise in the pit and at home that I can't think straight."

"Why did you bring me here?" she asked, although she knew. After all they had shared these past two weeks, what would happen tonight seemed inevitable. Good or bad, right or wrong—circumstances had rendered those words meaningless. Her body, purged of tears, rested against his, sensing his deep need.

He stopped outside the entrance to the last oven. "Please, don't make me go home."

She touched the space between his eyes, pressing gently until the crease there softened. "When you come here, what do you think about?"

"You," he said. He lowered his head, rounded his shoulders, and carried her inside. "Only you."

Chapter 21: Clare
June 23, 1933
The Vigil of St. John the Baptist

Liebe Clara,
Letzte Sonntag, habe ich Deirdre und ihre neue, shöne, gesunde Tochter besucht...
Last Sunday, I visited Deirdre and her beautiful, healthy new daughter...

Clare set Trudy's letter on the kitchen table and wiped her eyes.

Masha the tinker, to whom the letter was addressed and who had furtively delivered it to Clare's back door, sat across the kitchen table, sipping tea. "Good news or bad?"

"A fine girl," Clare said. "Margaret Patricia, but they're calling her Molly." She cleared her throat and read aloud. Three-week-old Molly was christened and, though a bit colicky, was nursing well. Deirdre, also well. Billy's mother had been present for the birth, which had gone without a hitch. A lovely woman, Trudy declared, and well off, even now. Her husband owned a produce warehouse and two grocery stores in Pittsburgh's fashionable East End. The oldest son ran one; Mr. McKenna, assisted by Billy, the other. Middle son Joe had finally been persuaded to turn in his deputy badge and return home to learn the family business. A good decision on Deirdre's part, marrying into a grocer's family, Trudy opined. Even in hard times, people had to eat, and East Enders ate better than most.

Masha drained her cup and patted the fresh stationery that she'd brought with Trudy's letter. "Thanks for the tea. I'm trading in Smock next week. If you want me to mail another one, get it to me by Friday." She gathered up Clare's payment, a yard of tatted lace.

Clare gazed at the bottom of the letter, where Trudy had written Deirdre's address in a firm hand. Clare could put the letter in her pocket and walk down the alley to Kamila's. If she asked, Kamila would hand her however much money would get her to Pittsburgh. She rose on rubbery legs and tried to imagine herself standing on a platform at the Uniontown train station. She closed her eyes, gritted her teeth. Tried and tried and tried—and failed.

She lowered herself back onto the bench, grasping, for the first time, the enormity of her neighbors' courage. Kamila, Concetta, Mirta—all had willingly turned their backs on everyone and everything they'd ever known. They'd packed shabby trunks and journeyed to a land so distant and different it could only seem like a dream. Such trust they'd had—in their men's ambitions, in their own abilities to make new friends and new homes for their children, no matter what. What a coward she was in comparison! Brought up speaking a foreign tongue, yet born here, an indisputable American. But no pioneer.

The only thing between her and Pittsburgh was a frayed screen door. Such a flimsy barrier—yet it might as well have been a brick wall topped with barbwire. She'd heard Fin call Frick's mines *captive* more times than she could count. The term referred to their partnership with a steel company, which guaranteed a market for their coal.

But captivity took many other forms. The Brotherhood. The Company store. The immutable prison of gender.

The dark, solitary cell of one's conscience.

She picked up Trudy's letter and reread the part about Katie. *I wish I could pay the whole convent dowry, but fifty dollars is all I can manage. I have approached my pastor Fr. Lambert Daller, who was touched by my account of Katie's vocation. He offered the use of our parish Lyceum's auditorium for an evening of entertainment and refreshment, the proceeds of which will be donated to Katie's cause. St. Marienkirche has an excellent reputation for theatrical productions, especially the annual Passion Play. The choir is filled with talented singers, and our organist plays the piano as well as anyone I've heard in concert at the Carnegie Institute. All have agreed to perform on Katie's behalf. A printer, also a parishioner, is making posters and handbills. Fr. Daller suggested a patriotic theme for the Fourth of July...*

Something in Clare's chest twisted painfully as she tore the letter in half and burned it in the stove. The laundry basket loomed. Reason settled over her like a coarse shawl. She added coal to the embers and hefted the irons onto the burners. Unfolding the board, she heard a familiar cadence on the steps.

Kamila opened the door. "I was on my way to the store when I saw Masha sneaking out your gate. Did Trudy write back?"

Clare fitted the perforated rubber cap onto the sprinkling bottle. Unable to resist, she pointed it at Kamila's empty hands. "Forgot your shopping basket?"

"*Pffft!*" Kamila seated herself emphatically on the bench and eyed the stationery. "Who're you writing to now?"

Clare draped Fin's Sunday shirt over the board, smiling proudly at Kamila, mother-in-law to a high school principal, a banker, and a railroad inspector. "My granddaughter's name is Margaret Patricia. Her grandfather is an East End grocer. She'll have fine food and new dresses. Maybe even a piano." With a potholder, she lifted an iron from the stove.

"If Deirdre had to run off like that, thanks be to God she picked a boy who comes from something." Kamila's thick finger tapped the table, setting the stationery aquiver. "Have you heard from your cousin? Did she send Katie's convent money?"

Clare sprinkled a shirtsleeve and applied the iron, sliding it hard through a cloud of steam. "You don't enter the convent loving any man but Jesus. A blind man can see that Katie loves Jack, and he's over the moon for her."

Kamila wagged her head. "Katie's meant for Indiana State Teachers' College, just like my girls. I'll get you the name of the person to write to about a scholarship—for Katie *and* Norah."

As the steam cleared, the white shirt changed to vivid Fourth of July bunting. Trudy's letter had taken ten days to reach Clare. By now, store windows throughout Deutschtown displayed posters for Katie's benefit. Tickets had been sold. Rehearsals were in full swing.

All on account of a mother who should have known better than to beg.

"A scholarship only pays for classes. The college has jobs for girls who need to work for their room and board. Katie and Norah will just go—" Kamila snapped her fingers—"and once they're gone, what's Fin going to do about it? Jump on the train and go after them? *Pffft!*" She got to her feet with a satisfied smile. "Let me tell you, it's easier to ask forgiveness than permission. Your girls will come home at Christmas with straight A's, and the next thing you know, Fin's bragging in the hoist cage."

She was gone before Clare could disagree. Once Fin made up his mind, there could be no asking, much less forgiveness.

Chapter 22: Clare
June 25, 1933
Feast of St. William, Abbot

Fin went off with his baseball mitt, saying he'd be home for supper. Norah left soon after, running to catch the streetcar to visit Helen and her new baby in Buffington. Katie changed from her Sunday dress into an everyday frock and morosely set out for Beetown, where she'd spend her fourth straight afternoon looking after The Queen's young sons. She'd been hired to come every day and amuse Hal and Georgie while The Queen drank tea in her parlor with nicely dressed Beetown women or visited them in their parlors or went out shopping.

In the quiet kitchen, Clare beat eggs and sifted flour, preparing dough for gingersnaps. Paul Visocky hurried with his brothers and father down the alley as she wondered—what would prompt a mother to pay a stranger to take her place? According to Katie, the afternoons seemed interminable. The boys were unpleasant children—spoiled, whining, constantly bickering—but who could blame them? They wanted their mother's attention, not that of a patch girl, who played with them solely for money.

Clare set down the sifter. Who was she to question the motivation of a rich woman—or any other? Whatever The Queen felt about her boys, it surely wasn't fear.

When Clare looked up from the mixing bowl, Shorty Dvorsk and Mike Zoshak strode past her back gate. Concetta's husband and sons lingered at theirs, nodding at Stan and Mike as they passed. The Tonellis waited until the two other men were out of sight, then entered the alley, heading in the same direction.

Clare set down her spoon and went into the living room, moving the window curtain just enough to survey First Street. As she suspected, it was vacant. She was about to let the curtain drop when movement caught her eye. She focused on the slender gaps between the houses facing hers. She stared until her eyes watered. Until she was convinced—and uneasy. In two's and three's, with calculated spaces in between, The Hive's men and boys walked purposefully south, just as Fin had. She had no idea where he was going—where any of them were going—but she was sure it had something to do with the union.

She returned to the kitchen and, with a nervous hand, worked a worn wooden spoon through the stiffened dough. Around and around like her thoughts, circling the disturbing fact of a mass male exodus from the patch. Around and around until her hand cramped. Until her worry gave way to a different disquiet as she formed the dough into balls. She intended them for Mirta Kukoc, whose house she'd avoided since Tina's funeral.

She'd told herself that the family had had its fill of visitors, however helpful and solicitous. What they needed now was quiet time in which to heal. Their wound—so deep, so grievous—wouldn't mend as swiftly and simply as Katie's torn-up hands. She'd told herself that to encroach on their privacy now would be wrong. Every day prior to the funeral, she'd delivered food to Mirta's house, handing it to an aunt or cousin over the threshold. Clare had never been able to step over it. She couldn't bear the thought of meeting Mirta's eyes.

Mirta had had two daughters. Now, only one.

A tear splashed onto the cookie sheet. Clare wiped it away with a corner of her apron. The pain of losing Deirdre still gnawed. At times, Clare's longing racked her insides like excruciating hunger. But Deirdre lived. After four years, it was possible to think of her without crying. Occasionally, Clare could even think of her and smile. Mirta, however, inhabited a hellish trap. How to remember Tina apart from the recollection of her hideous death? Entering Mirta's kitchen, Clare would be a cruel reminder of her loss. But it was equally cruel to stay away.

When Clare carried the heaping plate of gingersnaps into the Kukoc backyard, she was met with a hard stare from Branka, now Mirta's only daughter. Branka knelt in the garden, hands hidden by carrot fronds. She offered no greeting, clearly hoping Clare would take the hint and leave. Clare forced herself to smile at Branka and approach the house. Two weeks had passed since Jack had planted a white cross on the slate dump, yet Drastovic and half a dozen relatives stayed on. The tale-teller greeted Clare at the kitchen door. Crumbs flecked his salt-and-pepper beard. His eyes settled greedily on the cookies. "*Keksi*. Very nice! Please, sit, have coffee." He motioned her inside.

Men with shaggy mustaches and women shawled and scarved in black surrounded the table. A young cousin entered the kitchen, supporting Mirta. A skeletal face peered from the dark cave of her *babushka*. Her skin wore the yellowish cast of an old cheese.

Drastovic placed the cookies on the oilcloth-covered table, crowded with cups and a coffee pot. The guests sampled the gingersnaps and nodded approval. Mirta lowered herself onto a stool, and the cousin stepped behind, a reassuring hand on each hunched shoulder. Clare squatted before the stool and clasped Mirta's hands, chilled and limp. "Ginger," she said finally, glancing at the table, "is good for the stomach."

Mirta's eyes were uncomprehending, but the cousin left her to collect a handful of cookies. She whispered to Mirta and offered her one. As Mirta chewed, Clare and the cousin exchanged glances. *This is good*, the young woman's expression assured Clare.

Meanwhile, Drastovic presided at the table. Occasionally, someone laughed and was quickly hushed. When that happened, Mirta's eyes widened, as if surprised that such a sound existed. She stared at the table—longingly, it seemed—as if perceiving a chasm permanently separating her from people capable of laughter.

She refused another cookie and took Clare's hands. "Thank you for so many times bringing supper."

Mirta turned and spoke rapidly to the cousin. "She is saying, give *keksi* to her mama," the young woman explained. She patted Mirta's shoulder and, taking the last cookie from the plate, went upstairs.

Mirta peered at Clare with red-rimmed eyes. "Soon, we must be having *vjenčanje*. Janko and Katie." Her fingers tightened, as if pressing her meaning into Clare's skin. "*Vjenčanje?* Making a wedding, Janko and Katie? Very soon."

Something turned in Clare's stomach that ginger wouldn't soothe. She saw Katie clad in a white gown and veil. Then another Katie in a drab black habit.

Katie's meant for Indiana State Teachers' College.

You don't enter the convent loving any man but Jesus.

"This house is wanting, very much, *sreća.* Being happy." Though halting, Mirta's speech was determined. "*Umorni smo u ovoj kući. Previše plakanja.* In this house, we are tired. Too much crying."

Branka came inside to wash her hands. She eyed Clare sullenly. "Tommy Tonelli's out in the alley, looking for you. He says you have company."

Surely Tommy was mistaken. Still, Clare was relieved to rise, stiff-kneed, and say goodbye. Handing back the empty plate, Drastovic waved her out the door. "*Keksi* very good. Thank you, goodbye, come back soon."

Tommy stood outside the gate, stuttering and gesturing wildly. "H-h-hurry! Your g-girl's b-back. W-with a b-b-baby."

Clare nearly turned her ankle in the alley's rutted dirt. Tommy galloped beside her, thrilled to have prompted such a dramatic reaction in someone who wasn't his mother. When she reached her gate, her eyes misted, blurring the figures by the fence. Tommy darted into his own yard, finally managing to blurt out Deirdre's name.

For a moment, Clare stood stock-still, unable to do anything but look. Then Deirdre smiled and beckoned, bringing some withered part of Clare back to life.

Concetta held Molly, cooing to her in Italian. When Clare reached for the warm pink bundle, Concetta smiled ruefully. "If I am only knowing, I will be some way telling Rosie, say to your boss you are sick and run home very fast from Beetown."

Concetta took the plate, freeing Clare's right hand to reach for Deirdre, soft and solid, smelling of lavender and milk. Molly bleated like a lamb as they cried and laughed at the same time. Deirdre straightened her hat, its charming little brim encircled by a lilac ribbon that matched her flowered dress. Lifting Molly to her shoulder, she nodded at the woman beside her. "I'd like to introduce my mother Clare Sweeney."

Though the woman's bobbed hair was deep brown, not red, Clare knew at once that she was Billy's mother. Clare extended a chapped hand—and noticed with horror a cinnamon-brown crescent of cookie dough lodged beneath each ragged fingernail.

"So glad to meet you." Mrs. McKenna's smooth oval face, like those of the bosses' wives, was lightly powdered. Attired in a navy-and-white seersucker dress, she looked as stylish as The Queen.

Clare saw herself as clearly as if a mirror had dropped in front of her. Every inch a downhiller missus—limp-haired and dowdy in a dated shift. Compared to Billy's mother, she looked no better than Masha the tinker.

"My Mollydoll's hungry," Deirdre said, patting the whimpering baby. Though her waist was as trim as a girl's, her lace-trimmed collar draped full, womanly breasts. She turned toward the house. "Let's go inside. I'd love a nice cup of tea."

Clare searched her pockets for a hankie to slide between the infant's bubbling mouth and Deirdre's pristine collar. It struck her then that Deirdre probably had another dress just as fine. Perhaps more than one. Billy's father could afford to dress Clare's daughter as handsomely as his wife. Then it occurred to Clare that Deirdre was now his daughter, too.

In the kitchen, Clare babbled apologies for the clutter as she hurried mixing bowls into the sink. She cleared a place on the table for teacups, silently thanking every saint and angel that she'd made so many gingersnaps. She slid the remaining cookies onto the plate, filled the kettle, urged her guests to sit. The stove needed coal, and she smudged her skirt shoveling it. Back to the noisy pump to wash her sooty hands, to pry the hardened dough from beneath her nails.

As she scurried around, Mrs. McKenna tenderly arranged a pink receiving blanket over Deirdre's shoulder, a modest drape for the nursing mother. Here was the woman who had tended Deirdre during her pregnancy. Fashionable, impeccably polite—and she had taken Clare's place.

Clare hated her. Wanted her dead, gone, never to have existed.

Bile rose in the back of Clare's throat. Her body quaked, full to bursting with such fierce, despicable desire. She pumped and pumped and scraped beneath her nails until her envy, like the dough, slowly dissolved. This well-off woman was essential to Deirdre's new life, the future into which Clare had blindly, desperately dispatched her. Clare's hate would cast a shadow over Deirdre, over Molly, over every good thing they already had and what was yet to come.

The kettle hissed. Clare dried her hands and filled the teapot. Deirdre, still nursing, petted Molly's head. "Mrs. Tonelli told me Rosie and Mike Zoshak are engaged. Please give her my address, so she can write and tell me all about it."

Mrs. McKenna removed her gloves and tasted a gingersnap. "Light as a feather! I'd very much like the recipe if it's not a family secret."

Clare glanced into the yard, and her tongue turned to stone. Fin opened the gate, slapping his mitt against his hip. Concetta stopped scattering chicken feed to call his name, louder than necessary, as a warning. They conversed briefly as Clare watched, paralyzed. What on earth could she do—hurry the visitors out the front door like bootleggers on the lam?

Fin crossed the porch before she could move. He stopped on the threshold and fitted the glove onto his left hand. Punched it with his right fist. The sound of knuckles against leather, unremarkable on a ball field, lifted the hairs on the back of Clare's neck.

Deirdre passed Molly to her mother-in-law and turned away to quickly button her dress. Turning back, she reached for the baby, sated and drowsy. "Surprise, Pap! This is Margaret Patricia, your very first grand—" Her voice trailed off as she looked uncertainly at Clare.

Fin fixed his gaze on the wall. A tic set his right eyelid quivering. "Who gave you the right to be overruling me?" he shouted.

"Gracious, look at the time," said Mrs. McKenna, consulting her delicate gold watch. "We really must be going. My son Joe is meeting us at the train station."

"Look at her, Pap." Deirdre folded the bonnet brim away from Molly's face. Only Deirdre would dare approach him now, pitting her considerable will against his. Though the mother of a child, she was still child enough herself to believe she could succeed.

Fin whipped the mitt from his hand and hurled it to the floor, just missing Deirdre's shoes. "I will not be made a mockery of in me own house!"

Mrs. McKenna drew Deirdre toward her. "Thank you for the tea, Mrs. Sweeney. I hope you'll visit us soon in Pittsburgh." Keeping herself between Fin and her new daughter, she guided Deirdre to the door.

Deirdre glanced back at Clare, her face crumpling with disappointment. *Has nothing changed since I left? Nothing at all?*

When they'd gone, it was this look as much as Fin's fists that doubled Clare over, then knocked her to the floor.

Chapter 23: Katie

Norah closed the bedroom door and leaned against it. "You're not a virgin anymore," she said with toneless, switchboard-operator inflection.

"How would you know?" Katie countered. *Verdammt!* A flat denial was called for. Katie didn't want to know how Norah had gained this information. "Open the door," Katie said. "If I'm late for dress rehearsal, The Queen will bite my head off."

Norah, predictably, didn't budge. "How can you be a nun if you've known a man?"

Trust Norah to put it like that. *Known a man.* Only a girl who behaved like a nun could make love sound like a catechism lesson. As far as Katie knew, Norah had never let Paul so much as kiss her. "You know a man, too," Katie hedged. Dress rehearsal started in an hour. She should've been seated in The Hall's basement while Betty applied her makeup.

Norah stalked around the bed. "The nuns will find out. They have a doctor examine you."

Katie caught her breath. "Betty wasn't examined."

"Are you sure?"

"She would've told me," Katie said. And in excruciating detail. Nothing entertained Betty more than shocking someone. *I think God is tricking you...*

"Have you both confessed? What if there's an accident, and Jack dies in the pit? He'll go straight to hell." Norah seized Katie's shoulders. "What if you're pregnant?"

Katie pulled away. "I started my period yesterday."

"Your luck won't hold forever. What about next month?"

"Trudy will send the money, and I'll be gone." Could Katie have sounded any less convincing? An angel dropping two hundred and fifty dollars on their doorstep seemed more plausible now than Katie leaving. Only when she lay in the abandoned oven, Jack's body covering hers, could she forget the slate dump looming outside. Mutti's bruised face, Pap's dark muttering, day after tedious day minding the Finch boys—everything fell away

171

like the ground beneath her feet when Jack carried her into the oven's soothing darkness.

The first time had been her gift to him. She hadn't intended to repeat it. Her longing for a second time had surprised her. She'd begged God for the strength to resist. After the third time, she'd hoped only that they wouldn't get caught.

Norah sat on the edge of the bed, arms and legs crossed. One foot impatiently beat the air. Katie sensed its urge to kick some sense into her. "You aren't going anywhere," Norah said. "Trudy can't possibly come up with so much money. Even if she does, how could you let Jack risk his soul for you, then walk out on him? That's as bad as fornication."

"You sound like the Mistress of Novices. Maybe you should enter, too."

"For goodness sake, Katie, just marry Jack and be done with it."

"It's not that simple!" Katie cried. Surely Norah wrestled with some version of this. Otherwise, she'd be Mrs. Visocky by now, having babies like her friend Helen, instead of working at Wright-Metzler's as Paul lingered hopefully in the background. Katie flung herself onto the bed. "I wish I was Deirdre, and Jack was Billy, and we could just run away."

Norah's head dropped onto the quilt beside hers. "Leave, then. Both of you."

Katie stared at the whitewashed ceiling, as empty as the lives lived out beneath it. "His parents won't leave Tina. He won't leave them. If I marry him, I have to stay, too."

Norah clasped Katie's hand. "It could be worse. He'll never hit you." Her grip tightened. "What do you think Pap will do if you get pregnant?" When Katie shuddered, Norah released her hand and sat up. "Then make sure it doesn't happen."

Katie regarded her know-it-all sister with skepticism. "How?"

"You eat seeds," Norah whispered, "after—each time."

Norah's earnest expression stopped Katie from laughing. "Who told you *that*?"

"I figured it out." Norah glanced at the closed door, then back at Katie. "Do you really believe Mutti lost all those babies by accident?"

172

***

"The Queen's mad as a hornet, so pretend you've been here all along," Betty warned, hurrying Katie down the steps to The Hall's basement.

Katie was reaching for the dressing room door when The Queen surprised them from behind. "Where's your costume, Kathleen? Your makeup?" She tapped her silver watch. "Stage etiquette requires a dress rehearsal to start on the dot, just like a real performance."

"I was—in the ladies' room. It's my time of month," Katie said.

The director frowned and lifted a peremptory finger. One's time of month was endured, that finger implied, not discussed. "Get her ready. Fast," The Queen told Betty. "The curtain rises in ten minutes." She stalked away, calling to Sobena to dim the house lights.

When the door closed behind them, Betty chirped, "I say we slip The Queen a nip of something before she strangles someone." She turned to the rack, where the saint's costume was crowded by faded, patched dresses. At the rack's far end hung Branka's, a striped hand-me-down from Tina. Betty slipped the white satin gown from its hanger and handed it to Katie. "We'll both get our heads cut off if you miss your entrance."

Katie stepped behind a four-paneled screen painted with peacocks and blossoming trees. Sobena claimed it had come from The Queen's own bedroom. In The Hall's gray basement, its ceiling crisscrossed with pipes, the screen looked more theatrical than the stage set.

A scarlet tunic soared over the screen, along with Betty's command: "Get a move on!"

The tunic was no sooner over Katie's head than Betty pulled her to the makeup table, littered with brushes, lipsticks, and powder puffs. She thrust a mirror into Katie's hand and stuffed her hair into a tight net, securing it with bobby pins, emphatically jabbed to induce a headache. Then Betty took up the round tin of thick beige cream that The Queen called, strangely enough, *pancake*. With brisk, capable fingers, Betty coated Katie's face.

The door swung open, admitting Sobena, a winged angel with a stage manager's clipboard. Frantic pink patches shone through the layers of snowy powder masking her cheeks. "The Queen says, five minutes or else!"

"Tell Joey Dvorsk to sneak a shot of whatever's in his flask into The Queen's tea. Her maid's in the kitchen, boiling water," Betty advised, calmly rouging Katie's cheeks. "Better yet, have Joey distract her maid—she's sweet on him, you know—while someone else spikes the pot. Trust me, in five minutes, The Queen will be purring like a kitten."

"I'd like a nip myself. She's run me ragged since I walked in the door," said Sobena.

Betty snickered. "I think, deep down, she'd love to play St. Barbara herself. Betcha anything she wanted to be an actress, but her snooty parents had a fit and married her off quick to King Frick's cousin." Betty waved a rouged hand at Sobena. "Hurry up! Find Joey!"

As a damp brush outlined Katie's upper eyelids, she marveled at Betty's smooth transition from convent to coal patch. In less than a month, the former postulant had brought herself up-to-date on a year's worth of quarrels and liaisons, leaked secrets and broken promises. It was news to Katie that Joey favored The Queen's maid, a sturdy Irish orphan trained by The Queen's mother and dispatched to Beetown. "I thought he had his eye on the motor boss' daughter," Katie ventured as Betty tilted her head back to do the lower lids.

"That's what Mrs. Dvorsk likes to think. Who'd want a maid for a daughter-in-law, instead of an upperhiller?" Betty powdered Katie's face and, stepping back, appraised the results. "Know what? I'm not half bad at this. Maybe I should go to Hollywood. I could make a big heap of money doing Jean Harlow's movie makeup."

"What about nursing?" Katie asked as Betty fitted the flowing wig onto her aching head.

"The doctor's paying me a little bit to help out in his office. It's all right unless someone's bleeding. Blood makes me vomit," Betty replied through clamped teeth and bobby pins. One by one, they left her mouth to gouge Katie's skull. "It's got to be tight," Betty said when Katie complained. "St. Barbara loses her head, not her hair."

Katie studied the garish face in the mirror. The girl beneath the pancake was no longer the Katie who nearly fainted with delight when the cast list was posted. Who calmly delivered the high school valedictory speech. Who sat for an hour in Fr. Kovacs' tiny parlor, patiently answering questions about her vocation. Without warning, Tina had vanished, taking that Katie with her.

Who, then, was this painted-up person left behind? This brazen stranger eager to shed her clothes in a coke oven? The pageant's audience surely would see through the pancake and satin. How could a girl of questionable virtue and dubious vocation convincingly play a saint?

The Queen had nothing but praise for the cast, lined up onstage for the concluding ritual known as *notes*. "The audience is in for a memorable experience tomorrow night," she gushed. Her smile, so uncommonly serene as to seem affectionate, moved from one player to the next. Joey and his pals could barely keep straight faces. Sobena nudged Katie and pointed to the wings. Betty stood just offstage, sipping from an imaginary teacup with a primly lifted pinky.

The Queen's dreamy gaze settled on Katie. "My dear, you have taken a character from ancient history, a woman about whom we know very little, and brought her unforgettably to life. I believe you are the most splendid St. Barbara ever to grace this stage."

Katie felt Sobena stiffen as The Queen's compliments continued. Last year's saint, understandably, felt slighted. Not mentioned, let alone commended, was Sobena's last-minute willingness to take on the angel's role, in addition to the thankless job of stage manager. "She's tipsy," Katie whispered to Sobena. "She'll read me the riot act tomorrow when she checks your notes and sees how many times I needed prompting."

Sobena didn't reply.

It took Katie the better part of an hour to change and scrub the grease from her face. The other girls departed quickly, performing only a cursory wipe with a passed-around rag. Wearing make up was such a novelty that they relished a leisurely walk home, pursing unnaturally rosy lips, batting eyelashes darkened with a stick that resembled a sliver of coal.

The doorknob rattled, and a muffled male voice called Katie's name. Toweling her face, she opened the door. She expected to see Joey, gloating over his prank. Instead, she found Jack, who offered her a pink rose and quick kiss. "I sneaked in and watched from the balcony. The Queen's right. You're the best St. Barbara ever."

Katie thanked him for the flower, its delicately scented petals just beginning to open. "You watched the whole show? I thought you didn't want to spoil the surprise."

Jack's expression changed. For the first time, he wore a seasoned miner's face—stoic, vigilant, suspicious—uncannily similar to Pap's. "I can't come tomorrow. You said dress rehearsal's just like the real thing." His finger traced the line of Katie's jaw. "This was even better. You did it just for me."

She gripped his hand. "Why can't you come? Did someone get sick?"

"Nothing like that." He glanced down the corridor at Betty, rounding the corner with Sobena's wings, and backed away. "I'll see you at the fireworks tomorrow night."

"He left in a hurry," Betty observed, carrying the wings into the dressing room. She hung them on a rack separate from the other costumes. "When are you leaving for the convent?"

Katie draped the stained towel over the back of a chair. "I don't know."

Betty assessed the makeup table, drifted with ivory face powder. "No point in redding up. I'll just have to do it all over again tomorrow." Leaning over a mirror, she lightly applied pink lipstick and quick dabs of rouge. Fluffed out her bob with swift strokes of a brush. As she left, she called over her shoulder, "The trunk's all packed. Just say the word, and it's yours."

Katie pictured Betty darting around The Hall, then slowing to a hip-swaying stroll when she saw Jack. *Wait up!* she'd call. Politely, he'd oblige. As they walked down the alley, she'd stumble in a rut. Clasp the hand he offered a moment longer than needed to regain her balance. *Katie's taking my old trunk to the convent,* Betty would say. *She's leaving any day now.*

Like a movie, the scene gave way to side-by-side images. Katie, modest in postulant black, danced with a mop; Betty, radiant in bridal white, danced with Jack.

Everyone caught the sharp edge of The Queen's tongue the following evening. "Ten prompts!" she fumed, pacing beside the makeup table as Betty—gleefully, it seemed to Katie—impaled her scalp with bobby pins. "You knew those lines like the back of your hand, then—" she snapped pink-lacquered fingers—"gone!"

The dressing room, which had rustled and hummed with costume adjustments and nervous conversation, went silent. The Queen's puzzled blue eyes moved from one wary face to the next. It wasn't until her gaze fell on Branka, inexpertly applying lipstick, that a door to her memory seemed to open. A flush rose into her powdered cheeks. She'd certainly been told. *A girl died in an accident on the slate dump. Another one injured, but not mortally.* Had she wondered, even for an instant, what had prompted girls to climb the dump in the first place? Katie imagined her instructing the maid to send flowers, making a note to recast the angel and pilgrim, then putting on a sunhat and going outside to play croquet.

Branka continued sloppily coloring her mouth. Sobena squatted beside her. Drawing back the spotless bell of her sleeve, Sobena held out her hand to receive the lipstick. "Open your mouth, just a little," Sobena instructed Branka after Betty had wiped away the red smears.

Sobena's voice cracked the shell of tension enclosing the room. The girls resumed dressing and making up their faces, their voices lowered to a murmur. When The Queen urged them to hurry, nobody so much as glanced in her direction.

From the first rehearsal, The Queen had warned players never to *search the house.* What she meant was *don't peek at the seats to find your mother and all your cousins.* Katie had never disobeyed this rule until that night. The execution scene began, and she moved downstage center, hands clasped over her heart, to deliver her final speech. She'd been directed to lower her eyes, demure and virginal, as she forgave Dioscorus—Joey, pacing upstage with his gilded wooden sword—and offered her soul to God. Instead, she gazed out at the rapt faces, some openly weeping. She spoke her lines without hesitation as she searched the audience, row by row, for Jack.

At the very back, Norah stood with Mutti, her bruised face swathed in a shawl. Not surprisingly, Pap wasn't with them. Katie supposed he'd sit with a teammate, but couldn't locate him. Her eyes roamed the balcony as she intoned her own benediction. Surely Pap would come, if only for the right to brag about fathering the finest Barbara ever and dispel, once and for all, the shameful shadow that runaway Deirdre had cast. As for Jack, how could he say that he loved her, then stay away? If not for sickness in his family, then what?

A chill coursed through her. *You're not a virgin anymore.* Norah hadn't repeated the tired adage—*why buy a cow if you can get free milk?*—but with all her talk of risked souls and fornication, it must have crossed her mind. The last time Katie and Jack had gone to the coke yard, he continued to talk about marriage. If he'd suddenly wearied of her, why had he sneaked into dress rehearsal and brought her a rose? Surely Betty hadn't turned his head already, not with Katie still here, eager to enter the oven and open her body to him.

The stage lights shone like a thousand suns. Though drenched in sweat, Katie shivered as she knelt at Joey's feet. Sobena waited in the wings, holding the large, white-gowned rag doll that served as Barbara's headless body. She'd carry it toward the painted mountain backdrop as an electric flash of lightning felled Joey. A tear rolled down Katie's cheek and dropped onto the scuffed stage floor. Like St. Barbara, Tina had been buried in a mountain. Her role and Katie's had tragically become one, but only Tina, who'd died a virgin, deserved to be called a saint.

Chapter 24: Clare

July 1, 1933
Feast of the Most Precious Blood of Our Lord Jesus Christ

Every young woman in The Hall reminded Clare of Deirdre. She forced her eyes away from the ones with babies, only to have them stray back. When Katie wasn't onstage, her gaze wandered the dim aisles. She craved just a glimpse of Molly's bonnet brim peeking over Deirdre's lacy collar. She was so distracted that she didn't see the curtain fall. Norah had to pull her to the exit as the audience cheered and applauded.

"Katie was wonderful," Norah said as soon as they were outside. "Deirdre couldn't've done it nearly as well."

"Deirdre made the right choice." Clare drew the shawl from her sweating head and pretended not to notice as Norah assessed the swelling above her left eye.

"Tell me again about Deirdre's dress," begged Norah.

Clare described the stylish skirt and layered lace collar. She saw the costume as clearly as if Deirdre stood in front of her. Even when she'd picked herself off the floor after Fin's punishment, she had seen her lost daughter through a dark mist of blood.

Norah sighed with envy. "If only I'd been at home."

She surprised Clare by turning into the alley. "Aren't you going to the ball field for the fireworks?" Clare asked.

"Everyone's still at The Hall, waiting on the players to change." Norah's hand strayed to the band of her pale straw hat to stroke the tiny fan of gray-blue feathers. The hat had arrived damaged at Wright-Metzler's and sold as-is for a quarter. Every evening for a week, Norah had hunched over the torn straw, smoothing and stitching. Masha had sold her navy ribbon to cover the repairs, and she'd gathered the feathers while picking berries. It was the one new thing she owned, and she wore it with palpable pride. Tonight, however, her forehead wrinkled beneath its brim. "What if Trudy sends the money and Katie changes her mind?"

Clare felt as if she stood in the middle of a bridge that she'd convinced herself was still too distant to be crossed. She gripped Norah's arm. "Has Katie said something to you?"

Norah's fingers released those reassuring feathers. She nibbled her bottom lip. Clare knew she was arguing with herself. How much to tell? What to hold back?

She'd always been the quiet one, looking long and hard with deep-pond eyes, listening while her sisters chattered. She saw and heard more than she ever let on, storing every gesture and half-finished sentence in her memory's spacious, ordered cupboard. While her tireless hands worked switchboard wires or curtain stretchers, her mind retreated to that cupboard like an inventor to his laboratory—studying with a fresh eye, alert for meanings previously unseen. It frightened Clare to imagine the discoveries she'd made and hidden there, patiently waiting for the perfect moment to expose them.

She drew Clare closer and whispered, "Jack went with Pap to a secret union meeting tonight. A local meeting to follow up last Sunday's big rally in Uniontown."

Fear rose in Clare's throat. Who had told her this? "That's impossible. Deputies are everywhere. Organizers could never get the word out, much less find a place to meet."

"A farmer near Ralph let them use his field. Deputies are watching the streetcars and main roads. The men are taking back roads and following train tracks." Norah's mouth snapped shut. The less Clare knew, the less she might let slip and be punished for.

"Are you sure Jack went, too?"

Norah regarded Clare with loving exasperation. "Jack was waiting in the alley while we ate supper. Didn't you see him? He stayed behind the outhouse till Pap opened the gate. Then they went off together, but not to the pageant." Quickening her pace, she added, "At Helen's shower, Mrs. Zekula said Katie's applying for a scholarship to the teachers college. She could use Trudy's money for board."

Liebe Trudy, vielen Dank, aber Katie hat sich anders besinnen...

At that very moment, Trudy and other Deutschtown women were busily baking for tomorrow's benefit at St. Marienkirche's Lyceum.

Dear Trudy, Many thanks, but Katie changed her mind...

They didn't notice Paul Visocky until he walked beside them. "I saw you leave early and thought maybe you got sick or something." He looked quickly at Clare, then at the ground, clearly unnerved by her bruises.

"Nobody's sick," said Norah, patently brusque.

It was all Clare could do not to shake the girl. Why on earth had she made sheep's eyes at Paul all through high school, only to turn chilly the minute they'd received their diplomas? From the dogged way he courted her, it was clear that he didn't understand either. Unless Norah changed her tune, and quickly, he'd likely take up with another girl, eager for a husband and babies. Who wouldn't jump at the chance to marry such an industrious young man? Paul had never met a broken motor he couldn't fix. Good times or bad, he'd never lack for work.

Clare invited him in for a cup of tea, then hurried ahead, hoping Norah would treat him with more than cool courtesy. Clare was foraging in the pantry for raspberry preserves, Paul's favorite, when the screen door banged. "Set out the cups, Norah," she called.

It was Katie, however, who flung herself into the pantry. Tear-streaked makeup stained her cheeks. "Jack didn't come. His whole family was there, even *Baka*. I thought he cared for me, but I was wrong." She covered her face with her hands and, sobbing, fell against Clare.

"*Käthi, Liebchen, sachte, sachte.*" Darling, there, there. Clare pried Katie's face from her shoulder. "Of course Jack loves you. He wouldn't've missed it without a good reason."

Black puddles surrounded Katie's red-rimmed eyes. She looked chillingly similar to the hysterical girl carried home from the slate dump. Drawing a shaky breath, she added, "Pap didn't come either."

Clare argued with herself—what to tell, what to hold back—then cupped Katie's slick cheeks. "Jack and Pap went to a secret union meeting. You can't let on that you know."

Horror claimed Katie's face. "They'll get arrested. We'll get thrown out of our—"

"Your pap knows how to get past the deputies." Lord knows, he'd successfully dodged them for years.

"Jack said he'd meet me at the fireworks." Katie's tone risked a faint ring of hope.

Clare's mind soared like a buzzard above the wooded, hilly landscape between Ralph and The Hive. If the men avoided the roads, it was a hard two-mile walk. Without incident and with luck, they were probably heading back. "Jack will be there. Your pap will keep him safe."

Katie frowned. "Jack's never said a word about the union. He always wears his Brotherhood pin."

The door banged again. Clare called to Norah to check the kettle, recalling those seemingly uneventful evenings. The girls washing dishes. Fin and Jack on the porch steps. Fin talking. Jack listening.

Fresh tears welled in Katie's eyes. "Will they leave the Brotherhood? And lose their jobs?"

"Of course not. Pap won't risk another eviction."

Katie's greasepaint-smeared face remained unconvinced. "They don't care about that Brotherhood committee they voted on, do they?"

Norah poked her head inside the pantry. "Tea's ready." She took in Katie's expression and added quietly, "Paul's pap went, too. And Mr. Lubicic. A lot more than I thought."

"But the Hall was packed," Clare said. Then again, aside from Katie, to whom had she paid attention? Not miners, but mothers with infants' heads lolling on their shoulders. The only man she recalled seeing was Kamila's husband Anton, and only because he'd sat next to his oldest daughter, cradling her six-month-old.

Norah rolled her eyes. "Sure, The Hall was packed—with cousins and grandmas from all over the county. The deputies were too busy checking the ones coming in to see who was sneaking out. Trust me, the men will be back for the fireworks. And they'll make sure the bosses see every last one of them, so nobody gets suspicious." She took the jar from Clare's hand. "No raspberry?" When Clare shook her head, she was out the door, informing long-suffering Paul, "Too bad. It's blackberry or nothing."

Clare stood with Katie near third base, pretending to admire the red whirligigs sparkling in the sky. Fin materialized out of the darkness to stand next to her. "Everyone's saying how grand she was." He nodded at Katie, who clasped Jack's hand, then disappeared into the crowd.

Some contrary part of Clare wanted to know more than Norah. "Katie missed a line in the first scene. Couldn't you tell?"

He shook his head. "'Twas nothing. She covered herself well. Nobody noticed."

A shower of silver stars painted his upturned face with light. If he suspected that Clare was testing him, he gave no sign. The false stars' light faded too quickly for her to check his pants and boots for thistle heads and caked mud, evidence of a backwoods trek.

She tried again. "Katie said Jack didn't come. She was terribly disappointed."

Fin's only response was applause for a pair of golden starbursts high above middle field.

She breathed deeply. "She didn't see you either."

Fin observed the red and blue Roman candles, then gave her a sideways glance. "I was up in the balcony with Dal Visocky. His Sobena did well as the angel."

Didn't he trust her? Or was she too inconsequential to merit an explanation?

Fin lifted a hand and exchanged nods with Big Bill, standing with Maeve and Emma not far away. Another brilliant explosion ignited the sky. The Brotherhood pin, with its clasped hands and enameled shield, gleamed on Fin's breast pocket.

How much longer would he be willing to wear that tiny tin mask?

Chapter 25: Katie

"It's not important," whispered Jack.

His mouth stopped Katie's before she could ask again. His fingers, practiced now, slipped beneath her blouse. Her brassiere straps slid from shoulders that he lifted with ease from the quilt. The cloth grazed her skin as lightly as his lips, tracing the curve of her chin. When they moved to her breast, she forgot the question he'd evaded as they'd crossed the coke yard. She forgot Norah's warning about being careful. Instead, she heard Betty. *God's tricking you...* Indeed, He'd tried, but Jack had intervened, saving Katie from Betty's mistake.

Christ's intended bride wouldn't unbuckle Jack's belt and slide eager hands beneath his opened pants to hasten their shedding. She wouldn't shiver with delight each time Jack's hands undid her buttons. Christ's bride would come here only to seek the miracle of an angel in the shadows, to hear a holy voice summoning her.

"Love, my love," Jack whispered, his skin warming hers. "*Ljubavi moja.*"

She needed no further summons. She sensed the presence of the unseen angel that was Tina, who did not judge them, but simply loved them as much as they loved each other. Tina kept watch, her wings spread across the oven's entrance, securing them inside.

Jack's hands trembled with urgency, even as they attempted to delay the miracle. A ragged nail scratched the inside of Katie's thigh. She winced and felt his caught breath between her lips. "Does it hurt?" he'd whispered the first time, and she'd assured him, no, because that pain had been so forgettable, compared to the wonder of the rest. Her hands assured him now, urging his hips, his hard-muscled back. He cried out as the miracle rose through her body, a cradle for his, rocking until both were breathless.

"Marry me," he said when he could speak again. "Please. Say, *I'll marry you, Jack.*"

She said it. Said or unsaid, it made no difference. The first miracle had married them.

His smile imprinted her mouth. "I hope we have a child," he whispered. He rolled onto his back, taking her with him. "*Kći*. A daughter, who looks just like you."

Kći. At the sound of that word, she forgot where she was. A daughter. She heard Mutti, tenderly describing Deirdre's Molly until Norah interrupted. *What do you think Pap will do if you get pregnant?* Jack moaned with pleasure beneath Katie, but, for the first time, the miracle dissolved within her like a bud withered by unexpected frost.

In less than a year, she, too, could be tending an infant—but not like Deirdre. Deirdre's wedding, which Trudy's letter had described as *lavish* and *elegant*, had been a fitting preamble to a comfortable future. In stark contrast, Katie would marry in St. Barbara's amid homegrown flowers and shabbily dressed guests. Though Pap would grumble about the hunkie custom, Jack's friends would build an arch over the Sweeneys' front gate, entwined with crepe paper by Branka, Norah, and Jack's girl cousins. Jack's mother would suspend two dolls, a girl and a boy, from the arch. When they returned from church, Jack would cut them down, giving Katie the girl and keeping the boy, ensuring they'd have at least a daughter and a son. *I kći i sin.* There'd be a gypsy band, a roasted pig, and a tub full of shattered dishes, each broken to buy a dance with Katie. And when the music ended, she'd face a future shadowed by secret meetings, the slate dump, and the memory of Tina.

Jack's contented heart pulsed against Katie's cheek. "You're cold," he said, drawing the quilt over them. When she continued to shiver, he rose from the quilt and collected her clothes, draping her with his shirt as she struggled with her underpants' snarled drawstring. Gently, he moved her trembling fingers and loosened the knot. In the darkness, his sure hands clothed her, then himself. He'd speak to Pap tomorrow, he said, then his parents, then the priest.

He was placing the rolled-up quilt by the oven's back wall when she remembered the question he'd left unanswered. "Where did you go last night?" When he didn't reply, she

185

clasped his arm. "If we're going to marry, we shouldn't keep secrets from each other."

Still silent, he led her outside, where the cool night air held the faint scent of smoke. She stifled a cry when she glimpsed the hill behind the ball field. A large cross burned on each side of the flagpole. The white-hoods' robes glowed like Sobena's pageant-costume wings. Horses stood in a bulky huddle, their flanks streaked with flickering light. The hooded men marched around the crosses, singing to the accompaniment of a throbbing drum.

Onward Christian soldiers, marching as to war, with the cross of Jesus going on before.

Katie shrank against Jack. "They know about your secret meeting."

Jack's body stiffened. "If you know, too, then it's no secret, is it?"

She'd just held him, kissed him, indeed, married him in every way that mattered. Now, watching in horror as the Klansmen fell into formation, she wondered who he was becoming. He walked away quickly without glancing back to see if she followed.

Christ, the royal master, leads against the foe, forward into battle, see his banners go.

She ran, stumbling over rubble, until she seized his arm. "They'll see us. Let's go back to the oven until they're gone."

He kept walking. "*Kukavice!* Let them see me! Only cowards wear hoods."

You're marrying a coward, she nearly told him, but knew he wouldn't hear.

"*Ja ne skrivam svoje lice iza maske!*" he shouted

I don't hide my face behind a mask. She understood just enough Croatian to know that he wanted to do something dangerous. Something Pap might do, like drinking himself onto the store's roof to sing out his rage against King Frick's hump. Jack, as far as she knew, did not touch whiskey. Then again, how much did she know anymore, aside from his love?

Hell's foundations quiver at the shout of praise...

186

She fixed her eyes on the rough ground, yet the crosses still burned before them. Would the torch-bearers' wives be waiting when they returned home, proudly taking the hoods and robes to wash and press? Or were the hoods and robes stored in a secret place, laundered by someone paid to keep silent? Did the wives simply nod, as Mutti did, when their men said they were going out? Did they lie awake, night after night, fearful and alone?

Would Katie do likewise, once she became Mrs. Jack Kukoc?

Brothers, lift your voices, loud your anthems raise...

When Katie turned to scan the hillside, a broken brick tripped her up. Her head struck something hard and sharp as she hit the ground.

Jack dropped to his knees beside her, his face stricken. "Jesus, you're bleeding." He stripped off his shirt and pressed it against her hair. "I've got to get you home."

She managed to sit up even as glowing crosses whirled dizzily around her. "Jack, listen to me. You've got to hide. They found out who went to that meeting. Any minute now, they'll ride down the hill, and you can't be at home when they get there."

Bleeding, she'd succeeded in capturing his attention. They ran toward the ovens, pursued by strains of the relentless hymn.

At dawn, Katie entered the kitchen. Mutti caught her up in a long, tight hug as Norah paced and scolded. "We've been up all night, worried sick. Why didn't you come home?"

"The gate's knocked down." Katie struggled to see Mutti's face. "Where's Pap?"

"*Los,*" Mutti murmured, stroking Katie's shoulder, her cheek, her hair.

"Gone where?" Katie asked, pulling away. "Did the white-hoods get him?"

"*Mein Gott, was ist mit dir passiert?*" Mutti cried, discovering the tender knot of bloodied hair. My God, what happened to you?

187

Norah pushed between them and peered at Katie's wound. "It's not deep, but it needs cleaning." She took the kettle to the sink and began pumping.

"What happened to Pap?" Katie cried as Mutti pressed her gently into a chair.

Norah slammed the kettle onto the stove as if attempting to smash a bug. "Two horsemen broke through the gate. They trampled the garden and rode right up to the porch. I told them Pap was gone, nobody knew where, and they should just leave us alone."

Katie's scalp throbbed beneath Mutti's thorough inspection. "You *talked* to them?"

"If I hadn't, they'd've come inside and ruined more than the garden." Advising Mutti to wash her hands, Norah headed for the pantry. Over her shoulder, she asked severely, "Where *were* you all night?"

As Mutti worked the pump, it occurred to Katie that she could deliver the explanation of her choice as convincingly as St. Barbara's death scene. *We were walking by the tracks when we saw the crosses. Jack hid in the woods. I ran to the coke yard and hid in an oven.* But when Norah emerged from the pantry with the iodine bottle, her narrowed, know-it-all eyes surely read every line of the script writing itself in Katie's mind.

"We were walking by the coke yard when they lit the crosses. We hid in an oven so they wouldn't see us. I tripped and fell." Katie touched her head, grateful for the bloody evidence. "Jack wanted to bring me home, but it was too dangerous."

"You spent the whole night in a coke oven," said Norah.

Mutti turned away from the sink. "*Mit* Jack."

Katie looked from one weary face to the other, then nodded. She was no longer onstage, pretending to be someone she was not. The ones pretending, Jack had explained, were the men who'd sneaked off to Saturday night's meeting. They'd joined a Brotherhood they had no respect for. They'd elected employee committee representatives they called *Dan Phelan's pit spies* when no boss or deputy was within earshot. What Jack didn't say was how long they were willing to keep pretending.

188

"The Company's police superintendent in Scottdale somehow finds out where the union meetings are. He has deputies dress up like miners and mix with the men. The deputies make lists of who they see," said Norah. She lifted the steaming kettle from the stove. Her tone was matter-of-fact, as if describing how to brew tea. "That's how the Klan knows whose gardens to ruin. They support the Brotherhood one hundred percent."

Mutti's mouth opened, then immediately closed. Katie suspected that she didn't want to know how Norah had come by her information.

As if reading their minds, Norah added, "A window in the machine shop was open. Paul overheard Mr. Phelan talking to the deputy." She flapped a hand at Mutti. "I'll take care of Katie. Go upstairs and lie down."

Mutti kissed Katie's cheek and left the kitchen. Norah waited until footsteps sounded overhead, then filled a cup with water. Setting the cup on the table, along with a saucer and spoon, she drew a creased envelope from her pocket. She unfolded it and poured tiny, shriveled kernels onto the saucer. "Crush them into powder," she said, handing Katie the spoon. "Then pour the powder into the water and drink every last drop. You should take them right after, but, obviously, you didn't have them in the oven."

We really were hiding, Katie could insist, but what was the point? "Do you take them?" she asked, even though she knew the answer. When Norah snorted, she persisted, "Aren't they a sin, too? Like—"she hated how Norah described her time with Jack—"fornication?"

To her surprise, Norah let out a sigh. The self-righteous gleam in her eyes vanished, and pinched-at-the-corners confusion took its place. "I guess they are a sin. I should've gotten rid of them after Deirdre left. She was always so reckless, I thought she'd need them sooner or later." Norah's shoulders sank. "Then a girl at work started crying one day. She was scared of what *her* pap would do if— Well, I felt sorry for her, that's all." Another sigh. "It just seems—I don't know—unfair somehow. That it's the girl who always has to be scared. That

Mutti—oh, give it here." Norah pulled the spoon from Katie's hand and ground it hard against the saucer. "You want a nice, fine powder, so it's easy to drink."

That Norah would keep such a secret, and a sinful one, to boot, left Katie speechless. Maybe her sister wasn't as prudish as she let on. Maybe she *had* let Paul kiss her. Gathering herself, Katie finally said, as if it made up for anything, "We're getting married."

Norah didn't even look up. "Well, of course. You stayed out all night together." The spoon stopped. "Do you want to have a baby right away?"

"No!" Katie snatched the spoon. When Norah approved the powder's consistency, Katie added it to the cup and drank. Finished, she asked, "Where do you think Pap went?"

The question was barely out of her mouth when footsteps pounded the back steps. A sobbing Negro woman threw herself against the screen. "They be taking my boy in the night and hanging him from a tree!" cried the woman, tearing her hair. "They be whipping his pa, making him watch. Now he be bleeding himself half-dead."

Norah eased the door open, and the woman collapsed at her feet. Before Katie could move, Mutti ran downstairs and into the kitchen. "Essie," she said, kneeling to take the woman in her arms, stroking her torn hair as tenderly as she'd stroked Katie's.

Josiah, Essie's husband, died two days after her son Willie's lynching. Three other Negro miners also had been hanged. Mutti went door to door, asking for donations to pay for two coffins and train fare for Essie, her three daughters, and Willie's widow to return to Alabama. They collected nearly fifteen dollars, which Mutti took just after sunset to Niggertown.

Each afternoon, returning from The Queen's house in Beetown, Katie passed women whispering over back fences. *Vaš muž? Vostro marito? Ón férjemet?* Your husband? Is he back? Some stopped Katie and, after looking up and down the alley, asked about Pap.

"Still gone," she said, after looking, too.

By Friday, Pap was the only man in The Hive who'd not yet come home. Katie crossed the railroad tracks, fingering the bills in her pocket, her final payment from The Queen. Tomorrow, she and the boys would leave to spend the rest of the summer at her parents' seaside home. Though glad to be freed from policing the boys' daily battles, Katie regretted that those two pocketed dollars would be her last wages. She took a detour from her usual route to pass the ball field. If Pap were to return, he might well seek out his teammates before heading home.

In Pap's absence, Jerry Visocky, Paul's brother, was covering first base. He leaped for, but missed the pitcher's high, hard throw. The ball bounced into the weeds.

"Sorry, fellas, I'll get the next one," called Jerry. Red-faced, he ran to retrieve the ball. When he noticed Katie, he waved his glove. Mr. Donovan stood and lifted his catcher's mask. Like every other boss, he was ready to pounce on any careless comment about Steamshovel's whereabouts. Mr. Tonelli had spread the word that Pap was ailing from a harsh bout of miner's asthma, but the bosses were growing suspicious.

"Pap had another bad night. He might not make it tomorrow," Katie shouted. As she'd hoped, Mr. Donovan lowered his mask and yelled at Jerry to stop yapping and play ball.

Later, as Katie set the table for supper, Pap walked through the kitchen door. Dirt caked his clothes and lined the creases of his hands and face. "They were needing help in Niggertown, digging all those graves," he said, his only explanation.

Mutti's face couldn't seem to decide whether to weep or smile. At last, she said, "You did a good deed, helping out there."

Without washing his hands, Pap sat in his chair. Crumbs of dirt fell from his pants onto the floor. Norah clapped a hand over her mouth as she entered the kitchen. Lifting the pot of beans from the stove, Mutti gave her head the tiniest of shakes. When Pap bent over his bowl, a leafy twig dropped from his hair onto the table. Mutti picked it up, tucked it into her apron pocket, and said nothing. For the first time ever, Pap did not pause to cross himself and recite, *Bless us, O Lord, and these, Thy gifts...* He simply took up his spoon and ate.

Norah waited until he'd finished a second helping before reporting, "The white-hoods broke the gate, but Paul fixed it."

Pap wiped his bowl with a crust of bread. "Paul's a good lad. If he asks, you should marry him."

"He hasn't asked," Norah said crisply, rising to clear the table. She nudged Katie on her way to the sink. "Tell him."

When Pap shifted his gaze, Katie noticed that even his eyebrows were clotted with dirt. She'd lived her whole life surrounded by filthy men, but this dirt was different than bug dust. Pap wore this dirt with the same raw defiance that the Klansmen wore their hoods. The muddy footprints he'd left on the floor silently proclaimed, *there's no turning back.* What covered Pap wasn't just soil, but intention.

His earthen brows lowered. "What is it I need telling?"

"Jack will be coming to talk to you. Tonight, maybe," Katie said. "About us."

"Jack's a fine lad, too. The other lads respect him. He understands what's worth a fight," Pap declared, pushing back his chair.

Mutti closed her eyes. Under the table, Katie clasped her hand. *Kukavice.* Cowards. Jack had said it with such scorn. Like Pap, he didn't understand what was required of women. Told to keep quiet and out of the way, they both dreaded and longed to hear their angry men's latest plan.

Norah returned to the table for more dishes. "I'll heat your bath water, Pap. You don't want to scare Jack off, looking like Tarzan the Ape Man, fresh from the jungle."

"Trust me, lass, 'twill take more than a wee bit of dirt to scare Jack." Pap opened the door and stepped onto the porch. Halfway to the outhouse, he didn't hear the bowl slip from Katie's hands, nor see the white shards scatter, impaling the mud.

Jack arrived in time to help Katie drag the washtub outside. Pap stood in the doorway, so Jack didn't kiss her, though she knew he wanted to. He touched her hand and followed Pap into the living room, a dim space with an old couch and armchair that Pap sat in when he listened to Pittsburgh Pirates baseball games and Fr. Coughlin's *Catholic Hour* on the old, static-racked radio. The room had seen three wakes, but never heard a word about marriage.

Katie took care watering the tomato plants, each gleaned from a different missus' garden two days after the crosses had burned. Paul appeared at the gate and swung it appraisingly before crossing the yard. "Looks like it's holding up all right."

"Thanks for fixing it," Katie said. Though the alley appeared vacant, she recalled Mr. Donovan's attention at the ball field and raised her voice. "Pap's feeling better now. I think he'll make it to the ball game tomorrow after all."

Paul grinned. "Jerry will sleep better, knowing that." His grin widened when Norah came outside, adjusting her hat. "We're going to Uniontown to see *College Humor*. George Burns and Gracie Allen are in it. Want to join us? I hear it's really funny."

Norah steered Paul toward the gate. "She can't. Jack's inside. He and Pap have things to talk about."

Paul glanced at the alley before asking, "About the union?"

"*Shhh!* Of course not," said Norah. "About him and Katie."

Paul opened the gate for Norah, then turned to wave at Katie. His gaze lingered for a moment on the porch. No doubt, he imagined himself climbing those steps and following Pap into the living room, hoping Norah would eventually give him the encouragement to do so.

Katie finished watering and sat on the steps to wait. It wouldn't be right to hover in the kitchen, brazenly eavesdropping on Pap's conversation with his future son-in-law. The crickets began to sing, just as they did each evening in the coke yard. Warmth rose into Katie's cheeks. How wonderful it would be to love Jack in their own bed, without worrying that a patrolling deputy would find them and cause a scandal. It seemed as if the girl who'd helped Betty carry the trunk across that same yard had been Katie's much younger sister. That naïve girl had believed in fairy tales: a small fortune would come in the mail, evil was speedily vanquished, and everyone lived happily ever after.

She started when Mutti sat beside her. "*Du willst ihn?*" Mutti asked, drawing Katie's head onto her shoulder. He's what you want? When Katie nodded, Mutti pressed against her, filling her ear with an urgent whisper. "*Sobald das Hochzeitfest fertig ist, gehen sie fort. So schnell wie möglich, fahren sie nach Pittsburgh oder Akron.*" Breathing deeply, Mutti glanced back at the house, then continued, "Go, before the trouble starts."

Katie stared at the nervous woman who'd issued absurd instructions. Leave right after the wedding? Go to Pittsburgh or Akron as quickly as possible? "What trouble?" Katie asked.

Mutti shook her head. She glanced back again, squeezing Katie's hand with contagious alarm. "Now, Jack will do anything for you. Now, he'll listen to you."

Katie's pulse quickened. "What about later?"

"I don't know," Mutti whispered. She got to her feet as Jack and Pap entered the kitchen.

Pap shook Jack's hand and opened the door. "Clare, this lad is wanting to join our family. What do you think about that?"

"I think it's wonderful," Mutti said. She smiled at Katie, but only with her mouth. *Tell him*, her eyes urged. She crossed the porch and kissed Jack's cheek.

"I tried to talk him into joining me for a drop to toast his future happiness. But no, he'd rather be out strolling with our Katie," Pap said. He clapped Jack's shoulder. "See you tomorrow at the ball game, then."

"Thank you, Mr. Sweeney," Jack said. "I'll be good to her, I promise."

"Mister, me arse. I'm Fin to you now, lad. Save *mister* for those bastards up the hill."

"Such talk, Fin, and in front of your daughter, to boot." Mutti opened the door and motioned Pap inside. Her eyes sought Katie's. *Jetzt.* Now.

Jack clasped Katie's hand, and they ran across the yard and into the alley. Behind the outhouse, she gave him the kiss he'd wanted. "*Ljubavi moja,*" he whispered. "My sweet love. I've never been as happy as I am right now."

Now. She took a deep breath. "Will you do something for me?"

"Anything, Katie." He kissed her. "Anything in the world." Laughing, he kissed her again.

"After the wedding, I want to leave. Go to Pittsburgh, Akron, wherever you want."

She might have been a burning cross, he released her that quickly. "Leave here? Why?"

"At least, think about it. My sister lives in Pittsburgh. We could—"

"Your sister ran off with a goddamn pussyfoot." Jack reached for her again, stroking her face with repentant fingers. "I'm sorry, Katie, I shouldn't've said that. Let's just be happy now, all right? Let's be happy together right here."

She pressed a hand against his mouth. "Listen to me. There's going to be more trouble."

He pulled away. "There needs to be a lot of trouble, and after it's over, everything will be better, I promise." He kissed her again. "Jesus, Katie, you're shaking like a leaf."

She turned his face toward the slate dump. A column of hooded torch-bearers filed slowly up The Dirty Hill.

Chapter 26: Clare

July 14, 1933
Feast of St. Bonaventure, Bishop, Confessor, Doctor

Clare's hands trembled as she took the envelope from Masha. Concetta leaned over the fence. Clare drew out a cashier's check from Workingmen's Savings Bank & Trust Company, 800 Ohio East, Pittsburgh, for $168.50. Trudy had included a note.

Liebe Clara,

The benefit for Katie was a great success. Surely the convent will accept her with this dowry, given her circumstances and those of our nation. Fr. Daller and our parishioners send their best wishes and hope Katie might visit St. Marienkirche someday...

I had the pleasure of seeing Deirdre and darling Molly last weekend. Both are well and happy. Mrs. McKenna, who joined us for a light lunch, dotes on the baby. She told me that, after raising three sons, she's delighted to finally have some female companionship...

Clare didn't realize she was weeping until Masha offered her a tattered hankie.

Concetta touched the stationery. "Sad news?"

Clare showed Concetta the check, but her frown indicated that she saw only a piece of fancy paper. Clare pointed to the figure. "If I take this to a bank in Uniontown, they'll give me that many dollars."

Concetta clapped her hands. "*Tanta generosità!* Who is sending?"

Clare put the check back into the envelope and stowed it in her pocket. "I'll write to Trudy and send it back."

Concetta was aghast. "All? Not to be keeping Katie something for *il matrimonio?*"

"Don't tell Katie," Clare implored Masha and Concetta. "It will just confuse things."

Masha headed for the alley. "Is your cousin coming to the wedding?" she called over her shoulder.

196

How had Clare overlooked this? Of course, Trudy had to be invited. Invited, and apologized to profusely. However, considering the effort she and her church had expended to help Katie become Christ's bride, Clare doubted that she'd come. Or that she'd ever write to Clare again. Trudy, lost—and with her, Deirdre and Molly.

If Clare closed her eyes and concentrated, she could still retrieve images of Deirdre in the lavender dress and Molly's sleepy face on the lacy collar. But after just three weeks, those images had begun to lose their focus. Deirdre's features were still distinct, but Molly's had turned fuzzy. She might have been any drowsy baby.

Concetta touched her hand. "Will not go away, these dollars, this bank?"

A valid question. The Beetown bank had been closed for nearly a year. "No, the dollars won't go away. I think times are better in Pittsburgh."

Concetta nodded. "Every night the fire-crosses, here is better only than *prigione e inferno*."

She'd said it so often that Clare no longer needed a translation. Prison and hell.

Kamila appeared, whacking the gate with a broomstick to remind Clare that she'd promised to pick coal. Clare explained her new dilemma as they walked to the slate dump. Kamila simply rolled her eyes. "So Katie changed her mind—*pffft*! Girls do that all the time. Let me tell you, better now than after she entered. Betty could've saved us a lot of trouble *and* money if she'd thought things through."

Kamila's pace slowed as they crossed the tracks. Slower still as they approached the dump. When they reached the base of the first hill, she stopped and tipped her head back, squinting at the sooty heaps. A deep breath lifted, then lowered her broad bosom. Her fingers tightened around the broomstick till her knuckles blanched. "May as well get it over with."

For a month after Tina's death, no one, not even the Lubicic twins, had approached the dump. Then, in one's and two's, coal-pickers had trickled back—nearly all women—dragging their sacks and baskets. A few older children had ventured out, but none brought cardboard for a swift descent with a filled sack. Each coal-picker now carried a makeshift probe like a divining rod. *If only she'd carried a stick...climbed more slowly...been more careful...* Judgments passed among them as they crossed the tracks. Gripping canes, broomsticks, and barrel staves, they warily scaled the slopes. Assured each other—and themselves— that it would never happen twice in one summer.

Clare and Kamila began to climb.

After an hour, Kamila muttered, "It's all picked over. We need to go higher." She stabbed the dirty stones above her before planting her foot. "Seems sound enough," she said with forced bravado.

Stab, tap, step. With this cautious rhythm, they continued their ascent of the smallest hill. Nobody ventured onto the heap scarred with the wide, rust-brown trail. Dan Phelan had ordered the tipple crew to suspend dumping on this mound, marked at the summit with a cross.

Kamila whistled between her teeth as she discovered a plum-sized piece of coal. "Let me tell you, this is the last time," she declared, adding the nugget to her sack. "A whole morning up here, and for what? Maybe enough to boil a cabbage. *Pffft!*" She passed Clare the broomstick so she could probe her digging spot. "Now that we're getting the Brotherhood raise, I'm not risking my neck on this deathtrap again."

Clare pried out a chunk the size of an egg. She wore old gloves darned too often to wear to church. After just an hour, the fingertips had turned sticky with a paste of soot and sweat. "That raise couldn't've come at a better time," Clare agreed. A full ten percent, started when The Hive's Brotherhood had elected its representation committee.

Much as she loathed Fin's choice of words, she couldn't argue with his assessment of the election. *Not a hunkie, mick, polack, dago, or nigger in the lot. Just one union doesn't give a damn about your last name or skin color, and that's John L. Lewis' union.* Only the almighty Lewis could convince Fin to consider a Negro his equal.

Stab, tap, step. "The newspaper said they're cleaning up the Kyle mine. Gates and Edenborn are back up and running. Why rock the boat with union talk when our men are getting five-day weeks again—and a raise, to boot?" Kamila asked.

Clare remained silent. Not every man was rocking the boat. According to Fin, Anton talked nonstop about how he'd put himself up for the committee once he became a citizen.

"The newspaper says the Company ordered scales for the tipple," Kamila continued. "Fin's pestered the bosses for years about that. What's he got to complain about now?"

Clare, of course, had heard about the scales. Hell would freeze over, Fin had insisted, before his wagons got weighed. *I'll be believing in scales, like fairies, as soon as I see one.*

Clare nearly shared this opinion with Kamila—then, just in time, checked herself. Her comment might well pass from ear to ear until it reached Dan Phelan's. The words congealed, filling her throat until it ached. When she was sure she could speak lightly, she said, "Oh, you know Fin. He's not happy unless he's bellyaching about something."

"Every night, those awful crosses." Kamila's broomstick-thrusts sent cinders flying. "The white-hoods are warning Communist troublemakers not to spoil things for everyone."

Clare thought hard before replying, "The United Mine Workers aren't Communists. Even the President says they've got the right to organize."

"That big-talking Grindstone miner, Martin Ryan? He's a Communist, for sure, and a fornicator, to boot. Anton says he's lived with ten different women." Kamila gripped Clare's arm. "Who's going to walk Katie down the aisle if Fin gets himself thrown in jail?"

Did she truly think Clare hadn't considered this—not once, but every waking hour? Clare managed a weak laugh. "If Fin lands in jail, he can keep the Lubicic twins company. I hear they stole a cow this time."

Kamila waved off old gossip and appraised the sun-washed slope. "I can't stand one more minute up here." When Clare said she'd give it another hour, Kamila handed her the broomstick. "Sometimes you're just as stubborn as your husband."

Two hours later, Clare probed-tapped-stepped her way back down. She'd thought of nothing but what to write Trudy, yet shrank from telling the truth. Her only satisfaction: a half-filled coal sack. When she neared the bottom, she heard shouting. Fearing another accident, she wheeled and scanned the dump, which was nearly vacant. The noise swelled, carried on a ribbon of smoke from the coke yard.

It was nowhere near quitting time, yet the yard swarmed with blackened miners. Thumping their buckets, they milled around a crumbling oven near the gate. Smoke poured from its eye. Two and three at a time, men emerged from the throng and approached the jamb. They flung small white papers into the fire and something else, small and shiny.

The others cheered. "It's '33, not '22—'33, not '22!" they chanted.

No boss was visible. A loaded wagon rose up the hoist cage, indicating that work continued in the pit. The yard boss stood in the lamp house doorway. A lamp man pushed past him and strode across the yard. The crowd opened a path, chanting the man's name. Hands clapped his back as he headed for the oven, pulling his wallet from a back pocket.

Then it dawned on Clare. They were burning their Brotherhood cards.

Fin elbowed his way toward the oven. He raised his arms, quelling the noise. A stocky man Clare recognized as Dal Visocky broke out of the crowd, pushing a rusty wheelbarrow. He steadied it beside Fin, who stepped inside. From this mean pulpit, he preached to his flock.

"The Brotherhood is dead!" he shouted. "These men are your brothers. Every local across this state, in mines and mills and factories—they're your brothers. John L. Lewis, the union, and the President himself are with us. If we stand together, we'll beat Thomas Moses. We'll get our scales and our checkweighman. We'll see prosperity yet! Are you with me?"

The men's roar passed through Clare like a wind bent on blowing down any door in its way. Sooty fists punched the air. A fresh chant rose with the smoke. A dust-covered man joined Dal, and they hoisted Fin onto their shoulders. The crowd turned away from the oven, heading for the tipple. Clare caught her breath when she realized who, with Dal, was carrying her husband. Jack, the union's young recruit, following his new father straight into what surely would be war.

Chapter 27: Clare

July 17, 1933
Feast of St. Alexius, Confessor

Less than an hour after Clare had packed his lunch, Fin returned home and banged his bucket onto the kitchen table, as gleeful as if he'd just hit a grand slam. "Big Bill took me check off the board and gave it back. *We've got enough help today,* he said. Told Jack the same damn thing." Before Clare could respond, he added that Mike Zoshak, Vlade Lubicic, Shorty Dvorsk, the Tonellis and Visockys, and many others also had been turned away. The lamp man who'd burned his card had been reassigned to the barn, mucking out the draft horses' stalls.

Clare's hands wrung beneath the dishpan suds. "What about tomorrow?"

"Tonight comes first." He assumed his first-base stance: feet planted a yard apart, left palm open and receptive to the repeated *smack!* of his right fist. "They've called a meeting at The Hall. The bosses will be writing up two lists. One for the Brotherhood and one for the United Mine Workers local. They won't be ignoring us ever again."

She groped beneath the foam for something solid to hold onto. "What if they fire you?"

Fin slung his jacket over the back of his chair. "If they fire me, they'll have to fire the whole lot. Then they'll be struggling to hump enough goddamn wagons to keep the steel mills running. They can't line their pockets without us breaking our backs. We'll gladly keep breaking them, but only if they follow the President's recovery bill and let us choose our own union." He looked at Clare with the focus of a hunter stalking a deer. "Are you with me, then? If not, it'll go hard with you because I'll not be backing down now."

When had it not gone hard? When had he ever backed down? She drew a deep breath, but still felt as if she were suffocating. "Is Anton with you?" she managed to ask.

"Spineless hunkie. His wife's had him on a leash for twenty-odd years. She's pulling it so tight now, 'tis a wonder he's still got his head." Fin moved to the door and stared through the screen. "Thank God, 'tis July. If we're put out into a tent, we won't freeze this time."

Clare gripped the edge of the sink and took in, with a glance, her homely kitchen. Worn table, two chairs, the girls' bench. Yellow muslin curtains, painstakingly cross-stitched by Norah. Pots hanging from a wooden rack that Fin had made when they'd first married. Her gaze fell on the rust-frilled stove. Cossacks had dented the flue in '22, when they'd emptied the house, then dumped the wagonload into a field. "What about the ball team?" she asked.

"Without us, they'll be down to a catcher and left fielder." Fin turned away from the door. His gaze crossed the room like a slowly outstretched hand. "'Tis bigger than baseball, Clare." He said her name so quietly it startled her. "Marty Ryan's organized Grindstone. They're organizing in Maxwell, Gates, Lambert, and Palmer. Not just Frick mines, but others, too, all over the county." He stepped toward her. "I'm asking you again, are you with me?"

He'd never asked before. Only commanded.

"Katie's wedding," she hedged. "It's less than a month away."

"There'll be a wedding. Jack will see to that." Fin's brow tightened. "For the love of Christ, Clare, give me an answer. Are you with me, yes or no?"

That she had preferences, even trivial ones like a color or ice cream flavor, had never seemed to cross his mind before. Their marriage—lived out exclusively for worse and for poorer, shadowed by three dead sons and his whiskey-sickness—clearly had come down to this one question. Not trusting her voice, she nodded.

"'Twon't be easy, seeing this through to the end. But you'll not regret it, Clare." He opened the door and, with swift, jubilant steps, crossed the yard.

In the deliberate speaking of the name he'd forced upon her, had he finally seen her as separate from himself? Not something he owned, but someone?

His jacket slid off the chair onto the floor, so she dried her hands and retrieved it. A crumpled pay envelope fell out of his pocket. As a United Mine Workers member, would he ever receive one again? She smoothed it flat on the table. Two weeks' wage was marked at the top, followed by the customary deductions. She turned the envelope over, where pumpkin-colored print identified H.C. Frick Coke Company as a division of U.S. Steel. Sandwiched between that heading and the Company's safety motto was a block of words she'd never bothered to read before.

Abraham Lincoln, in his address to the Workmen's Association in 1864 said: "Prosperity is the fruit of labor; property is desirable; is a positive good in the world. That some should be rich shows that others may become rich, and hence is just encouragement to industry and enterprise. Let not him who is houseless pull down the house of another, but let him work diligently and build one for himself, thus by example, assuring that his own shall be safe from violence when built."

Safe from violence. It might have been an intercession intoned by Fr. Kovacs. *Dear God, please keep us safe from violence. Who livest and reignest, Amen.* She threw the envelope into the stove, then, sick at heart, filled a pail. The floor needed cleaning, and, though she felt drained of anything but dread, she knelt to do it. Wondered, with each rasp of her scrub brush, how much longer she'd have a floor to wash.

How soon before they'd be living in a tent, pitched just inches from those on either side? She closed her eyes and heard wailing children, barking dogs, angry conversations—all mingling until the entire encampment was blanketed by a grating, inescapable hum. How would she bear it this time without Kamila?

She was working the scrub brush under the table when Tommy Tonelli appeared at the door, waving a piece of paper. "F-for you. S-s-sstore Miss g-gave me a n-nnickel to b-bring it."

She wished she had a penny to bolster Ada Smiley's delivery fee, but Tommy's cheek accepted a pat from her puckered hand before he dashed away. She unfolded the paper and read:

The Sweeney family's reservation of the Heath Community Hall basement for the afternoon and evening of Saturday, August 5, has been declined. The Hall facilities are no longer available.

The inked loops of Dan Phelan's signature bled into a pale blue pool beneath her damp thumb. The paper quivered as fury worked its way from her heart to her hands. She left her soapy kitchen, stalked through the dim cave of the living room and out the front door. For this errand, she would not keep discreetly to the alley.

She crossed Main Street, daring the oncoming streetcar to run her down. Someone called her name, but she didn't turn, didn't hesitate. She started climbing The Clean Hill. By the time she opened the Keatings' petunia-bordered gate, she was breathless. The same purple-and-white blooms lined the slate walkway to the front porch. Her hands no longer dripped, but her skirt and the bottom of her apron clung damply to her knees. Grass spread around her like a bright green lake with brick-rimmed islands of yellow roses. Not a bean or cucumber plant in sight.

Four wide-eyed little girls warily approached the screen when she knocked. In the lead, Maeve's daughter Emma. They regarded Clare as if she were the doctor, brandishing a hypodermic needle. "I need to speak to your mother," she told Emma.

The girls backed away, stumbling over each other. One began to cry. From the back of the house floated a lilting voice. "Is everything all right?"

Emma wheeled and ran down the hall. "There's a missus here, and she's all wet!"

Clare opened the door. The fearful children shrank against the wall. On any other day, she would have stopped to reassure them.

In the kitchen, Maeve and three other bosses' wives sat at a table spread with teacups, cookies, and playing cards. Seated at the table in Maeve's adjoining sewing room were Maggie Phelan, Bridget Donovan, and two women Clare didn't recognize. Surprise registered on every powdered face but Maggie's.

Maeve rose quickly. "Is someone hurt, Clare?"

Clare thrust the paper into her hand. "For a start, Katie's feelings, once I show her this."

Maeve took an uncommonly long time to read two sentences. When she looked up, her face looked like that of a miner's missus watching Cossacks drag her table out the door. Behind her, the women stirred and murmured.

"Is there some emergency?" Maggie called from the sewing room.

Maeve glanced back at her guests. Perhaps she looked beyond them—out the screen door, across the lawn, past the vivid zinnias bordering the back fence. Perhaps that glance was all she needed to remind herself where she lived, and who she was. What the wife of the man who'd written the letter expected her to say. When she looked back at Clare, her expression had smoothed like pond water over a thrown rock. It happened so quickly that Clare wondered if she'd imagined the sorrow that had been there just moments before. Maeve handed back the letter. "It's too bad, Clare."

Maggie glanced at her wristwatch. "Can we please get back to the game? It's Dan's birthday, and I'm making a roast for supper. I can't stay past two."

Clare snatched back the letter and stalked out the kitchen door. Behind her, someone laughed. The sound, like a hard wind, pushed her around the house, down the walkway, into the street, and down The Clean Hill. All the way down.

Chapter 28: Katie

"We don't need their goddamn hall," Jack declared. "They can't deny us the church." He crushed the letter and threw it at the outhouse. "Or your yard. Or—" his voice rang with defiance— "the alley. That's plenty of room, without the bosses and their spies."

The setting sun cast long shadows across the yard. A breeze carried the faint, irregular cadence of hammering over the fence. Jack took Katie's hand and pulled her toward the gate, but she pulled back. "Where can we go? Deputies are everywhere," she said.

"We'll find someplace. Your Irish luck will keep us safe."

Katie's heels ground into the dirt. "Nobody's safe. Norah said there was trouble on the picket line in Maxwell."

"What the hell does a switchboard girl know about pickets?"

"She read it in the paper. Everyone in Uniontown is talking about the strike."

Jack's arm slid around Katie's waist. His tone softened. "Let's go over to Beetown. The dance hall's windows will be open. We can listen to the music and dance outside."

They skirted the gate, broken again by the Klan and, this time, not repaired. Walking down the alley, they passed six more just like it until they reached the Zekulas', which remained intact. Jack found a rusty can and heaved it over the whitewashed slats into the vacant yard. Bing Crosby's voice floated from the house. *Why don't you remember, I'm your pal. Say, buddy, can you spare a dime?* The sound of hammering, louder now, competed with the music.

Four gates later, Jack booted a stone through another fence, just missing a boy who crossed the yard to the outhouse. "Goddamn red!" the boy shouted. He made a rude hand gesture, then bent to find his own stone. Jack pulled Katie away before he could throw it.

By the time they reached Railroad Street, Katie couldn't keep still any longer. "Everyone's hateful, or scared, or both. It's bad luck, getting married now."

"*Ljubavi*, don't, please." Jack's tender fingers wiped the tears from her cheeks. "Next week, the strike will be over. And the week after that, you'll be my wife."

"There's never been a strike this big over in a week. Paul told Norah—"

Jack's hands pressed Katie's cheeks until her lips could no longer make words. "Until Paul walks the picket line, whatever he says isn't worth listening to, let alone repeating."

Jack will do anything for you now. Now, he'll listen. Mutti's assurance beat like a frantic drum in Katie's ears. Had the time Mutti promised already passed? Hard as it was to imagine Pap as a love-struck newlywed, Mutti surely had known such a time, too, or she wouldn't have spoken. What she'd left unsaid was how long that time might last, how soon the rigors of the pit, snake-inscribed envelopes, and the lure of Boyle's Beer Garden would end it.

Jack's hands fluttered beside her cheeks like skittish birds. "Your face, your sweet, perfect face. Katie, I'm so sorry." His fingertips lighted on her cheeks, her chin, as if making sure they were still intact. "I'm a stupid brute. It's not your fault, what's happening." He drew back, and his hands clenched. "If I could just take a swing at Dan Phelan or any of those upperhiller bastards, I know I'd sleep better tonight."

He'll never hit you. Norah might've been standing right behind Katie, predicting a future that no longer seemed secure. "It's worse than the last strike," said Katie, her voice shaking. "Then, at least, we were all on the same side."

Over Jack's shoulder, she saw the throng of workmen and deputies at the mine yard entrance. The fence, fortified with barbwire, had failed to keep the pickets far enough away from Brotherhood members reporting for work. A special freight had arrived with a load of lumber for a wooden ramp that rose over the fence and into the yard. Mounted deputies had chased away strikers when construction began. Now, guarded by the deputies and supervised by the yard boss, workmen erected high walls on either side of the ramp. Pickets had thrown stones at Brotherhood members working the Colonial mines. Katie feared that these new barriers, however high, wouldn't discourage The Hive's strikers from doing the same—or worse.

Jack brought Katie's hand to his lips. "C'mon, let's go and dance. Tomorrow, I'll be back here on the line, and I want to remember how it feels to hold you." He regarded her solemnly. "I'm doing this for you. For the family we'll have." Color rose in his face. "I can't afford a ring. But as soon as this is over, I'll buy you one with a diamond. And rent us our own house."

"I don't need a diamond," she said, though she knew he didn't hear. He was already describing the house they'd have, with a new stove and maybe even a washing machine. She leaned against him, letting his determination wash over her like rain, dissolving her impulse to contradict. The wish she'd cherished was to have a safe haven. Their own home, their own bed. Their love sanctioned at St. Barbara's, then left alone. None of this could happen, other than the wedding, until the strike resolved.

Like Pap, Jack hadn't worked a day since he'd burned his Brotherhood card. The house they'd planned to move into after the wedding had been given to a new young couple. The husband was said to be a cousin of the Brotherhood's employee committee chairman. After the wedding, Katie would move in with Jack's family. What did it matter where they lived, he'd said, as long as they were together?

Oh, but it did matter! She'd forced herself to smile and say, *of course*. Jack's mother had told Katie repeatedly how happy she was with her son's intended wife. Even so, happiness didn't make the Kukoc house any bigger than the Sweeneys'. Jack and Katie would share *Baka*'s room, while his brothers slept on pallets beside their parents' bed. Branka would take the couch downstairs. "Don't worry," Jack had assured Katie. "*Baka* sleeps like a log." He'd winked, clearly unconcerned about privacy, but Katie couldn't imagine how the miracle could occur with an old woman snoring in the next bed.

The party following the wedding also posed a problem. Norah, the sole Sweeney wage earner, was offered extra shifts by her sympathetic boss, whose brother was the checkweighman for a union-shop Crabtree mine. Norah brought home just enough to pay rent and buy some groceries, but not nearly enough to feed a horde of wedding guests. Every invited missus had assured Mutti that she'd contribute a roasted chicken or pot of goulash, a fresh-baked cake or pie to the backyard party. No mention had been made of a roasted pig or gypsy band. Or a gown for Katie, who knew better than to ask.

Jack steered Katie away from the work crew at the mine gate. Beside the tracks, the deputies' horses paced, tossing their heads. Paul, stacking boards at the top of the ramp, saw Katie and waved. Jack looked pointedly away, tightening his grip on Katie's hand. She kept her other hand clamped to her side, but allowed Paul a quick smile. The moment he'd picked up a hammer, Paul had become a scab in Jack's eyes. Like Norah, he took any extra job he could find, including a weekend shift in a Brownsville car repair shop. Though his brothers and father sided with Pap, they openly admitted that the ramp-building money kept a roof over the Visockys' heads. While scavenging for coal by the railroad tracks, Sobena had confided to Katie that Mike Zoshak's younger brother Andy had proposed. But with eight mouths to feed, her parents couldn't undertake the expense of a wedding until the strike ended.

"You're so lucky," Sobena had said wistfully. Katie had nodded and quickly changed the subject. Luck, that of the Irish or anyone else, had taken leave of The Hive the day the Company had passed out the Brotherhood booklets.

The construction noise receded as Jack and Katie neared the railroad tunnel. Her eyes strayed to the crest of The Dirty Hill. Charred crosses loomed in the gathering twilight—three withered warnings to the pickets to return to work. According to Pap, Pittsburgh Coal Company miners had struck, too, partly in sympathy for the Frick miners and partly to force out their own company's Brotherhood. As a result, crosses burned nightly throughout Fayette County.

Picking her way through the tunnel's gloom, Katie longed to ask Jack, what if walking out now—with the six-day week reinstated and so many mines reopened—was a mistake? Jack had made it clear that he didn't believe what the Company told the newspapers. Like Pap, he believed that President Roosevelt would step in any day and force Thomas Moses to obey the new recovery law and recognize Lewis' union.

As Jack had predicted, the Beetown dance hall had opened every window. Cheerful strains of *Tiptoe Through the Tulips* greeted them as they circled the building. "Remember when we saw the gold digger movie with this song? And Norah got sore because I kissed you before they turned down the lights?" Jack asked.

Katie laughed at the memory of her blushing sister's scolding. Jack drew her into his arms beneath a maple's rustling canopy. With his cheek pressed to her forehead, she no longer smelled the garbage bin behind the hall or wondered who might be watching from inside. His boots scuffed gravel, and a pebble found its way into her shoe. It bit her heel as he spun her away, then back. The streetlight's glow filtered through the branches, wrapping them in shadows like fine black lace.

Later that week, Norah returned from work and handed Katie a folded newspaper. Sinking into Mutti's chair, she said, "They've sent in state troopers. It's all over the front page."

Katie spread the paper on the table. With Mutti's breath warming the back of her neck, she read aloud the account of Major Lynn G. Abrams obeying Governor Pinchot's order to deploy Troop A from Greensburg to Fayette County. Smudged photos of tents and uniformed men appeared beneath the headlines. Mutti's arm found Katie's shoulders. She wasn't sure if it was for her comfort or Mutti's.

"My friend at work invited me to stay in town till the strike's over," said Norah. "She invited you two also. Her sister just got married, so they have a spare bedroom."

"No." Katie's response was as quick and emphatic as Mutti's.

Norah regarded them with barely contained exasperation. She rose from the chair and planted her index finger on a smaller headline. "Read this."

"Go on, Katie." Mutti lowered herself into Pap's chair, gripping Norah's hand.

Katie read slowly, dread churning like spoiled food in her stomach. Wayne Smell, an assistant foreman in Smock, had been sent to the hospital. A brick thrown through his car windshield had fractured his skull. Charles Riggins, the fire boss, had his car wrecked before being attacked by pickets with stones and clubs. A Grindstone deputy also had suffered a fractured skull. Another deputy's ear had been severed.

"*Gott in Himmel!*" Mutti kneaded Norah's hand. "Have we turned into animals?"

"That's not all," Katie said, swallowing hard. Two Colonial miners had been shot.

Norah freed her hand from Mutti's and took the paper from Katie. "Here's the Company's official statement. Thomas Moses says, '*This concern has no quarrel with the United Mine Workers of America, but we do not think our men want recognition with the United Mine Workers.*'" She looked from Mutti to Katie and back again. "What do you think Pap and Jack will say about that?"

"Jack doesn't believe what the papers say," Katie said and, for once, was glad of it.

"They arrested a Filbert striker for beating up a boss." Norah's voice had gone flat. She folded the paper. "I won't stay in Uniontown without you, but I really wish you'd change your minds. There's nothing we can do here except worry."

Mutti's eyes glittered as she rose. "We need to cook for your pap. Wash his clothes. Keep house, while we still have one."

"Our rent is paid. They can't put us out," Katie protested. If the Sweeneys got evicted, so would the Kukoces. Marrying into a crowded house was bad enough. A tent was unthinkable.

Katie pulled the paper from Norah's hands and shoved it into the stove. As it caught fire, she turned to Mutti, filling the kettle for tea. "How long do you think it will take before things are good again?"

The pump handle stalled in Mutti's grasp. Flames danced in her eyes. "They've never been good."

Chapter 29: Clare

July 29, 1933
Feast of St. Martha, Virgin

Clare sifted weevils from the flour Katie had brought from the county relief truck. A tentative knock rattled the screen. When Clare looked up, the sifter, bugs and all, dropped back into the sack. The knock surprised her more than the visitor. If Kamila ever practiced that convention, it wasn't at Clare's door.

"I know Fin told you not to talk to me," Kamila said, making no move to turn the knob. "He's not here, is he? I've got something for Katie."

"He's not here," Clare said, then remembered what she'd never needed to tell Kamila. "Please come in."

Kamila entered, carrying a lumpy pillowcase under one arm. Her eyes cast about the kitchen, searching for something to look at other than Clare. "Is Katie home?"

Clare went into the living room and called Katie's name at the foot of the stairs. After fetching the flour and a small sack of beans, Katie had returned to her bed, standing on tiptoe beside the window. From this vantage point she occasionally glimpsed Jack on the picket line. She'd leave the window if Clare summoned her, then hurry back to her post as soon as the task was completed. "Cup of tea?" Clare asked Kamila, reaching for the kettle with a flour-powdered hand.

Kamila shook her head. "I can only stay a minute." She shifted her weight from one foot to the other. "Katie hasn't got a wedding gown, has she?"

Clare bent over the flour sack and folded down the top, hoping Kamila hadn't noticed the sifter. "We can't manage a new dress right now. It's a shame, I know, but—"

"That's what I thought," said Kamila. When Katie entered the kitchen, Kamila pushed the pillowcase into her hands. "I've got wedding clothes that might fit you." Kamila's cheeks had turned ruddy. She thrust her hands into her apron pockets. "If you want them, that is."

Trying not to seem overeager, Katie opened the makeshift sack and drew out a long veil. Its lavish lace trim trembled in her hand. She gazed at it for a moment, then reverently set it aside. A tear glittered on her cheek as she unfolded the gown.

"Tatted all that lace myself. Might as well get some use out of it," Kamila said to Clare. Turning to Katie, she urged, "Try it on. You'll probably have to take it in some."

Katie carried the gown into the pantry. Moments later, she emerged—a fairy-tale bride. The satin-lined lace dress was cut in princess lines with a flaring skirt. A wide flounce around the neckline formed a short cape. "I never dreamed I'd wear a gown this fine," said Katie.

Kamila shook out the veil and placed it on Katie's head. Pinched the sides of the dress bodice. Her hands settled on her hips. "Looks a little yellowed there on the right. You might try sponging it with vinegar."

Tears flowed unchecked down Katie's cheeks even as she smiled. "Do you like it?" she asked Clare. "Do you think Jack will like it?"

"*Pffft!*" said Kamila. "He's a damn fool if he doesn't."

Clare couldn't speak. Her throat was packed solid with shame and gratitude, relief and regret. Despite the strike, she hadn't lost Kamila. At least, not yet.

It was hard to tell who moved first, but a moment later, Katie was weeping on Kamila's shoulder. Kamila wagged her head. "Laughing one minute, crying the next. That's a bride the week before her wedding. Let me tell you, it only gets worse."

"Thank you," Katie sobbed, "so very, very much. Won't you please come to the wedding? And your girls, too? Everyone, even the babies?"

Clucking her tongue, Kamila untangled herself from the veil. "Better hang it up so the wrinkles fall out." She looked at Clare, who knew exactly what she was thinking. Fin wouldn't allow any Brotherhood man—or his family—to step so much as a foot into the Sweeneys' yard.

Clare had never hugged Kamila, and she could hear the *pffft!* if she tried. Still, how could Clare let her walk away, as good as shunned? Clare touched her hand. "Please come to the Mass."

Kamila considered this as she reached for the door. St. Barbara's was the only place in The Hive where everyone—bosses, Brotherhood men, and strikers—could still gather. With tension, but without incident. "I'd like that," she said, stepping outside. "The girls will, too."

Norah came home from work, bringing a newspaper with the largest, blackest headline yet: **MARTIAL LAW IN COUNTY**. Sheriff Harry Hackney, surely up to his neck in one of the Company's deep pockets, had refused to cooperate with state police. Fed up with Hackney's insubordination, Governor Pinchot had deployed two battalions of Pennsylvania National Guard to Fayette County to deal with the nightly cross-burnings, gunfire, and tear-gas bombs.

Fin staggered across the porch, undone, not by whiskey, but two round-the-clock shifts on the picket line. His drooping eyelids forced themselves open when he noticed the paper. "'Tis war, then," he said, falling into his chair. His bucket slipped from his hand and dropped onto the floor. Clare filled the kettle and set it on the stove, then sliced bread for a baked-bean sandwich. "Not hungry," he muttered, shedding his boots.

Clare set the plate in front of him. "Eat. You're no use on the line if you can't stand up straight." Did she imagine a tic lifting the corner of his mouth? For the first time since the third Finbar's birth, he was satisfied with her. She'd shed her doubts about Marty Ryan and the union. They wouldn't get The Hall back for Katie's wedding, but maybe in the long run they'd get every downhiller even more. "Eat," she repeated. "Then go to bed."

"Aye, Mammy," he said, his brogue as thick as the sandwiched beans. Even Norah's taut lips relaxed long enough to smile.

"Is Jack still down there?" Katie asked.

Fin nodded. "I told him to go home as soon as someone comes to relieve him. We don't want him nodding off on Saturday before he says, *I do*."

Norah petted the feathers of her hat, nestled like a cat in her lap. "I know Katie's supposed to move in with the Kukoces, but wouldn't it be better if Jack came here? His family is bigger than ours. I can sleep on the couch. We hardly ever use the living room anyway."

Katie threw her arms around Norah, nearly knocking her off the bench. "Do you mean it? You wouldn't mind?"

"If I didn't mean it, I wouldn't say it," Norah said, her voice muffled by Katie's hair. "Go on now, before you crush my hat."

"Jack's more than welcome." Fin got to his feet. "I'll be setting the alarm for five. Make sure me bucket's ready." He nodded at Norah. "You're a good lass. When this is all over and done with, I expect we'll be planning another wedding."

Norah waited until he'd gone upstairs to complain. "Why is everyone in such a sweat to marry me off?"

Katie hugged her again. "I want you to be as happy as I am. You're always so good. You deserve to have a pretty gown and a party—" she giggled—"and Paul, of course."

Norah shrugged Katie off. "All this hugging and kissing and good-girl talk, you'd think we were acting out *Little Women*."

"If we were, you'd be Meg," Katie said gaily, holding Fin's bucket to her chest. She extended a hand to clasp that of an invisible dance partner and twirled across the kitchen.

Norah gathered up the newspaper. "A girl at work is lending me her bridesmaid dress. Her sister got married in December, so the dress is navy blue. Is that too dark for August?"

Katie stopped twirling and dizzily handed Clare the bucket. "I think it's lovely. Why don't you and Paul get married in December? Then *I'll* wear the navy dress."

"Provided you're not—" Clare held the bucket low on her belly, and Katie blushed.

"For crying out loud," said Norah. "You two should go on the radio. You'd give Gracie Allen a run for her money."

Clare took the bucket to the sink and removed the bottom compartment, emptying the dregs of Fin's coffee. The compartment slipped out of her hand and clanged into the sink, so she didn't hear what sent the girls running outside. Then Fin careened downstairs, wearing one sock and carrying the other. "What on earth?" she asked, but he didn't answer. The door slammed behind him. By the time she'd joined them on the porch, she'd counted six gunshots.

Fin ordered them to stay inside as he tied his boots. Then he dashed across the yard and through the gate. Clare huddled with the girls at the window. Doors slammed on all sides. Boots pounded porch steps. The alley streamed with the shadows of running men.

Clare moved to the door. Opening it, she spoke with a fierceness that echoed Fin's. "Norah, keep your sister inside. And stay away from the windows. No telling where they'll shoot next." She was down the porch steps before Norah called after her. She walked faster, knowing that a woman was no more welcome on a picket line than in a hoist cage. Norah's voice was soon lost in the cacophony of barking dogs and banging gates.

Gunfire persisted as Clare emerged from the alley onto Railroad Street. Against the backdrop of the newly constructed ramp, men and horses milled about. Barrels filled with God-knows-what flamed around the perimeter. The flickering light lashed the men's faces and horses' glistening necks like yet another weapon.

She should have been daunted by the rifles' eruptions. Part of her acknowledged the folly of her presence as she slowly approached, strangely captivated by the brawl's herky-jerky dance. Wheel and jab, charge and retreat. Her stomach turned when a striker tottered, his forehead bloodied by a rifle butt. She pressed her back against a fence, her gaze darting from face to face in search of Fin and Jack.

The acrid scents of gunpowder and smoke undercut the tang of fresh-cut lumber. A spooked horse reared, upending a barrel. Fire spilled across the ground, greedily igniting sawdust and wood chips left by the ramp's construction. A thin, ragged wall of flames illuminated the melee as effectively as footlights on The Hall's stage.

Clare's breath caught when she saw Dal Visocky drag Shorty Dvorsk away from the crowd. His shirtfront was dark with blood. Masha the tinker helped Dal prop him against her cart. A horse lunged away from the flames, and Masha ran toward it, a bucket dangling fom her hand. She took out a tomato and, jeering, flung it at the deputies. Five more followed, splattering in the dirt. The sixth exploded against Deputy Harrison's badge. He seemed momentarily dazed by the pulpy redness marring his navy jacket. Then he shouldered his rifle.

The next red explosion occured on Masha's chest. She toppled backward, collapsing in a heap as if she had no bones. "Help her! She'll be trampled!" Clare shouted at the impervious mob. Tears stung her eyes, blurring Masha's limp form. She could do nothing to help the woman who had so often helped her.

"Hold your fire!" Deputy Harrison shouted. As dust swirled around them, the uniformed men obeyed. Rifles lowered. The deputies and their horses drew back. The strikers massed at the foot of the ramp. In the no-man's-land between them, the bloodstained pile of rags that was Masha reposed beside a rusty shovel. Out of the murmuring huddle of miners, a lone rock arced through the smoky air, striking the neck of a black horse. It bucked in a frenzied circle, nearly unseating a young officer. Somehow he steered the horse clear of Masha's body.

A man emerged from the strikers' ranks and bent to collect another stone. He straightened up, and his eyes narrowed as he took aim. It was Jack, transformed by firelight and fury into someone Clare barely recognized.

The mounted deputy drew a pistol from his belt. As the scream left Clare's throat, Jack snatched the rusty shovel from beneath the horse's hooves. The strikers moved forward, brandishing picks and shovels. The deputies raised their rifles as Jack, the shovel, the deputy, the pistol, and the horse collided. The shovel dropped between the horse's legs. Jack's hand locked around the deputy's, fighting for the gun. The agitated horse, tripped up by the shovel, stumbled over Masha. Its right foreleg buckled. As it pitched sideways, the deputy slid off the saddle and onto Jack. They landed in the dirt, entwined and writhing like wrestlers.

218

Clare screamed again when hands gripped her shoulders and hauled her backward. "*Gott in Himmel*, have you lost your mind?" Norah shouted.

Clare tried to tell her that it was Jack on the ground beside the downed horse—Jack and a deputy and the deputy's gun. But Norah plowed forward, dragging Clare down the alley, ignoring the *crack!* of a final gunshot.

For more than an hour, horses galloped. Tires squealed. Two ambulances raced down First Street. From time to time, Clare went outside and stood on the back porch. Shadowy figures congregated by every fence. Wives and daughters huddled and whispered and wept. Brotherhood women, union women—labels no longer mattered. Differences dissolved when men ran off into the night, and someone fired a gun.

Clare's head felt like a stone; her body, like nothing at all. She returned to the living room couch, where Katie had cried herself to sleep. Her head lay in Norah's lap.

It was almost midnight when a banging door roused Clare. Sound asleep, Katie curled in a ball beside her. Clare tiptoed into the kitchen, where Norah pumped water into the kettle. Fin sat at the table, unlacing his boots. A bright patch of blood painted his left cheek.

"It's just a scratch," said Norah. "Water and iodine will take care of it."

Rage and sorrow, like opposing armies, did battle on Fin's face. "'Tis bad," he said, freeing his feet from the boots. "A deputy shot in the chest. Dal and Shorty shot, too. They'll live, though it'll be awhile before Shorty's back on the ball field."

Törichten Mann! Foolish man! Who thought of baseball on a night like this? "What about Jack?" Clare asked, gripping the back of her chair.

Fin's head dropped into his hands. "God help the poor lad. They arrested him."

Norah shoveled coal into the stove. Her eyes advised Clare to keep quiet and let her ask the questions. "What's the charge?"

219

Fin sighed, then lifted his head. "They're saying he shot the deputy."

Sinking into her chair, Clare couldn't contain herself. "The one on the black horse?"

Norah threw up her hands at the gaffe. Fortunately, Fin was too distracted to notice. "It was all a hurly-burly," he said. "Jack and the pussyfoot got so tangled up, you couldn't tell who shot who." Fin threw his boots toward the door. "It would've ended sooner if that goddamn gypsy woman hadn't started flinging tomatoes."

"You mean Masha?" asked Norah with a hard glance at Clare. *Count your blessings*, that look advised, *that he didn't see you down there.*

Fin snorted. "Stupid bitch had no business on the picket line. Harrison shot her. They took her body away in a wagon."

"What happened to the deputy? The one they say Jack shot?" Clare prompted.

Fin raked back his hair. "I saw him lying there before the ambulance came. Didn't look much older than Jack. His horse knew more about keeping the peace than he did."

Clare white-knuckled the arms of her chair, fighting the impulse to shake her husband till he told the story she wanted to hear. But Fin, being Fin, would tell it his way or not at all.

Norah filled a bowl with warm water and wet a clean towel. Fin winced as she applied the compress. "For the love of Christ, lass, are you trying to scrub me skin off?"

Norah dipped the cloth back into the bowl. "What happens to Jack if that deputy dies? Will they charge him with murder?"

They weren't prepared for the scream. No one, not even sharp-eyed Norah, had noticed Katie standing in the doorway.

Chapter 30: Katie

Entering the Beetown jail, Katie felt as if she'd stepped onto a movie set with soot-gray walls and scarred desks. Naked bulbs leaked light that somehow felt cold. Even colder were the faces of the uniformed men. Some sat at the desks. Others hurried past, carrying papers and looking at her as if she were a chair carelessly left in their way. She forced herself to stand in front of the largest desk, where a gray-haired deputy talked on a telephone.

"Look what the cat dragged in," he said when his conversation ended. It took the rude gestures of two men at neighboring desks before Katie realized that he was referring to her.

"Please, sir," she said, taking care to speak respectfully. "I'd like to see Jack Kukoc."

He squinted at her over half-moon glasses. "Who?"

"The patch kid from the Heath brawl last night," said a tall man across the room. Katie might have thanked him for offering helpful information until he added, "Sonofabitch who killed an officer."

He didn't! she nearly cried. Pap had said that, during a scuffle, the deputy had shot himself. But, clearly, none of the officers believed that one of their own would do such a thing. "I'm his sister," Katie said, hoping that might make a difference. Surely a jailed man would be permitted to see family.

"Is he allowed visitors?" asked a young deputy.

"Frisk her," said the officer with glasses. "Make sure she's not carrying a file or a knife."

"Oh, I'm not! I wouldn't!" Katie protested. *Frisk her.* Would they really do that to a girl? The men smirked and nudged one another. If only she'd brought someone along—but Norah had to work, and Mutti was sitting with Jack's mother.

The young deputy rose from his desk and approached Katie. For a terrifying instant she thought that he intended to drag her into another room and touch her in a way that nobody touched a decent girl. Instead, he led her into a hall that turned darker with each step as the bulbs got smaller, weaker, and further apart. Picking through a ring of keys, he opened a metal door that groaned like Jack's grandmother when her knees hurt. Behind the door was the darkest hall yet. A single bulb lit a narrow walkway lined on each side with black iron bars.

"He's down at the end," said the deputy, jingling his keys. "You've got five minutes. I'll be standing here the whole time, so don't try to pass him anything. I've never locked up a girl, but I will if I have to."

She stumbled over a loose brick in the floor and fell against the bars to her left. Behind them, the man lying on a pallet swore and shook his fist. "Watch where you're going. I'm trying to get some shut-eye."

She felt her way carefully, each foot tapping the space just ahead as if she were on the slate dump. Slowly, her eyes adjusted to the gloom. Each cell contained two pallets and two men. They regarded her the same way the deputies had. Some smoked cigarettes, turning the air thick and stale. At the end of the walkway was a cell less than half the size of the others. It contained a single pallet, where Jack lay, one arm thrown across his eyes. Katie hesitated, wondering what the deputy would do if she reached through the bars to touch Jack's hand.

"Look alive, Kukoc, your sister's come to see you," the deputy shouted.

Jack sat up slowly, his expression masked by the poor light.

"Jack, it's Katie," she whispered. "Come closer, so we can talk."

He didn't move. "I know who you are." His flat tone shook her to her core.

She raised her voice. "Please, Jack. I can only stay five minutes."

When he approached, she almost regretted her request. His face appeared nearly as gray as the walls. "You shouldn't've come. It just makes things worse," he said.

Her eyes filled with tears. His face blurred. "I had to make sure you're all right."

His voice turned rough. "Yeah, I'm all right. This is a luxury hotel, compared to where I'm going next."

"Where *are* you going next?"

He turned away quickly, and she realized that he, too, was weeping. "Forget about me."

"Pap said the union will get you a lawyer. We'll postpone the wedding till they let—"

"Two minutes!" shouted the deputy.

Jack glanced over his shoulder. "You're free," he said hoarsely before flinging himself onto the pallet.

Free? Well, of course she was free. She was outside the bars, and he was inside. But that would change, and then they'd get married. "Jack, look at me," she implored. "You'll be free, too. Probably not by Saturday, but surely—"

He kept his back toward her. "John L. Lewis himself couldn't get me out of here."

"But, Jack, surely you didn't shoot that man." As the words left her mouth, she recalled their walk to the dance hall. *If I could just take a swing at Dan Phelan or any of those upperhiller bastards, I know I'd sleep better tonight.* No, it wasn't possible. No matter how angry Jack got at the bosses and Brotherhood men, he wasn't capable of murder.

"You're—free," Jack repeated, his voice breaking. His shoulders shook, just as they had in the churchyard the night she'd told him she was entering the convent.

Then she understood. He'd given up hope—and her.

"Please, turn around. Jack, let me see you!" She was shouting, but it made no difference. Jack might have been a brick in the floor, the lock on his cell, a thing incapable of hearing.

"Time's up, sister," the deputy called. "Blow him a kiss and say goodbye."

"Jack, *listen* to me!" She glanced down the walkway, startled by men's faces pressed against the bars. One man began to laugh. She turned away, sickened by this human zoo. Already, it had turned Jack into someone she hardly recognized. "I'll wait—a month, a year, as long as it takes!" she shouted as the deputy hurried toward her. She tried to rattle the bars and get Jack's attention. But the bars wouldn't rattle, and Jack wouldn't turn around.

The deputy grabbed her arm. She hardly felt the bricks beneath her feet give way to a wooden floor. Her hands still felt the cold metal she'd gripped in vain. Her eyes still strained to navigate the cell block's unnatural twilight. The deputy pushed her through another door, and she found herself outside, shocked by the brutal blueness of the sky.

It took most of the afternoon to walk through Beetown, then up and over and down The Dirty Hill. Taking the shortcut through the railroad tunnel would have required Katie to pass the dance hall, a building she never wanted to see again. When she finally reached The Hive, there was no way to avoid the picket line. She fixed her eyes straight ahead, ignoring the men and their urgent questions. *Did you see Jack? Are they treating him all right?* She couldn't bring herself to stop and face them, to say the name of the caged man who no longer wanted her. She paused only a moment at the Kukoc gate, then moved on. She found Mutti at home, staring at a closed book on the kitchen table. She rose when Katie opened the door. "*Hast du ihn gesehen?*" Did you see him?

Katie toppled forward into Mutti's arms. Mutti stroked Katie's hair until she could say, yes, she'd seen Jack.

"*Er ist nicht verletzt?*" Mutti persisted. He's not hurt?

Katie shook her head.

Mutti lifted Katie's face. "We all know he's innocent. They're blaming him to make the strikers look dangerous."

"He sent me away."

Mutti looked puzzled. Then she caught her breath. "Oh, my poor child."

"Tomorrow will come, then the next day, and the next, until it's Saturday. I can't be here then." Katie took a deep breath, but it wasn't deep enough. The kitchen might have been filled with coke cinders, pushing all the good air away. There was not enough air left in this house or anywhere in The Hive to let her say one more word, much less keep her alive.

Her gaze fell on Mutti's book. *The Door*. She flinched, her eyes assaulted once more by the punishing sun that had greeted her when she'd been forced out of the Beetown jail. Jack would leave that grim building through a different door, and, unlike Katie, he wouldn't be permitted to walk back home.

Mutti eased Katie onto the bench and went into the pantry. She emerged with a small sack of beans and placed it on the table beside the book. "Open it. Go on," she urged Katie, whose lungs still labored. When Katie shook her head, Mutti untied the string. She drew out an envelope, folded down into a stiff square.

When Trudy's check lay before Katie, she drew sufficient breath to ask, "How soon can I leave?"

Chapter 31: Clare
August 3, 1933
The Finding of the body of St. Stephen, the First Martyr

Twelve thousand men were now on strike. Fin insisted it was just the beginning.

Thomas Moses refused to attend what the newspaper called Governor Pinchot's *peace conference* between the Company and United Mine Workers. Instead, he closed the mines.

After Clare had shown Katie the cashier's check, Katie had gone to her bedroom and stayed there. When she wasn't sleeping, she sat at the foot of the bed. A rosary dangled from her hand. Each time she moved, it swayed like a pendulum. Marking phantom time—the empty minutes between the future she had lost and the one she couldn't yet grasp.

Fin had been gone for two days, looking for someone in the union who could help Jack.

Could anyone, even God, help Jack now?

Kamila and Betty brought the trunk filled with convent clothes and took away the pillowcase and its contents.

"How is she?" Kamila asked.

Clare just shook her head.

She had two daughters. In two days, she'd have only one. With each scrape of cloth down the washboard, each stitch of her darning needle, each stir of a spoon, she murmured a new litany. *Katie will go to college. Katie will become a teacher. Katie is alive.*

Alive.

Fin returned as Clare set the table for supper. "Did you—" she began, then thought better of it. The look on his face told her that there was no miracle in the making for Jack. He was lost.

Chapter 32: Katie

Norah fell asleep quickly, but Katie lay awake, listening to the church bell chime each quarter-hour. Would it be easier to sleep, surrounded by the soft breathing of a dozen other girls, knowing that the following day would be much the same as the one she'd just completed? Knowing that, day after day, all that was required of her was obedience?

Would the daily ritual prove soothing: rising and praying, studying and praying, working and praying, and praying yet again before retiring?

Even if it took years, would she eventually believe that, despite Betty's insistence, God was not a trickster? That He heard, even if He didn't answer Katie's prayers?

In the morning, they walked—a solemn, silent procession of three—to the streetcar stop. Katie kept her eyes on the sidewalk. Behind her, angry shouts from the picket line drifted up First Street. She nearly put her fingers in her ears, then stopped herself. It seemed only right to walk with the bowed head and clasped hands of a postulant.

Perhaps, if she assumed, over and over, this posture of piety, she might slowly gather up the tatters of her soul. Remake it—breath by breath, prayer by prayer—into something serviceable, something that would sustain her. Something that belonged to a girl who had chosen this path as a vocation, not an escape.

It seemed impossible that she'd once thought this was everything and Jack, nothing. When they reached Main Street, she averted her eyes from the churchyard. Only now did she understand, down to her bones, how Jack had felt when she'd told him to give her up.

Pap carried the trunk onto the streetcar, then got off and crossed his arms. "Be a good lass, then. Don't give the sisters any trouble."

Katie promised that she wouldn't. Mutti, weeping, hugged her for a long time and made her promise to write soon and often. She promised that, too.

The streetcar driver called out, impatient to be on his way. She boarded and pressed her face against the smudged window. Her hand lifted and waved to her parents, who got smaller and smaller until the streetcar turned a corner, erasing them altogether.

Only then did she allow herself to turn around. Through a scrim of trees, she glimpsed the First Street houses. The barricaded mine gate and the men clustered around it. Rising above them, the slate dump and The Dirty Hill. On its summit, three tiny black crosses mocked her.

Remember? In the coke yard with Betty? You begged God for a sign.

Part Three
La Femme

(Norah, 1941)

Chapter 33: Clare
April 14, 1941
Feast of St. Justin, Martyr

> *Mr. and Mrs. Karol Cverna*
> *request the honour of your presence*
> *at the marriage of their daughter*
> *Grace Elizabeth Cverna*
> *to*
> *Mr. Paul Cyril Visocky*
> *on Saturday, the third of May,*
> *nineteen hundred and forty-one*
> *at three o'clock in the afternoon*
> *St. Barbara's Church*
> *Heath, Pennsylvania*

Why did Clare weep, reading what she already knew? Up and down every street in The Hive, each missus surely stood in her living room, admiring—not crying over—the elegant invitation that had been delivered by Grace's lanky young brother. "Gotta hurry," he'd told Clare. "I've got a chemistry test tomorrow, but Ma said I had to pass these out first."

Had his mother instructed him to make each delivery by way of the front door? Or had it simply been understood that such an abundance of expensive paper—the invitation card, two more concerning the reception, a tiny sheet of tissue, and assorted envelopes—should not be diminished by a trip down an alley?

Clare carried the packet to the kitchen and arranged the cards on the table. Though a handful of recent weddings in The Hive had been preceded by similar invitations, none were those of downhillers. It seemed an affectation, not to mention an unnecessary expense, to formally invite people to an affair that they'd written on their calendars as soon as Fr. Kovacs had first announced the banns at Sunday Mass.

Paul, of course, didn't need to pinch pennies—but he was the last man on earth to put on airs. This lovely paper assemblage was, pure and simple, a proclamation of the bride's joy. And, Clare suspected, the groom's immense relief.

On the envelopes, someone—probably Grace—had carefully written their names.

Mr. and Mrs. Finbar Sweeney
Miss Norah Sweeney

Miss Norah Sweeney. *Miss.* Clare's eyes filled. Again, the words drowned.

Though she stood within arm's reach of the stove, she was overcome with a sudden, bone-deep chill. Time had reversed, and she stood once again in the outhouse, shivering in the in-like-a-lion early March night. Through a chink in the warped wood, she watched Paul descend the back steps, hands jammed in his coat pockets. Her palm pressed the door, but refrained from pushing it open.

Paul tore off his cap and flung it onto the frozen ground. His breath collected in a milky vapor around his bared head. A bright full moon revealed every anguished plane and hollow in the face he tipped toward the sky. The cloud of his breath thickened. Clare's neck ached in sympathy for the boy, sustaining such an awkward posture.

That's when it struck her. Paul was no longer a shy, awkward youth, faithfully squiring Norah to school dances and church socials. Nor was Clare's daughter still that quiet, modest girl, allowing him to carry her schoolbooks as they waited for the streetcar. No longer a boy, Paul wanted boys and girls of his own. His younger siblings Jerry and Sobena had five children between them, and Branka, married to his brother Bob, was pregnant with their first. Paul owned a successful Uniontown automobile repair business that displayed his name on a prominent sign—but no one to pass that name on to.

That cold night, he'd lowered a face marked in the moonlight with two silver streaks. In Clare's experience, only funerals were capable of driving a man, born and bred in a hard-luck hole like The Hive, to tears. Slowly, he'd bent, retrieved the cap, and fitted it onto his bowed head. He'd stalked across the yard, canted forward as if bucking a strong wind. The gate had snapped shut. His footsteps had crunched through the alley's brittle crust of snow, turning softer and faster until the sound had died.

Teeth chattering, Clare had gone back inside, telling herself that she couldn't imagine the reason for Paul's sorrow. She'd returned to an empty kitchen. Norah had gone upstairs to bed. She hadn't responded to Clare's knock on her door.

In the morning, Norah left for work before Clare could find a way to mention Paul. As she ironed, she told herself that the distress on his moonlit face had been caused by something other than her daughter. A problem at work, perhaps a difficult customer. Clare peeled potatoes and heated Fin's bath water, still the busy optimist, holding onto hope that Paul would appear after supper as usual. But he didn't. Not that evening nor any that followed.

They'd never spoken about what had happened that night. Why Norah had sent him, so saddened, away. But Clare knew. She regarded the beautiful and terrible invitation on her kitchen table, and her heart pulsed with the answer to that unvoiced question. *Because of me.*

Chapter 34: Norah

Lavish crepe paper swags hid most of the pipes crisscrossing The Hall's basement ceiling. Tall vases massed with white lilacs stood in the corners. Greenery studded with creamy roses and gardenias stretched the length of the wedding party's table. A four-tiered wedding cake stood in the table's center. Shuffling past in the punch line, Norah paused beside the vanilla-scented monument. On the top tier, a celluloid couple smiled coyly beneath an arch of shirred white netting. Norah stepped out of the line and folded back the scrap of veil from the tiny face of the bride, a blue-eyed blond like Grace. Paul, no doubt, had made sure of that. Of all the men Norah had ever known, only Paul faithfully attended to details—which surely accounted for his success at diagnosing and treating ailing automobiles.

"How on earth did the Cvernas manage a spread like this, with Karol out on the picket line all last month?" someone said behind Norah. "And a bakery cake, to boot—"

"Agnieszka told me Paul paid for everything, even Grace's trousseau."

"It doesn't seem decent, a man picking out a girl's—"

"Paul didn't pick it out. He sent Agnieszka and Grace to a fancy new shop in Uniontown and told the owner to send him the bill. Agnieszka said his business is so good that he hired another mechanic last week. That makes five all together. Who'd've thought he'd do so well for himself, tinkering with cars?"

"Still and all—"

"Let me tell you, if someone had offered to pay for Betty's gown, I would've jumped for joy."

Norah's fingers froze, pinching the toy bride's veil. *Jesus, Mary, and Joseph, please don't let Mrs. Zekula notice me handling Paul's expensive bakery cake.*

"Did you hear Paul just bought a big hou—"

"Three bedrooms, Agnieszka said. All brick. The church is only two blocks away. She told me Paul goes to Mass every morning before work. My girls all married nice fellas, but not one goes to daily Mass, not even during Lent."

"Young people these days—"

"*Pffft*! It's all on account of movies. You heard about that new picture, *Ziegfeld Girl*?"

Norah realized that she was holding her breath and cautiously, quietly let it out. *Please, St. Barbara and all the saints and angels...*

"The Legion of Decency list said that film is—"

"Scandalous, my Anna said. Girls parading around in nothing but spangles and feathers. Irene pestered morning, noon, and night, till Anna gave in and took her."

"What was Anna—"

"That's just what I said. I said, 'Anna, what were you thinking, exposing a thirteen-year-old to trash like that?' Next thing you know, my granddaughter will be bleaching her hair and sneaking off to smoke cigarettes in the alley, just like Jean Lubicic. Oh, hello, Norah."

Norah pulled back her hand, only to drop her purse. Ignoring it, she turned as slowly and gracefully as Lana Turner, balancing a spectacular headdress on a glittering Broadway stage. Politely, she greeted Mrs. Zekula and Mrs. Dvorsk. *I've seen* Ziegfeld Girl *three times and thoroughly enjoyed every last spangle.* Should she say it and endure a rant from her mother's best friend? It might be worth it, simply for the fleeting fun of watching Mrs. Zekula turn red-faced and bug-eyed. For the remainder of the reception, amusement would almost certainly be in painfully short supply.

Layered in stiff aqua organdy, Mrs. Zekula stepped around Norah to inspect the cake. "For heaven's sake, the bride's missing. Do you see it on the floor?"

"Just this," said Mrs. Dvorsk, beating Norah to her purse.

Thanking her, Norah peered around the ruffled mountain of Mrs. Zekula. The doll was nowhere to be seen. Mrs. Zekula pointed. "Look here, the icing's all smeared."

"Nothing down here," said Mrs. Dvorsk, lifting the edge of the tablecloth. "Maybe one of the kids ran off with her. Those rotten little Zoshak boys, I wouldn't put it past them."

As if cued, Sobena and Andy's sons raced past the table. Mrs. Zekula's gloved hand closed around the five-year-old's shirt collar and lifted him, kicking and yelping.

"Here she is!" Mrs. Dvorsk triumphantly plucked the tiny bride from a cluster of ferns.

"No more running around like a wild Indian, you hear? It's a wedding, not a circus," Mrs. Zekula told the dangling boy. She gave him a brisk shake before lowering him to the floor.

Norah might've laughed at his small, horrified face if she hadn't noticed the sugary white streak across the knuckles of her left hand. As Mrs. Dvorsk reunited bride and groom, Norah excused herself and headed for the door at a pace closer to that of a wild Indian than a Ziegfeld girl. Knowing glances followed as she searched her purse for a hankie to clean her hand. Her name surely figured in every conversation. The rustling streamers overhead echoed the guests' collective opinion. *Foolish girl. Did she think he'd wait forever?*

At last, she was through the door—and, God forbid, face-to-face with Paul and his brother Bob, smoking cigarettes in the hallway. When Paul greeted her, she wadded the sticky handkerchief in her fist, shielding it with her purse.

"See you later, pal," said Bob. He nodded at Norah and returned to the reception.

An excruciating moment passed before she thought to say the obvious. "Congratulations, Paul." Another extended pause. "Grace's gown is lovely." Her cheeks warmed. Would he guess that she knew who'd paid for it?

Paul just grinned. Crooked and wistful, that grin might have belonged to Jimmy Stewart, the earnest, in-over-his-head senator in *Mr. Smith Goes to Washington.* "Girls always notice the dress, don't they?" he said. The smoke from his cigarette floated languidly toward her. His shirt collar splayed across his suit jacket's lapels. Since childhood, he'd never worn dress clothes tidily. Resisting the impulse to straighten his tie, her hand twitched behind her purse. Had he noticed? "You look nice yourself," he added.

Did he recognize her Easter frock, poorly transformed with fresh eyelet on the collar and cuffs? Or was he simply being gallant, like Fred MacMurray's character in *Alice Adams*, when Katharine Hepburn did the same thing to an evening gown? Norah flapped a dismissive hand. "Oh, this old thing."

"Girls always say that, too, even if they just cut the tag off." He took a drag, then tapped the cinder into the glass ashtray in his left hand. Yet another detail attended to. Any other man wouldn't think twice about dropped ashes. The glass saucer trembled. Until that moment, Norah hadn't considered the possibility that Paul, likewise, had hoped to avoid this encounter. His neck had turned pink above his starched collar.

"Your sister made a lovely bridesmaid." *Gott in Himmel*, she'd said *lovely* again. His lips curved around the cigarette. He'd noticed. Neither words nor ashes escaped his attention.

"She's making noise about marrying that Edenborn pitcher, but Pap says she has to finish nursing school first." Paul ground out his cigarette. "Sorta makes me nervous, thinking I might land in the hospital someday and have my kid sister taking care of me."

He shuddered, and Norah found herself laughing. Putting people at ease came as naturally to him as breathing. Even idiots who drove their cars into trees never got scolded. He simply offered them a cup of coffee and patient explanation of the necessary repairs in his office at Visocky Automotive, the newest member of Uniontown's Chamber of Commerce. She'd heard that from Ada Smiley, whose father had once depended on Paul to keep the Company store's delivery truck in good running order. Once word had gotten out that Paul was courting Grace, wasp-tongued Ada—who'd never had a date, much less a boyfriend—had taken every opportunity to let Norah know she thought her a complete fool, hooking a fish as fine as Paul only to throw him back.

Their laughter faded. Norah drew herself up, wondering how on earth Katharine Hepburn, the greatest actress who ever lived, would play this scene. If only Norah had command of an aristocratic New England accent. At last, she said, "It's terribly rude of me, keeping you from your guests."

Paul's eyes dropped to the ashtray. "You're not rude. You see things and call 'em what they are. Fellas do that, but not too many girls have the guts."

If she truly had guts, she would've walked away from The Hive years ago, with or without him. She forced a laugh. "Not very feminine, is it?"

He shrugged, his neck still ruddy. Perhaps he thought of his bride: dimpled Grace, barely twenty, who'd never held an opinion her mother hadn't held first. Grace would give Paul a baby a year, if that's what he wanted, and still keep her Dorothy Lamour figure. Cook sumptuous Sunday suppers. Vote for the candidates he supported. Defer to his choice of radio programs.

He dipped his head, and a lock of hair fell across his forehead. Instinctively, Norah's hand strayed from the screen of her purse. Panicked, she drew it behind her back, clenching sticky fingers that had nearly given her away.

"You're exactly who you are, that's all." This time, Paul looked straight at her. "You've never pretended to be anybody else. I've always admired that."

Norah stepped back, away from a compliment she knew to be sincere. Fifteen years of courtship had taught her his every gesture and expression. Without saying goodbye, she fled to the ladies' room.

When she opened the door, she nearly collided with Mrs. Keating, who seized her arm. "I've been looking all over for you."

The previous summer, Dan Phelan had been promoted to the Company's Scottdale office, and Big Bill had become The Hive's assistant superintendent. A month after the Phelans' departure, Superintendent Finch and The Queen had returned to Pittsburgh. The new Superintendent's wife had made it clear from the outset that, with four young children and another on the way, she had no time or energy, much less interest in directing the pageant. It was also quite clear whom she considered the logical person to take it over. If Big Bill was her husband's second-in-command, then his wife, by extension, was hers.

Mrs. Keating steered Norah away from the crowded mirror, where a pastel huddle of young women earnestly refreshed their lipstick. With her back literally against the wall, Norah had no choice but to listen as Mrs. Keating whispered the sketchy details of a scandal that had revealed itself just that morning. Jean Lubicic, this year's St. Barbara, had admitted to being five months pregnant. Mrs. Keating threw up her hands. "What was I thinking, casting a Lubicic? The pageant's next month, and I've lost my saint."

The cake had lost its bride. Mrs. Keating had lost her saint. And Norah had lost her prize fish to Grace. Norah realized that she was smiling, albeit grimly, when Mrs. Keating scolded, "This is hardly a joke. We have a reputation to keep up. People come from as far away as Pittsburgh to see the pageant. Bill's sister says our fireworks are the talk of the East End."

"Deirdre lives there now. She must have mentioned it to her neighbors."

Mrs. Keating frowned. Twelve years had passed, yet Deirdre remained notorious, as much for her last-minute abdication of the inaugural pageant's prized role as for eloping with a Cossack.

"Your Emma's old enough for the part," said Norah, beginning to suspect where this conversation was heading. A trickle of sweat inched down her back.

Mrs. Keating let out an impatient breath at the mention of her daughter. "Emma has terrible stage fright. The only sensible plan is for you to play St. Barbara." Norah opened her mouth, but Mrs. Keating's peremptory finger cut her off. "Don't be making excuses now. You've helped two sisters learn those lines. You've seen the production twelve times."

"So has Betty Zeku—"

"She just got married. St. Barbara was a virgin, for heaven's sake. It wouldn't be right."

Norah knew for a fact that four previous St. Barbaras—one of them Katie—hadn't considered virginity a prerequisite for the role. For a giddy instant, she considered whispering in the director's ear. *I'm not a virgin either.* She'd have to admit to the lie in the confessional, but the look on Mrs. Keating's face might be worth the extra penance. Mrs. Keating, however, wouldn't keep this revelation to herself. The looks on other faces—especially Ada's—would dog Norah for weeks, if not forever. Of course, none of this would be as unfair as the indelible stain it would leave on the otherwise spotless reputation of Paul, the only male with whom Norah had ever kept company. She might well be a fool, but she'd never been mean-spirited and didn't intend to start now.

"You'll do it, then." Mrs. Keating drew a deep, satisfied breath. The pageant's reputation was clearly secondary. Most at stake was her own.

Norah took a frantic mental census of The Hive's teenage girls whose maidenheads, as far as she knew, remained intact. "What about Jean's sister?"

"Jesus, Mary, and Joseph! Do you think I'd be taking another chance on a Lubicic?" Mrs. Keating opened her handbag and took out her compact. It opened with a no-nonsense click, a sound that, in Mrs. Keating's opinion, clearly sealed the deal. She dabbed her nose with the powder puff. "You're a good, steady girl who takes responsibility seriously."

"I'm almost thirty!" Norah protested. "That's not a girl, that's an old maid!"

The room went silent. The wide-eyed faces reflected in the mirror regarded her with conspicuous relief. Finally, she'd given voice to her folly—and fate. Hence, any conversations on the matter no longer qualified as venial-sin gossip, but bald restatement of fact.

Mrs. Keating's compact snapped shut. "You don't look a day over twenty-one." Her pronouncement broke the silence as effectively as a backfiring dump truck. She glided triumphantly toward the door, saying, "I'll give you the script after Mass tomorrow. Rehearsal starts at seven sharp. A smart girl like you will easily have the first scene memorized by then."

A smart girl would have said, *absolutely not*, with the regal authority of Hepburn dressing down John Knox in *Mary of Scotland*. Neither girl nor smart, Norah of The Hive slumped against the wall and contemplated what could only amount to abject humiliation. The oldest St. Barbara had turned twenty the week of the '37 pageant. Dioscorus, played by a stuttering thirteen-year-old, had looked more like the saint's son than her father. Even Hepburn would be challenged as this year's lead, supported by a cast whose oldest member, Grace's sixteen-year-old brother, played small parts that kept him only briefly onstage.

And if onstage humiliation weren't bad enough, Norah would be deprived of the one thing that made spinsterhood bearable. She'd miss a month of Saturday matinees on account of weekend rehearsals. *Citizen Kane*—written up in every movie magazine—had just premiered in New York. What if, by some miracle, it came to Uniontown before the pageant was over?

"How *could* Paul have thrown you over for that little nitwit?" someone hissed in Norah's ear. "So what if Grace is half-Slovak? That Old Country stuff doesn't matter anymore."

Norah bleakly regarded Helen Zekula Novak, clad in a pink twin of the frock Hepburn had worn while knocking down Cary Grant's brontosaurus in *Bringing Up Baby*. Helen balanced her year-old daughter on one hip, and Norah nearly knocked them both down by dropping her heavy head onto Helen's shoulder. "In three weeks, I'll be the laughingstock of Fayette County. Jean Lubicic's out of the pageant, and I'm taking her place."

"Oh, darling, surely not. You're much too old."

Norah lifted her head. "Apparently I'm the only goddamn virgin available." She shook off Helen's shocked finger, pressing her profane lips.

Helen lowered her squirming daughter to the floor. "Is Jean—"

"Go ask your mother. She probably knew before Jean did."

Helen pinned her toddler between her knees and put an arm around Norah. Lowering her voice, she said, "Everyone thinks it's a rotten shame Grace stole your fella."

Summoning, at last, the equanimity of her favorite actress, Norah said coolly, "I never had the slightest intention of marrying Paul." She slipped free of Helen's arm and hurried from the room, leaving her friend as wide-eyed as Cary Grant upon his first encounter with Baby the leopard in Hepburn's Park Avenue apartment.

Chapter 35: Clare
May 3, 1941
The Finding of the Holy Cross

Paul's cousin the *Starosta,* or master of ceremonies, offered toast after toast of *slivovica* and *palenka,* traditional spirits concocted for the reception. At the main table, Grace blushed each time someone tapped a glass with a spoon. Other spoons joined in, until the newlyweds conceded to Polish custom and kissed. Meanwhile, Dal Visocky, Paul's father, draped an arm around Fin's shoulder. They shouted and swayed, draining their glasses of firewater. Before the '33 strike, they'd barely spoken, but now Fin called Dal *hunkie* as a term of affection. Seated beside Clare, Norah stonily eyed the gypsy band, tuning their instruments beside the dance floor.

When they began to play, the *Starosta* made his way toward them. "Dance?" he asked Norah. She hesitated, then surprised Clare by accepting.

Her seat was vacant for less than a minute before Kamila slid into it. Now that Roosevelt had finally outlawed the Brotherhood, Clare no longer had to pretend to hate her—or the wives of other miners who'd succumbed to Company pressure to join. "Wait'll you hear this," Kamila said. "Jean Lubicic went and got herself pregnant. Maeve kicked her out of the pageant."

"Girls don't get themselves pregnant," Clare replied.

"You'll never guess who the new St. Barbara is," Kamila added. A cat with a fresh canary in its throat had never looked so smug.

Clare was more concerned about Veronika Lubicic, whose oldest daughter had had trouble written all over her from the day she'd taken her first step. Worn out with six subsequent children, Veronika could do little to keep Jelena on the straight and narrow. Before opening a pool hall that did a brisk business in the numbers racket, Peja and Duje had distinguished themselves as the county's most accomplished and frequently jailed livestock thieves. Jelena had followed suit, perfecting cons and petty thefts of her own. She told anyone who'd listen that she was bound for Hollywood to take up where the late Jean Harlow had left off. Thanks to religious applications of peroxide, her hair bore an uncanny resemblance to that of her idol. She took to calling herself Jean, ignoring everyone (especially her parents) who addressed her otherwise, until the new name caught on. Since the cast list had been posted, Veronika had not stopped smiling, so elated was she that the girl had finally put her talents to credible use.

Another nudge from Kamila. "Go on, guess who's got the part now."

Clare was momentarily distracted, having spotted Veronika across the crowded hall. Her six-year-old son clutched her skirt. Jean, not surprisingly, was nowhere to be seen. No doubt she'd be dispatched in disgrace to a distant relative to wait out her time. "God bless her," Clare said. "God bless them both."

Kamila scooted her chair closer. "Maeve and Emma sat in the pew in front of me at the wedding. Let me tell you, they weren't praying. Maeve threatened to lock Emma in her room if she didn't take the part, and Emma said, 'Fine, go ahead.' *Pffft!* Maeve lets that girl walk all over her."

With the band so loud and male guests so boisterous, Clare could barely hear Kamila. Jana Dvorsk wove around tables cluttered with the remains of *kolbassi* and sauerkraut, *holupki* and *pirohi*. Pulling up a chair behind Clare, Jana asked, "How did Maeve talk her into it?"

Concetta Tonelli took the chair to Clare's right. In the brief lull between the fiddler's final note and the guests' applause, she shouted, "They are saying one more time you are St. Barbara's mother!"

Concetta had the grace to blush, but the damage had been done. The tipsy crowd, primed with *palenka* to celebrate anything, roared its approval. The dancers parted to reveal the *Starosta* dropping to one knee, a reverent pilgrim before the new saint. Cheeks flaming, Norah raised her hands to her chest, wringing them in what Clare recognized as agony at the attention. Everyone else saw Katie, delivering the saint's death-scene speech eight years earlier in what was still considered the role's penultimate performance. On the fringe of the crowd stood Fin, a half-filled glass in hand, grinning drunkenly as Dal and Karol, Grace's father, congratulated him.

Norah elbowed her way off the dance floor. The *Starosta* downed another shot and cried, "The bride is lost! Who will find her?"

Chaos broke out as the mock bride-hunt began. Chairs were overturned; tablecloths, lifted. Children scampered and shouted, making a show of peeking into corners. Kamila rose, unable to resist the Slovak custom, then reached over and grabbed Clare's arm. "For heaven's sake, look alive. It's a wedding, not a wake."

She pulled Clare after her rustling, ruffled bulk and called Grace's name, echoed throughout the hall. As Kamila pretended to seek a bride who'd changed her mind, Clare looked in earnest for her daughter, who, apparently, had had hers made up for her.

"I found her!" shouted Grace's mother, leading her through the crowd. They were followed by the bridesmaids, four giddy blond buttercups in frilly yellow gowns.

Tradition demanded that the groom now be escorted from the hall. "By force, if necessary!" the *Starosta* shouted. "Call the deputies, fellas, if he won't go peaceably!"

Paul made a hasty exit with his brothers. Grace stood in the center of the cleared dance floor as the bridesmaids sang, "*Nasa mladajak sosna...*" *Our maiden has sprouted like a pine...* The maid of honor carefully removed Grace's veil and began to fold it. The *Starosta*, however, snatched it and draped the lacy layers over Grandpap Cverna's cane. Kamila and Jana pinned Clare between them as they joined in the singing. "*No more can she wear ribbons in her hair.*" The song was supposed to be mournful, but everyone smiled. Unlike a wife's hard lot in the Old Country, Grace's marriage was an enviable achievement.

Clare recalled other Slovak weddings, when the veil had been replaced with a starched white *cepec*, or kerchief, the traditional head covering of a married woman. Anna, Kamila's oldest daughter, had worn the cap only until her groom returned. Helen—who'd dropped the final *a* from her name to make it sound more American—had pronounced the custom old-fashioned and refused to participate. To Kamila's dismay, her other daughters had followed suit. Grace, apparently, felt likewise, since her mother produced no *cepec*. Paul and his brothers were permitted to return as the *Starosta* capered, flapping the veil like a flag and proclaiming that he'd sell it to the highest bidder.

The band struck up a waltz, and Paul rejoined his bareheaded bride. He announced that, while the waltz was his, the next song would begin the traditional bridal dance. Jostling good-naturedly, men lined up for a turn on the floor with Grace. Karol went off to find a hat large enough to hold their donations. The *Starosta* exhorted the guests to applaud Grandpap Cverna, who'd bought the veil for twenty dollars, a sum so generous that he'd get his cane back for free. A little boy got the bright idea to climb onto a table and grasp a ceiling pipe. He swung like a monkey, snarling the streamers, until his mother hauled him down. Impervious to the hubbub, Paul and Grace glided across the floor.

Kamila fumed. "*Pffft!* They're doing it all wrong. The bride's dance comes *before* the capping. And where's the *cepec*? I know for a fact Agnieszka made one. She told me so at the store last week."

"She told me yesterday Grace wouldn't wear it." Jana's head wagged. "Such a shame."

Leaving them to commiserate about young people's flagrant disregard for tradition, Clare made her way toward Maeve. She stood beside the punch bowl, chatting with the pit boss' wife. Forgoing a greeting, Clare demanded, "Why can't Jean's sister play St. Barbara? Or one of the Cverna girls, who still *are* girls?"

Maeve greeted Clare politely. Her expression, however, would have frightened a mule. "I was daft, casting a Lubicic in the first place. I'll not be making the same mistake twice. And," she took a dainty sip of punch, "none of the Cverna girls auditioned."

"Neither did Norah. You can't tell me there's nobody else."

Maeve turned away. Clare had been dismissed, and not for the first time.

She found Norah standing in front of the ladies' room mirror. She held her powder puff, but made no attempt to use it. Her eyes, as startlingly blue as Fin's, blazed in a face no longer flushed with shame. Framed with hair as dark as bug dust, her features had become a stiff white mask. In a lifeless tone, she asked Clare's reflection, "Did they cut the cake yet?"

"They just started the bride's dance," Clare replied.

If Norah were a little girl, Clare would have gathered her in and let her weep away her disappointment and shame. If she were a little girl, however, she'd have no reason to weep. Paul would still be a little boy. There would be plenty of time to ensure that their story would have a different ending.

Why had Clare never considered the possibility of this unhappy chapter? How could she have failed to foresee that, when Norah contemplated her future, duty—as Norah defined it—would trump desire? "Do you want to go home?" Clare asked.

"I want to step through this mirror like Alice in Wonderland. Failing that, I guess I could step in front of the streetcar." Norah opened her purse and dropped the powder puff inside.

Clare clasped her hand. There was more to her upset than embarrassment. She visited Uniontown's Penn and State theaters as faithfully as Mass and Confession. Though the comparison was surely blasphemous, Clare was sure that the weekly outing, briefly immersing her in lives so different from her own, sustained her as much as Holy Communion. Gently, Clare suggested, "Maybe they'll hold over the movies they've got now. Or show Westerns for a couple weeks."

Norah pulled away. Her purse snapped shut. "I'll just have to offer it up."

Chapter 36: Norah

A church bell chimed the quarter-hour, reminding Norah that her lunch break was nearly over—yet she lingered before a bay window banked with potted palms. This had to be the shop where Grace had chosen her gown and, according to Helen, most of her trousseau. Unlike the large, serviceable wooden signs identifying the neighboring dry cleaner and shoe repair, the shop displayed only a small pink oval beside a door painted the same shade.

La Femme Charmante
Distinctive clothing and accessories
Monday through Friday 10 until 5
Saturday 10 until 4
And by appointment
Rosalind Hamilton, Proprietress

In the window, three mannequins modeled frocks that glowed like precious gems in the midday sun. Peach, lavender, and apple-blossom pink, all of them silk, for only silk possessed such sheen. Wright-Metzler's best dresses shone, too, but under no-nonsense department store lights that cheapened them, rendering them mere clothing fit for Uniontown closets. These filmy confections—paired with tinted straw clutches and hats (oh, such hats!)—might well grace the wardrobes of Jean Arthur, Barbara Stanwyck, and, especially, Katharine Hepburn.

Something moved behind the mannequins. Norah backed away. A woman placed a baby blue patent leather handbag beside a white ceramic urn dripping with ivy, then artfully threaded a leafy strand around the purse's handle. Her hands, tipped with perfect coral nails, touched the purse with the care and appreciation such a stylish object deserved. When the woman retreated, Norah inched forward to study the window's rosy satin swag. A gold cord, as thick as her wrist, gathered the folds in the window's left corner. The drape was fine enough for a

Broadway theater or—her nose grazed the cool glass—the window of a Hollywood boudoir.

Unbidden, an image of The Hall's worn velvet curtains came to mind. She sighed, succumbing to yet another futile examination of conscience. What had she done to so offend heaven? How had she unwittingly earned the heavy penance of playing the daughter of a fourteen-year-old? He stood a full foot shorter than she! Mrs. Keating had spent most of the previous evening's rehearsal re-blocking the execution scene, fuming at smart aleck cast members who'd urged the diminutive Dioscorus to play his part on stilts.

Norah gaze shifted to the mannequins' shoes, only to realize that a woman inside the store regarded her with curiosity as keen as her own. The woman smiled and drew back the swag. Norah fled. She punched in at Wright-Metzler's an embarrassing nine minutes late.

For the rest of the week, she dodged her friends to spend each rainy lunch hour under her umbrella. She hovered beside a parking meter in front of the shoe repair. Determined to behave more discreetly, she contented herself with an oblique view of La Femme's window. A pink handbag now reclined in the ivy, along with a straw picture hat, its brim encircled with a filmy fuchsia scarf. By Tuesday, she'd memorized the window's every detail. The shop's customers, each dressed to the nines, received the same scrupulous attention.

She made quick, furtive sketches of hats, frocks, and handbags in a notepad she'd purchased at the 5&10. The pad slid in and out of her pocket during each evening's interminable rehearsal. While the other players behaved like the children they were—name-calling, shadow-boxing, pinching, pulling hair—she pored over her sketches between exits and entrances.

Eager for an excuse to skip rehearsal, she volunteered to take a Saturday shift in place of a girl who'd begged off to attend a wedding. Another girl failed to show up, leaving the switchboard short-handed. Within an hour, Norah had disconnected three calls and transferred two more to the wrong departments—shameful performance for a supervisor. By noon, her scalp throbbed beneath the headset. Swallowing two aspirins, she fled the noisy lunchroom and stalked through Better Dresses to the elevator. No longer did she need to avert her eyes from the mannequins, whose frocks she'd once coveted with sinful fervor. Only La Femme's dresses, and those of its customers, tempted her to flagrantly break the Tenth Commandment.

When she reached the shop, she eagerly assessed a new display of hats. Her eyes lingered on a floppy Panama trimmed with a pink-ribbon plait and cascade of roses. Before she could take out her notepad, the shop's door opened. Stepping outside was the woman whose attention she'd done her best to avoid. Dressed in strawberry silk, the woman beckoned. When Norah backed away, the heel of her left pump lodged in a sidewalk crack. Freeing it required the most desperate and unfeminine of movements.

She lurched down the sidewalk until she reached the bakery, where the heel gave way. Her left ankle painfully buckled. The broken heel skittered into the street, where a taxi promptly ran over it. Gritting her teeth, she limped back to the store. She tried to recall a movie scene in which the plucky, stylish heroine found herself in a similar fix and turned it into a triumph—but her throbbing ankle was too much of a distraction. She was simply a dowdy patch girl who'd broken her shoe, venturing too close to a place where she didn't and never would belong.

On Monday, Norah borrowed Mutti's scarred brown oxfords and left her broken pump at Mr. Simons' shoe repair. She'd resolved to spend the rest of her lunch break at the library, comparing her sketches to fashion magazine photos—but couldn't help noticing that La Femme's window display had changed yet again. One mannequin modeled a black linen suit, which bore an uncanny resemblance to a Hepburn costume in *Stage Door*. The second wore white linen sailor slacks and a billowy silk blouse—identical to Jean Arthur's attire in *Only Angels Have Wings*. Netting—white on the left, black on the right—enveloped each mannequin's head, then bloomed into an extravagant bow. Had someone told Norah that a head wrapped up like Jordan almonds in a wedding favor could appear elegant, she would have encouraged that someone to purchase eyeglasses. Was it possible that La Femme's owner had Hollywood connections?

Before she could turn away, who should emerge from the shop but—*Gott bewahre,* God forbid—Mrs. Cverna and Grace. Each held a large pink shopping bag. They paused on the threshold, and Grace fluttered a hand sheathed in an ivory glove. "Thank you so much for your help, Roz!" she called. "I don't know how we'd manage without you." Atop her blond head was the striking rose-trimmed Panama hat that had caught Norah's eye the previous week.

Norah backed into the shoe repair's shaded entryway, awash with relief when the pair turned in the opposite direction and headed toward the bank. Hungrily, she studied the peplum of Grace's ecru linen jacket, bobbing prettily with each step. She remained in the shadows as Grace and her mother crossed the street. Halfway down the block, they paused beside a shiny convertible the color of vanilla ice cream. Grace unlocked the driver's door and climbed inside, leaning across the seat to open the passenger door for her mother. They deposited their shopping bags in the back seat, heads tipped toward each other. Norah was sure she heard their laughter—and why not? Who wouldn't revel in a shopping spree on the first sunny day in a week?

They replaced their hats with scarves that Norah knew, just knew, were pure silk chiffon. Grace donned sunglasses, then half-turning, slowly backed the car up just a bit. Turning around, she paused to say something to her mother, then pulled forward. The car glided away from the curb, its chrome bumper shimmering in the sun.

Grace could drive.

Norah stood stock-still well after the car had turned the corner and disappeared. Was that really bashful, tongue-tied Grace? That self-assured woman who'd called La Femme's saleslady by name, who wore a daring hat and handled a car—a convertible, no less—with ease? In less than two weeks, Grace had transformed from a nothing-special patch duckling into an enviably elegant city swan.

It was easy to imagine Katharine Hepburn behind that spotless convertible's wheel. Hair sheathed in silk, eyes shaded by chic dark glasses, she cruised along a road bordering the ocean as palm trees flashed past. Beside her, Paul praised her skillful driving. For one brilliant instant, Hepburn vanished, and Norah took her place. An instant was all Norah could bear.

The following day, Norah spent her lunch hour at the 5&10. She paced the millinery aisle, checking and rechecking price tags, then chose a cheap Panama hat and a yard of navy ribbon. As she counted coins into the cashier's palm, her eyes strayed to a colorful display of artificial flowers. "Just a moment, please," she told the cashier. She had to squeeze around a stout, tongue-clucking woman who held a lampshade the color of mustard.

She selected three white spider mums and a cluster of tiny daisies. The sticky green wrapping on their wire stems left grass-colored fuzz on her worn white gloves. "Sure you're all finished?" asked Lampshade Woman as she returned to the counter. "Some people have jobs to get back to, you know."

Norah laid the flowers on the counter. "I'd like these wrapped, please."

"Aren't *we* putting on the ritz? This ain't Wright-Metzler's, y'know," said Lampshade Woman. The woman's loud, red-flowered dress and barren straw hat reflected shockingly common taste in business attire. She plopped the shade onto the counter. Its chocolate-brown fringe, Norah noticed, puckered on one side.

"I expect good service, no matter where I shop," Norah replied. She smiled at the cashier, who looked barely sixteen and probably hadn't finished high school. As the girl rolled the flowers in tissue paper, Norah decided not to point out the lampshade's flaw. Some people wouldn't recognize quality—or its lack—if it bit them on the nose.

The cashier handed Norah her bag. She hesitated, then asked, "Did you buy your hat at Wright-Metzler's, miss? Feathers are in fashion this summer, aren't they?"

Setting down the bag, Norah removed her much-mended, eight-year-old straw hat. She'd found the feathers snagged on a blackberry cane the summer Katie had entered the convent. "You'll look charming in it," she said, handing the hat to the astonished girl. "The straw is such a becoming shade for your hair."

On Friday, Carol Ann—who'd left the switchboard to sell ladies' gloves—blocked the lunchroom door, demanding to know Norah's destination. "You gobble your sandwich and run out every day like the place just caught fire," she said. "C'mon, spill the beans. What's his name?" The other girls giggled, egging her on, until Norah masked her chagrin long enough to invite Carol Ann to come along.

"It's not a fella," Norah said as they left Wright-Metzler's. Though La Femme's existence was hardly a secret, she felt as if she were about to give up a precious possession. "It's just a dress store." Her tone and the shrug that followed seemed as sacrilegious as feeding Communion hosts to Mrs. Tonelli's chickens. "It's next door to the shoe repair, so I noticed—"

"Oooh, fun! We've got almost an hour to poke through the clearance rack." Carol Ann quickened her pace when thunder rumbled in the distance. Her umbrella boisterously rapped the sidewalk. "Is that where you bought your new hat?"

Norah touched the Panama's brim, its right side rolled and beribboned like the one Grace had purchased at La Femme. She longed to nod, smug as a girl routinely mentioned on the newspaper's society page, a girl who drove a convertible as if she'd been born behind the wheel—then caught herself. Once Carol Ann saw La Femme's display, she'd know Norah was lying. "I bought the ribbon and hat at the 5&10 and copied one I saw in the shop window," Norah admitted. "I bought flowers, too, but they didn't look right, so I left them off."

She pointed to La Femme's door as a woman emerged from the bank on the corner. For a long, horrifying moment, Norah beheld Grace, arrayed like a film star in ivory linen and the rose-trimmed Panama, peering in amusement at the patch girl in faded blue dotted Swiss and a ridiculous dime-store replica of her own expensive hat. Norah reached up to pull the wretched imitation off her head when she realized that the approaching woman wasn't Grace at all. She was almost as old as Mutti. She wore a bargain basement dress and far too much rouge and didn't give Norah so much as a glance.

"You should go to Hollywood and make movie costumes. Maybe you'd meet Veronica Lake," said Carol Ann, oblivious to Norah's discomfiture. Since accompanying Norah to *I Wanted Wings*, she'd styled her blond hair to droop, as Lake's did, over her right eye.

Norah stopped in front of the shoe repair. "Only rich people shop there," she cautioned as Carol Ann and her click-clacking umbrella made a beeline for La Femme's window. "I'm going to check on my shoe. I'll just be a minute."

When Norah entered, Mr. Simons peered around the curtain to his workroom and threw up hands stained the same dirty brown as Mutti's shabby shoes. "How many times I hafta tell you, sister? Not till next week! I got a wedding party, eight pairs they need dyed PDQ. Mrs. Hamilton, she sends me all the country clubbers. Money to burn, but patience? Ha!" Muttering like the bombastic Wizard of Oz, he ducked back behind the curtain.

Norah sighed and stepped outside, wishing she'd at least caught a glimpse of the country club shoes. A stiff breeze laden with rain swept across the street. A trio of bankers trooped down their building's marble steps, hands clapped to their hats. Norah forced open her old umbrella, puzzled by the vacant sidewalk. Perhaps Carol Ann hadn't found La Femme's window so impressive and backtracked to the bakery to indulge her sweet tooth.

La Femme's window warmed with a rosy glow as if, indeed, its curtain hung in a theater, and the first act was now underway. Behind the potted palms, Carol Ann conversed with the saleslady. *Gott in Himmel!* What had possessed a common shop girl to enter an establishment catering to the country club set? The saleslady wore a fashionable striped gray suit. In contrast, Carol Ann appeared merely presentable in a blouse and skirt that accentuated the five pounds she was always hoping to lose.

A burst of rain slapped Norah's back, soaking her straight through to her brassiere. Lightning flashed, drawing Carol Ann's attention to the window. *Come in,* she mouthed, frowning when Norah didn't move. She flapped her gloves—good ones, at least, purchased at Wright-Metzler's with her employee discount. The saleslady beckoned, too, leaving Norah no choice but to approach the pink door. Just as it opened, she noticed that the leather had split across the toe of Mutti's left shoe.

Carol Ann pulled her inside, announcing, "Mrs. Hamilton, here's my friend Norah Sweeney. She's spent every lunch hour for two weeks outside your store."

"What a lovely compliment," said Mrs. Hamilton. Her dark hair fell in soft waves to her shoulders. Parted in the middle and drawn back from her forehead, it was the same style worn by Hedy Lamarr on the current *Screen Guide* cover.

"Not two weeks," Norah protested. She'd gladly have stepped on Carol Ann's foot, but feared to draw Mrs. Hamilton's attention to the damaged oxford.

"Carol Ann tells me that you like my windows. I'm just tickled to death," Mrs. Hamilton added, her inflection remarkably similar to Vivian Leigh's in *Gone With the Wind.* "Why, look at you, you're soaked to the skin. We can't have you going back to work like that."

Mrs. Hamilton led Norah across rosy plush carpet insulted by her dripping hem. Beside floral chintz armchairs, dainty tables held copies of *Marie Claire,* a fashion magazine Norah had never seen before. She longed to inspect the alluring covers, but Mrs. Hamilton escorted her to the adjoining room, where mannequin brides flanked a rack of frothy white gowns. The velvet chaise against the wall was worthy of the Big Boss' mansion. On a low table, an open book displayed the pastel sketch of a wedding veil that seemed oddly familiar.

"Do you like that veil?" said Mrs. Hamilton. "I had one made up a few weeks ago. Pretty little blond. She married the nice young man who fixed my car."

I watched the pretty little blond's grandpap buy that veil for twenty dollars. At the time, the sum had seemed outlandish. Now that Norah had seen La Femme's refined interior, she suspected that Grace's veil had cost even more. She opened her mouth, about to remark that she'd attended the nice young man's wedding, then closed it. She hadn't spoken Paul's name since the reception. To do so here, surrounded by the glorious evidence of what she'd given up, would surely bring on humiliating tears. She was grateful when Mrs. Hamilton urged her through yet another doorway. She found herself in a hall lined with crystal-knobbed closets.

"Scoot inside a dressing room, sugar," said Mrs. Hamilton. "I'll go and find you something pretty." She regarded Norah with a practiced eye, no doubt seeing right through the drenched dress to the Sears catalog underwear. "Such a trim little waist, I'm simply green with envy. Go on, now. We don't want to ruffle your boss' feathers, sending you back late."

She retreated, leaving Norah as frozen as the mannequins. Mrs. Hamilton clearly expected Norah to wear that *something pretty* back to Wright-Metzler's, dry and stylish beyond her wildest dreams. Since this was hardly a satin-curtained relief office, Mrs. Hamilton also would expect payment—certainly much more than the three dollars in Norah's wallet.

Carol Ann's voice floated through the bride's room. "Blue is her favorite color."

"Jesus, Mary, and Joseph," Norah muttered, pacing in front of the dressing rooms. God helped those who helped themselves, but not a girl whose pride had escorted her into a jam that offered no graceful exit. Then she noticed a different door, larger, with a worn brass knob.

The door opened onto an office. Ledgers, an adding machine, and issues of *Harper's Bazaar* cluttered a large desk. On the coat rack hung a gray suede hat, its brim pierced with an iridescent peacock feather. An iron railing was visible through the lone window. Norah approached it, her decision made. If Hepburn, as Jo March in *Little Women*, could climb out a window and down a trellis wearing a crinoline, Norah could certainly manage a fire escape.

Despite her vanity, God hadn't abandoned her. She clambered over the sill and down the clanging metal steps, noticing with no small relief that it had stopped raining.

255

Chapter 37: Clare
May 17, 1941
Feast of St. Restituta, Virgin, Martyr

Fin looked up from his newspaper. "That cousin of yours and her kraut church, they're likely sending money to Hitler on the sly. Hoping he conquers the world, aren't they now?" He shook a finger at Clare. "You know he's got it in for Catholics, too, not just Jews."

Clare covered a kneaded mound of bread dough with a towel and floured the next batch. "Trudy's church wouldn't support that evil man. I hope someone shoots him dead, and soon."

"Sure as I'm an Irishman, your cousin's on Hitler's side. Working for a kraut company all these years. Katie's superior had no business sending her to teach Nazi sympathizers."

Clare sighed, careful to keep it soundless. If she had a dollar for every version of this conversation, she could buy herself an electric stove and a new hat, to boot. "Heinz is an American company," she reminded Fin. "It's been around longer than the both of us. And Katie's students are first grade children. They can't spell Nazi, much less know what it means."

A cloud of flour surrounded her as she dug into the dough, favoring her tender left wrist. Even if Fin noticed the bruise, he'd have no memory of how it had been injured.

"I'll be home late," he said, taking his hat from a nail by the door.

He was off to meet his pals at Boyle's for a shot and a beer or two before heading to the Lambert ball field. Someone would have a different paper, maybe the *Pittsburgh Post-Gazette*. They'd pass the smudged pages back and forth between innings. After the game, they'd return to Boyle's. Take up fresh glasses and the same rant Clare had heard since the '33 strike had died the slow, painful death of wasted effort—and Hitler had taken over both the German government and every newspaper's front page.

When Roosevelt had gotten his draft bill passed last September, she'd prayed that they'd take Fin. Her hopes, of course, had proven as futile as his picket lines. He was too old and knew it, and that knowledge fueled every hateful urge inside him. If only he took pride in his labor as so many miners did, calling themselves pit soldiers in the President's Lend-Lease army. Each time German bombers targeted Dublin, Fin's fists retaliated, and she ended up with at least one black eye.

Leaving the dough to rise, she took scissors into the front yard to cut peonies—fragrant, feathery globes of magenta and white. She heaped them in her basket, added three Mason jars filled with water, and headed for the cemetery. It was nearly two weeks till Decoration Day, when every plot behind St. Barbara's would be lavishly adorned. Everyone but the day-shift miners had left for Lambert, so she knew she'd have the cemetery to herself.

She no longer needed to pick coal, not with the War Board needing fuel, and the Company paying men round-the-clock to dig it. Fin had never earned so much—nor drunk so much away—but with Norah's wages, she was spared the need to climb the heaps that had brought the Kukoces and her Katie such misery. Whenever she nursed a bloody nose, she thought of Mirta's pain. Unlike hers, it would not pass. Every day, Mirta had to avert her eyes from the slate dump that had swallowed her daughter. Every moment, guard against longing for her son, who'd live out the rest of his life behind bars in Pittsburgh's Western Penitentiary.

Though Clare was grateful to be spared the strain of filling a coal sack, she missed the chance to play her old game. She didn't dare speak aloud in German the names of kitchen items or what grew in her garden, fearful that a breeze might carry a telltale syllable into an alert, disapproving ear. Many shared Fin's antipathy for *ihre Muttersprache*, her mother tongue. Only two German families still lived in The Hive. Before the Nazis had invaded Czechoslovakia, the Fieldings and Greenwalls had called themselves Feldmann and Grünwald. Even then, however, Clare had suppressed the urge to seek out

Sabine Grünwald or Annaliese Feldmann for *ein Klatsch*, a chat.

Instead, she'd taken to visiting her dead sons. For years, Norah had tended the plots, giving anyone who'd commented on Clare's absence a cold eye. Perhaps Clare had needed a grace period—if such a sinful woman as she could expect even a thimbleful of grace—before returning with any regularity to the site of those three quick burials.

In the quiet cemetery behind the church, the grass around the small white crosses was free of weeds, but the tulips Norah had planted were withered. Clare cleared away the dead leaves and arranged the peonies. A pair of red-winged blackbirds perched, twittering, on the fence. Across the yard, the Donovans' beagle worried a downed branch.

"*Der Hund hat einen Stecken gefunden,*" she told the Finbars. The dog found a stick.

She rocked back on her heels. Would the boys have wanted a dog? Would Fin have indulged his sons, finding some way to feed an animal even as he struggled to feed his family? Would he be watching one of them now—the new Steamshovel, a fine first basemen, who'd lead The Hive to yet another Frick League trophy?

Her sons. Clare imagined them—dark-haired and sturdily built like Fin. They stood alongside their sisters, young and happy. Innocent and irreproachable. How long would it have taken before each had become his father's faithful disciple, following Fin onto the ball field, into the pit, and night after night to Boyle's? How long before Clare or another woman or girl felt uneasy in their company?

She fixed her gaze on the church, blinking till the mist cleared. "*In diese Kirche,*" she told her lost sons, "*war ich auch verloren.*" In this church, I, too, was lost. "*Vier-und-zwanzig Jahre später, ist es noch so.*" Twenty-four years later, it's still the same.

No, not the same. It had only gotten worse.

They'd lived in The Hive just three days when Fin had marched Clare to St. Barbara's to register as parishioners. The old priest who'd preceded Fr. Kovacs had produced a thick leather-bound book and a pen. After writing his name, Fin had passed the pen to Clare. His hard look had reminded her of their agreement, as if the welts across her back had been insufficient incentives to obey.

Clare Finnegan Sweeney, she wrote, her hand trembling beneath the weight of Fin's scrutiny. Then she swayed, ambushed by vertigo. Whose feet supported her? Whose heart throbbed inside her chest? Her falsely named body, like a hand-me-down from a missionary box, simply did not fit.

Taking the pen, Fin wrote the girls' names below Clare's. The priest reminded them about Sunday Mass. "Nine o'clock for Polish, Slovak, Croatian, and English." He spoke the four languages well enough to preach what the Company prescribed: Christ's example in enduring hardship, gratitude for employment. He peered at their names. "You come from Ireland?"

Fin nodded, staring at Clare until she forced her head, heavy as stone, to nod, too. She swallowed the vehement protest that lodged painfully in her throat. *Nein, ist es nicht so! Meine echte Name ist Clara Pfingsten Sweeney. Ich bin in Amerika geboren, aber meine Eltern, viele Jahre tot, sind aus Bayern gekommen. Ich habe einen Ire geheiratet, aber ich bin keine Irin.* No, it's not true! My real name is Clara Pfingsten Sweeney. I was born in America, but my parents, long dead, came from Bavaria. I married an Irishman, but I'm not an Irishwoman.

Not Irish. No longer German.

They walked home in silence. Fin had said everything the night before. "You'll never be speaking that other name or a single word of Kaiser-talk again. 'Tis an insult to me dying brother, who'd be alive and well if the Huns hadn't burned up his lungs with their poisoned gas. 'Tis an insult to me and to me children."

His children. Clare might've laughed if she'd yet regained her breath. She was young then, married just seven years, believing that Fin could somehow be persuaded to become someone other than he was. "My name is my name," she'd argued that night. "I didn't gas Seamus, and my parents, God rest their souls, didn't either. They left Würzburg long before—"

Fin's belt had finished the sentence for her. The next day, wincing against the weight of a cotton dress across her back, she took the priest's pen and rejected her heritage. Clara Pfingsten, lost.

For weeks afterward, she heard an urgent whisper. *Wer bist du, Clara?* Who are you?

Unlike poor Seamus, Fin thought he'd won the war. Conquered the Hun beneath his roof. But Clare hadn't been conquered, not entirely. Despite the beatings and bruises, she held onto *ihre Muttersprache.* Secretly, she taught the girls. As children, they begged to play *Sprachschule,* language school. They hoarded the words as precious secrets, just like Clare.

Now she surveyed the cemetery, the church entrance, the streets—all were deserted. Smiling at the crosses, she stroked a peony petal. "*Schöne Blu—*" Her finger recoiled from the flower. Would the boys—Fin's boys—have been willing to keep her secret? Or would they, like their father, have considered each syllable an insult?

Fin had thought that changing her name was as inconsequential as drawing a coke oven. Creating a hole inside her, then filling it with something different than what had been there before. Did he believe that if she were no different than an oven, not so much as a crumb of old carbon remained, wedged in some dark corner? The core of that crumb held the heat of every fire burned there. Even Fin's belt, wielded with storied Steamshovel strength, couldn't fully extinguish the ember of who she was. Such a metamorphosis had to be her doing. Hers alone.

Two years after signing St. Barbara's book, undone by a beating and utter exhaustion, her transformation was nearly accomplished. Two years after that, the third Finbar died—and she no longer recognized herself. Clara Pfingsten had ceased to exist.

Wo bist du gegangen, Clara? Where have you gone?

The beagle loped across the cemetery plots, indifferent to treading on the dead. The blackbirds pecked at the grass. As their bloody epaulets flashed, it struck Clare that the Finbars weren't the only Sweeneys buried here. For years, Norah had diligently tended her brothers' graves. With each visit, she had interred a bit more of herself beside them.

Had Norah buried her heart that cold March night when Paul had left, never to return? Or had she waited until the ground thawed, until the Cvernas' invitation had arrived? On behalf of the world's most unworthy mother, she'd chosen the worst possible martyrdom. Buried while still breathing.

The blackbirds took wing. The peonies' heavy heads nodded agreement with the plan weaving itself like a black web in Clare's mind. She would tell Norah about her brothers. Upon hearing so horrible a story, Norah would surely reject Clare and leave The Hive. She'd regain her life before it was too late. Clare's first-born—lost like all the rest.

Clare sat in silence, breathing in the warm scents of grass and soil until her heart calmed. Then she rose and assured her sons, "*Wenn euere Schwester geht, werde ich auf euch aufpassen.*" When your sister leaves, I'll take care of you. Then, gripping the basket of shriveled tulips, she hurried home to see to the bread.

Chapter 38: Norah

Norah slipped her mended shoe into her raincoat pocket and shook out her umbrella before entering Wright-Metzler's. The manager had stressed that the floor be kept dry and safe for customers, despite what was turning into the wettest May in recent memory. She paused on the rubber mat inside the door, struggling with the balky umbrella.

Carol Ann leaned across the glove counter. "Guess who just walked in." She glanced sideways, then turned and waved. "She's back, Mrs. Hamilton!"

The slick umbrella handle slipped from Norah's panicked hands. This time she had no fire escape at her disposal. She forced a smile at the approaching woman in the smoky blue topper.

Mrs. Hamilton raised a gray-gloved hand in greeting. Its gauntlet-like cuff drooped elegantly over her coat sleeve. "Why, Norah Sweeney, imagine running into you here."

"I work here," said Norah, then realized how perfectly stupid she sounded. Mrs. Hamilton knew that, of course. She also knew what Norah did and how long she'd been doing it. All thanks to Carol Ann, who'd admitted to sharing these details while helping Mrs. Hamilton search La Femme's racks for the dress Norah had never tried on.

"I'm so pleased I ran into you, sugar," said Mrs. Hamilton. Her gray glove extended, giving Norah no choice but to clasp it.

"I'm terribly sorry I had to dash out the other day," said Norah, all too aware of Carol Ann, snickering behind her. She cleared her throat, wringing her memory for a Hepburn line that would salvage the situation. "The time had completely gotten away from me, and I—"

"I'd like to talk to you about something important, Norah," said Mrs. Hamilton, so smoothly that it didn't seem like an interruption. "Please join me for dinner after work. Do you care for Italian food? There's a charming little restaurant not far from my shop."

Carol Ann made a queer choking sound. Had their positions been reversed, Norah might well have done the same. A girl drips all over your shop, leaves without so much as a goodbye, wastes the time and trouble you took finding her something dry to change into—and you invite the ungrateful wretch to supper?

Norah frantically calculated the contents of her wallet. Given her ungracious exit during their last encounter, a refusal was out of the question. She'd order a green salad, claiming she was on a diet. Surely a salad couldn't cost more than a dollar. "I love Italian food," she said.

"Wonderful," said Mrs. Hamilton. "Come by the shop after you punch out. So nice seeing you, too, Carol Ann. I must stop in again and take a closer look at those gloves. Such an impressive selection." She glanced at the door. "Praise be, it stopped raining. I declare, if this dreadful weather keeps on much longer, we're going to find ourselves sprouting webbed feet."

"Holy Toledo," Carol Ann said when Mrs. Hamilton was safely out the door. Head wagging, Carol Ann regarded Norah as if she had, indeed, sprouted, not just webbed feet, but also feathers and a bright orange bill, and Carol Ann, more than anything, wanted them, too.

"I'd like you to work for me," said Mrs. Hamilton, arranging the white linen napkin in her lap. "That is, no pun intended, if you're not too attached to that switchboard."

Norah's hand twitched and knocked her napkin, cleverly folded to resemble a crown, onto the floor. Before she could retrieve it, a waiter swiftly gathered it up. Seemingly in the same motion he deposited another in its place. Her mouth suddenly and inconveniently went dry. "What," she rasped, "would you want me to do?"

"Assist customers, of course. I certainly don't have my own switchboard hidden away in a closet." Mrs. Hamilton opened her handbag and withdrew a red tooled-leather case. Instantly, the waiter reappeared and struck a match. "Thank you, Marco," she said as he lit her cigarette. Leaning back in her chair, she pursed her lips to expel a delicate stream of blue smoke. It

263

wafted toward a pastel mural depicting what Norah supposed was an Italian fishing village. "I don't expect an immediate decision, sugar, but will you consider my offer?"

Kick me, Norah nearly said. *Blow smoke in my eyes. Convince me this isn't the most vivid daydream I've ever created.* "Of course," she said before her arid, incredulous tongue pasted itself to the roof of her mouth. She leaned back, too, hoping she appeared nonplussed, a girl accustomed to receiving job offers during elegant restaurant suppers.

Mrs. Hamilton's cigarette tip glowed like an ember in Mutti's stove, an object that seemed a thousand miles away. "What do they pay you at Wright-Metzler's?"

Norah reached for her water glass. She'd no sooner drained it than Marco's pitcher set it brimming again. She waited until he backed away before blurting out her salary.

Mrs. Hamilton's tongue clicked. "Ridiculous. How old are you? Twenty-four?"

"Twenty-nine," Norah admitted. Her mouth still felt as if it was caked with sawdust.

"They're taking advantage, sugar. That happens so often to women in the workplace. My father taught me early on that the most desirable employer is always oneself." Smoke curled like a gauzy veil around Mrs. Hamilton's hat brim. "I'm prepared to pay double for the services of a mature young woman like you. With the war wreaking havoc in France, my customers need sound advice more than ever. I haven't been able to get a current issue of *Marie Claire* or any other Paris publication for over a year."

Norah's hand froze halfway to her water glass. Marco, the mural, the magic word—*double*—surely arose from an overactive imagination, a scene conjured to conceal the rain-streaked window of the streetcar, rattling inexorably toward The Hive.

"Father tells me quality fabrics will soon be impossible to come by. It will only get worse if America enters the war." Mrs. Hamilton shuddered. "Hollywood uses rayon now because it looks like silk under the lights. But truly, the very idea of a synthetic dinner dress makes my hair stand on end."

Norah nodded, as if the advent of rayon was every bit as regrettable as the Nazi occupation of Paris. Her heart, meanwhile, leaped at the prospect of sudden, stunning wealth. With a doubled salary, she could save up and buy Mutti an electric stove. And then a Maytag washing machine, just like Mrs. Zekula's. In time, perhaps, even a refrigerator.

Mrs. Hamilton ground out her cigarette in a cut-glass ashtray—immediately exchanged for a pristine replacement by the vigilant Marco. "Forgive me for talking business before we've eaten. Let's start with some warm minestrone to put the roses back in your pretty Irish cheeks."

Norah's eyes flew to the menu. How much did minestrone cost?

She started when Mrs. Hamilton's hand, furtive as Marco's, covered hers. "When I invite someone to dinner, sugar, I expect her to be my guest. If you reach for the bill, why, I'll have to forget my manners and spear your little old hand with my fork. Surely you wouldn't want me to engage in such rude behavior as that." After an unquestionably affectionate squeeze, Mrs. Hamilton's hand retreated.

Like a genie from a magic lamp, Marco reappeared with a pencil and tablet. "I highly recommend the scampi tonight, *Signora* Hamilton."

"Is shrimp to your liking, Norah?" Mrs. Hamilton asked.

Norah nodded, unwilling to trust her voice. Scampi, minestrone, the sole of her shoe—she'd gladly eat anything Marco's solicitous hand set before her.

"And please bring us a bottle of Chianti," Mrs. Hamilton added, smiling across the table at Norah. "I'd like to toast my new assistant."

Marco recorded the remainder of Mrs. Hamilton's order, none of which Norah remembered as he took her menu. Swallowing hard, she found the nerve to ask, "Why are you hiring me?" *I've never sold a thing in my life.* She had, of course, working in the notions section of the Company store. That retail establishment bore as much resemblance to La Femme as St. Barbara's worn costume resembled Hepburn's bridal gown in *The Philadelphia Story*. Would Mrs. Hamilton withdraw her offer if she knew her country club customers would be assisted by a patch girl who made over bargain basement dresses—and from the clearance rack, to boot?

Before Mrs. Hamilton could reply, Marco returned with a straw-covered bottle and two wine glasses. "Let my new assistant have the first taste," Mrs. Hamilton directed. Marco obligingly poured a small ruby pool into Norah's glass, then showed her the bottle's label as if it were suddenly of the utmost importance.

Norah had tasted homemade wine at the Tonelli girls' weddings, but never anything poured from a labeled bottle. After a cautious sip, she automatically declared it delicious— then realized it was true. Did wrapping a wine bottle in straw somehow enhance the flavor of its contents? She took another sip, knowing better than to ask.

"*Grazie, signorina*," Marco replied, patiently waiting until she set down her glass. With genie-like efficiency, he filled it, then Mrs. Hamilton's, before vanishing again.

Mrs. Hamilton lifted her glass and gently tapped its rim against Norah's. A slow, discerning sip. A satisfied nod. Lowering her glass, she said, "I'm hiring you because you have a sense of style. I've noticed how you trim a common hat or dress and make it special. That's instinct, sugar, something you share with Chanel and Schiaparelli. It's what my customers pay for. Not just the frock or handbag, but the eye of someone who can put together an ensemble that flatters the customer and makes her feel like she's the prettiest thing on two legs."

Two large swallows of wine washed the sawdust from Norah's tongue. The candlelight and cottages painted on the wall had become details from a movie in which she, incredibly enough, had been offered a starring role. This was how an elevator girl felt when Florenz Ziegfeld boarded and recruited her for The Follies. Still, Norah felt obliged to confess, "It's not really instinct. I saw it in a movie, six or seven years ago. *Alice Adams*. Katharine Hepburn was nominated for Best Actress."

Marco delivered steaming bowls of minestrone and a basket of bread nestled in another spotless napkin. "*Bene appetito*," he said before melting away.

Mrs. Hamilton smiled and sipped her wine. "I believe I did see that film. But it's been awhile, hasn't it? Refresh my memory while our soup cools."

"Well, Hepburn plays a poor girl, Alice, whose pap, I mean, her father isn't very successful. She's good and sweet and never complains about not mixing with girls who can afford new clothes and get invited to all the high-class parties. She just does the best she can with what she has, adding ribbons to a dress, or a new collar, some small thing to change the look even a little. She tries to pretend she's not poor, but this nice young fella finds out—that's Fred MacMurray—and falls in love with her anyway."

"So you learned your fashion tricks from a movie?" Mrs. Hamilton set down her wine glass and tasted her soup. "Not too hot now. Try it, sugar." As Norah obeyed, Mrs. Hamilton regarded her with a smile. "Have you a handsome suitor like Alice Adams?"

A noodle slid the wrong way down Norah's throat. She coughed and sputtered as Mrs. Hamilton urged her to take a drink of water. Dabbing her eyes with her napkin—was that bad manners?—she managed, at last, to speak. "I used to, but he married another girl. The young man who fixes your car? Paul Visocky? Him."

Jesus, Mary, and Joseph! What had possessed her to share something so deeply personal and painful with her future employer? Bad manners or not, she had no choice but to use her napkin again as a hankie. She couldn't bring herself to look at Mrs. Hamilton, who probably regretted that she'd offered a fine job to a girl who displayed such a glaring lack of professionalism.

"I'm so sorry, sugar. Mr. Visocky seemed like a fine person. Why, it just goes to show how appearances can deceive."

"Oh, not at all!" A scarlet-fever feeling burned Norah's face. "Paul *is* a fine man. We went steady for years, and he wanted to marry me, but I just couldn't leave—" Her lips snapped shut. She'd talked herself into a situation more embarrassing than her fire-escape exit.

"Not another word, my dear," said Mrs. Hamilton. "I've been unlucky at love myself. Let's talk instead about how much I'm going to enjoy having you as an assistant."

Norah nodded, forcing a wobbly smile. She took a shaky sip of wine, then quickly set down the glass. In addition to the daunting task of assisting La Femme's country club clientele, she'd have to wait on Grace. What if Paul accompanied his wife to the shop? How on earth would she possibly maintain even a semblance of professionalism then?

"The first order of business, sugar, will be outfitting you properly," said Mrs. Hamilton between spoonfuls of soup. "We want you looking like you walked straight off a page in *Vogue*. This, of course, is at the shop's expense. Could you possibly come by after work tomorrow so we can start assembling your professional wardrobe?"

Norah couldn't speak. She could barely bring herself to nod. A doubled salary and a *Vogue*-worthy wardrobe, to boot? Under such circumstances, how could she even consider saying no? If Grace—with or without Paul—came into La Femme, she'd have to pretend with all her might that she was Hepburn—and act accordingly. Surely assuming a movie star's demeanor would come more easily if she were actually dressed like one.

"Thank you," she said, forcing back tears. It simply wouldn't do to mop her face with her napkin a third time, despite what could only be considered a miracle. Maybe this was God's way of making up for the unearned penance of her role in the wretched pageant. Then an unnerving thought struck her. Perhaps this was God's reward. Perhaps He was assuring her that the heartbreaking decision she'd made that cold night in early March had been the right one.

"Wonderful! I'll expect you shortly after five." Mrs. Hamilton finished her soup and encouraged Norah to resume eating hers. "I believe that's quite enough business for now. Am I correct in assuming that you know almost as much about films as fashion?" She waved off Norah's emphatic denial. "Did you happen to see *Gone With the Wind*?"

"Four times! Although I still think Cukor or Selznick or whoever decided not to cast Hepburn as Scarlett O'Hara made a big mistake."

"Would you like to hear about the Atlanta premiere? I had the pleasure of attending."

Norah dropped her spoon into her soup—and left it there. "Tell me everything."

"She ate lunch with Clark Gable and Carol Lombard! And danced with George Reeves at the ball! He played one of the Tarleton boys. Remember that first scene when Scarlett can't decide who to go to the Wilkes' barbecue with?"

Pap rolled his eyes. "If she's good enough to hobnob with movie stars, what's she doing selling dresses in Uniontown?" he asked, shoveling pork roast into his mouth.

"It's complicated," said Norah. Her own dinner had gone largely untouched as she'd attempted to convey the wonder of the previous evening. "She comes from a well-off family in Athens, not far from Atlanta. Her pap owns cotton mills, successful ones. She has enough money to sit at home and have her maid wait on her morning, noon, and night, but she's always been involved in the family business. She's got a head for it, she says."

"Her pap's probably another King Frick. Filling his pockets while his workers barely scrape by. In Georgia, you say? Sonofabitch probably owns slaves, too."

"For heaven's sake, Fin, that was back in the last century," said Mutti, provoking a glare from Pap.

"She says I have fashion sense like Elsa Schiaparelli," Norah added proudly.

"Who's that? Mussolini's sister?" Pap countered.

"Of course not! Schiaparelli's a famous designer. She created—" Norah caught herself before mentioning German-born Marlene Dietrich's striking man-tailored suits. Giving up on Pap, Norah turned to Mutti. "Mrs. Hamilton went to college at Bryn Mawr when Katharine Hepburn was there! They didn't have the same classes, but she said she often saw Hepburn on campus. If you ask me, Mrs. Hamilton is every bit as elegant as a movie star. Even her name is elegant—Rosalind—like Rosalind Russell. But she said I should call her Roz."

Pap snorted. "Sounds like a dog growling."

"I'm just thankful she's given Norah such a fine job," Mutti declared.

Pap sent a sharp look across the table at Norah. "'Tis a pity we don't have movie stars lollygagging about, waiting to dance with you. It may be a fine job you're getting, but 'twon't be doing you much good, thinking yourself finer than you are on account of it."

Norah regarded him without, she hoped, a trace of expression. How could she have borne it if Roz had insisted on driving her home the previous evening? Simply talking about Roz in Pap's derisive presence seemed like a sin.

"Watch the time, Norah," Mutti warned. "I saw Maeve at the store this morning. She's counting on you to set a good example for the other players."

"She's the director. It's her job to make them do what she wants," said Norah.

Pap cut another slice of bread. "Remember, it's your name they'll be printing at the top of the program."

It's your name you're thinking of, not mine. Norah scraped her plate into the garbage bucket, handed it to Mutti, and left the kitchen without bothering to ease the screen door shut. Mutti's voice rose above the *bang!* "You forgot your script!"

"Don't need it!" Norah called back. It rankled her to admit that Mrs. Keating was right: she'd learned the role in no time. Still, try as she might, she couldn't imagine herself in costume, saying her lines before a standing-room-only crowd. Nor could she yet see herself wearing La Femme dresses that, Roz insisted, would tempt customers into purchasing their own. With such a miracle set to occur in just five days, how could St. Barbara's martyrdom, now in its thirteenth reprise, seem anything but stale?

Chapter 39: Clare
May 27, 1941
Feast of St. Bruno of Würzburg, Bishop

Liebe Clara,
Let me lay any fears to rest. Absolutely no one at St.
Marienkirche favors Hitler. Nor do they offer financial
support to the Axis alliance in Europe or equally dreadful
American fascist groups like the Bund. Indeed, I can no longer
bring myself to listen to Fr. Coughlin's radio program. I can't
shake my suspicion that he is mixed up with the Christian
Front...
As for Norah, you need not give her up. How often have I
urged you to leave? How often have I promised that such
action would not lead to destitution, but gainful employment
at Heinz...
I recently purchased a sound brick house with two large
bedrooms on Lockhart Street. The towers of St. Marienkirche
are easily visible from my front windows. I often see Katie,
sweet-faced Sr. Mary Gertrude, shepherding her small
charges...
I will welcome Norah with open arms, and you as well. I
have enclosed a check for sufficient funds to ensure that you
both may travel comfortably...
With all my love, Trudy

Clare smoothed the stationery, as if touching it somehow
allowed her to feel the curve of Katie's cheek, a lock of Deirdre's
hair, the sweet weight of the grandson she'd never seen. Thirty-
one years ago, she'd recklessly spent a week's wages to take the
train to Pittsburgh and meet Trudy for a restaurant lunch and
orchestra concert. Would Clare recognize her now—a
homeowner, an assistant chef in a Heinz factory test kitchen, a
self-sufficient woman making her own way in the world?

What better model for Norah?

Clare was startled by the mine whistle, signaling the day
shift's end. Her eyes darted to the clock, which told her that
she'd spent more than an hour woolgathering. She hurried

271

Trudy's letter into the stove, where it crackled and burst into flame. Before she could drop the cashier's check into the blaze, her hand drew back. Making her way into the pantry, she folded the check again and again, then pushed it deep into a sack of rice. Three times, she knotted the twine. Each knot, a wish. *Keep this, my daughter's fare to freedom, safe from my husband's eyes.*

With haste, she spread towels on the floor and placed the washtub in the center. She'd need a small miracle to have the tub ready when Fin arrived. Though the kitchen now had running water, Fin insisted that what flowed from the tap wasn't hot enough to clean a miner. She filled the kettle and two deep pots and set them on the stove. To the tub, she added a pail of tap water, hoping that just once he'd excuse a bath that wasn't steaming.

Pacing beside the stove, she heard his sarcastic reminder. *Beauty won't make the kettle boil.* She glanced down at her flour-sack apron, spotted with old stains. Were it not for her apron strings wound twice around her middle, her dress would dangle, shapeless as a curtain. As a girl, she'd done her share of primping, but the marriage bed had quickly cured her of foolish notions about the value of rosebud lips or a shapely figure. Fin cared nothing for her appearance, which may have explained why damaging it never seemed to engender regret. With no ball to throw or bat to swing, what energy left in him after a day spent wrestling with the coal-cutter had no outlet but lust. As long as she had legs to spread, she need not be beautiful, much less cooperative. She need only be.

It had taken her more than twenty years to realize that he derived as much satisfaction from demanding and hearing her *yes* as from the act itself. *Will you do your duty? Will you, will you,* night after night. *Yes.* Whispered and sobbed and moaned. *Yes. Yes. Yes.* But no more.

Though his strength would always enable him to have his way with her body, she had taken back her voice. He persisted in his demand—*Will you, goddamnit?*—but to no avail. Though he tried to slap and bite and choke that *yes* out of her, she remained inexorably mute. Despite his punishments, he'd never hear her speak her capitulation again.

A clap of thunder drew her attention back to the neglected tub and simmering pots. She checked the clock again. Forty minutes had passed since she'd heard the whistle, but there was still no sign of Fin. She dipped tepid water from the tub and replaced it with the contents of a steaming kettle. Returning the refilled kettle to the stove, she carried the bucket outside to the garden. Storm clouds clotted the sky, but she watered the tomatoes anyway.

Concetta stood at the Tonellis' gate, ignoring the rain that began to fall. "So late," she called to Clare. "Something bad, you think? We maybe should go see?"

Clare looked toward the slate dump. Kamila stood on her porch, rocking back and forth. A bubble of worry swelled in Clare's chest until Kamila flapped her apron. "They're coming!"

Clare ran inside to empty the heated water into a tub that was barely warm. Quickly, she refilled the kettle and pots as Fin opened the gate. He strolled with a spring in his step, in no apparent hurry to escape the rain. His bucket swung like a schoolboy's. As he neared the porch, she was stunned to hear whistling, a habit he'd abandoned the summer Jack had been arrested.

Unable to contain her curiosity, she stepped onto the porch. "A good day, then?"

"Not for Hitler. They had the radio on in the lamp house. A British battleship torpedoed the Bismarck. Sent the fucking boat and two thousand Nazi devils to the bottom of the sea." Fin tossed her his bucket, which she managed to catch, and went inside. Just before the door slammed, he called, "If I hear a word out of you, feeling sorry for those drowned bastards, I'll wash your mouth out with me soap, I swear to Jesus."

The unmistakable scent of whiskey trailed him across the porch. So that's why he was late, and the others with him. They'd all stopped at Boyle's to toast a well-aimed torpedo.

Warily, she entered the kitchen. He'd stripped to the waist and knelt on the towels, cursing his aging knees and back. Leaving the bucket inside the door, she hastened to the stove.

He plunged his hands into the tub. "What's this, then? Ice water for me aching bones?" He glared at her as she snatched a potholder and lifted the hissing kettle. "Are you trying to kill me with the shock?"

She stepped toward him, steam curling around her like incense from Fr. Kovacs' censer. For a moment, she felt as powerful as a Cossack. In her hand she held the means to blind Fin's eyes and blister his skin. To exact revenge for every torment he'd inflicted on her. The steam thickened into an opaque wall between them. She needed only to step through it. Swing the kettle. And aim.

"Are you thinking 'tis funny, then, standing there with your goddamn kettle while I'm left filthy and shivering? 'Tis a poor joke, tormenting your husband after a hard day's work."

Like a rush of wind, his words dissolved the steam. Blisters, blindness, grievous pain—such would render most men senseless. Fin's muscles and rage, however, were more powerful than boiling water. Clare's hand trembled beneath the kettle's weight. Only a roof fall—or bullet—could stop him. His bloodshot eyes narrowed. Did his whiskey-drenched brain comprehend how strenuously she was tempted?

An oily film glazed the tub water, mottled with gray droplets raining from his upraised hands. He coughed and spit black mucous onto a towel. When he looked back at her, his expression was as easy to read as a newspaper headline. *Go on. I dare you.*

Words squeezed past her pounding heart. "Careful now, so you won't get burned."

Fin drew back his arms. Dark rivulets streamed onto the towel beneath his knees. She crouched and tipped the kettle. He tested the water again and scowled. "'Tis a penance, this bath, but 'twill have to do."

Lathering his face and chest, he muttered as she refilled the kettle. She set it on the stove and, struggling to keep her voice steady, asked, "Shall I wash your back now?"

"Ah, no, why trouble yourself? 'Twould seem just heating water is too much effort."

"I was outside, watching the alley. Concetta was, too, and Kamila. We were worried—"

"Outside, the lot of you, gossiping when you should've been filling the tubs. If you'd had the sense to turn on the radio, you'd've known what's what. Don't be pretending you've no interest in what your goddamn *Führer*'s up to."

He rocked back on his heels. She emptied the pots into the tub, unable to think of a comment that might distract him. He watched in silence, giving her hope that this daily ritual would soon be over and done with.

She glanced at the clock, hoping that Norah wasn't getting off the streetcar. *Gott bewahre*, God forbid she should return just then and provide Fin with another target. Soon, soon, Clare had to find the words to tell Norah what sort of woman she steadfastly defended. And then steel herself for the sight of her daughter, turning forever away.

Fin's arms plunged back into the gray suds. He groaned softly, lungs rattling. His head dropped between hunched shoulders. Clare knelt behind him and soaped a fresh rag, then worked it as hard as she could up and down his back. Though she plied the cloth till her arms ached, his skin remained dusky. Any man who'd mined as many years as Fin had bug dust embedded in his pores. The stain could never be erased, not even with harsh strokes of a floor-scrubbing brush that some men insisted upon.

"All done," Clare said, drying his back with a towel. "I thought I'd pull some onions—"

She gasped as his wet fist seized her sleeve. His furious speech sent flecks of whiskey-tinged spittle onto her face. "I'm offered a chilly bath unfit for a dog. Then, for me privates, I'm left with liquid as black and cold as what's pumped out of No. 2? You'll empty this worthless tub onto your goddamn onions and fill me a fresh bath with water hot enough to brew tea."

Her arm throbbed in his grasp. "That will take time, Fin. I haven't yet started sup—"

"You're doubting me, then? Take a dip yourself, and you'll be changing your tune."

His other hand grabbed her hair and plunged her head into the sooty soup. Putrid water flooded her mouth and burned her eyes, shut too late. She spluttered and thrashed as her chin scraped the tub's bottom. Was this how it would end, her lot not so unlike those sailors lost with the Bismarck? Had this been his intent from the moment he'd entered the kitchen? Or had he sensed *her* fleeting impulse? Was this punishment for imagining that she and her puny kettle could fell the mighty Steamshovel?

He hauled her out of the water. "Are you agreeing with me now?" She coughed, unable to reply, and he interpreted this as hubris. "Ah, well, maybe you're needing a deeper drink."

Before she could catch her breath, she was plunged again. Her forehead struck metal. The blackness exploded like a sky filled with fireworks. Was that what they'd seen when the torpedo hit?

How did he know she'd be feeling sorry? No one should have to die like this.

Chapter 40: Norah

"I never imagined I'd be *studying* fashion magazines," said Norah, raising her voice over the restaurant's din.

Across the table, June and Carol Ann exchanged glances. Envy and surprise registered on their faces. And something else, too, something Norah couldn't name.

"We have to make do with *Vogue* and *Harper's Bazaar* until the war's over. Roz can't wait to go back to Paris and see the big fashion shows. And—" Norah leaned across the Cobb salad she'd barely touched—"she says she'll take me along!"

June and Carol Ann simultaneously lowered their forks. "You are the luckiest girl in Pennsylvania," Carol Ann declared. "I was sure you'd cooked your goose, climbing out her office window."

The waitress paused beside their booth, hefting a coffee pot. "You girls need a refill?"

Carol Ann offered her cup. As the waitress poured, coffee slopped onto the saucer and muddied the paper placemat. She nudged the cup toward Carol Ann and hurried away.

Aproned hips thumped the swinging kitchen door. A busboy's dish tub rattled. Someone guffawed, and a raucous hand smacked a table. Norah cringed. Why had she agreed to meet here? Four blocks away, Marco hovered beside diners who modulated their conversations, wore discreet dabs of *Je Reviens*, and refrained from punishing the furniture. She nibbled a slice of hardboiled egg, taking shallow breaths of air redolent with cigarette smoke, beef grease, and *Evening in Paris*, a fragrance so cheap and common you could buy it at the Company store.

June smoothed her pink gingham smock, gently rounded over the pregnancy that had prompted her retirement from Wright-Metzler's switchboard. Her eyes settled covetously on Norah's powder blue crepe. "I saw a photo of Ginger Rogers wearing a turban just like yours."

"Do you like it?" Norah turned her head, patting the curls clustered at her neck. "I sold three this morning. Roz says the best sales pitch doesn't use words. If you look good in something, nine chances out of ten, customers believe they'll look good in it, too." Her hand descended to her smartly padded shoulder. She couldn't resist brushing away a bit of lint, with her friends' eyes following her every move.

Carol Ann stabbed a tomato wedge, spraying pale red juice across Norah's placemat. "If your closet gets too crowded, I'll be happy to take a few dresses off your hands."

It may be a fine job you're getting, but 'twon't be doing you much good, thinking yourself finer than you are on account of it. Unbidden, Pap's warning jabbed Norah's insides with the vigor of Carol Ann's fork. Had Norah started to put on airs, looking down her nose at the coffee-stained table and cheap gingham, at everyone and everything inside the noisy diner? If she didn't take care, she'd lose her friends by acting like an upperhiller. She set down her fork and smiled at June and Carol Ann as if they were La Femme's best customers. "If I tell you a secret, will you promise not to spread it around?"

"About Paris?" asked Carol Ann.

"About Roz." Norah lowered her voice. "She's been married twice."

"Twice?" June's jaw sagged.

Carol Ann planted her elbows on either side of her plate. "Did her husbands run off?"

"Roz married right out of college to a boy she grew up with. Then she fell for someone else, an older man from Pittsburgh. He forbid her to work after she had a baby, so she left him." Norah sat back, proud of herself for recalling Pap's warning. No matter where she worked or how she dressed, she'd make sure Carol Ann and June knew she was still just one of the girls.

June rolled her eyes. "Why would a woman with a baby *want* to work?"

"Was he too proud to let her earn the money instead of him?" asked Carol Ann. "I read a story in *Love Fiction Monthly* about this girl who—"

"It's got nothing to do with money," said Norah, forgetting to keep her voice down. "Her pap's worth as much as the Mellons, and she'll inherit it all. Her ex-husband has money, too. Plus a lot of outdated ideas about what women should and shouldn't do."

"I certainly don't think being a good mother is outdated." June rested a proprietary hand on her smock and eyed Norah's dress as if its bodice buttons had changed into a scarlet letter. "Did she run off and leave her baby, too?"

"Of course not." Norah was beginning to regret her impulse to confide in a girl who apparently couldn't see past her own belly. "Roz bought a house in the East End near her ex-husband's so she'd be close to Aaron. She thought it was best for a boy to live with his father."

Carol Ann sighed. "She gave up her son. That's so tragic."

"Aaron's an odd name," said June. "I don't know a single boy—"

"Roz had a dress shop in Pittsburgh, downtown in Jenkins Arcade. A really successful one," Norah added, for June's benefit, "until the St. Patrick's Day Flood ruined it. After that, she said she'd never set up shop in a city with even one river, much less three. She has an old friend here, a banker's wife, who said she'd do really well, since anyone who's anyone in Uniontown goes to Pittsburgh to buy their clothes." Norah returned to her salad, wondering how she could change the subject.

"Rich people shop here," said Carol Ann. "I waited on the mayor's wife just yesterday."

"She left her baby in Pittsburgh? That's a mortal sin, if you ask me," June declared.

Norah breathed deeply before replying, "Aaron's seven years old, and he has a stepmother now, so he's not out roaming the streets. Roz hired me so she could take some Saturdays off and visit him without having to close the shop."

"Decent women wouldn't step one foot inside her shop if they knew about this," declared June. "I sure won't once I fit into regular clothes again." She bit primly into her club sandwich.

You couldn't afford so much as a belt from La Femme. Norah gnawed the inside of her cheek until she could speak civilly. "Divorce isn't against the law."

"As long as she's not Catholic," Carol Ann said earnestly. "She isn't, is she?"

"She's Jewish. Her family name used to be Himmelmann, but her pap changed it to Hamilton when the Great War broke out." Norah balled up her napkin and dropped it onto the table. "Changed it legally," she added, before June could deride that action as sinful, too.

June lowered her sandwich to her plate. "You work for a *Jew*? My husband says—"

"I work for Roz Hamilton," said Norah, "the kindest, most generous woman I've ever met." She slapped a dollar bill onto the table and slid out of the booth. Carol Ann called after her, but she made her exit without so much as a backward glance.

When thunder rattled the jeweler's window, Norah paused beneath its awning to open her umbrella. *Gott sei Dank*, thank God she hadn't left it in the booth with the small-minded girls she was no longer sure she wanted as friends. Mindful of her delicate dress, she huddled against the building to avoid the rain. Her umbrella's catch jammed. A spoke popped free and drilled the inside of her right wrist. The umbrella had no sooner fallen to the sidewalk than a voice, achingly familiar and completely unexpected, asked behind her, "Need a hand?"

Holding her bleeding wrist away from her dress, she turned to find Paul, dry and dapper as a banker beneath a large black umbrella. "What I need," she said, "is a bandage."

Before she could blink, she was holding his umbrella. With fingers faintly stained with automotive grease, he clumsily wrapped her wrist with his monogrammed handkerchief. "I'm a lot better with spark plugs," he admitted. "But this will keep you from spoiling your dress." He released her wrist, swathed in a fat cotton bracelet with a prominent navy **P**.

"I'll spoil your handkerchief instead." She tried to return his umbrella, but he had stooped to retrieve hers. "Now your back's all wet. I've spoiled your suit, too."

"It'll dry," he said. In a single motion, he straightened up and forced her navy umbrella open. It bumped the black one, with which Norah was attempting to shield his suit, and knocked it to the pavement.

"Jesus, Mary, and Joseph," she murmured, cheeks burning. The capricious wind swept beneath the awning, setting it aflutter and the black umbrella, like an unwieldy kite, aloft. With timing befitting the most carefully rehearsed movie pratfall, she lunged for its handle as he lunged, too. She recaptured his umbrella. Her navy one, in his hand, snagged her turban. It whirled into the gutter, brimming with water as dark as the contents of a miner's bathtub.

"Stay put," Paul said, then sprinted to retrieve her headpiece. Uncannily reading her mind, he called back, "If Abbott and Costello had seen that, they'd put us in their next picture." He returned to the awning and regretfully handed her the dripping turban.

She thanked him, pretending not to notice when their fingers brushed. He noticed the dangling spoke on her umbrella and, with a quick twist, snapped off the broken metal and dropped it onto the sidewalk. When they'd successfully exchanged umbrellas, gratitude washed through her. Just as he'd done so many times since they were schoolmates, he'd made an awkward situation, if not easy, then at least a little less awkward.

Rain drummed the awning and descended in a dull silver curtain behind Paul, who'd turned as quiet as she. The oil-stained ridge of his knuckles stood out like a bruise. He regarded her with an expression both endearing and alarming.

She remembered with startling clarity a long-ago argument with Katie, who'd called Paul handsome. Norah had been quick to set her straight: *Cary Grant is handsome. Paul is just ordinary.* Compared to aristocratic Cary Grant or rakish Clark Gable, Jimmy Stewart could seem rather ordinary, too. Now, however, against the stark backdrop of a downpour, Paul looked every inch the leading man—a workingman's leading man. "You look like a banker, decked out like that," she said, hoping the vigorous rain covered the catch in her voice.

He stared at the dropped umbrella spoke. "I had an appointment with a banker, as a matter of fact. I'm buying a new building. Business is good, and I need more space."

Her gaze dropped, too. "How wonderful." She might have been praising his shoes. Grace needed to be mentioned, so Norah did, staring at the soaked sidewalk. "I'm working at the dress shop Grace—" How on earth could Norah phrase this casually, an oh-by-the-way comment, not an I-was-spying confession? "I think I saw Grace driving—"

"A convertible?" said Paul, rescuing her again. "That was my wedding gift. I rebuilt—"

When Norah looked up, her eyes met Paul's. The knowledge embodied in his frank gaze startled her into an ungainly backward step. She righted herself quickly. She could not allow his hand, always at the ready to ease her way, to leave the safe haven of his pocket and touch her. She could not acknowledge with a syllable or the slightest gesture what she read on his face. *I would leave her if I had the slightest encouragement from you.*

How could the sidewalk, at this hour, remain so empty? The storm might have been apocalyptic, swiftly and stealthily drowning every other Uniontown inhabitant. She and Paul huddled beneath the awning, clutching their umbrellas like life preservers. Norah forced herself to turn and walk away. Lest she appear rude—she couldn't bear for him to think ill of her—she flapped the turban, a limp blue semaphore that signaled an ended conversation.

As she rounded the corner, an unfamiliar sensation overcame her. Lightheaded, she paused beneath the tom-tom of her umbrella to breathe deeply. She noticed her reflection in a shop window and studied the woman with the navy umbrella as if she had never seen her before.

I would leave her...

Power. This was the ineffable quality the woman in the window possessed. An altogether unexceptional woman for whom Paul Visocky, nonetheless, would abandon his new wife. The realization nearly upended her. Each day, she waited on the wives and daughters of the wealthy, envying their access to country clubs, fine restaurants, and Pittsburgh pleasures she couldn't begin to imagine. Compared to them, she was nothing, had nothing, or so she'd thought. Having witnessed Paul's unvoiced confession, she understood that she was capable, not just of ending his marriage, but claiming anything else she truly wanted and was willing to work for.

"Good gracious, you look half-drowned!" Roz exclaimed when Norah returned to La Femme. "I declare, I haven't seen so much rain since that dreadful flood in '36."

Norah set her umbrella in the brass stand beside the entrance. On the floor lay a folded paper bearing the moist gray imprint of her shoe. She picked it up and offered it to Roz, who'd taken the sodden blue turban in hand for closer inspection. "I'm sorry, Roz, I stepped on your mail. The postman must've dropped it."

Tongue clucking over the headpiece, Roz shot her a distracted glance. "It's probably a solicitation. Just throw it away."

Norah unfolded the paper. The sloppily printed words fairly leaped from the page.

NO PLACE HERE FOR CROOKED JEWS
GET OUT BEFORE ITS TOO LATE

"Roz," she whispered. The paper quivered in her hand. "Roz, look."

As Roz scanned the message, her lips drew together like a puckered zipper. She crumpled the paper and regarded Norah. "Let's get you out of those wet clothes. There's a robe in my office. This time—" she shocked Norah by smiling—"I trust you won't use my window as an escape hatch. Why, sugar, what's the matter?"

Norah covered her face with her hands. *You work for a Jew? My husband says...* Surely it wasn't possible for June already to have told her husband what Norah had told her, and for him to have scrawled those hateful words, then made his way across town to slip the paper under Roz's door. "It's all my fault," Norah admitted, lowering her hands. Overwhelmed with shame, she stared at the floor. "At lunch, I told my friends—"

"That I'm Jewish?" At the sound of Roz's rippling laughter Norah looked up in surprise. "Trust me, sugar, everyone in town—the butcher, the baker, and candlestick maker—knows that. And that I've divorced two husbands. And that Hamilton probably isn't my real name." Roz drew a hankie from her pocket and passed it to Norah. "Now dry that pretty face of yours. You're wet enough already."

"Aren't you afraid?"

"Frankly, I think my notorious past is good for business."

Norah obediently dabbed her eyes. "That note might've come from the Klan. It's still around, you know."

"Of course, I know. It's certainly not the first time I've received something like this."

Norah dropped the hankie. "Jesus, Mary, and Joseph."

Roz's laughter trilled again. "See there? I have a good, upstanding Christian in my employ, so nothing untoward is going to happen." She retrieved the hankie and eyed the crumpled paper. "I'd love to put a match to the damn thing, but I suppose I should follow orders and phone in a complaint."

Chilled by her clammy dress, Norah suppressed a shiver. "Whose orders?"

"The police." Roz spoke without a trace of concern, as if dealing with the law was of no greater consequence than a dropped hankie. "I've encountered some version of this ever since I can remember. Hateful people only have as much power as you give them. I assure you, sugar, I neither cower nor run from anyone."

Roz steered Norah into the bride's room, then retrieved a flannel robe from her office. "I keep it around to snuggle up in when I'm here late working on the books. Put it on while I phone the police station." Handing the robe to Norah, she snapped her fingers. "I was going to let you hold the fort this weekend while I went to Pittsburgh. However, I just reconsidered. We'll *both* go to Pittsburgh and see what our big-city competition is up to."

"Who will hold the fort then?" asked Norah. She realized she was wringing the robe and hastily draped it over her arm. *Who will watch out for Mutti?*

284

Roz waved the paper as if it were a magic wand. "I've closed on Saturdays before. And Friday is Decoration Day, so we'd be closed anyway. As long as Pittsburgh hasn't issued any flood warnings, I say we check into the William Penn Hotel and have ourselves a lovely time. Doesn't your sister live in Point Breeze? That's a hop, skip, and a jump away from my ex-husband. You can visit her while I spend time with Aaron."

Roz might as well have proposed that Norah go straight to Hollywood and present herself at Paramount Pictures for a screen test. "My mother—I can't possibly—"

"Of course you can. You have a promising career in fashion merchandising, and this will be your first business trip. Your mother can spare you for one weekend."

Norah felt a fresh surge of what had ambushed her on the street. No longer was she simply Mutti's daughter, a laughingstock St. Barbara, a stubborn spinster. She had a career, a promising one. She pushed away the image of Paul's face. He was part of her history, something she couldn't undo. The best way to forget him was to dive headlong into the remarkable new life Roz was offering her.

"I've never been to Pittsburgh," said Norah, suddenly and intensely giddy with anticipation. She nearly laughed, imagining Mrs. Keating's reaction to the news that St. Barbara would miss three rehearsals because she'd checked into the William Penn.

"What's this?" Roz asked, lifting Norah's bandaged wrist. Her eyes settled on the monogram, then rose to meet Norah's. "A painful encounter?"

"With my broken umbrella," Norah replied evenly. The wound began to throb. She hurried into the nearest dressing room and shut the door before Roz could ask another question.

Norah paused in surprise on the back porch. Half-past six—and Pap's washtub still occupied the middle of the kitchen floor. Not a whiff of supper hung in the air. "I'm home!" she called, uneasiness mounting when no one responded. She opened the screen and stepped inside, nearly tripping over two legs tangled in a grimy towel. With a cry, she dropped her purse and knelt beside Mutti, who lay in a cinder-flecked puddle beside the table.

Mutti shuddered as Norah lifted her head. A goose egg swelled on her forehead, purplish beneath the water's ashy scum. She began to cough. Thin gray vomit spilled between her lips, staining Norah's skirt.

"We need to clean you up," said Norah, trying to sound like a poised career girl who had a vexing situation well in hand. "Did you fall? Can you tell me what happened?"

"*Das Bismarck,*" Mutti whispered, "*ist gesunken.*"

"The Nazi boat sank? That's good news." Puzzled, Norah smoothed dank strings of hair back from Mutti's swollen forehead. How did a battleship figure in this mess?

Mutti opened eyes clogged with soot. "*Ist er blind? Tot?*" Is he blind? Dead?

"Who, Mutti?"

Mutti turned her head slowly and regarded the tub. "*Ich habe versagt,*" she said, shutting her eyes. I failed.

"You're going to be just fine," Norah assured the limp woman in her lap, the spent, sour-smelling woman who suddenly and profoundly disgusted her. "This won't happen again," she added fiercely, though she didn't believe it. *I assure you, sugar, I neither cower nor run from anyone.* Recalling Roz's declaration, Norah trembled with anger. "I'm going to Pittsburgh with Roz on Friday morning," she whispered, "and I'm not coming back till Sunday night. If you can't stay alive that long without me, it's not my fault." When Mutti stirred, Norah's pulse quickened. Had she heard?

Mutti's eyelids labored open. She breathed deeply, coughed, then breathed again. "I had my chance. I should have tried." She struggled to her feet, resisting Norah's attempt to take her arm. "When he gets home, I'll—" She took a step, swayed, then pitched sideways.

Norah sprang forward and helped Mutti to her chair. She nearly asked—*Did you hurt Pap?*—then dismissed the question as absurd. As Mutti muttered in German about the kettle, Norah filled it. The scab on her wrist throbbed as she shoveled coal into the stove. Right now, Paul might be reading the paper while Grace did the dishes. Or sitting with her on the couch, listening to *Riff Rhythm Quintet* on the radio. Or, upstairs in their fine brick house, trying to start their family.

Norah hurled the shovel into the coal bucket. Tight-lipped, she gathered towels and wiped up vomit. She felt Mutti's gaze following her, but kept her eyes fixed on the floor. She could already hear Mrs. Keating's rant about St. Barbara setting a bad example by being late that night for rehearsal. Hip-bumping the screen open, she dragged the washtub outside.

Black water cascaded over the side of the porch. Next door, Mrs. Tonelli stopped scattering chicken feed long enough to ask, "Your mama is needing maybe some help?"

Norah straightened up. If only she could nod and break the Sweeneys' unwritten code of silence. *My mother needs a new life, and quickly, before the one she has gets her killed. And I need a new life, too.* "No, thank you, Mrs. Tonelli," she replied. Forcing a smile, she took the tub back into the kitchen.

Chapter 41: Clare

May 30, 1941
Feast of St. Walstan, Penitent

"It's only three days," Norah lisped around a pearl-tipped hatpin.

"Enjoy every minute," Clare told her. "Make sure to ask Deirdre for new photographs of the children. Especially Will."

"I'm only going on account of my job," Norah said, sliding the pin through the black straw. The hat's short lace veil floated over the brim. She wore yet another new outfit, specially selected by her boss for the trip: a lightweight coat and matching dress, ivory piped with black. When she turned, the hemlines flared like morning glories.

Clare was about to brush away a speck of lint, then drew back her hand. Her chapped fingers might snag the fine fabric. "You look like a movie star."

Drawing on her gloves, Norah was quick to correct. "I look like a *career girl*. Don't forget to tell Mrs. Keating I'll be gone all weekend. She'll probably have a fit."

"You could play that part perfectly right now, and she knows it as well as I do."

Norah batted Clare's hand away from the handsome new leather suitcase. "I can manage."

So can I. If only Clare had the courage to say it. *I can survive without a captive saint beneath my roof.* Instead, she urged Norah to hurry so she wouldn't miss the streetcar. She suspected that Roz had offered to pick up Norah at home, and she was both glad and sorry that Norah had refused. A small, curious part of her wanted to meet the woman who treated her daughter with such kindness and generosity. But if Roz appeared at Clare's door, what on earth would Clare say to a rich, Southern, college-educated, Jewish businesswoman?

"If Mrs. Keating gives you a hard time, tell her I quit. That'll take the wind out of her sails," said Norah, stalking down the back steps. She wore tasteful pink lipstick and pearl earrings that gleamed against her hair's dark waves. The upperhiller wives'

Sunday best couldn't hold a candle to what Norah called her *professional wardrobe.*

"You should stay awhile longer," Clare suggested as they crossed Main Street. "Trudy would gladly put you up. She has a house now on the North Side. On Lockhart Street."

"I can't just go off gallivanting. I have a job, same as Pap. I have responsibilities."

Clare tried again. "You might at least visit Trudy."

The streetcar rattled into view. Norah boarded, calling over her shoulder, "It's a *business trip*, not a vacation. The only reason I'll see Deirdre is because Roz's son lives nearby."

Clare waved as the streetcar pulled away. Across the street, Ada Smiley stood in front of the store, supervising clerks as they hung bunting for the afternoon's Decoration Day parade. "Where's she off to, all gussied up and carrying a suitcase?" Ada called.

"A business trip to Pittsburgh," Clare replied. "She and her boss are staying at the William Penn." Clare knew it was petty, but she still felt positively elated when Ada gaped. Never had Clare stunned The Hive's pinch-faced busybody into silence.

Smiling, Clare headed for The Hall's auditorium. Maeve paced in front of the stage. She tapped her cheek with a pencil as she flipped through the papers on her clipboard. The players filed, silent as altar boys, into the first two rows. Maeve looked up, about to address her cast, then noticed Clare. "Rehearsals are closed to the public. You should know that by now, Clare."

Clare delivered Norah's message, taking care to keep her tone matter-of-fact.

"What kind of business could a shop girl have in Pittsburgh?" Maeve demanded.

Clare shrugged. "You'd have to ask her boss."

"That makes four missed rehearsals in one week." Maeve's pencil mercilessly beat her clipboard. "What kind of example is this for the rest of the cast?"

"They're *children*, Maeve. Norah is—a career girl." Clare congratulated herself for remembering the term her daughter held so dear. It struck her that she was enjoying this encounter even more than watching Ada's jaw drop.

Maeve turned back to the players, "Take your places for scene one. Where's my stage manager?"

"Sick, missus," ventured a girl in the second row.

"How sick?" Maeve asked.

Blushing, the girl sank in her seat. She whispered to the girl beside her, who sank, too. The boys in front of them began to snicker.

"Speak up!" said Maeve.

"Her monthly bill came early!" the girl shouted, covering her face with her script.

Laughter broke out. Maeve's face whipped toward Clare. "Here's a fine kettle of fish! No leading lady. No stage manager. I've got two weeks to be turning this sorry, disrespectful lot into real performers. How in heaven's name can I possibly be working that miracle when certain people take it into their heads to skip rehearsal at the drop of a hat?"

A chuckle escaped before Clare could suppress it. "Don't ask me, Maeve. I'm not the director."

Maeve's face turned ruddy. Before she could respond, Clare hurried outside, where the morning sun glanced off the streetcar tracks. Bunting fluttered from the porch of the Company store. As Clare turned toward it, the colors blanched. The light faded and, with it, Clare's amusement. By now, Norah was nearing Uniontown, exulting at the fairy-tale turn her life had taken. While she was off visiting Deirdre and experiencing city life, Clare would practice what she so dreaded to say. Then Norah would return, and Clare would say it—and Norah would pack her fine new suitcase again. Captive no more, she'd leave for good to live with Trudy.

After so many years, Clare could summon only a hazy mental picture of her cousin. How did she dress? What did she eat? The only kitchens Clare was familiar with were her own and those of her neighbors. What did a factory test kitchen look like? Surely it contained an electric stove, but how large? How many pots and pans? Did Heinz have more than one kitchen? Would Trudy make sure that Norah worked alongside her, at least in the beginning?

Clare paused in front of the church. These ruminations, however promising they might seem to her, would amount to little more than ashes for Norah. Compared to pretty dresses and business trips with the glamorous Roz, what possible allure would work in a pickle factory hold? Why would Norah abandon a rich patroness who treated her like a sister for a workaday cousin she'd never met?

Clare's feet turned purposeful, carrying her around the church to the cemetery. Her pace slowed as she approached her sons' splintery crosses. They regarded her like a three-member jury. *Tell us*, they commanded, *what you've never dared to tell anyone. Tell us exactly what you'll tell Norah.*

Clare dropped to her knees and wrapped her arms around her belly. Though her womb was long gone, the deep inner pain felt just like labor. She set her teeth and bore it, knowing that her memories wouldn't be birthed as easily as the three buried boys.

A year after flu had killed the first Finbar, his brother had entered the world. Whistling an Irish air, Fin had jigged around the bed with his swaddled son. The midwife had clucked her tongue and reclaimed the child, warning that such antics would bring on colic. Clare had put the second Finbar to her breast, gazing upon his whorl of dark hair, his tiny, flailing fists. Her heart had wrenched as she imagined pulling his eager mouth from her nipple and pressing the baby into the startled midwife's arms.

Take him away. Find him a home with a patient, gentle father. Take him now, before he catches Fin's whiskey-sickness. Before my heart breaks at losing yet another child.

Never known for generosity—except when treating his pals to whiskey—Fin took a bill from his wallet and handed it to the midwife, who nearly swooned with surprise. "'Tis the finest day of me life," he told her. "If I had a million dollars, I'd gladly give you half."

For three weeks, Fin was happier than Clare had ever seen him. The new Finbar, though beautiful and blameless, made her shiver with fear. His ceaseless colicky cries rang with the same ferocity as his father's rages. One endless night gave way to the next as she carried the wailing infant downstairs, so Fin's sleep wouldn't be disturbed. Hour after hour, she rocked and nursed and tried in vain to soothe the child, all the while praying for a miracle.

Help him withstand his heavy heritage. Help me shield him from his father's cruel example. Please, help me save some girl from marrying Fin's son and suffering deeply on account of it.

During those three weeks, she indulged the hope that the miracle had already occurred. Surely the presence of this longed-for boy would cure Fin's sickness, temper his nature. Her hope swelled as Fin indulged her, too. Having given him his heart's desire, she could do no wrong. Then the inevitable happened: he stumbled home late, reeking of the drink and raving about some Company injustice, and beat her for serving him a dried-out supper.

Exhausted by his rant, Fin stumbled off to bed, leaving her to pick herself up off the floor and face another sleepless night. She cradled the weeping babe against bruised ribs. Breathing as shallowly as possible, she guided his mouth again and again to her cracked nipples. Favoring her swelling ankle, she staggered back and forth across the kitchen, moaning each time his restless head thumped her tender collarbone. Darkness drained from the sky while she massaged his turgid belly and stroked his back. In the bleary blush of dawn, she sank into her chair with the inconsolable infant, aching down to her bones. Dimly, she heard the alarm clock ring, the thud of footsteps overhead. She mounded towels in the laundry basket and relinquished her weeping son just long enough to feed Fin breakfast and pack his bucket.

Before he departed, Fin bent over the basket to regard the child, thrashing and shrieking. "Starving the wee lad are you? Letting himself cry himself sick before troubling yourself to feed him?" Before she could protest, he drew back his hand and struck her jaw, knocking her against the stove.

Somehow she got to her feet and carried Finbar upstairs to the bedroom. His small fists pummeled an invisible target. She recoiled, face throbbing, as those tiny fingers turned dusky, each knuckle embedded with bug dust.

"Was ist mit ihm los?" What's the matter with him? She turned to find eight-year-old Norah in the doorway, worrying the yoke of her nightgown. "Should I get the doctor?"

Clare sensed that she asked, not just for Finbar, but also for her limping, wincing mother. "*Keine Sorge. Er hat nur Hunger,*" Clare assured her daughter. Don't worry. He's just hungry.

Two small white teeth gnawed Norah's lower lip. Her eyes fixed on Clare's, seeking an answer to the question she dared not speak aloud. *What happened last night after I went to bed?*

"Close the door while I feed him," Clare said. "Go back to bed with your sisters."

The door swung shut. A formidable roaring filled Clare's ears, overwhelming the baby's cries. She swayed, nearly falling, then forced her eyes open to behold an angel. Radiant and smiling, he rose from the cradle and held out his hands. The dregs of strength ebbed from her arms. She released the infant and let herself fall, embraced by darkness as black and silent as the shaft of an abandoned mine.

How long did she remain in this strange limbo? She recalled only that, when she emerged, she was sprawled across the bed in which her children had been conceived. Not so much as a whimper rose from Finbar's cradle. The door whined, nudged open by a smoky draft filtering through the window screen. She tiptoed out of the room so as not to wake her son, mercifully asleep.

Clare was stirring a pot of oatmeal when Norah screamed. Clare took the stairs two at a time. In the bedroom, Norah stood beside the cradle, hands pressed against her face. Her narrow shoulders heaved with sobs. Clare dropped to her knees and gathered up Finbar. Still and pale, his body flopped like a rag doll. Clare shouted at Norah to run for the doctor. Through the smudged window, she watched her son's soul rise like a perfect pearl through the cinder-clogged air.

The doctor assured her that the second Finbar, like so many other infants, had succumbed to crib death. She didn't believe him. Something dire had happened during her sojourn in darkness, something that had surely been her fault.

293

Chapter 42: Norah

"First time here?" asked the bellhop. He turned as he walked and held out his hand. Flustered, Norah fumbled her purse's clasp. "Your key, miss," he added, shaking his head to assure her that Roz's tip had been more than adequate. "These old locks can be tricky."

Norah waited meekly while he opened the door to her room. As he motioned her inside, she realized that he'd quickly sized her up as a wide-eyed bumpkin and was doing his professional best to put her at ease. "Oh my!" she exclaimed, then clapped a hand over her mouth. She'd just confirmed his assessment.

"Pretty swell, huh?" he said, removing a luggage stand from the closet.

"It's like walking onto a movie set," she marveled, taking in the satin-pillowed chaise and polished dresser, the wide bed with its royal canopy.

The bellhop set her suitcase on the stand. "It's called a duchesse bed. The thing hanging over it is a tester." He laughed at her expression. "Believe me, I didn't know that either till I got this job. They teach you the swanky lingo while you're in training."

Norah crossed the room to the window. Smoky clouds couldn't completely obscure her tenth-floor vista of stately skyscrapers, boxy warehouses, and automobiles—so many automobiles!—reduced to the size of toys. Grimy bridges spanned a river the color of soot. She motioned to the bellhop. "Is that the river that caused the St. Patrick's Day flood?"

He joined her at the window. "They all did. That one's the Allegheny. On the other side of us is the Monongahela. There to the left, they call that The Point. That's where the two rivers meet and turn into the Ohio."

"Those buildings across the bridges, are they part of Pittsburgh, too?"

294

"That's the North Side." He pointed to the right. "See those big smokestacks? That's the Heinz plant, where they make all the pickles and ketchup."

She caught her breath. "Is Deutschtown over there, too?"

He shrugged. "I guess so. I'm one hundred percent American, so I sure wouldn't live there. 'Specially not now, with Hitler raising hell every day."

"Only the Indians," she said crisply, "are one hundred percent American." She gave him a cool look. "Thanks for the information."

He shuffled his feet, awkwardly contrite. "I'm sorry I cussed like that. Don't tell anyone, okay? I could lose my job." Slowly, reluctantly, he reached into his pocket and held out the bill he'd received from Roz.

Why on earth would she—a career girl with promise—be intimidated by a boy who carried bags and unlocked doors for a living? She drew herself up, haughty as Hepburn. "I don't take bribes. I don't snitch on people either."

She waited until the door closed behind him, then turned back to the window. White smoke poured from the Heinz factory towers, changing the dark clouds around them to a light gray. Her gaze shifted left to a hazy clot of smaller buildings that intuition told her was Trudy's neighborhood. Somewhere in that haze was St. Marienkirche's convent, where Katie was grading papers or praying for Jack. Just down the street, Trudy busied herself in the house that belonged solely to her. Tomorrow, she might attend a concert, meeting a friend for a restaurant supper before the performance. On Sunday, she'd go to Mass and chat with Katie, then spend the afternoon taking a walk or visiting a museum. This was how an independent woman lived. Owning, if not a house, then at least every moment of every day of her life.

The doorknob rattled. "Ready, sugar?" Roz called.

"I'm coming!" Norah replied, even as she lingered at the window. Stripped of its satin drapes, it might have framed a view of The Hive's sky, back when she couldn't step outside without crunching coke cinders between her teeth. Suddenly she was eager to leave the movie-star room and enter a world awash in smoke, a world that seemed unexpectedly familiar. A rush of tears surprised her, and she paused to dry her eyes. "Coming!" she called again, recalling that brief time when she'd supposed smoke was just that, merely vapor, not a wall.

"Tell Roz you've decided to pursue your career somewhere else," said Deirdre, arranging in a crystal vase the gladioli Norah had brought. She looked pointedly at Norah, seated at the kitchen table, stirring sugar into her tea. "No fairy godmother is waiting behind the outhouse to turn you into Cinderella. If you want things to be different, you have to change them yourself."

Deirdre turned away to admire her arrangement. If she'd added, *just like me,* Norah would have upended her teacup onto the table's bright red enamel and stalked out the front door. "It's easy to say that now," she called as Deirdre carried the vase into the living room. "You've been away so long you don't remember what it's like."

Children's voices floated in from the backyard. Through the open window, Norah watched pigtailed Molly, a red-haired, eight-year-old replica of her mother, scold younger sisters Meg and Ginny for improperly spacing croquet wickets. Year-old Will crowed in his wooden swing, patiently pushed by Hattie, the young Negro maid.

Deirdre returned and poured herself a cup of tea. Twelve years of comfortable city life had changed the restless, headstrong Sweeney sister into a serene, self-assured matron. Her perfectly waved hair and smart clothes, the nonchalance with which she'd shown Norah around her spacious, modern house—all hallmarks of her impetuous leap from The Hive to the lofty, improbable realm of the well-to-do. She wrinkled her lightly powdered nose and reached for the sugar bowl. "When Mutti writes, all she says about Pap is that he's working six-day weeks. I assume that means he can afford to get twice as drunk before he beats her."

Though liberally sugared, Norah's tea tasted bitter. The image of Mutti, lying half-drowned on the kitchen floor, gnawed at her conscience. What if she returned home to find Mutti dead?

Deirdre flapped a manicured hand, dispelling what felt like a smothering cloud of coke smoke that had appeared out of nowhere to envelope the table. "Let's talk about something else, something fun. Who'd you throw Paul over for? Mutti wrote that he married Grace." Deirdre planted dimpled elbows on the table and rested her chin in her hands. She might have been twelve again, wondering aloud how it felt to be kissed.

"Nobody." How calm Norah sounded! Though it pained her to credit Mrs. Keating, perhaps the cranky director actually had taught her something about acting.

"You gave Paul the brush-off for no good reason?"

"I have plenty of reasons." For a moment Norah considered telling Deirdre about her rainy-day encounter with Paul. She'd noticed a copy of *Love Fiction Monthly* on Deirdre's nightstand. Her confidence could well be a lurid headline: *Miss Goody-Two-Shoes Admits Her Feelings for a Newly Married Man!*

Deirdre directed a no-nonsense look across the table. "You've lived so long with a martyr you're turning into one yourself."

"I'm a *career girl*. Paul wanted to start a big family right away, and I'd rather—"

"You'd rather live with a drunk and his punching bag and play-act a role you're ten years too old for." Deirdre rolled her eyes. "Oh, don't have kittens. Your boss won't pick you up for hours. Or are you planning to walk home?"

Norah hadn't realized she was standing. She lowered herself onto the chair, painted the same cheerful red as the Formica countertops. "I came here for a visit, not the third degree."

Deirdre reached across the table and clasped Norah's hand, a gesture so disarming that Norah's eyes filled with tears. "Want to hear a secret? Billy won't be back from his convention till Wednesday, so you're the first to know."

Norah blinked as hard and fast as she could. Two tears dropped anyway, leaving dark blots on her suit jacket's pale yellow lapel. "Tell me."

Deirdre produced a lacy hankie and passed it across the table. "I'm pregnant. Can you imagine? I finally lost the weight I gained with Will, and now I'll be back in those ugly smocks by Labor Day. I'm no different than a patch missus, popping out a baby every other year."

Norah laughed as she dabbed her eyes. "You're an East Ender with a house straight out of a magazine and a husband who makes lots of money." Norah flicked the hankie toward the backyard, where Hattie lifted Will from his swing. "And there isn't a single tomato stake out there. That's about as different from a patch missus as you can get."

Deirdre went to the window and beckoned to Hattie. "Let's go for a walk. I want you to see a local landmark. Will needs a nap, and he'll fall asleep right away in his buggy."

Norah followed Deirdre into the backyard, where a sturdy blue baby carriage was parked under the porch eaves. As Will, red-faced and fussy, passed from Hattie's arms to Deirdre's, Norah admired the sloping green lawn bordered with neatly clipped hedges and snowball bushes laden with white blossoms. Though Norah had never seen the Big Boss' Beetown property, she doubted it could be any finer than this.

Deirdre efficiently bedded down her thrashing son, then set off across the yard with the buggy. Norah surreptitiously checked her lapels, relieved that the tears had dried without leaving stains. They rounded the house and proceeded down the sidewalk. Every dwelling they passed displayed a greenhouse or gazebo, fish pond or fountain. "Roz calls this part of town Millionaires' Row."

Deirdre smiled, leaving Norah to surmise that the runaway deputy with whom her sister, in turn, had run away might someday be a millionaire himself—or was already. "Five years ago, Billy's father said self-service grocery shopping was sheer nonsense. Now he's renovating his stores into supermarkets. He even went with Billy to the convention," Deirdre said proudly.

"Is it wonderful, being rich?" asked Norah.

Deirdre threw back her head and laughed. "It's better than being a patch missus. But it doesn't mean nothing bad ever happens. The children get sick, Billy works late, things break and have to be fixed." Deirdre gently maneuvered the buggy over the curb so as not to rouse her dozing son. "And there are things I never dreamed of, like giving a formal dinner party. What should I serve? Who should sit next to whom? Who *shouldn't* sit next to whom? It's important for Billy's business, so I have to do it right. Lift the front end, will you?"

They hoisted the buggy onto the opposite sidewalk. Deirdre turned left onto Homewood Avenue. Will murmured and rolled over. Norah stroked his cheek, sticky with tears and sweat. If fairy godmothers existed, would she ask to change places with her sister? She noticed Deirdre's smile and hastily withdrew her hand. Among millionaires or miners, housekeeping was still housekeeping. Deirdre, who'd never done anything else, couldn't possibly understand the satisfaction of a real career. Thrusting her hands into her pockets, Norah asked, "Where's this landmark you're so interested in?"

Deirdre pointed. "See that turret? Guess who lives there. I mean, *lived* there."

"How would I know? I don't mix with the same set as you and Billy."

"We don't mix with this person either because he's dead. Go on now, guess."

The homes they'd already passed deserved to be called mansions, but none claimed as much manicured lawn or as many stately trees as the property Deirdre indicated. Gables and windows of every size and shape embellished the gray brick castle's four stories. It was grand enough to be Hepburn's home—or the set for a movie. Atop its columned front porch was a spacious balcony, much like the one where she danced with Jimmy Stewart in *The Philadelphia Story.*

Deirdre's pace slowed. "It's called Clayton. King Frick lived here before we were born. Now it belongs to his daughter Helen, but she prefers to live in New York. They say everything is right where the Fricks left it when they moved. Wouldn't you love to snoop around inside?"

Norah felt the sidewalk tilt beneath her. "I'd love to—to set fire to the place. And hire a band to play while it burned to the ground." When her incredulous sister stared, she added, "If Frick owned it, it's a sin. If his daughter had a conscience, she'd sell it and—and—"

Deirdre's arm crept around Norah's waist. "Give each miner and coke drawer who's still alive a few dollars? For heaven's sake, Norah, where are you going?"

Norah broke away and scooped pebbles from the gutter. Glaring at two women who strolled on the opposite sidewalk, she shouted, "It's a monument to cruelty!" She began to run, her gait clumsy in two-inch heels. She glanced back just once to see her flushed sister jogging behind the shuddering blue boat of Will's carriage.

The pebbles burned inside her fist. If only they were embers that would reduce King Frick's castle to a smoking ruin. She threw herself against the wrought iron gate until it gave way, then sprinted toward the house. Smug beneath drapes and awnings, dark windows regarded her with disdain. The trees rustled, lending the house a sardonic voice. *I've stood through the Homestead steelworkers strike, an attempted murder, and no end of harassment from that goddamn miners' union. Do you think you and your silly little stones can bring me down?*

Crossing the lawn, she veered toward the greenhouse. Each glass pane presented a glittering target. She stopped short when a man in muddy overalls rounded a tall cluster of rhododendron bushes. The man pushed a wheelbarrow heaped with dirt and regarded her as if she were more of the same. "Whaddya think you're doing? This here's private property."

Panting, Norah remembered her fist. In one swift motion she swung her arm, unlocked her fingers, and released the stones. She flung herself in the opposite direction. Anticipating a triumphant crash, she heard only the gardener's bluster.

Deirdre pulled her through the gate. "What on earth has come over you?"

Norah shrugged out of her jacket and slung it over her shoulder. Her silk blouse, wet enough to wring, was surely ruined. She lifted the hair from the back of her neck, wishing for a stiff breeze and a bolt of lightning to accomplish what she and her stones could not.

Casting wary backward glances, Deirdre scolded, "What if you'd gotten arrested for trespassing? I wouldn't be able to hold my head up around here."

Norah glanced back, too. The greenhouse sparkled in the sunlight, utterly intact. Her steps turned leaden. Something *had* come over her. No doubt it was the same something that had prompted Pap to sing the wagon-hump song on the store porch. To burn his Brotherhood card. To curse and stone the Cossacks. Deep inside, like a dark seam of coal, she, too, carried rage that had nowhere to go.

She was startled when Deirdre called out and waved. A woman in a plain brown dress and modest hat stood on her sister's front porch. Deirdre turned to Norah. "Surprise! I invited Trudy for dinner. We wanted Katie to come, too, but she wasn't allowed to leave her convent."

Trudy hastened to meet them. "*Wilkommen, Liebchen*," she whispered, drawing Norah toward her. When they separated, a broad smile stretched Trudy's round cheeks. Her bright blue eyes might have been Mutti's before patch life had dulled them. Her hand caught Norah's chin, gently turning her face right, then left.

"*Was machst du*?" asked Norah. What are you doing?

"Looking," said Trudy, "for Clara, your mother."

Chapter 43: Clare

June 2, 1941
Feast of St. Blandina, Slave, Martyr

Norah described a grimacing gargoyle perched on the roof of a downtown bank, a forty-one-story Gothic tower called the Cathedral of Learning, a special streetcar climbing a narrow track up the side of Mount Washington. It was after midnight, but they ignored the clock as tea cooled in their cups. Norah handed Clare new photographs of Deirdre's children. Clare pored over them, her heart turning over at the sight of Will, her first grandson. Carefully, she hid them inside the lining of her sewing basket.

Clare's weary eyes stung as if scratched by cinders, but Norah's remained wide, brighter than the bulb overhead. She paused to sip her tea, no longer the spinster resigned to a future graced only with stylish dresses and Saturday matinees. What she described was where she belonged. Surely she realized now that her future lay outside The Hive.

From time to time, she reached across the table. Her fingertips grazed Clare's forearm or elbow, then withdrew. She was assuring herself that her mother had miraculously kept herself intact during her absence. Clare pretended not to notice. The voice of her conscience fairly shouted. *Jetzt! Heraus mit der Sprache!* Now, speak up—before Fin returns from Boyle's.

Norah clasped her hand. "Is something wrong?"

Clare shook her head. Through the window, she saw Fin stumble into the yard. Quickly, she gathered the cups. "Hurry up to bed. Your pap's too tired to hear about your trip now."

Norah's chin lifted. Her face hardened as she opened the screen. "Hello, Pap. I'm back home, safe and sound."

He tripped on the porch steps, and she hurried to help him. "Get away from me," he snarled, shoving her aside. "You, with your fancy clothes, looking down your nose—" he motioned to the yard—"thinking me home is just a pile of shit."

The cups wobbled in Clare's hands. Tea spattered the floor. She set the dishes on the drainboard and snatched a towel. "Come inside, Fin," she called. "I'll make you some coffee."

"'Tis not coffee I'm needing," he said. He gripped Norah's shoulders and shook her with each word. "'Tis—the—respect—of—me—own—daughter." Releasing Norah, he moved toward Clare, crouching to wipe up the puddled tea. His boot struck her hip and sent her sprawling. "Made another mess, did you?"

Norah tried to step between them. "It's my fault, Pap. I spilled my tea, and Mutti—"

He slapped her. "What filthy word are you speaking straight to me face?"

Clare struggled to her feet. "She's exhausted, Fin. She doesn't know what—"

Before Clare could stop him, he hit Norah again. "Here." He pushed her toward Clare. "Another mess to clean up."

As pain swelled in her hip, Clare held the towel to Norah's bloody nose. Held her tongue as Fin's boots thumped the stairs. To confess now, on the heels of such punishment, would be cruelty even she wasn't capable of. She drew Norah, shuddering, against her shoulder and repeated like a litany, "I'm so sorry. So very, very sorry."

At dawn, Fin left with his bucket, speaking not a word about the daughter who'd insulted his ears with Kaiser-talk. As always, the drink had washed his memory perfectly clean. An hour later, Norah skipped breakfast and rushed out the front door, but not before Clare saw the bruises. What would Roz say when she saw them? Would Norah tell the truth or, as ashamed as her mother, make up an excuse?

Clare's hip ached, but she had no time to coddle herself, not with a week's worth of dirty laundry awaiting her attention. The radio announcer intoned, *"For a wash that's deep clean, sparkling clean, use deep-cleaning Oxydol. Deep-cleaning, deep-cleaning, deep-cleaning."* Clare turned up the volume so she'd hear *Ma Perkins* over the rasp of cloth against her washboard. *Ma Perkins* gave way to *Mary Marlin, Vic and Sade,* and *Pepper Young's Family* as Clare worked through the stack of

Fin's crusty, blackened shirts: boiling, scrubbing, rinsing, then scrubbing again.

She paused for a sandwich when the news came on. The report was somber. The Allies had withdrawn from Crete. Her appetite, fanned by three hard, steamy hours, receded. She imagined Fin, seating himself in a black niche and opening his bucket. His fists clenched as word reached him: *Hitler wins again.* The image persisted as the day dragged on, a tedium of steam, scraped knuckles, and radio static. At last, she hung the last damp sheet on the line. All too soon, it would be evening. Fin would go off to Boyle's—and, having waited far too long, she would speak to Norah.

Clare limped back into the kitchen, where organ music subsided. *"The true-to-life story of mother-love and sacrifice..."* said the announcer, introducing *Stella Dallas*, her favorite serial and daily reminder to start supper and Fin's bath. Her hands quaked as she set the tub on the kitchen floor. The radio voices dissolved into an unintelligible drone. She was grateful for the weight in her stomach. Dreading Fin's homecoming was familiar. It distracted her from the novel terror of confronting Norah.

For a heady instant, she regarded the bath water almost lovingly. A pale yellow bruise lingered on her forehead, a grim souvenir of the Bismarck's sinking. Had Fin succeeded the day the Bismarck went down, her secrets would have drowned with her. She wouldn't feel them now—tenacious fingers that squeezed her throat. Her knees folded, placing her beside the tub like a supplicant before the altar. *Spare me, please, the need to horrify my daughter.* She leaned toward the water's quivering reflection of cowardice. Closer. Closer still.

"Hey, Missus!"

Dazed, she straightened up and regarded the screen, pressed by a boy's face. Concetta's grandson, dark-eyed and dimpled, waved a towel-wrapped bundle. He laughed as she wiped her dripping nose with her apron. "It's not Halloween," he said when she opened the door. "Why are you bob—" He peered at the tub. "No apples?"

"I dropped a pin in the water. I was trying to find it."

An innocent, he believed her. Would Norah, who had buried her innocence with her unborn siblings, believe Clare, too?

"From Nonni," he said, handing her the bundle.

She peeked inside the towel and thanked him for the pizzelles. He pounded down the porch steps, leaping off the last with outstretched arms. "Watch out, mister!" he told Fin, opening the gate. "There's a pin in your bathtub!"

Fin entered the kitchen. "A pin in me tub? What kind of foolishness is that?"

Clare shrugged and took his bucket, her arms liquid with relief. He hadn't yet heard about Crete.

Norah didn't return home until Clare was clearing the table. Fin, who hadn't commented on or even seemed to notice his daughter's absence at supper, had already left for Boyle's. Clare set a plateful of reheated chicken and potatoes in front of Norah, but she barely touched the food. Rising, she scraped the plate into the garbage pail and turned toward the door.

Before she could open it, Clare caught her arm. "I need to tell you something."

"Not now," Norah said. "If I miss another rehearsal, Mrs. Keating will have a fit."

Clare stepped in front of her daughter, blocking the door. Her frantic heart threatened to block her throat. "I did something terrible. Twenty-two years ago."

A dent appeared between Norah's brows as she calculated. She reached around Clare, groping for the knob. "Please, let me go." A note of fear rang in her voice.

The air felt thick, as if laden with cinders. "The second Finbar? I killed him," said Clare.

Outside, the crickets ceased chirping. The wind stopped agitating a loose upstairs shutter. A faraway dog cut short its howl. The entire world, as if stunned by her assertion, turned silent.

"I put him in his cradle. I took a pillow off the bed. I pressed it over his face and held it there." Clare's voice broke. "Until he stopped breathing."

Norah's expression wavered between confusion and sadness. "That's a lie."

"I killed him so he wouldn't—"

"You put him in his cradle. Then you fainted." Norah held up her hand when Clare tried to interrupt. "You told me to go back to bed, but I didn't. I stood outside the door. When the wind blew it open, I saw what happened."

Desperately, Clare contradicted, "I distinctly remember—"

"What do you remember?" Norah countered. "That you hadn't had a decent night's sleep in weeks? That Pap beat you so hard you could barely walk? That you almost fell asleep standing up? You nearly fell over, but you caught yourself just in time to put him in the cradle."

What did Clare remember? Darkness. Only darkness.

Norah grasped Clare's shoulders. "I tried to wake you up, but I couldn't. He was kicking and crying in his cradle, but I ran away because I thought you were dead." She shuddered. Her hands dropped to her sides. "I hid under my bed until I heard you get up and go downstairs. Then I went back and found him." Her voice faltered, then dropped to a whisper. "He was dead, and it was my fault for running away."

"*Your* fault? Do you still believe that?" When Norah refused to answer, a sob rose in Clare's throat. How could a child bear such excruciating knowledge, much less keep it to herself? "Why didn't you tell me?" She reached for Norah's quaking shoulders, but Norah backed away.

It was worse, much worse than Clare had imagined. Two children had died that day.

Norah's gaze fixed on the floor. "I couldn't even tell the priest. I still feel like a liar each time I leave the confessional. I thought that taking care of the graves would be my penance. But it wasn't enough."

"*Mein Engel!* Oh, my angel, there was nothing to confess! The doctor said—" Clare's certainty that, in those unremembered minutes, she had committed the most heinous offense imaginable dissolved like salt in a steaming pot. Again she reached for Norah, as much to keep herself upright as to comfort her daughter. "It was crib death. You couldn't stop it. Nobody could."

Norah backed away. Her eyes seemed focused on something far in the distance. A fly breached the space between them. Its faint whine broke her trance. She pointed at Fin's bucket on the drainboard. "You were afraid, weren't you? You thought they'd be just like him."

Had Clare been so transparent? Frantic, she tried again. "The third Finbar—so tiny and weak, yet he refused my milk. He knew what kind of mother I was. I let him starve—"

Norah silenced her with a slap. "He didn't know anything. He was born too early, that's all. It's not your fault that he died."

Clare's scalded cheek was the only part of her body she could feel. How could she twist this wretched history into something incriminating, something to turn Norah against her and send her packing?

Norah's face was awash with tears—and pity. She spoke so softly that Clare strained to hear. "I wonder which is better, to be an angel or a survivor. The way things happen here, it seems like even God isn't sure."

"Do you hate me?" Clare asked. Everything inside her stopped as she awaited the answer.

"Do you really think I'd believe you could do murder?" Norah wiped her cheeks with the backs of her hands and pushed past Clare. "I'm late."

Clare groped for a chair. She'd never touched a drop of whiskey, but how she craved it now! Then she noticed the bundled towel at the end of the table. Slowly, she unwrapped Concetta's pizzelles. She broke off the edge of a brittle anise-scented waffle and raised it to her lips. The first bite tasted like dust. The second bite, no better. The cookie had dwindled to a fragment before her tongue detected a faint note of sweetness.

It took her more than an hour to eat the six pizzelles. The backyard dimmed from gray to purple to black. Golden flashes of fireflies perforated the darkness. Like voices from a distant radio, the Finbars' whispers rose and fell. *Not your fault. Not your fault. Not your fault.*

Chapter 44: Norah

"Norah Sweeney, did you leave your head at the William Penn Hotel?"

The papers on Mrs. Keating's clipboard fluttered as she stalked down the aisle. Following close behind, the stage manager carried her own clipboard as if it were a fifty-pound block of ice. The look she gave Norah spoke louder than Mrs. Keating. *For crying out loud, wake up!*

Indeed, Norah felt as if she were trapped in a nightmare that dragged her from the blazing stage to a silent bedroom containing a cradle and a lifeless child. Stage to bedroom, bedroom to stage, back and forth until she hardly knew just where she stood.

"Give her the line," said Mrs. Keating, dropping into a front row seat and fanning herself with the clipboard. She glared at the stage, abuzz with whispers. "Pipe down, all of you! If I hear another word you'll be copying the whole script as punishment for wasting my time."

The stage manager read in a monotone, "*Oh, builders, I beg thee, fashion three windows in my bathhouse wall. Each time I enter, I will be reminded of the Blessed Trinity—Father, Son, and Holy Ghost.*" She looked up at Norah. "Got it?"

Norah nodded. The words wafted past her like smoke. All she'd heard was *ghost.*

Mrs. Keating looked pointedly at her watch. "Can we *please* be moving on, then?"

A boy who played a builder raised his hand. "Missus, may I be excused?"

"Absolutely not," snapped Mrs. Keating. "Norah, it's your cue."

"Please, missus," the boy persisted, "I gotta go number two real bad."

Without waiting for permission he darted from the stage. Norah watched him run, wishing that she, too, could escape—from this stage, from this town, from the damning echo of her own confession. *He was kicking and crying, but I ran away.*

She'd pushed away the memory of that cradle, banished it again and again, until forgetting had become as automatic as breathing. Only rarely did the image of a baby's lifeless face ambush her like a disturbing frame from a movie. She quickly substituted another scene, funny or romantic, from a film she'd recently seen. Over time, she'd all but convinced herself that what she recalled had been devised by Hollywood, a scene briefly projected onto a screen before giving way to another, and another, each a vivid fiction.

"Your cue, Norah!"

The auditorium seats cracked into red fragments like pieces imprisoned in a kaleidoscope. Norah rubbed her eyes. "I'm sorry. Can you please repeat the line?"

Mrs. Keating leaped to her feet and approached the stage, beckoning to Norah. She leaned over the footlights and, without lowering her voice, warned, "If you ruin all the work I've put into this pageant, I'll see your family thrown out of The Hive, lock, stock, and barrel. Is that clear, or do you need me to be repeating that?"

Norah nodded. The stage lights overhead punished her with waves of heat. If only this rehearsal and the conversation that had preceded it were products of delirium. For the life of her, she couldn't recall a word from the script, the name of the film currently playing at the Penn Theatre, or even what Mutti had made for supper.

The boy returned. With prompting, Norah recited the bathhouse instructions. The compliant builders installed the trinity of windows. Then, silence.

Mrs. Keating threw up her hands. "Jesus, Mary, and Joseph!"

The stage manager yawned extravagantly before chanting, *"Keep me firm in my new faith, so my example may inspire my father to abandon pagan ways and follow the true path to salvation."*

Norah repeated the first phrase before memory pulled her back twenty-two years to that blown-open door. She watched Mutti, pale as death, topple like a felled tree onto the bed.

"The line, please!"

A girl who played a pilgrim ran onstage. "I can do it, missus! I know every line!"

"She's too old anyway," said someone else from behind the side curtain.

Amen to that. Norah managed a smile at the chubby girl, quivering beside the plywood bathhouse like a would-be starlet awaiting her screen test.

"Quiet!" shouted Mrs. Keating. "I'll not be changing the cast at this stage of the game. Norah, I expect better effort from a young woman of your—maturity." Snickers broke out, but silenced quickly after a hard look from Mrs. Keating. She motioned to the stage manager. "Give Norah your script, but just for tonight. Tomorrow I expect a perfect performance." She raised her voice. "Everyone offstage! Stagehands, reset for scene one."

The stage manager passed the script over the footlights, whispering to Norah, "You won't look so old once you put on the costume and makeup."

When Norah straightened up, Mrs. Keating regarded her with narrowed eyes. "What's that on your face, Norah? It looks like you walked into a door. Or was it someone's fist?"

"I walked into a door," Norah replied coldly before stalking offstage.

In the morning Norah huddled over her compact, dabbing on Max Factor foundation between streetcar stops. She pretended to ignore the stares of a little girl and her mother, a common, down-at-the-heels woman with no sense of discretion. The only opinion that mattered was that of Roz, whose perfectly arched eyebrows had shot up when she'd first seen Norah's battered face. Norah had stammered hopelessly, unable to recall the explanation she'd fabricated. Roz, however, had simply handed Norah a padded silk cosmetic bag. In a dressing room, Norah had concealed the bruises as well as she could.

When she reached Uniontown, she walked quickly, chin tucked against her collar. As she rounded the bank steps, a glittering expanse of broken glass spread out before her. She looked up to find three black cars and a motorcycle hugging the curb. An ambulance idled in the street. Its back doors were opened, revealing a cot draped with a sheet. A policeman shouted at the driver of an oncoming truck to turn around. Beside the motorcycle, a man in a dark suit scribbled in a notebook.

Norah heard her name called and turned toward La Femme. The display window had been shattered. Mannequins that Norah had dressed the day before lay in a heap like toppled bowling pins. A single potted palm remained upright, a pink scarf snagged on its fan-like fronds. Colors completely inappropriate for spring—black, rusty red, and a dreadful pea green—marked everything with streaks and spatters. Roz stood inside the window, her face and hands and powder blue suit stippled with a brighter red. She beckoned just before a man in a white coat drew her away.

Blocking the door, a bulky policeman waved Norah off. "Store's closed, ma'am."

Roz's faint voice floated from inside. "She works here, Officer. Let her in."

The policeman stepped back, and Norah entered a space she no longer recognized. Glass shards littered the carpet, now a slick swamp of spilled paint. Thick rivulets ran down the wallpaper. The chintz chairs were ruined, as were—Norah gasped at such sacrilege—the rack of summer frocks she'd unpacked just last week. Two policemen prowled the room, stepping over broken bottles. Roz and the man in the white coat had disappeared.

"What happened?" Norah asked. When the policemen didn't respond, she looked back at the doorway. The officer who'd admitted her had gone outside. What his body had screened was now visible. A large red swastika gleamed wetly on the shop's front door. Everything inside her turned hard and cold as she recalled the hateful message. **NO PLACE FOR CROOKED JEWS.** She forced herself to turn away.

Zigzagging around the wreckage, she found Roz lying on the chaise in the bride's room. Roz seemed oblivious to the stains her ruined suit had left on the velvet upholstery. Blood marred the center of her pale forehead. The man in the white coat wrapped gauze around her left hand. A bulky doctor's satchel gaped at his feet. On the table by Roz's head, a syringe and empty glass vial sat atop an old issue of *Marie Claire*.

Norah all but fell into the nearest chair, fleetingly comforted by the fact that it had escaped damage. "That awful letter, telling you to get out—"

"The bottles thrown through my window must be the author's calling cards. Each one filled with paint—and *such* unsightly colors," said Roz. Her dreamy tone sounded as if she'd just awoken from a sound sleep.

The medic propped her bandaged hand on a pillow and reached for his satchel. "There's still a piece of glass in your forehead. I'm going to remove it, but I'll cover up your blouse first."

"Oh, to hell with my blouse," said Roz, as sweetly flirtatious as Scarlett O'Hara. "Do you really think I'd wear these clothes again and remind myself of such an unpleasant incident?"

"All right then, ma'am," said the medic. "I warn you, this may be rather painful."

"I highly doubt it," said Roz. "Thanks to that injection you kindly provided, I feel like I'm floating on a cloud."

The medic's shiny tweezers probed the bloody clot on Roz's forehead. A powerful humming filled Norah's ears. The air became a sparkling blanket, heavy and enfolding. "Jesus, Mary, and Joseph," she murmured before everything went black.

When the darkness lifted, she found herself lying on the carpet. The medic held a small, foul-smelling bottle in front of her nose. Batting it away, she propped herself on her elbows. A bandage had been taped over Roz's forehead. "Are you putting her in the hospital?" Norah asked.

"I'd like to see him try," Roz said pleasantly. "Such a fuss over little old scratches."

"Those are cuts, not scratches, and some are rather deep. You definitely need to see a doctor," said the medic. He turned to Norah. "Go home, miss. You're still white as a sheet."

Norah sat up. "I'm fine now. I'll go with her to the hospital."

"That's kind of you, sugar, but completely unnecessary. Call my maid and tell her to take the streetcar over here. She can drive my car to the hospital and pick me up." Roz touched her forehead and winced. "You may take me to the emergency room, but I refuse to be admitted. As you can see, I have quite a bit to attend to here."

Mr. Simons, the shoe repairman, stumbled into the room. His hands raked his hair into wild gray tufts. "It's an outrage, I tell you! Hitler's devils, right at our doorsteps!" He looked at Roz and gasped. "*Mein Gott*, missus, what have they done to you?"

"Nothing that a few stitches and a good insurance policy won't take care of," Roz replied.

"Did they break your window, too?" Norah asked Mr. Simons.

"They painted on it. Such terrible words, that terrible symbol." He slumped against the doorjamb. "I am ruined. No customers will come to me now. Nobody will take the risk."

"What risk?" asked Norah, but Mr. Simons hurried away, muttering and wagging his head. Norah turned to Roz. "What about your customers?"

The medic helped Roz to her feet. "I doubt my customers scare so easily." She smiled faintly at Norah, but her tone had changed from flirtatious to flat. "Call my maid, then go home, sugar. There's nothing you can—"

"There's plenty I can do," said Norah. "Just tell me."

Roz glanced back as the medic led her away. "Call a glass company. Have them send someone over to replace the window."

"I'll take care of it right away," Norah said. Buoyed with fresh purpose, she hurried into Roz's office and closed the door. Cloistered in the cluttered space, she could almost forget the disaster just two rooms away. Almost imagine that the office belonged to her, a successful shopkeeper who neither cowered nor ran away when attacked by the Klan. She seated herself at the desk and phoned the maid, who began to cry. "Roz isn't badly hurt," Norah assured her. "She'll be back at work tomorrow, and so will I."

313

One task accomplished. Norah paged through the telephone directory, which listed a dozen glass companies. Roz, naturally, would want the best—and know just whom to call. If only Norah had thought to ask before the medic had taken Roz away. Then again, Roz might not have been able to recall a name or phone number, considering the cloud she floated on.

Before Norah could stop her fingers, they were dialing again. A brisk female voice answered. "Visocky Automotive Works. How may I help you?"

Taken aback, Norah nearly hung up. Foolishly, she'd expected to be greeted by the owner, not his receptionist. "I need to speak to Paul."

"Mr. Visocky isn't available at the moment. If you'd like to make an appointment for automotive services, I'll be happy to assist you."

The confidence with which Norah had spoken to the maid vanished. She could have been a greenhorn miner boarding the hoist cage for the first time. "Tell him Norah Sweeney is calling."

"As I said before, Mr. Visocky is not available to take calls."

"He'll take one from me," said Norah, more forcefully than she'd intended. She leaned back in the chair and closed her eyes. She was back on that drenched sidewalk, stunned by Paul's unspoken assurance. *I would leave her.* She forced her eyes open. *Please, St. Barbara, don't let him think I want anything more than advice.*

The receptionist's tone turned icy. "I'll see if he's in. Hold the line."

The phone took on the weight of a brick in Norah's damp hand. No matter what she said or how she said it, he'd hear an invitation. She was about to hang up when his voice, alarmed, leaked from the heavy receiver. She raised it to her ear. "Someone vandalized La Femme," she said, her tone as business-like as she could make it. "Could you recommend a glass company to replace the front window?"

"Are you all right? Were you there when it happened?"

"Roz was. They took her to the hospital. Whoever did it painted a big swastika on the door." Norah touched her face, surprised to find it wet.

"Are you there all by yourself?"

"The police are here." A sob escaped. Norah pressed her fist against her mouth, grateful that Roz wasn't there to witness such a shameful loss of composure.

"I'll be right over."

Norah's fist dropped, thumping the desk. The adding machine's keys rattled like metallic laughter. "No!" she cried. "I'm fine! I just need the name of—Paul?"

The line had gone dead.

Norah stayed in Roz's office, reading and rereading the glass company listings. She'd called Visocky Automotive again, only to be informed by the frosty receptionist that Paul was unavailable. Her hand rested hopefully on the phone. Surely he'd think twice. Call back. *If it was my window, I'd hire Mr. So-and-so. He's the best man in town.*

When someone knocked, she leaped to her feet, knocking the receiver off the desk. "Come in," she said, hauling it up by the cord. She seated herself again, promising St. Barbara she would stay in the chair, no matter what.

A policeman opened the door. "There's a fella here about the window." He allowed Paul to enter, then shut the door behind him.

As if sensing her unease, Paul froze, hat in hand. "Are you sure you're all right?"

"I shouldn't've disturbed you. I'm really sorry." She turned the phone book around and pushed it toward him. "Who would you recommend?"

Three minutes later, it was done. His oil-stained fingers closed the directory. The wedding band swam like a dull gold fish. When he walked around the desk, she held up her hand. Imagined it speaking, since she could not. *This was a big mistake. Turn around and leave before it gets any bigger.*

He took her hand in both of his. "You're cut, too," he said. He reached for his pocket, then peered intently at her palm. "False alarm. Just paint."

Was this a sin, allowing her hand to be clasped? "I didn't want you to come," she said. Was that entirely true? If she wasn't sure, was it a lie?

He drew her to her feet. "Then why did you call?"

To an observer, they'd appear to be shaking hands. A professional leave-taking, nothing more. "I didn't want to make things here any worse," she said. She could tell that he didn't believe her.

"As soon as they board up the window, go home and don't come back. Whoever did this hates Jews, but they hate you, too, for working here." His hand tightened. "Promise me you'll find another job."

His entreaty so surprised her that she forgot to keep her distance. "Roz isn't afraid," she said. "Neither am I." She shivered as he released her hand, as his arms encircled her.

"How did you hurt your face?" His mouth tightened. After so many years, he knew better than to ask.

"I don't want this to happen," she said, believing it until he kissed her.

His mouth lifted. "Do you want me to stop?"

She felt each word, soft as down, against her lips. "Yes," she said. "But not yet." Surely, she decided, resting against him, given the awfulness of everything that had happened that day and the day before, she could allow herself this one fleeting gift.

Chapter 45: Clare

June 4, 1941
Feast of St. Buriana, Hermitess, Penitent

Fin's coughing woke Clare. The mattress shifted as he leaned over the side of the bed to spit phlegm into the jar. He settled back onto his pillow and began to snore. She was about to close her eyes when she noticed a flickering in the window. It reminded her of the old days, when hundreds of charged coke ovens filled the night with dancing shadows. Unsettled, she slid out of bed, careful not to rouse Fin, and tiptoed downstairs.

Norah stood at the kitchen window. She turned when the floor creaked, then silently turned back. Clare crept toward her, stifling a gasp when she saw the flaming cross in the alley just outside their gate.

For the first time since they'd traded confessions, Norah reached for her hand. "Hear that?" Norah whispered. "The white-hoods are riding away. They must've tied their horses further up the alley."

Clare stared at the cross, at once mesmerized and repulsed. "What on earth brought them this time?"

She was startled when Norah's chest thudded against her. She stroked her daughter's hair as she sobbed. When Norah lifted her face, the dying fire illuminated the contour of her swollen cheek. "Paul said they'd try to scare me because I work for a Jew."

"How would they know that? When did Paul—"

"I called him." Norah's chin dropped onto her chest. "I'll go to confession in the morning."

"For calling him? A phone call isn't a sin." Clare regarded her daughter's drooping form. Norah had come home yesterday in obvious distress, yet offered few details about the shop's damage and Roz's injury. What was she holding back?

"Paul came to the store. I shouldn't have let him in. I'm so ashamed."

Clare pried Norah's chin from her chest. "What are you ashamed of?"

Fresh tears dripped onto Norah's nightgown. "For loving him when he belongs to someone else. And for letting him still love me." She drew a shaky breath and told Clare the rest of the story.

Fin smashed the charred remains of the cross before departing for work. "She's not to be leaving the house," he told Clare. "Go to the store by yourself to get the paint. And don't be telling every Tom, Dick, and Harry why you're in need of it."

He threw the blackened boards into the garbage bin, then took his bucket and strode down the alley. Standing on the porch, Clare watched other miners pass. Each eyed the graffiti on the Sweeneys' outhouse. Half a dozen swastikas surrounded a prominent warning.

JEW LOVER BEWARE

The sight of the gate and fence, spattered with black, unnerved her as much as the words. From where she stood, the dark stains resembled something other than paint.

She entered the kitchen, where Norah stood at the window. The purple bruise on Norah's cheek stood out against her pale skin. Clare took in her attire—a smart gray suit—and shook her head. "Your pap says you have to stay home."

Norah's laughter caught Clare off guard. "He's a fine one to give orders. Has he ever stayed away from a picket line?"

"He's a big, stubborn man," Clare reminded her. "If the Klan comes after you, he'll stand up to them. But you can't, *Liebchen*. Not by yourself." She forced herself to add, "Paul can't protect you. He's got a business of his own. If they saw him at your shop yesterday, it could go badly for him, too."

Norah wilted like a parched seedling. "I have to go to church. Pap won't deny me that."

If Fin had heard Norah's story, he'd insist on a trip to the confessional—but he'd beat her first, so harshly that the priest's penance, however stringent, would seem like a blessing in comparison. "Don't tell him anything. He'd never understand," said Clare. "Change your clothes and eat something while I go to the store for paint. I need you to help me cover up—that."

She motioned toward the outhouse. "When we're done, then you can go to church."

On her way to the store, Clare offered and received the usual *good morning*'s, but every missus replied with her attention fixed somewhere other than Clare's face. The store clerks barely glanced at her, then quickly turned away. Shoulders bowed from the weight of two heavy cans, Clare met Branka Kukoc Visocky on the way home. Branka stared down at her pregnant belly and passed Clare in silence.

Though saddened, Clare wasn't surprised. Every store-bound woman who'd passed her gate had made an immediate and wise decision to put as much distance as possible between herself and the Sweeneys. She'd keep that distance as long as she perceived—or her husband decided—that The Hive was under Klan surveillance. Too many crosses had burned over the years for anyone to take this warning lightly. Women were whispering over their fences to neighbors. Miners, likewise, were circulating the news underground. Until something else occurred, something noteworthy enough to dispel this epidemic of dread, the Sweeneys would be pariahs. Clare set the paint cans by the fence, resigning herself to the fact that she'd be shunned.

Inside, Norah nibbled a piece of dry toast. She indicated her faded housedresss. "Is this proper painting attire?"

"You're the fashion expert," Clare replied, relieved to see Norah's halfhearted smile.

For the next two hours, a veritable procession of women and children passed—each glancing at Clare and Norah, then quickly looking away. Though Clare understood their concern, it still pained her when Kamila and Concetta allowed her only cursory nods. Like the others, each wrestled with conflicting loyalties. Which came first, their family's safety or an old friend's need? Like everyone else, they succumbed to fear. Over the years, the Klan had ruined more gardens than Clare could count, but never had a cross-burning targeted a single household—and at such close range.

The black paint bled through two coats of white, so Clare returned to the store for a third can. When they had emptied it, the outhouse and fence were as before—just another outhouse and fence, albeit cleaner than the neighbors'. Sunburned and spattered, she and Norah scrutinized their efforts, brushes at the ready to subdue a stubborn shadow.

"If it needs another coat, I'll do it when I get back from confession," Norah said. She ran inside to change her dress.

When she emerged, Clare followed her into the alley. "Straight to church and straight back, you hear? And don't ever tell your pap I let you go."

Clare rinsed the brushes and left them on the porch to dry. Back in the kitchen, she switched on the radio, then switched it off, unwilling to hear any more bad news. She filled a pail with sudsy water and knelt with her scrub brush, plying it with hard strokes across the dusty floor. She was dragging the bucket out the kitchen door when she realized that Norah's confession was taking an unusually long time. She regarded the clock, whose indifferent face informed her that her daughter had been absent for more than an hour. She scrambled to her feet, upending the bucket. Gray water cascaded across the porch. She dashed across the yard and threw open the gate, past caring that her fingers smeared the fresh white paint.

The alley remained vacant for however long she stood there, straining for a glimpse of Norah. Then a sound rose up behind her, a sound more dreadful than that of the white-hoods' galloping horses. In the middle of the workday, the mine whistle shrilled the seemingly endless alarm that signaled disaster.

Within seconds, the alley flowed like a river. Clare's frantic neighbors nearly knocked her over in their haste to reach the mine. Concetta darted past, crossing herself. The whistle kept screaming. Clare turned and followed the others. Her pulse grew louder with each step until the alarm was subsumed by the rhythm of her yearning.

Endlich ist er tot. At last, he is dead.

Chapter 46: Norah

Roz looked up from a stack of papers. "I believe I told you to stay home, sugar. The cleaners are doing a fine job, all things considered."

Norah nodded. She'd nearly tripped over one of the men, kneeling by the door as he pulled up carpeting. "I'd've come sooner, except—" She caught herself. Roz was not to know what had happened to the Sweeneys' outhouse. "My mother needed help."

"Sit down, Norah." Roz indicated a chair heaped with other paint-stained dresses. "Just put them on the floor." Weariness edged her voice. Her Hedy Lamarr waves were drawn back into a careless French twist. A bandage on her forehead accentuated the pallor of her face, bare of makeup. Her eyes shifted between Norah and the door until she got up to close it. "Actually," she said, returning to her chair, "it's good that you came. I have something to tell you."

"The new glass should be ready tomorrow. Once the plywood's gone, the cleaners will have a lot more light," said Norah. She noticed the telephone directory on Roz's cluttered desk and quickly looked away.

"Thanks for taking care of the window." Roz shook her head and sighed. It was a helpless sound, utterly out of character for Uniontown's resident Scarlett O'Hara, the tough cookie frosted with Southern-belle charm. "I don't know when I'll reopen. To be honest, I'm not sure I will reopen. I've never experienced anything quite like this before. And I certainly don't want you hurt by it."

Was this the same woman who'd insisted she never cowered? "But you told me—"

"I'm terribly sorry, sugar, but I have to let you go. I'm sure Wright-Metzler's will take you back."

Norah sprang to her feet. "You said your customers don't scare easily. Well, I don't either." If she took three steps, she'd stand precisely when Paul had stood, making her promise that she'd find another job. She blinked back tears. In the confessional, Fr. Kovacs had insisted on a more difficult promise, intended to break what was left of her heart.

"You've been a fine assistant, Norah, but my mind is made up. I've already called my best customers. Most of them wouldn't come to the phone." Roz breathed deeply before adding, "I had to talk to their maids. Everyone knows what happened here."

I am ruined. A day earlier, Mr. Simons' rant had seemed no more than the temporary hysteria of a frightened old man. Watching Roz write out a check, Norah filled with what was surely the same heavy despair. It was all she could do to accept the check, fold it, and put it in her pocket. One hundred dollars. Two days earlier, it would have been a fortune. The sum now seemed irrelevant.

Roz extended her hand, and Norah shook it. Then she walked out the door, a career girl in need of a new career.

Norah righted the overturned bucket on the back porch before entering the quiet kitchen. The stove, which should have been heating Pap's bath water, was cold to the touch. Instead of plates and cutlery, a basket heaped with clothes that needed mending sat on the table. She was about to go upstairs when she heard the sirens. She opened the front door just as six ambulances raced down First Street. Nearly tripping on the front steps, she ran after them.

An agitated crowd parted at the mine gate to let the screaming vehicles pass, then closed behind them. As Norah approached the tracks, she encountered Branka, crouching and cradling her swollen belly. "What happened?" she asked, enduring Branka's shocked, bloodshot gaze.

"Everyone's saying it was an explosion. Didn't you hear the whistle?" When Norah shook her head, Branka's head dropped onto her knees. "Bob's still down there."

Norah rose and hurried toward the crowd, searching the throng of taut, frightened faces for Mutti's. Like a catfish rising darkly from the creekbed, a dizzying possibility surfaced in her mind, but she pushed it back down. *What if Pap—* Another push, and another, until her forehead throbbed. She forced her way into the assembly as conversations hummed around her.

"God help us, it's just like the Marianna blast. Over a hundred gone."

A miner's voice, strident with hard-earned authority, disagreed. "Marianna, my ass. It blew up in November. Explosions happen in the winter."

A woman countered, "What about the blast in that Ohio mine, Willow Grove? It happened in March, just last year."

Norah cried out when fingers gripped her arm. "I thought I'd lost you, too," Mutti breathed into her ear.

They wormed their way out of the crowd and sat on a railroad tie with arms entwined. Each head propped the other. "Do explosions ever happen in the spring?" Norah asked.

"I heard it was fire damp. Something set it off, maybe a locomotive spark."

Norah breathed deeply, then asked, "Has anyone come up yet?"

"Twenty or so, right at the beginning. Some had trouble breathing, on account of the gas. The doctor sent them all to the hospital," said Mutti.

Norah hesitated, afraid to say it, afraid to hear herself say it. "Was Pap—"

Mutti shook her head. She rocked back and forth as she related the rest. Mr. Sestak had gone down with some other bosses to check gas levels. They'd come back up almost immediately. Rescue teams had arrived from neighboring patches. They'd been put on stand-by with The Hive's squad until the bad gases cleared. Fr. Kovacs was also waiting with the medics. Mutti sighed and stopped rocking. "People tried to sneak under the gate, but the deputies beat them until they turned back."

"What if Pap's dead?" As soon as the words emerged, a space opened inside Norah. For as long as she could remember, that space had been solid with fear.

"I don't know," Mutti said tonelessly. She stared at the ground for a long time before asking, "Did you really go to confession?"

Norah nodded. If only Mutti had forgotten and spared her the reminder.

"What did Fr. Kovacs say?"

"I'm not allowed to see Paul—" At the sound of his name the empty space inside Norah grew larger, becoming a wound too deep and wide to possibly heal. "I'm not allowed to call him or have anything to do with him again."

Mutti drew Norah's head to her chest. "You shouldn't have turned him away. Especially not on my account."

"It doesn't matter now." Norah lifted her face and considered the distraught families keeping vigil at the gate. She looked past them at the towering slate dump, the rows of dispirited houses, each as shabby as the next. Nothing here, not one thing seemed the least bit important. Everything was lost— including her fear. "If Pap's dead, we can leave. We can go to Pittsburgh, to Deirdre's house or Trudy's."

Mutti looked at the ground. "We don't know anything yet."

Norah glanced over her shoulder before whispering, "There's no point in pretending. Everyone's saying, *maybe, if only*, but they're thinking, *when will they tell me he's dead?*"

"I'm afraid to believe anything right now," Mutti whispered back. She got to her feet and, stumbling like a sleepwalker, began to pace.

At sunset, the Big Boss' shiny maroon Cadillac crossed the tracks. Deputy Harrison unlocked the gate. Behind him stood a dozen uniformed assistants, billy clubs in hand, poised to hurt anyone attempting to follow the car. At sundown, they lit fires in barrels. Old Smiley and Ada arrived in the store's delivery truck to hand out ham sandwiches and bottles of ginger ale. Norah took a sandwich for Mutti, who refused it. The single bite Norah was able to chew and swallow formed a painful lump in the center of her chest.

Mutti kept pacing, and Norah doggedly followed. Around sleeping children curled like limp kittens against their mothers. Around aged men and women who knelt in the dirt, plying rosary beads and murmuring Old Country languages. Norah averted her eyes from men who wept openly, unashamed. If the worst didn't happen, joy would override recollections of unmanliness. If it did, nobody would recall anything but the worst.

From time to time, Mutti's shoulders slumped. She'd stop suddenly, swaying as if ready to collapse. The moment Norah touched her, she'd draw herself up and walk on. Each pause seemed slightly longer than the one before. Just once she allowed Norah to take her arm. Hesitated, then ventured, "What if—"

"We'll leave," Norah whispered fiercely. She felt in her pocket for Roz's check. "As soon as we know for sure, we'll pack my suitcase and go to the Uniontown train station."

"There has to be a funeral," Mutti said faintly.

Norah hadn't considered this. All she could think of was leaving. Leaving and not looking back.

"He may be all right."

Norah stopped Mutti's mouth with her hand. "Don't say that. Don't even think it."

With each passing hour, new rumors spread. The General Superintendent had called from Pittsburgh and ordered the bosses to seal the mine. The rescue teams had been sent home. More rescue teams were on the way. The hoist cage and fan were hopelessly damaged. The chief engineer's crew had just finished repairs.

Mutti stopped beside a barrel and stared into the flames, then listed drunkenly. Norah hurried to catch her. "You need to sleep," Norah insisted, laboring across the tracks with Mutti draped like a weighty shawl over her shoulder. "I'll wake you up if anything happens."

She lowered Mutti onto a patch of grass and sprawled beside her. A thousand stars twinkled overhead. Fr. Kovacs' voice drifted down from heaven. *Go in peace and sin no more.*

Was it a sin to wish someone dead who truly deserved to die? If his death made others' lives worth living? Norah chose a star and whispered, "I wish a ton of rocks fell on top of Pap." Tears of shame, hope, and unexpected grief coursed down her cheeks. "And he died right away, without suffering." She'd allow him that much mercy.

At dawn, Norah opened her eyes to fresh commotion. Women snatched up drowsy children. Men milled around the gate. A voice rose above the clamor. "The cage is coming up!"

In an instant, Mutti was on her feet. She grabbed Norah's hand, and they pushed into the crowd. Someone trod on Norah's right heel, separating her foot from her shoe. "Wait!" she begged, but Mutti's grip only tightened. Oblivious to flailing arms and bumping hips, she forged ahead, dragging a limping Norah behind her.

The hubbub grew louder by the moment. Each outburst was giddy with relief. "See him there, at the back of the cage? Black as a nigger, but alive, thank Jesus!"

Someone called, "Big Bill, is everyone accounted for?"

The shouts abruptly changed to murmurs that trailed off into silence. Pinned between two husky men, Norah felt hairs rise on the back of her neck. She struggled to stand on tiptoe, to see the gate.

Norah and Mutti inched forward until Norah's fingers closed around the top bar of the gate. To the left stood Deputy Harrison, his club propped on a bulky padlock. A row of his grim-faced assistants blocked the way to the tipple. Outside the lamp house, cars and ambulances parked at odd angles. Yard men, bosses, and a dozen dirty miners huddled around the head frame. White-coated medics hovered by a large gray tent. Four men in business suits convened beside the mine office door. Big Bill was nowhere to be seen.

Norah gripped the cold metal bar, ignoring the hips and elbows buffeting her back. St. Barbara's bell chimed seven o'clock, then seven-thirty, then eight before a tall man left the group at the head frame and headed toward the crowd. Deputy Harrison raised his club. "Pipe down!" he shouted. "Big Bill's coming!"

Big Bill stopped well behind the row of assistant deputies. "Two rescue teams are underground now, searching for—" He coughed, covering what Norah sensed was a slip-up. He'd started to say *bodies*. "For survivors," he went on. "Twelve more men have come out. Their family members can see them as soon as the doctors allow."

"Let me in now!" begged a woman. "I can bandage as good as any doctor!"

"Be patient," Big Bill urged the restless crowd. "A state inspector just went down with Frank Sestak to check for pockets of black damp and after damp. We'll send down another crew once they say it's all right."

Mrs. Zekula forced her way to the gate. "You think the fellas trapped in there are having a picnic? Send down everyone you got!"

In vain Big Bill waved both arms, but the mob refused to quiet. "The cable's moving!" someone cried. "The cage is coming back up!"

Big Bill ran back to the head frame, now swarming with men. Mutti's head dropped onto the gate, sending a quiver through the metal. The shudder rose through Norah's fingers into her arms, her chest, her jaw. Every muscle thrummed as she peered through watering eyes at the grid that enclosed the hoist cage.

The crowd roared as the cage lurched to a stop. Inside, sooty men wore pale masks attached to oxygen tanks. Some stood upright, supporting others. A few clung to the bars of the cage. The medics hurried forward with stretchers. Someone unlatched the door. Orderly as dominoes, the miners fell through it. After twelve had been carried off, a trio still huddled in the corner. Big Bill, who'd never broken stride, entered the cage and, with the medics' help, carried out the remaining men.

The blackened figures seemed indistinguishable to Norah. She was shocked when Mutti lunged toward Deputy Harrison. "That's my husband!" Mutti shouted. "Open the goddamn gate and let me in!"

Perhaps it was the surprise of hearing such language from polite Mrs. Sweeney that prompted the deputy to obey. Clubs raised, his assistants stepped forward. He glanced back and shook his head before opening the lock. Deferential as a William Penn bellhop, he motioned Mutti and Norah forward, then slammed the gate before anyone else could follow.

Norah ran clumsily, hobbled by her shoeless foot. Mutti sprinted ahead, shouting at the medics to wait. Ignoring her, they carried Pap's stretcher into the tent. Panting, Norah caught up with Mutti when Big Bill and Mr. Donovan blocked her way. "You can't go in yet," said Mr. Donovan, trying to take the arm Mutti refused to yield.

Within moments, men surrounded them. Brushing dust from his pinstriped lapel, Mr. Phelan said, "Calm down and listen, Clare. The blast triggered a roof fall in Fin's section. The rescue squad had to tunnel through a good ten feet of rubble to get to him. Anton Zekula saved the day, beating on his bucket so they knew where to dig. Fin's in a bad way, the poor devil. His leg got caught—"

"You've always wanted him dead, and the union with him. So don't let on you're bothered by his condition now," Mutti snapped. "If you really give a damn, go down in the cage yourself and rescue someone else."

Norah could not have been more surprised if Mutti had magically transformed into Roz—the old Roz, who neither cowered nor ran. Mr. Phelan looked as if he'd been kicked by a mule. Tight-lipped, he nodded at a medic, who pointed at the tent. "This way, ma'am."

When the medic drew back the flap, Mutti recoiled, backing into Norah. The stench of vomit and loosed bowels wafted toward them. White-coated doctors and medics zigzagged from cot to cot like bloodstained ghosts. Somber Fr. Kovacs moved more slowly, raising his right hand and tracing a cross above each miner. In his long black cassock he resembled nothing if not an angel of death.

"D'you see him, missus?" asked the medic.

"Over there." Norah pointed. "They're putting something on his leg." As they proceeded through the maze of cots, she tried not to notice the oozing wounds, the limbs splayed at sickening angles. There was no way to stop her ears against the plaintive cries.

Norah tripped over an oxygen tank and bumped into a cot. Its occupant, whose face was too dirty to recognize, screamed. Then another man screamed, and another, until it seemed as if the canvas walls, straining to contain such a maelstrom of misery, might split at the seams.

Suffused with shame, Norah joined Mutti at the foot of Pap's cot. Their escort knelt to help a pair of medics hold Pap down while a doctor bound his left thigh to wooden splints. Rust-stained gauze covered Pap's forehead and right eye. "Go to hell, the lot of you!" he shouted, revealing teeth and a tongue as black as his tattered clothes. "Stop this torture and let me die!"

"Die, then," Norah whispered. She glanced at Mutti. Neither she nor the medics seemed to have heard. Norah closed her eyes and wished with all her strength. *Die and leave us in peace.*

Pap howled. Norah opened her eyes. Her gaze fell on the bloody window torn in his pants. A deep gash above his right knee oozed blood. Mutti shrank against her. Norah's insides contracted around the sinful wish that she knew, despite so much blood and dirt and palpable pain, would not be granted.

Mutti's pale face appeared frozen. A single tear inched down her cheek. Anyone who saw her would behold a worried but grateful wife. Norah, however, watched the tear's slow trail and knew that it had escaped from a deep well of despair. Mutti had insisted on entering the gate to confirm with her own eyes what she wouldn't let herself believe outside it. Like Norah, she'd expected to see Finbar Sweeney's corpse.

A second doctor appeared with a syringe. The medic struggled to restrain Pap for the injection. "Don't worry, missus," he said to Mutti. "His leg's broke, but he should come through all right if he'll just—" he leaned against Pap's rebellious shoulder—"hold—still."

On the neighboring cot, Mr. Zekula pressed a swollen hand against his chest and began to cry. "God bless him, Clare. When the roof caved in, Fin pushed me out of the way. Ran quicker'n a rabbit, just like the old days when he was stealing bases. He saved my life, no doubt about it. Anybody says a word against Fin, you send him to me, and I'll—"

"For the love of Christ, Anton, quit your goddamn caterwauling! Me eyes were so full of dust, I couldn't see what I was pushing. If I'd known 'twas you, I'd've saved me strength,"

Pap retorted. His left eye opened long enough to take in Mutti and Norah. "Who the hell let you in here?" he said before a coughing fit overcame him.

The first doctor secured the splints and wearily straightened up. "Give him oxygen," he instructed the medic. To Pap, he said, "Listen carefully, mister. You broke your left femur, the big bone inside your thigh. The injection should help with the pain. I'm sending you to the hospital. In the meantime, lie as still as you can if you want to keep your leg." He turned to Mutti. "You can stay with him till they bring the stretcher."

The medic hovered with the oxygen mask, but Pap knocked it to the ground. His bloodshot eye turned glassy. His voice slurred. "Go home. 'Tis no place—f'ra woman."

The medic retrieved the mask and lowered it onto Pap's face. Norah regarded his limp form, trying to remember how he'd looked when he'd run like a rabbit around the ball field. Had he ever been happy? Had swinging a bat and hitting home runs given him whatever fleeting pleasure that she and her sisters and Mutti could not?

The canvas flaps parted to admit a stream of women. Branka dropped to her knees beside Bob's cot, clasping and kissing his hand. Mrs. Tonelli and Mrs. Lubicic raced to the tent's opposite end, calling their men's names. Huffing like a locomotive, Mrs. Zekula flapped her hankie as she approached. "A miracle, thanks be to God!" she proclaimed before bending to gently wipe her husband's dirty face.

In one's and two's, the wives and mothers kept coming, filling the tent with soft weeping and murmured reassurances. As women and doctors and medics crisscrossed the makeshift ward, Mutti still did not move. Stiff as a splint, she stood beside Norah, watching as Fr. Kovacs blessed Pap. Medics brought a stretcher and carried him away. Not once did Mutti attempt to lay so much as a finger on her broken, bandaged husband. Even after the tent flap dropped behind him, she remained motionless, staring at the empty cot as if the world had shrunk to this one place, leaving her nowhere else to go.

Part Four
Deutschtown

(Clare, 1941)

Chapter 47: Clare
June 8, 1941
Feast of St. Melania the Elder, Pilgrim

Norah stripped dresses from hangers, leaving the bereft wires pinging against each other. She slung the frocks over her shoulder as if they were of no greater importance than soiled bed sheets, then turned to the rickety dresser. Each drawer screeched as she yanked it open. Her hands, quick as birds, plucked nightgowns, petticoats, and stockings from their neatly folded repose. They soared from her fingers onto the bed, where Clare sat, refraining from comment. A lace-edged corselette fluttered onto Clare's lap. She stroked it, mindful not to snag the silk.

Norah finally broke the silence. "You could still come with me. I've got more than enough money for two train fares." Her shoulders flounced when Clare didn't reply. Returning to the closet, she retrieved her red hatbox and leather suitcase. They would accompany her, as they had on her first business trip to Pittsburgh. This time, however, neither she nor her luggage would be coming back.

Clare pretended to misunderstand. "How would that look, me taking a vacation while your pap's in the hospital?"

Norah drew a deep, exasperated breath. "This is hardly a vacation. I need a job. My prospects are much better in Pittsburgh." She set the box on the dresser next to her straw hat and black patent handbag. The suitcase landed on the bed. Its hinge nicked Clare's hip.

Clare pretended to believe her. Though Norah parroted *better prospects,* they both knew that her leave-taking had as much to do with losing Paul as finding a new position. "I wish you'd ask Roz for a letter of recommendation," Clare said. "Surely she knows other shopkeepers—"

"Not in Deutschtown. I want a job I can walk to so I can save the streetcar fare." Norah struggled with the suitcase clasps. Her cheeks flushed. Clare suspected that she would like nothing better than a letter from Roz. To get it, however, she

333

would have had to return to Uniontown and risk an accidental encounter with Paul. "I can't expect Trudy to put me up forever," Norah went on. "I need to make my own way."

"Trudy's family, not a boarding missus. You can stay as long as you like."

"Trudy's used to her privacy. Anyone would be after so many years. Frankly, I'd like some myself." Norah flipped back the top of the suitcase, forcing Clare to slide to the head of the bed. Clare was shocked when Norah scooped up every last belt, blouse, and brassiere, then tossed the tangled collection into the suitcase. Her prized wardrobe flung about like so many rags. Clare had watched her beat rugs with more reverence. As if reading Clare's mind, Norah straightened up, hands on hips. *Go on*, her posture dared, *scold me*.

Clare remembered her as a skinny little girl, refusing help as she'd staggered outside to the clothesline with a basket of sodden laundry. Tears stung Clare's eyes. She lowered them, realizing that she'd succumbed to habit and folded the wayward corselette. She offered it to Norah. "By the time you get to Trudy's all your clothes will be wrinkled."

"Trudy owns a house. I'm quite sure she owns an iron." With a flick of her wrist Norah unfolded the corselette, dropped it into the suitcase, and snapped the latches. She pointed to the closet. "I left some dresses for my friend Carol Ann. I don't know when she'll come and get them. Please don't throw them out, or she'll be really disappointed."

"When have I ever thrown out a dress?" Clare nearly pinched herself. She'd expected their parting to be pleasant, never imagining her daughter would desire otherwise.

Norah smiled, triumphant. She might have been Maeve, slyly goading Clare into an impulsive remark. "You can start," Norah said, "by throwing out the dress you've got on. You've bleached every speck of color out of it."

Clare stared, open-mouthed, as Norah quickly turned her back. Clare braced herself for another stinging comment until she noticed her daughter's quaking shoulders. "You can leave without us being angry at each other," Clare said.

Keeping her back turned, Norah pulled a hankie from her pocket. It took her an inordinately long time to use it. When she finally spoke, her voice was thick with tears. "He's not your penance, you know."

Clare rose, pretending again to misunderstand. "I don't mind visiting the hospital every day," she said lightly. "I always run into someone, usually Concetta or Veronika. We ride the streetcar back together. And the nurses are all so kind—"

"Haven't you been punished enough?" Norah turned so swiftly that her candy-striped skirt swirled like a pinwheel. Sunlight pierced the dimity curtain. Her damp cheeks shone. "God forgave you for—everything—a long time ago. Do you think He sits up in heaven, saying, *attaboy, Fin! Go on, teach her another lesson for using those seeds!*"

What did Clare of all people know about forgiveness? She knew only that she wanted Norah to leave and be happy before it was too late. Now it dawned on her that her daughter knew her far better than she'd ever imagined.

Clare dropped back onto the mattress. The suitcase tipped and fell to the floor. The latches popped open, spilling clothes onto the rag rug. A dainty eyelet nightgown splayed across Norah's shoes. She kicked it aside as if it had bitten her. "Pap beats you on account of who he is, not what you did. And he's never, ever going to change."

Clare couldn't meet her eyes. "A brush with death can profoundly alter a man."

Norah threw up her hands. "Deirdre's right. There's no reasoning with a martyr." She knelt and stuffed her clothing back into the bag.

"What else does Deirdre say?" Clare asked, not at all certain that she wanted to know.

Norah reached beneath the dresser to retrieve a stocking. She sat back on her heels and inspected it with a sigh. "Snagged," she said, cramming it in with the rest. "I'm sorry," she added. She might have been apologizing to the stocking since she refused to look at Clare.

Watching Fin carried out of the hoist cage, Clare had been sure he'd die within the hour. But in yet another display of

Steamshovel strength, he'd cheated death. Keeping her a wife. Keeping her here. "Your pap may never walk normally again," she said.

Norah slammed the suitcase shut and got to her feet. At last, she looked at Clare. "Maybe he got what he deserved."

Clare shook her head. "Nobody gets what they deserve. Karol Cverna didn't deserve to die. Majella's husband didn't deserve to lose his sight. Or Mike Zoshak, his arm."

Clare held out her hand, but Norah stalked to the dresser and fussed with her straw hat. Adjusted the veil. Repositioned the pearl-tipped hat pin that Roz had given her.

Clare kept her hand outstretched as she rose. "Let me carry your hatbox."

Norah's mirrored expression stopped her cold. "You may not come with me. Not without a suitcase of your own."

"*Liebchen.*" Clare's hand dropped to her side. "You know I don't have a suitcase."

Norah pulled a folded bill from her purse and hurled it onto the quilt. "Buy one."

Clare lingered on the front porch long after the streetcar had taken Norah away. Since the last ambulance had departed, The Hive had turned eerily quiet. Cars filled with Company officials and state inspectors rolled slowly up and down First Street. Only the church bell's chime and the occasional shout of a child reminded her that a semblance of normal life continued.

Four days had passed since the accident, which had killed twelve men outright. Concetta's husband Alfie, her nephew Pasquale, and ten more clung to life in the hospital where Fin recuperated. Despite a severely broken leg, three cracked ribs, a concussion, and eight lacerations deep enough to require stitches, Fin was expected, barring infection, to recover. Vlade Lubicic, Shorty Dvorsk, Paul's brother Bob, and twenty-six others with extensive injuries also were out of immediate danger. Anton had returned home, his broken wrist encased in a plaster cast. Forty-seven others with similarly minor injuries also had been discharged. Thirty had emerged unscathed. The last sixteen, cut off from escape by a prodigious roof fall in the mine's deepest section, had been dug out by a rescue team just the previous day. Miraculously, they'd suffered only from dehydration.

For the first time in thirteen years, the pageant had been cancelled.

The mine whistle hadn't sounded since it marked the explosion. Dan Phelan, quoted in Uniontown's *Evening Standard*, stated, *"The Company is confident that an official investigation, now underway, will determine the exact cause of the blast."* Stringent measures, he promised, would be taken to prevent the recurrence of such a tragedy. When asked when No. 2 would reopen, he replied, *"When it is determined to be completely safe."*

Reading that, Clare couldn't decide whether to weep or laugh. Had a completely safe mine ever existed?

Frank Sestak swore up and down that not a trace of bad gas had registered on his safety lamp when he'd inspected the mine the morning of the accident. He insisted that a spark from a locomotive or coal-cutter had encountered just enough volatile dust to trigger the blast. Meanwhile, the hoist cage rattled up and down, carrying men and tools to brattice damaged ceilings and clear rubble. A new mound rose in the slate dump.

The tolling church bell startled Clare. She'd stood for a whole hour doing absolutely nothing. Pulse pounding, she ran inside and snatched her sewing box before Fin found out that she'd wasted— Then it struck her. He'd never find out.

The sewing box slipped from her hands and hit the kitchen floor in a flurry of spools. Freed from their hiding place, photographs of Deirdre's children fluttered like autumn leaves. Clare regarded the mess with wonderment, then knelt to collect the photos. If not later today, then sometime tomorrow, Norah would hear these children's laughter. Sliding the pictures into her pocket, Clare was momentarily subdued by envy. Then wonderment took hold again.

Giddy as a girl, she tacked the photos to the wall beneath faded images of John L. Lewis and the Sacred Heart. While she washed dishes or scrubbed clothes she could look at Molly,

Meg, Ginny, and dear little Will—and pretend that they looked back lovingly at her.

"*Guten Morgen, meine Lieblings,*" she said. Good morning, my darlings.

Clapping a hand over her mouth, she looked over her shoulder, aghast at such carelessness. One of Concetta's chickens meandered across the backyard. It paused beside Clare's garden and turned its beady gaze on her, a woman with fewer wits than a hen. She lowered her hand. Laughter bubbled out of her throat into the quiet kitchen. For the first time since she'd stepped inside it, no reason for fear existed.

Habit compelled her to collect and stow the sewing things, but she indulged herself by placing the box like a bulky centerpiece in the middle of the table. St. Barbara's bell marked the quarter-hour, reminding her to change into her good dress, and quickly, if she intended to catch the next streetcar. She kissed her fingertips and touched the cheek of each pictured child. "I'm going to visit your *Opa*. I'll be back in time for supper."

Hurrying upstairs, she resolved to write to Deirdre and request new photos, not just of the children, but also Trudy and Katie. An odd impulse sent her into Norah's bedroom. The giddiness she'd felt in the kitchen expired like a blown-out candle. She smoothed the rumpled quilt on the bed. Surely Norah would return to visit. Unlike Deirdre, she'd left without bad blood between herself and Fin. In a rare moment when he hadn't been raving with pain, he'd agreed that, given the vandalized dress shop and burning cross, Norah was wise to leave. She'd visit once she'd found a job, and learned her way around Deutschtown, and caught up with her sisters, and played with her nieces and nephew—and gotten over her anger at Clare.

The closet door hung ajar, revealing a clutch of empty hangers and the four dresses promised to Carol Ann. A strangeness overtook Clare, stronger than the silly desire to adorn her kitchen table with a sewing box. She slipped the blue crepe from its hanger. Her apron and housedress dropped to the floor. The delicate fabric slid over her head and down her body like a cool breeze. She adjusted the shoulder pads in front of the dresser's speckled mirror. None of the drawers contained the matching turban that had looked so striking on Norah. All she'd left behind was a stack of movie magazines. Clare carried them to her bedroom, leaving the drawer hanging open like an incredulous mouth.

Exiting the hospital elevator, Clare met Peggy Foley, the head day-shift nurse. Peggy straightened her starched white cap with one hand and grabbed Clare's wrist with the other. "Screaming Meemie's at it again. Maybe you can reason with him."

They entered the ward, lined on both sides with beds separated by white curtains. A gravely injured miner occupied each bed, and all appeared to have been rudely awakened from sleep. Those whose necks weren't immobilized nodded at Clare, but nobody smiled. Seated in a stiff chair at her husband's bedside, each missus regarded her with a mixture of weariness, annoyance, and pity.

A torrent of profanity from the bed in the back corner rolled down the aisle. "Goddamn whores! You'll be cracking me ribs all over—" Coughing aborted the tirade.

Behind the corner curtain, Fin wrestled with a sheet as two student nurses desperately tried to hold him still. The sheet covered his torso, leaving his legs exposed. The right was heavily bandaged above the knee. The left lay on a pillow, with the knee resting in a sling. A contraption on the foot of the bed and a metal pole fixed overhead held the sling and its pulley in place. A small trapeze attached to the pole dangled above Fin's chest. He was supposed to use it to support himself—carefully, and only with orderlies' help—when being bathed or using the bedpan. Dr. Murphy, the surgeon who'd set Fin's broken femur, called the assemblage Russell traction and claimed it had saved many a limb. Provided the patient was, indeed, patient, a virtue Fin had never demonstrated outside the batter's box.

Stepping around a frantic young nurse, Peggy planted her hands on Fin's heaving shoulders. She shared Kamila's hefty build, but even her strong arms trembled from the effort of restraining him. "Mr. Sweeney, if you keep ranting and raving, you just might lose your leg."

Fin's mouth closed. His cheeks labored as if his tongue worked to dislodge a bit of food from between his teeth. He ceased his thrashing just long enough to spit in Peggy's face.

Clare's cheeks burned with shame. Peggy didn't so much as flinch. "Get me a towel," she told the student nurse at her side. To Fin, she said, "If it takes a straitjacket to make you behave, then I'll order one. In the meantime, I'm calling the doctor."

"Call the whole fucking police force!" Fin freed an arm from the tangled sheet and swung at Peggy, who forced it back onto the mattress with a prizefighter's finesse. "May the devil swallow you sideways! Get me a bottle of whiskey and leave me in peace!" he shouted, trying to shake her off. The snowy gauze wrapping his forehead was now stippled with blood.

The student nurse returned with a towel, rolling her eyes at Clare. Mortified, Clare glanced at the window, aglow with sunshine. Despite the commotion, she heard her daughter's assertion. *He's never, ever going to change.*

"Wipe my chin," said Peggy, tilting her face as the young nurse obliged. "Go find Dr. Murphy. Tell him to come PDQ, before I accidentally-on-purpose break his patient's neck."

"Go on, I dare you!" Fin challenged. "They don't call me Steam—" A paroxysm of coughing seized him. Black phlegm bubbled in the corners of his lips.

"Suction. Hurry," the unflappable Peggy told the remaining student, who fumbled implements on the bedside tray. The student struggled to slide a rubber bulb syringe between Fin's stubborn lips. "Frankly, Mr. Sweeney, if coughing stops you from cursing, then I'm all for it," said Peggy.

"Bitch!" Fin gasped, his chin flecked with dark mucous. "Whore!"

"Shut your goddamn trap, Steamshovel!" someone shouted from the far end of the ward.

Dr. Murphy strode around the curtain, followed by the student nurse. The surgeon was tall and sturdy as a miner, a fact that, under different circumstances, might have earned him at least a modicum of Fin's respect. With Peggy's help, the doctor swiftly delivered an injection. Ignoring Fin's snarls, he inspected the sling and adjusted the pillow.

Fin closed his eyes and moaned. "May you roast in hell, you sonofabitch. I'd send you there meself this very minute if I wasn't chained like a convict to this goddamn bed."

"Now there's an idea. Would you prefer chains to a straitjacket?" said Peggy. She might have been the hostess at a garden party, asking Fin if he liked coffee more than tea.

Clare hesitantly approached the bed, displaying the paper she'd purchased at the corner newsstand. "Please, Fin, lie still and rest. I'll read you the sports page."

Peggy exchanged a look with Dr. Murphy, who nodded. She slowly lifted her hands from Fin's shoulders. He regarded her, bleary-eyed and unresisting, as a student nurse smoothed the sheet and drew it up to his bristly chin.

"Nurse Foley has my permission to use whatever means necessary to secure the traction. I've never used a straitjacket on a patient, but that doesn't mean I never will. Listen to your wife, Mr. Sweeney, and stop carrying on," the doctor said before departing.

Fin looked Clare up and down, clearly confused by the blue crepe dress. "Who's that?" he said, his unfocused gaze moving to the ceiling. "Never seen her before in me life."

Chapter 48: Katie

The convent parlor smelled like the furniture polish applied that morning by the new novice. Katie seated herself in a wing chair by the window and carefully arranged the folds of her habit. She hoped she looked like a real nun, not a girl playing dress-up. Aside from the novice, Katie, at twenty-four, was the youngest sister in the convent. She twisted around and peered at her reflection, cut by the leaded glass panes into small diamonds. It was impossible to tell if her freckles had faded even a little.

She heard voices in the hallway, then the familiar swishing sound of a long skirt's hem skimming the floor. An old nun appeared in the doorway, her wrinkled face nearly as pale as her snowy wimple. She made a show of ushering Norah inside. "Have a nice visit now," she said, closing the door behind her.

Katie had resolved to be sedate and serious, the perfect picture of a young woman who'd dedicated her life to God. However, as soon as the door latched, she sprang from her chair. Treading on her tunic's hem, she pitched headlong into Norah. Their arms tangled in her veil as Katie righted herself. Giggling, they settled into a long embrace. Katie gladly would have made it even longer, but Norah stepped back and held her at arm's length.

"Is my face dirty?" Katie asked. "There aren't any mirrors, so—"

"Your face is as pretty as it ever was." Another quick hug, and Norah released her. "I just needed a few minutes to see past Sr. Mary Gertrude clothes and find my Katie." She stepped forward and lifted the edges of the black veil away from Katie's cheeks. "Doesn't your head get awfully hot, all wrapped up like that?"

Katie nodded. "You get used to it. Except in July and August, when you just have to offer it up." She took Norah's hand and twirled her like a dancer. How fine her sister looked in the ivory dress and matching coat. "Mutti wrote that your new boss gave you pretty clothes, but I never expected anything like this. Look at us—" laughing, she pulled Norah beside her—"black and white, like two piano keys. Did your boss give you the hat, too?" She peered at her sister, who had suddenly stopped smiling. "What's wrong?"

"Didn't Mutti tell you what happened?"

Katie led Norah to the prim velvet couch by the fireplace and sat beside her. "Mutti hasn't written for a good two weeks. Trudy stopped me after Mass on Sunday and said she'd gotten permission for you to visit." She took Norah's hand in both of hers and squeezed gently. "It's so good to have you here! Tell me all the news."

Norah breathed deeply. "What would you like to hear first? How the Klan vandalized La Femme? Then burned a cross in the alley behind our outhouse? Or how the mine blew up? And Pap got hurt and went to the hospital?"

"Mutti should have sent a telegram!" Katie cried. "How bad is Pap hurt? Who else?" She interrupted Norah's grim litany of names and afflictions only once. "Is Mr. Kukoc all right?"

Norah nodded. "I think I'd stop believing in God if another awful thing happened to the Kukoces." She grinned wryly. "I guess I shouldn't say that in front of a nun."

"Being a nun doesn't mean I stopped being me." Katie stroked Norah's sleeve. "Will Pap be a cripple?"

"Nobody knows yet. His leg's strung up with a pulley and a sling. He's not supposed to move it, but he always gets worked up. The nurses have to give him shots to knock him out. Can you imagine a worse job than being his nurse?" Norah shuddered. "I'd sooner be a honeydipper and clean outhouses."

"I'll pray for them all, especially Pap. I'll start a novena as soon as you leave," Katie declared. Norah's shrug puzzled her. "You're praying, too, aren't you? I know he's done bad things, but he's still our pap. It's God's place to judge, not ours."

Norah rolled her eyes. "Fine, let God worry about him. And Mutti, too, and the whole damn patch. I'm sick of worrying. It's worn me out." She blushed and lifted a hand to her mouth. "I can't believe I just cursed in a convent. Is that a mortal sin?"

Katie clasped Norah's hands and kissed them. "I don't care! I've missed you so much! I couldn't believe it when Trudy said she'd fixed it so you could visit. The rules are so strict about us going out. I've only seen Deirdre twice, when she brought her girls to Mass at St. Marienkirche—and that was before Will was born." Someone knocked, and she turned toward the door. "Come in!"

"Can't!" replied a cheerful voice. "Unless you want me to drop your tea."

Katie darted across the room to admit Sr. Paula Marie, her best friend. Paula had entered the same year and, at twenty-seven, was the nun closest to her in age. Paula deposited the tray on the table in front of the couch, then turned to appraise Norah. "Heavens, you don't look at all alike. I thought you'd be a freckle-face, just like Gertie here."

Katie lifted the napkin covering a plate and clapped her hands. "Sugar cookies! Go on, Paula, take one. It's not fair we should have them all."

"Of course it is. It's not every day you have a visitor," said Paula, heading for the door. "I'll leave you two to catch up. Clock's ticking, you know."

"What clock?" Norah asked, filling her teacup. "And what's the big deal about a few cookies?" She bit into one and wrinkled her nose. "They're kind of stale."

Katie plucked the cookie from Norah's fingers and popped it into her mouth. "We only have dessert on special holy days, so I'm not going to waste a bite," she said thickly. She'd never dream of speaking with her mouth full in the convent dining room. But with Norah beside her, she could almost pretend that they were back on the bench in Mutti's kitchen. Glancing at the clock above the door, she added, "We've got less than an hour before someone comes to show you out. Visitors can only stay—"

"An hour!" Norah threw up her hands. "You put up with this? It's like being in jail."

A sugary lump lodged in Katie's throat. It took three swallows of steaming tea to dissolve it. Mouth stinging, she set down her cup and declared, "The convent is *nothing* like jail."

"I'm sorry." Norah sipped contritely from her own cup, then dabbed her lips with a napkin. "Do you ever hear from Jack?"

Katie regarded the cookie in her hand before returning it to the plate. Paula wouldn't believe her, but the treat had lost its appeal. "I'm not allowed to correspond with a man I'm not related to."

"Couldn't you sneak out a letter?"

"If I'm not willing to obey the rules, I shouldn't've entered in the first place." Katie stared at her hands, twisting on her lap. "The penitentiary they sent him to is just a few miles away. It's hard sometimes, knowing he's so close. Some days I wish I could go there, just to see it. Not inside—" She shuddered, recalling the dismal Beetown jail. "Maybe it's better that I can't."

A long silence passed before Norah said, "Gertie." She repeated the name softly, then shook her head. "Sr. Mary Gertrude. It doesn't seem to suit you."

"If it weren't for Trudy, I wouldn't be here. It only seemed right to take her name."

Norah nodded. Her tone turned wistful. "Do you ever wonder if you made a mistake?"

"I'd certainly rather be here than The Hive. I'd rather be *anywhere* than The Hive."

Norah threaded the napkin between her fingers. "Me, too."

Katie swept the crumbs from her lap onto the tray. Hoping to change the subject, she asked, "What came between you and Paul? I thought for sure you two would get—" The torment in her sister's expression took her aback. "It's all right. You don't have to tell me."

Norah looked away. "Maybe someday. But not now."

Katie hesitated before admitting, "I may not be here much longer."

Norah's face whipped around. "*Gott in Himmel*, you're not sick, are you?"

"Oh, no, nothing like that." The taste of sugar had fled Katie's tongue, leaving behind a familiar bitterness that only exhaustive prayer could dispel. How could she have overlooked the obvious? Norah's visit couldn't help but stir up memories that Katie struggled, day after day, to suppress. Despite stringent rules intended to keep her separate from the outside world, the convent, like St. Barbara's tower, was not as impregnable as she'd thought.

She took Norah's hand. "Sr. Lidwina Weber, a missionary nun, started a motherhouse and novitiate in San Antonio. The Catholic schools there really need teachers. Especially young ones like me."

"Where on earth is San Antonio—in Spain?"

"Texas." Katie couldn't help but smile. "For heaven's sake, Norah, it's not the end of the world. Believe it or not, a lot of German people live there. It'll be like Deutschtown, only with cattle ranches instead of the Heinz plant."

Norah snatched back her hand. "It might as well be the end of the world. I just got here, and now you're leaving. Can't you tell them you don't want to go? They can't force you—or is that a rule, too?"

The windowpanes had transformed the sunlight into little rainbows, strewn like jewels around the parlor. Katie slid her arm across the back of the couch. A small, vivid spectrum painted the palm of her hand. She closed her fingers as if she were a child again, believing that she could catch and keep something as ineffable as it was precious. Believing that a rainbow might accomplish what years of prayer could not. As she watched, the window darkened, and the light drained from her skin.

"Nobody's forcing me. When I heard about Sr. Lidwina, I asked if I could go." She made herself look at Norah as a tear, then another, rolled down her cheek. "This place seems like a completely different world to you. But, to me, it's still too familiar. That probably sounds ridiculous, doesn't it?"

She expected Norah to argue. Instead, her sister opened her purse and took out a lace-edged hankie. She leaned across the couch and dried Katie's face. "It's not ridiculous at all. It's why I left The Hive."

Chapter 49: Clare

June 15, 1941
Feast of St. Germaine Cousin, Mystic, Patroness of Abused Children

Clare opened the front door, surprised to see Big Bill, hat in hand, dressed in the dark blue suit he'd worn earlier in the week to Pasquale Tonelli's funeral. Her grasp tightened on the knob. "Did something happen? Was there another—"

"Nothing's happened, Clare," he assured her. "I'm here on behalf of the Company." He took in her grubby hands and apron, soiled with garden dirt. "I'm sorry to disturb you, but I have something important to tell you. May I come in?"

Wondering what could possibly be too important to say across a threshold, she motioned him inside. Convention dictated that, if the assistant superintendent put on a suit and presented himself at your front door, you seated him in the living room. She hesitated as a contrary spark ignited in her belly like a match struck against the sole of a shoe. With a nod, she led him into the kitchen. She sat in the chair at the head of the table. The other chair was heaped with rags that she kept intending, then forgetting to tear up and weave into a rug. Big Bill looked around, then lowered himself onto the bench. The table was strewn with library books, newspapers, and Norah's old movie magazines, so he set his hat on the bench beside him. He glanced at the drainboard, stacked with three days' worth of dishes that Clare had scraped and rinsed, but not yet washed.

Go on, she silently dared him. *Comment on my untidy kitchen.*

She smoothed her apron and clasped her hands, assuming the posture she adopted each Sunday when Fr. Kovacs occupied the pulpit. Big Bill regarded her with outright bewilderment. In his opinion, she'd committed yet anther sin of omission. She had asked him—a boss, no less—into her home and failed to offer, at the very minimum, a cup of tea.

He waited, giving her the chance to recognize her error, apologize, and clear the table sufficiently to accommodate a cup

347

and saucer. Deep inside her, that contrary spark flared again. She settled against the back of the chair and refrained from even a perfunctory pleasantry about the mild weather. The clock's second hand lurched forward twenty times before Big Bill cleared his throat and pointed at the photographs tacked to the wall. "Lovely children."

She nodded, knowing he expected her to eagerly offer names and ages. If she hoped to approach even the semblance of a courteous hostess, she'd then defer to him. Inquire about his fourteen grandchildren and six college-educated sons' commendable professions, none of which had anything to do with mining. Instead, she studied the floor, silently counting the crumbs of dirt she'd tracked in from the garden.

Finally, he said, "Well, it's like this, Clare. The Company doesn't want you to worry one bit about your rent or groceries. While Fin's laid up, you won't be charged for rent. You'll also get a weekly allowance at the store until he's working again. Free and clear, not credit."

He paused and smiled. He'd offered what he and the Company considered a generous concession to the wife of a man their mine had nearly killed. It was her turn to speak or, better still, shed copious tears of gratitude. Taking care to remain expressionless, she said nothing.

"You don't have to worry about the hospital bill either. Dan Phelan guarantees that the Company will cover every cent, no matter how long it takes for Fin to get back on his feet." He cleared his throat again. Grudgingly, she gave him credit for recognizing his poor choice of words. "No matter how long it takes," he repeated, "you and Fin will be taken care of."

He nodded, satisfied that he and the Company had done their part to assuage her fears. She nodded, too, so he wouldn't think her comprehension so compromised by upset over Fin's situation that he needed to deliver his speech again.

She expected that, having discharged his task, he'd make an expeditious exit, then pause on the sidewalk to consult a list pulled from his pocket. He'd proceed to the next house, the next injured miner's missus. Instead, he sat, neck ruddy above his shirt's starched white collar, as if someone had nailed his shoes to the floor. Had he been instructed by Dan Phelan to hold his ground like a deputy intimidating pickets until hearing the missus in question utter the magic words? *Thank you! Oh, thank you and God bless you! And bless Mr. Phelan, too!*

A wasp thudded softly against the window screen, then, whining, looped around the porch post. Twenty years ago, Big Bill had leaned against that post, wearing overalls and work boots, an ordinary miner like every other boss. They'd labored in the pit and played on the ball field, all the while talking about bringing in the union. Then a strike had begun. For reasons they'd kept to themselves, Fin's former friends had surprised the patch by refusing to walk out. Perhaps, like Masha the gypsy, they could see into the future. To ensure their fortune, and that of their children, and their children's children, they chose the side that, strike after strike, would win. And on account of all that winning, they slowly and inexorably changed.

A dog barked, dispelling Clare's useless reminiscence. A breeze rustled the pages of the *Evening Standard*, where a front-page headline announced the freezing of German and Italian assets in U.S. banks. She studied her dirty hands, then fixed her gaze outside, where half the garden remained to be weeded. Her right foot, unbidden, began to tap. Could the assistant superintendent tell she preferred to keep company with dandelions, who knew better than to patronize anyone owning a hoe?

Big Bill got to his feet. Taking up his hat, he looked piously at the faded picture of the Sacred Heart. "Fin's been a hard worker all these years. The Company will do everything possible to take care of him in his hour of need."

Though she wished he'd chosen to deliver his official assurances at Fin's bedside, she knew exactly how Fin would respond. *Hard worker, me arse! I've broken me leg and ruined me lungs in your goddamn gassy pit, and what do you do in return? Think yourself grand as God for paying the doctors to fix me up, so I can go back down and do it all over again. I'll stay a cripple, and gladly, if it means Dan Phelan has less money in his fine suit pocket at the end of the day.*

349

She stalked to the back door and opened it, unintentionally admitting the wasp. This unexpected ally circled Big Bill's head like a British bomber over Hamburg. Flapping his hat, the assistant superintendent made a swift, humbled exit.

Chapter 50: Clare

July 10, 1941
Feast of St. Amalberga, Mother of Saints

Day lilies bloomed in buttery profusion along the backyard fence. The garden's flowers became hard green buttons that swelled into peppers, tomatoes, and crookneck squash. Clare's plans to freshen the curtains with extra embroidery and weave a new rag rug went unfulfilled. Instead she read six novels, borrowed with her brand new card from the Beetown library. Kamila's daughters passed on *Anthony Adverse* and *Gone With the Wind* to Kamila, who then lent them to Clare. On a whim, she purchased a large box of candles, enjoying their cozy glow while reading in bed after dark. Sometimes she read long into the night. Sometimes all night.

Each time she stepped inside the store, Ada Smiley took obvious pleasure in informing her that she had received no mail from Pittsburgh. She told herself that Norah simply needed more time to get settled.

One by one, the injured miners mended and returned home. A small article in the *Evening Standard* noted the reopening of Heath No. 2. "*State and Company inspectors concur that a spark of indeterminate origin set off a small blast in an inactive room near the main haulageway, resulting in several incidental roof falls. All damaged ceilings have been bratticed, and locomotive tracks and electrical lines are now restored to full working order.*" The notice concluded with a quote from Dan Phelan: "*The Company deeply regrets the tragic loss of life and limb and stresses enforcement of the Company motto—Safety, the First Consideration. The resumption of operations has been welcomed by miners and Company officials alike. Each desires to do his part in filling the nation's war orders in support of the Allied cause overseas.*"

Reading between the lines, Clare was sure they still didn't know what had happened and probably never would. She was equally certain that the Company lamented the loss of revenue

351

during the shutdown as much as the deaths and dismemberments. She didn't mention the article to Fin. He'd rant and rave upon hearing Dan Phelan's statement and, once again, dislodge his traction. She told him only that No. 2 was back in business, to which he responded with a grunt.

Clad in black to mourn her late nephew, Concetta rode the streetcar with Clare that afternoon. Her spirits had risen considerably since her husband had been moved to Fin's ward. Alfie had not only recovered from the pneumonia that had set in shortly after his hospitalization, but had also come through four subsequent surgeries, the last to amputate his gangrenous right foot.

"God is giving him a miracle," Concetta told Clare as they disembarked in Uniontown. "But still he is angry, calling his new name Alfie *le zoppo*, the man who is lame. I am every day telling him to say the rosary as thank-you to *Madre* Maria. To live with one foot is very much better than keeping two foots, but being dead."

Clare pictured Fin, lying four beds away from Alfie. Though possessing both feet, Fin might also end up *zoppo*. Crippled. Like Alfie, he took little pleasure in being alive. Unlike Fin, however, Alfie was polite as a priest to the hard-working doctors and nurses and saved his complaints for Concetta.

Rosie waited on the sidewalk outside the hospital, holding the hand of her five-year-old daughter and balancing the baby on her hip. Because children weren't allowed in the wards, Concetta would visit first, then come outside and amuse her granddaughters while Rosie visited husband Mike Zoshak, plagued with a lingering infection in what remained of his left arm.

Rosie asked about Deirdre, but Clare was too ashamed to admit that Deirdre hadn't written in weeks. "Oh, just the usual for a pregnant mother. Trying to keep her breakfast down and take care of four little ones. She's praying for Mike," Clare said, hoping that it was true.

Before they remembered to ask about Norah, Clare excused herself and went to the newsstand to buy a paper. Norah still hadn't sent so much as a postcard.

Concetta went inside ahead of Clare, so she was alone when she encountered Peggy in the doorway of the ward. "Your husband's leg is on the mend," said the nurse, shaking her head in apparent disbelief. "I thought for sure he'd compromised the traction. But they took x-rays this morning, and there's a limited callus on the femur. That means new bone is forming around the break. His ribs are perfectly sound."

She peered quizzically at Clare. It took a moment before Clare realized that other wives reacted to such news with a radiant smile or tears of joy. Perhaps they even hugged the nurse. Clare, however, could scarcely breathe.

"He's still not completely out of the woods," Peggy continued. "That gash in his right leg seems to be healing well, but there's always a risk of infection. Overall, he's making a remarkable recovery, probably out of sheer cussedness."

"Have you told him this?" Clare asked.

"Dr. Murphy did," said Peggy. Someone in another room called to her, and she hurried away.

Clare could barely feel her feet as she made her way into the ward. On the right, Veronika Lubicic arranged photographs on the blanket covering Vlade. They smiled as Clare passed, laboring to fill her lungs. On the left, Concetta and Alfie argued spiritedly in Italian. Concetta caught Clare's eye and threw up her hands. *What's a wife to do?*

What, indeed? What wife, upon receiving news of her husband's amazing recovery, felt as if a room the size of two backyards was rapidly compressing? In a matter of moments, the hospital walls would crush her as effectively as a roof fall in a mine.

"You're late," said Fin as soon as she stepped around his curtain. "Gossiping with your friends, no doubt, while I lie here suffering. At least you had sense enough to bring the paper."

Clumsily she unfolded it, revealing the banner headline: **GERMANS ADVANCE, CROSS DNIEPER RIVER IN UKRAINE.** Her knees gave way, and she nearly fell into the bedside chair. "The nurse says the bone in your leg is healing. Is the pain any better?"

"Only when the stupid bitch troubles herself to give me the shot. Should be working in a prison, that one, taking pleasure the way she does in tormenting people."

"Would you like me to read you the baseball scores?"

"Wouldn't you rather be telling me how your *Führer*'s army is taking over the world?"

He slapped the front page, knocking the paper from her grasp. The pages scattered across the floor. "He's not my *Führer*, Fin." Her response was automatic, toneless. As she retrieved the paper, her head seemed to swell, becoming so heavy that she feared her neck would snap. It required prodigious effort to straighten up and cling to the pages he irritably rapped again. Though the muscles in his arms had wasted, he still managed to jab her shoulder. He chided her for being careless, being late, being unsympathetic for what he'd suffered to put food in her stomach and keep a roof over her ungrateful head.

Her fingers turned thick and stiff as she struggled to fold the paper. To distract Fin, she said, "Big Bill said the Company won't charge us for rent or groceries while you can't work. And they'll pay every cent of your hospital bill."

She found the sports page, but before she could locate the baseball scores, he shouted, "Will they be buying groceries for the rest of me life if I end up a goddamn cripple?"

"Your leg's mending well, Fin. There's no reason to think you'll end up lame."

"Don't be contradicting me! You're out playing cards, having yourself a fine time. Always thinking of yourself, while I lie here in misery. If you had even half a heart, you'd bring me a bottle of whiskey like you promised. But I suppose that's too much trouble, now isn't it?"

You know as well as I that I've never been a card-player. I read, you foolish man! I thought I'd forgotten how, but all I'd forgotten is how much I enjoy it. Before she could defend herself, she realized that, to Fin, reading a novel had no more merit than a game of bridge. "I never promised to bring you whiskey, Fin. You know the doctor wouldn't allow it." She scanned the newsprint, but the letters and numbers ran together like scurrying ants. "Just give me a minute till I find the baseball—"

"You're wishing I died in the pit, aren't you now? Stoned to death in the dark and saving you the trouble of coming here every goddamn day. Don't be lying to me, for I can see the truth plain as daylight on your face."

The shudder started deep in her belly. Her quivering fingers mashed the paper into a crude square. Dropping it onto Fin's chest, she stalked out of the ward.

In the quiet kitchen, Clare scrambled an egg, cut bread, brewed tea. She barely tasted the simple supper as she devoured *Gone With the Wind*, propped against her sewing box. She imagined the heat rising from her cup as the air in Atlanta as it went up in flames. She accidentally knocked her knife onto the floor, and the clatter transformed into rattling carriage wheels as desperate residents fled the embattled city. Her tea cooled as she read on, hungrier for the story than her food, until Rhett declared his love for Scarlett and departed to fight for what was surely a lost cause.

She marked the page with an old pay envelope and closed the book. Outside, the sky had dimmed to purple. Fireflies' tiny lanterns twinkled throughout the backyard. Cornstalks rustled in the garden. A breeze filtered through the screen door and passed over her grandchildren's photos like a gentle hand. Their corners trembled with what she imagined as a child's pleasure at having captured her attention. *Oma, pleeeease put away your book and play with us!*

Smiling, she rose. "*Oma* has to do dishes now. I've let them go so long that every plate and cup is dirty. Now what do you think of that?"

As she soaped and rinsed, the echo of Peggy's brisk voice assailed her. *He's making a remarkable recovery.* She stepped back from the sink. There would be no infection. Fin's thigh bone would mend perfectly, just like his ribs. He'd come home with two sound legs, expecting to find each pot thoroughly washed and neatly put away. Immaculate floors, upstairs and down. Each windowpane, spotless. The books, the photos, the candlestick by her bed—none could be in evidence.

He'd come home and, within days, summon sufficient strength to harshly put her in her place if she sewed on a button that he decided was crooked. As Norah had predicted, he'd come home and resume life exactly as it had been before. Though he'd cheated death, he had not been altered in the slightest. And never would be.

Her chest tightened, just as it had that afternoon at the hospital. The towel dropped to the floor. Gasping, she crossed the kitchen and sank into her chair. With Fin in the hospital, she inhabited a fairy tale, leaving dishes unwashed for days. Sweeping the kitchen floor only after supper and the other rooms, not at all. Reading during meals and in bed, hour upon blissful hour. Time typically spent laundering filthy work clothes, buying food and cooking it in sufficient quantities to fill a miner's belly, packing the workday bucket, preparing the daily bath—all given back to her, a hitherto unimaginable gift to do with as she pleased.

Much as she savored the freedom to conduct fanciful conversations with her grandchildren's pictures, the summer's most precious gift was freedom from fear. No step, no gesture, no drawn breath need be second-guessed. She lived, where, not so long ago, she'd merely survived.

Twisted and limp, the towel lay on the floor. She saw a body in its place—a woman, cringing in anticipation of another hard kick, even as she told herself she deserved it, and more. Each slap and bruise added to a tally that would never fully absolve her of her sins.

Fighting for air, she stumbled outside, down the porch steps, and into the center of the yard. Fireflies danced around her. The vise in her chest slowly loosened. She tipped back her head and regarded the vast darkness. Breathing deeply, she imagined it as God—enveloping her, an insignificant creature, who dared at long last to believe in redemption.

Chapter 51: Deirdre

Will banged his spoon against the tray of his high chair until Deirdre looked at him. Then he gleefully hurled it for the umpteenth time onto the kitchen floor.

"Billy, could you please pick it up?" Deirdre asked, setting down her knife and fork. Her hands hovered on each side of her untouched dinner. Which to massage first—her throbbing temples or her belly, punishing her with cramps for eating a leftover bowl of Hattie's spicy gumbo for lunch? Supper's mingled aromas of carrots, potatoes, and roast beef suddenly turned her stomach. She looked away from the laden table, from her husband and sister and four noisy, fidgeting children, and out the window above the kitchen sink. Framed by strawberry-print curtains, it afforded a view of the carriage house-turned-garage. The upstairs windows glowed, and Hattie could be seen through them, moving about in her compact kitchen, undoubtedly reveling in the ease of cooking just for herself.

Molly's voice, robust with eight-year-old outrage, drew Deirdre's weary attention back to the table. "Playing with your food is bad manners, Daddy." For added emphasis, Molly vigorously shook her head, whipping copper-penny pigtails from side to side. Her pink bows came undone, and a loosened ribbon flicked Deirdre's arm.

Having retrieved Will's spoon from the checkerboard linoleum, Billy used it and his fork to beat a Gene Krupa drum solo on the high chair tray. Will shrieked with delight when Billy passed him both utensils. The banging resumed, less rhythmic but twice as loud.

Though seated in a father's rightful place at the head of the table, Billy's behavior was no better than the children's. "I'm playing with silverware, not food," he explained, winking at Deirdre, who rolled her eyes. Tweaking Molly's braid, he snatched her fork.

"No fair, Daddy!" Molly glared across the table at Meg and Ginny. They sat, giggling, on each side of Norah, who made a poor attempt at keeping a straight face.

"For heaven's sake, Billy," Deirdre began, then opted to let Molly, the family deputy, pass judgment on further breaches of table etiquette. Deirdre caught Norah's eye. "Doesn't this make you want to run right out and find a fella to marry, so you can enjoy this kind of entertainment every night?"

Grinning, Norah countered, "Why would I spend money on a wedding when I can come over here and enjoy your family for free?"

Billy wiped a smear of mashed carrot off Will's face and transferred it to the tip of his own nose. Molly huffed and threw up her hands, sparing Deirdre the need to remove hers from her complaining belly.

"For heaven's sake—" Deirdre shook her head and gave up. How was it possible to love a man for his comical nature and simultaneously want to strangle him on account of it? As if reading her mind, Billy smiled contritely. From his necktie down, he was all businessman. Above the tie, he was the family clown, staining his nose to match his hair. Deirdre squelched the urge to hurl her cutlery—just like Will, just for the hell of it—onto the spattered floor. In a mere ten hours, the airy red-and-white kitchen had transformed from Hattie's spit-polished realm to an embarrassing display of sticky countertops and unwashed dishes. Small fingerprints in hues ranging from grass-green to mud-brown tattooed the low cabinet doors. Deirdre sighed and turned to Molly. "Hold still, so I can tie your ribbons."

"When you get married, can I be your flower girl, Aunt Norah?" asked Molly.

"Me, too!" said Meg, tugging Norah's sleeve.

"I'm *not* getting married." Norah gave Deirdre a look. *See what you started?*

"Where's Hattie?" asked Ginny. Kneeling on her chair, she reached for the basket of dinner rolls and knocked over her cup of milk.

Deirdre held her breath as a cramp waxed, then waned. "Billy, please stop laughing and wipe it up. And while you're at it, wipe the carrots off your nose."

Billy sopped up the puddle with his napkin. "If I can't laugh, neither can Norah."

Molly shook her finger at crestfallen Ginny. "You spill your milk *every single night*."

"I want Hattie," said Meg as Ginny began to cry.

Will's spoon sailed across the table and landed in Norah's mashed potatoes. Billy apprehended his fork before Will could send it in the same direction. "How about a roll, son?" he asked, taking one from the basket.

"He'll just throw it," Molly warned.

"Son, you may not throw this roll," Billy said solemnly, placing it before Will. Turning back to his salad, he asked, "Can anybody guess where these tomatoes came from?"

Will tore the roll in two. Cramming one piece into his mouth, he hurled the other at Molly. She glared at Billy. "I *told* you so."

"That you did, Mollydoll," Billy agreed. "How about feeding your brother some of those potatoes you're pushing around your plate while I finish my salad?"

Deirdre's hands reluctantly abandoned her belly. She leaned across the table to wipe Ginny's damp cheek. "Daddy will get you some more milk as soon as he wipes his nose."

"I'll get it." Norah carried the cup to the counter, where hard-earned experience had taught Deirdre to place the pitcher during mealtime.

"Just fill it halfway," said Deirdre, wincing as another cramp commenced.

Norah touched Deirdre's shoulder. "Are you all right?" she asked softly.

"Just tired," Deirdre replied. "It's been another long day in the nuthouse."

Billy speared a tomato wedge and paused to admire it. "All the way from California. Mark my words, the day will come when we'll stock fresh blueberries in December." He popped the tomato into his mouth and chewed with relish.

"Will Hattie give me my bath?" asked Meg.

"Mama will," said Billy. Checking his watch, he slid back his chair and looked apologetically at Deirdre.

She let out a noisy breath. "This morning, you said—"

"I know, I know, but something came up at the warehouse."

"Don't you pay people to take care of what comes up there?" Deirdre said, as annoyed with herself as with Billy. She was about to cry, for God's sake, on account of a stupid warehouse. She should have been grateful that Billy had left the office in time for a family dinner, however chaotic. The waistband of her skirt pinched, intensifying the cramps. Just three months along, and she was already fat.

Billy bent to kiss her cheek. "Sorry. I'll be back in a few hours."

"You always say that!" she called after him, hoping he'd forgotten about the carrots on his nose. It was downright petty to want Billy to enter his company's warehouse looking like a clown, but she didn't care. Molly the Deputy eyed her as if she were yet another petulant little sister. She eyed Molly right back. *Just wait till you're pregnant, and it's your maid's night off.* If only Will would stop banging on his tray! Massaging her temples, she said as sweetly as she could, "Mollydoll, please wipe the potatoes off your brother's face and take him out of his high chair."

"I'll put you to bed," Norah told Ginny, who'd climbed into her lap. "And Meg, too. Maybe your mama will let us borrow her bubble bath."

Deirdre blew a kiss to Norah. "God bless you. Take the whole bottle."

Meg and Ginny squealed and clapped their hands. Molly shouted over them, "I want a bubble bath, too!"

Ginny leaned forward, shaking her finger at Molly and upending her refilled cup.

"Jesus, Mary, and Joseph!" Deirdre burst into tears. She'd taken holy names in vain, and in front of impressionable children. She wiped her eyes, then realized that her underpants felt as damp as her face. Crying over spilled milk—and wetting herself, to boot! Nothing this humiliating had happened during her previous pregnancies. "Excuse me while I go to the bathroom."

Norah rose and deposited tearful Ginny back on her own chair. "Are you sure you're all right, Deirdre? You look, I don't know, kind of—"

"Pregnant?" Deirdre forced a laugh. A stabbing cramp turned her laughter into a gasp. Her panties had gone from damp to downright wet. Why on earth had she and Billy decided to try for another boy? Why did something go wrong at the warehouse every time he made it home for supper?

She felt a hand on her back and realized that she'd slumped against the counter. "You should lie down," Norah whispered in her ear. Turning to the children, Norah said, "Molly, listen to your mother and get Will out of his high chair. Then take him and your sisters outside to play while I put your mama to bed. After that, we'll have a bubble bath party."

"Mama, are you all right?" Meg's voice quavered.

Deirdre managed to straighten up. "Just tired, sweetie. Be a good girl now, and listen to Auntie." Gratefully, she watched Norah herd the children out of the room. "I wet my pants," she admitted when her sister returned. "My belly aches, and my dress is too tight—"

"Good Lord!" Norah grabbed a napkin and wiped Deirdre's legs. "You're bleeding." She pressed the cloth into Deirdre's hand. "Put it between your legs, so you don't drip on the floor."

Deirdre hobbled to the powder room with the napkin clamped between her thighs. When she let it drop, the cloth was sodden with blood. It streamed down each leg, seeping inside her shoes, pooling around her toes. A savage cramp doubled her over. Dimly, she heard Norah tell her what she already knew. Like Mutti, bleeding through Mrs. Tonelli's bed sheet, Deirdre was losing her baby. Overcome with shame, she sank to her knees and laid her head on the cool pink tiles. Was this her punishment for fretting over a messy kitchen, a thickened waist, a hardworking husband? "Please call the doctor," she murmured.

How long did she lie there, hands cradling her belly, trying to keep her second son from spilling all over the powder room floor? Her skirt clung, heavy and sticky, to the backs of her thighs. She pressed her knees together, but it was no use. Like a defiant heart, her womb kept pulsing. Relentlessly emptying. The air filled with a strange scent, at once sweetish and metallic, as if she lay amid piles of wilting flowers and old coins.

Norah returned and lifted Deirdre's head to place a folded towel beneath it. "The doctor's on his way. Hattie took the kids upstairs. I called the warehouse, and whoever I talked to said he'll send Billy home as soon as he shows up. What else can I do?"

As helpful as Norah had been—indeed, an angel could not have done better—she couldn't possibly understand. "Write to Mutti," Deirdre whispered. "Tell her to come."

Chapter 52: Clare

July 25, 1941
Feast of St. James the Greater, Apostle, Patron of Laborers

"I figured you'd be here," said Kamila, weaving around the graves. "Keeping company with the dead or the bedridden. Or sitting in that empty house all by yourself, which isn't much better." Grunting, she lowered herself onto the grass beside Clare, then jerked her chin at the Finbars' decrepit markers. "Those three crosses look as old as Methuselah."

"I've been meaning to paint them. I just haven't gotten around to it," Clare admitted.

"*Pffft*! Too busy reading. I've never been one to bad-mouth a reader, Clare, but a reader and a hermit are two different things." Kamila softened her tone. "Anna and Helen are bringing their kids over after lunch. If you come, too, we'll have a foursome for bridge."

Clare caught her breath, recalling Fin's assessment of women's card games. "That sounds like fun, but I need to go to the hospital."

Kamila plucked a handful of grass and studied the blades. "Veronika Lubicic says Fin keeps everyone in the ward up half the night, cussing like there's no tomorrow. You know what they say, Clare. You can't teach an old dog new tricks."

Hoping to change the subject, Clare said, "I heard Vlade may come home next week."

"And I heard Fin's bone is healing so well they're calling it a miracle." Kamila tossed the grass aside. "Why he got a miracle and not poor Karol Cverna, who never raised his voice, much less his hand—well, you can't help but wonder sometimes at the unfairness of it all." She gave Clare a sharp look. "I'm not trying to be mean. I'm just speaking my mind."

Clare tried again to reroute Kamila's train of thought. "Norah sent a letter. She's working at the Heinz plant, giving tours to visitors. Katie may be sent to teach school in Texas sometime next year." Now Clare was the one looking at the grass. "Deirdre had a miscarriage. They took her to the hospital for a D&C, but she's back home now."

Kamila threw up her hands. "If one of *my* girls lost a baby, I'd be on her doorstep so fast it'd make your head spin." She pointed at the crosses. "You can't do a thing for those boys now."

Clare rose onto her knees. "I need to go to the hospital."

Kamila gripped Clare's arm before she could stand. "I'm probably committing a bad sin by saying this, but I'll take my chances. Fin's made his bed, but you don't have to lie in it with him the rest of your life. God knows why St. Barbara saved him, but she did, so let her look after him. He can beat the living daylights out of her holy card whenever he has too much to drink."

A flush stained Kamila's face. Clare sensed that her own had gone stark white. Though rivaling Ada Smiley as the most outspoken woman in The Hive, Kamila had never talked so frankly about Fin. Clare's mouth opened and closed like that of an expiring fish, but she didn't know how to reply. *You can't teach an old dog new tricks. He's never, ever going to change.*

Kamila released Clare's arm. "If you excuse him just one more time, I'll never speak to you again. It drives me crazy when you say he doesn't know what he's doing. Ask anyone, and they'll tell you the same thing."

The noon sun shone without mercy. Sweat rose on Clare's forehead, in the small of her back, between her folded legs. Every secret was leaking out of her into the glaring light of day. She knew that Kamila wasn't bluffing, so she remained silent. The only words Kamila would listen to were those that had kept Clare up most of the night. Words that she feared she lacked the courage to say.

"He'll leave the hospital no different than he went in, Clare. When he comes home—"

"No!" Clare's outburst startled a pair of crows roosting on the cemetery fence. They took flight amid raucous remonstrations. Swaying in a jar on an adjacent grave, a cluster of black-eyed susans gazed straight through her. Even the air forcing itself into her lungs exhorted her to admit it. She couldn't bear the thought, much less the reality of living with Fin again.

Kamila fanned herself with a fallen sycamore leaf. "Fin may not be a baseball hero anymore, but there isn't a missus in this patch who'd sit on her hands and watch him go hungry. It's no trouble to cook a little more goulash or bake an extra loaf of bread. Lord knows, you've done as much for other families." With effort, she got to her feet. "Anyway, it's not forever. Anyone who can handle a coal-cutter can certainly learn to boil an egg." Hands on hips, she regarded the weathered crosses. "When Anton's cast comes off, I'll have him give them a good sanding and a fresh coat of paint." She strode out of the cemetery, calling over her shoulder, "Think about what I said."

Clare watched her cross the streetcar tracks and head down First Street. When Agnieszka Cverna, Karol's widow, emerged from the store, Kamila waited for her to catch up. Clare knew that, before they reached Agnieska's gate, Kamila would have her fourth for bridge.

The crows ceased their harangue and circled St. Barbara's steeple. Cicadas hummed. Clare turned to the crosses. "*Vergib mir. Bitte, vergib mir,*" she begged her sons. Forgive me. Please, forgive me. "I acted out of fear, not hate. Only fear." She walked on her knees from one cross to the next. From each, she broke off a chip of gray-white paint and wrapped the chips in her hankie.

She walked home and placed the carefully folded hankie in her handbag. Leaving it on the table, she removed the sack of rice from the pantry. She drew out Trudy's check, along with the five dollar bill that Norah had left like a dare the day she'd departed for Pittsburgh. Grains of rice pattered onto the floor as Clare unfolded the check and stowed it in her purse beside the hankie. If she hurried, she could make it to the Beetown bank before it closed.

In the Western Union Telegraph office, Clare's hand shook so violently that the brief message she'd written was nearly illegible. The clerk, a pretty little redhead like her Katie, went over it word by word, copying it onto a fresh form in a firm hand.

"He won't admit he needs new glasses. We don't want to take a chance on him getting it wrong," the clerk said, lowering her voice as if the bespectacled telegraph operator could possibly hear over the *clack-clack-clack* of his machine. Her kindness brought Clare close to tears, a state she'd teetered on the brink of since leaving the house.

The clerk displayed the neatly copied form. *ARRIVING TOMORROW BY TRAIN. CLARE.*

"Would you like me to put down the time your train gets in?"

"I—I haven't bought my ticket yet," Clare admitted. *Gott in Himmel*, such a simple undertaking, yet she was as incompetent as a child.

The clerk patted her hand. "I'm sure they won't leave you stranded. You're going into Penn Station, right? It might help if you put *morning* or *afternoon* after *tomorrow*."

"Afternoon," Clare said, drawing a deep breath. People rode trains all over the country, morning, noon, and night. She'd never been one of those people, but surely she had sufficient intelligence to get herself from The Hive to Pittsburgh if she had most of a day in which to do it.

"Very good," said the clerk. "Now I need the recipient's address."

"Lockhart Street, number—" Clare hesitated. What if Norah and Trudy had plans after work, perhaps eating supper at Deirdre's? Clare could very well find herself stranded at this Penn Station if nobody read her message. "Can you send a telegram to the Heinz factory?"

The clerk dimpled. "Of course. Full-rate or by mail? Full-rate costs more because it's delivered by a courier."

Clare opened her handbag. It contained money enough for a lifetime of telegrams. "Full-rate," she said, the first words she'd uttered that day with absolute assurance.

Clare was waiting for the elevator when Kamila's daughter Betty crossed the hospital lobby. Betty's lips bristled with bobby pins as she removed her nurse's cap. Clare was surprised that they hadn't encountered each other before. "Better hurry," Betty said, taking the pins from her mouth. "Visiting hours end in ten minutes."

"That's all I need," Clare replied, tucking the newspaper under her arm.

Betty gave her an odd look, then shrugged. "Tell Katie I said hello next time you write."

Clare refrained from saying that she'd deliver the greeting in person.

On Fin's floor, a student nurse met her outside the ward. "I'm sorry, Mrs. Sweeney. We waited as long as we could, but your husband just wouldn't settle down. Dr. Murphy insisted on sedation. I'm afraid you won't have much of a visit. He's pretty groggy now."

"Please don't apologize. I'm quite late today. The doctor did what he thought was best." Clare nearly hugged the dear girl, so earnest and helpful, doing her utmost for a man who didn't notice and probably wouldn't give a damn if he did. "I'll just be a few minutes."

The nurse motioned Clare into the ward, clearly relieved to be spared another scolding. Fin's coarse ravings surely had blistered the girl's ears before Clare had arrived. She made her way past the beds, a few now empty, smiling at Vlade, Alfie, Mike, and the others.

"Shoulda been here an hour ago, missus," said a Lubicic cousin, whose right leg was strung up in a traction like Fin's. "Steamshovel nearly took the roof off with his hollering."

"Good thing the roof here ain't made out of coal," Mike Zoshak added. "We'd all be buried up to our necks again, right, boys?"

The ward erupted in guffaws. Before stepping behind Fin's curtain, Clare regarded the beds and their battered, laughing occupants. Because they had no other prospects, most would return to work in the place that had nearly killed them. They knew this as well as Clare. But though many had been deprived of an arm or a foot, not one had lost his sense of humor. At a time when Clare most needed courage, what truer, finer models could she possibly behold?

When she reached Fin's bed, he labored to lift his head from the pillow. She expected him, groggy or not, to reproach her for tardiness, and he didn't disappoint her. "Where've you been? Out on the town with your girlfriends, leaving me here—" He

367

coughed faintly, his head lolling from side to side. "No heart, that's what you have. No pity."

She placed the *Evening Standard* on his bedside table and said, "That's enough, Finbar Sweeney." His glassy gaze fixed on her as if he had never seen her before. It struck her then that, indeed, he hadn't. The woman standing before him, the woman his absence has allowed her to become was unrecognizable to him. "I'm leaving tomorrow on the train to Pittsburgh, and I'm not coming back."

He blinked and squinted, attempting to clear his vision. His arm slid from beneath the sheet. Pointing a finger at her, he said thickly, "Whad'jou juss say?"

"You have a sickness, Fin, and it has nothing to do with your leg. The drink may eventually kill you, but I'm not willing to die on account of it, too. The doctor says your leg will be all right. You may not be able to do without whiskey, but you can certainly do without me."

"You've no right—" he began, eyelids drooping. He fought to keep them open, to clench his swaying hand into a fist. "Desertin' your—"

Regarding that harmless fist, she felt her voice strengthen. "The only way I can stop you from hurting me is to go away."

His arm dropped onto the sheet. His eyes closed. Had he heard? His chest rose and fell, air rattling in and out. Like his fist, his face had turned slack and uncommonly peaceful. Though no longer the agile, idolized first baseman, he looked years younger. She couldn't help but wonder—had he worked for a company that allowed the union, would their lives have turned out differently?

One thing remained to be said. She bent toward his sleeping face. "*Ich vergebe dir.*" I forgive you.

She had drawn back the curtain when he startled her by shouting, clear as a bell, "You'll burn in hell for this, Clare!"

She didn't look back. "I'll take my chances."

Chapter 53: Norah

"What's a doctor doing in there?" asked a boy, pressing his nose against the bottling plant window. He pointed at a bespectacled man in a white cap, coat, and apron, much like Trudy's test-kitchen uniform. Making a note on his clipboard, the man motioned to an assembly line worker to remove a bottle of ketchup from the conveyor belt. The worker snatched a bottle and placed it in the carton held by a white-uniformed assistant.

"He's the ketchup doctor!" shouted another boy.

Norah raised her voice above the children's laughter. "He's a scientist who makes sure no germs get into the ketchup or anything else we make. He'll take those bottles back to his laboratory and test their purity. Heinz is one of the first American companies to have a department called quality control."

The teacher paced behind her class. "Who can tell me what 'quality' means?" she asked. The children ignored her. She turned to Norah. "If we stand here much longer, they'll be completely hypnotized by all those bottles whizzing past."

"Let's move on," said Norah, whom the children also ignored. As usual, she was running a good ten minutes behind schedule. Children were always captivated by the pipes and funnels, the enormous metal vats, and seemingly endless column of ketchup bottles snaking along swift conveyor belts.

"Pay attention, class!" The teacher hurried to separate two boys, who elbowed each other to claim a spot next to the window.

"Let's go see how pickle jars get their labels," said Norah, making sure to smile. "Do you like pickles?" she asked a little girl, pigtailed and prim like Deirdre's Molly, who stood on tiptoe at the fringe of the group.

The girl ignored her. Holding the naughty boys by their ears, the teacher delivered a spirited scolding. The children closest to the glass discovered that breathing hard produced a patch of steam in which they could print a name or draw a funny face. "No fair!" shouted the little girl, hopping from one foot to the other. "You're fogging up the window!"

Without consulting her watch, Norah knew that she was now at least fifteen minutes behind. And on Thursday, to boot, when it seemed that every school in Pittsburgh dispatched a rambunctious group to tour the factory complex known as The House of 57 Varieties. Clapping her hands, she raised her voice again. "Who wants a prize?"

The little girl pointed down the corridor. "There's the ketchup doctor!"

As the white-coated pair approached, a boy wriggled out of the group. "Mr. Ketchup Doctor, are there germs in those bottles?"

Norah motioned to the teacher. "We need to move on."

The young assistant's crooked smile was a painful reminder of Paul's. "Ketchup doctor—there's a good title for you, Dave." He nudged the man with the clipboard, and the bottles in his carton clanked against each other.

"What happens if germs sneak inside the bottle?" the boy persisted, tapping the assistant's carton. "Does the ketchup turn green?"

"Our quality control scientist needs to get back to his laboratory," said Norah. Averting her eyes from the assistant, she attempted to move the boy out of the way.

"I have a son about your age. He's full of questions, too," said Dr. Ketchup. He bent and tousled the boy's curly hair. His white lab coat strained in the front to accommodate a small paunch. Though he grinned at the boy, the genial expression excluded his dark eyes. Deep wrinkles surrounded them like tiny birds' nests. Were wrinkles, like thick glasses, an emblem of his profession, the inevitable result of hours spent squinting into a microscope? A poor judge of age, Norah decided that his was anywhere from thirty to fifty. His eyes, however, looked as if they belonged to eighty-year-old Grandpap Cverna.

The man straightened up and addressed the group. "Raise your hand if you'd like to see a scientist's laboratory."

Hands shot into the air. "Are you a *mad* scientist?" asked the boy.

The man's grin vanished when he faced Norah. Staring past her shoulder, he asked, "Will an impromptu detour unduly complicate the remainder of your tour schedule?"

Unduly? Was he making fun of her, or was this how scientists talked? At the end of the corridor, she saw her friend Joanne leading another school group. Joanne's face told Norah to gather her charges and get a move on. "Take them anywhere you want," she told the scientist. "As fast as you can."

Turning back to the children, he raised his clipboard like a drum major's baton. "Everyone choose a partner. If you stay together and behave yourselves, the young lady leading your tour will give you a prize at the end. Ready? Set? Follow Dr. Ketchup!"

The children eagerly paired up and, like The Hive's *Figlii di Italia* band members, high-stepped after the scientist and his assistant. "Is it true about a prize?" asked the teacher, bringing up the rear with Norah.

"A pickle pin," Norah replied. Watching the bobbing clipboard, she couldn't help but wonder—were the mad scientist's glasses smudged, or was he being *unduly* sarcastic, referring to her as young?

Norah punched in on Monday morning beneath an unsmiling portrait of President Lincoln. Above the time clocks, the motto etched in the stained glass window seemed to murmur sternly, just like Fr. Kovacs delivering her penance in the confessional. *Temperance and labor are the two real physicians of man.* She returned her time card to its slot and glared at the motto, taking grim pleasure in using her facial muscles for something other than the requisite tour-guide smile. She'd obeyed the priest and departed The Hive, certain she'd be rewarded with a promising new career. She was grateful, of course, when Trudy escorted her from Penn Station directly to the Heinz employment office, where she was hired on the spot. But by the end of her first day, she knew that tour-guiding wasn't a career. It was simply a job, and it paid even less than Wright-Metzler's.

She made her way to the women's dressing room, her face averted from windows overlooking downtown skyscrapers. Pittsburgh's busy sidewalks and elegant department stores lay just across the river, but she had yet to find the energy, much less the time to cross the Sixteenth Street Bridge for anything other than an occasional visit to Deirdre's.

Changing into her uniform, she caught sight of herself in the full-length mirror attached to the adjacent row of lockers. She looked hard at the reflection of the slump-shouldered woman who'd turn thirty in less than a month. As girls dressed and chattered and primped around her, she closed the door of her locker and rested her forehead against it. It wasn't yet eight in the morning, and already she was tired. She no longer wanted to smile and be courteous and helpful. She'd used up that part of herself taking care of Mutti, and switchboard callers devoid of patience, and country club women dithering over kidskin purses. Who could blame her for dreading another day-long parade of disorderly youngsters?

"Look alive, Norah!" someone called.

She sighed and pushed herself away from the locker. Glancing back at the mirror, she made herself smile. She pretended that someone slightly out of focus stood beside her. Someone kind and patient and as different from Paul as Claude Rains was from Jimmy Stewart. Someone who wanted to take care of her.

On Wednesday morning, the mad scientist was inspecting steaming pots in Trudy's test kitchen when Norah and her tour group stopped outside its window. The high school students fidgeted as Norah indicated six people eating soup in the adjoining room. "The employees at that table have been specially selected for their exceptionally developed sense of taste. They sample food created by our test chefs, as well as—"

A boy rapped on the window and shouted, "Can I be on your committee? I skipped breakfast, and I'm starving!"

To the chagrin of their teacher, the boy's classmates closest to the window followed his example, tapping the glass and pointing emphatically at their gaping mouths. Accustomed to tour groups, the tasting committee, like Trudy and the chef she assisted, paid no attention. The scientist, however, looked up from the jar he was filling with pale yellow broth. When he noticed Norah, he frowned and gave an odd little bow. Maintaining her tour-guide smile, she hastened to direct the boisterous students to the auditorium for a lecture about company founder H.J. Heinz. As they departed, she glanced back to check for stragglers. The scientist's attention had not returned to his jar, but remained, disconcertingly, on her.

"I'm sorry we disturbed you," she mouthed, wringing her hands in an exaggerated pantomime of apology. Then, cheeks burning, she committed a tour guide's cardinal sin: running to catch up with the group she'd carelessly allowed to escape.

Norah confessed her transgression to Joanne as they took their seats in the auditorium for the lunch-hour organ concert. After describing the scientist, she asked, "Do you know who he is? I'm afraid he'll report me, letting those kids carry on like that."

"He must be the new bacteriologist," said Joanne, settling back in her seat. "My aunt's a stenographer in quality control. She told me his name, but I can't remember now—Steiner or Steinberg, something Jewish. He's a genius, she said. His office wall is covered with university diplomas."

His eyes are unspeakably sad. These words stalled on the tip of Norah's tongue as her mind wrapped itself around another one. *Jewish.* Was that the source of his sadness? Had he, like Roz, been threatened or attacked by the Klan? "Who told your aunt he was Jew—"

"Shhh!" Joanne nudged her as lights dimmed. "The music's about to start."

Employees from the packaging plant to the president's office filled about a third of the hall's three thousand seats. Shadows claimed the intricately plastered ceiling, inlaid with shiny bits of aluminum. The enormous murals on the balcony walls turned dim. Sonorous chords from the pipe organ flowed around Norah, soothing the headache induced by students clamoring for samples of pickles and spaghetti. How many more were already filing through the visitor's entrance?

She tipped back her head and closed her eyes, sinking into the soft plush seat. Something rustled behind her as a latecomer took a seat. Fleetingly, she wondered if it was Trudy, who never missed a concert. *Turn around*, nagged Norah's conscience. *Ask her if Dr. Genius complained to your boss about those rotten kids.*

Something sharp jabbed her ribs. Music had given way to the hum of conversation as employees filed out of the hall. Glowing chandeliers had transformed the ceiling into a vast field of glitter. "Hurry up, sleepyhead! We've got groups scheduled for the whole afternoon," called Joanne, hurrying toward an exit.

As Norah hauled herself upright, someone tapped her shoulder. *Gott bewahre*, it was the sad-eyed scientist. Hands thrust in his pockets, he rocked back on his heels, the picture of a disgruntled genius. She realized she was wringing her hands, replicating her pathetic performance outside the test kitchen. She hastily clasped them behind her back. "I'm so sorry. I shouldn't have allowed those kids to be so noisy. I promise it won't happen again."

The scientist's eyes sank deeper into his mournful face. "On the contrary, it is you who deserves an apology. I seriously compromised your tour agenda last week by absconding with those little rapscallions for an unscheduled visit to my laboratory. Will you please forgive *me*?" *Me-me-me* echoed throughout the empty auditorium, whose superlative acoustics transformed his question into a taunt.

She stared, taken aback as much by his inflated language as the unexpected apology. Was he mocking her, a genius' sarcastic way of getting even? "It was my fault—I should have tried harder to—" Jesus, Mary, and Joseph, she was wringing her hands again! She gripped the seat back, determined to regain some semblance of poise. "Please excuse me. I've been informed that a number of rapscallions are waiting for their afternoon tours."

Before she could escape, Dr. Genius began to laugh. He *was* mocking her. His sad eyes all but disappeared, obscured by wrinkles and glasses and tears of cruel mirth. He wiped his face with a crumpled white handkerchief yanked from his back pocket. When he offered it to her, she realized to her horror that she had started to cry.

"I must apologize again," he said as she dabbed her cheeks. "I have a—regrettable tendency to become insufferably verbose whenever I'm—" When she returned the handkerchief, he gave a stiff little bow. His face had turned almost as red as the seats' upholstery.

"Are you telling me I deserve to be fired?" Perhaps she did deserve it—for ingratitude, and for her group's bad behavior. *It may be a fine job you're getting, but 'twon't be doing you much good, thinking yourself finer than you are on account of it.* How Pap and June and Carol Ann would laugh if they saw her now, no longer a dressed-to-the-nines career girl, but a uniformed babysitter.

Dr. Genius vigorously shook his head. His glasses slid halfway down his nose. "Miss Sweeney, I assure you, I'm here to impart to you nothing of the kind. I sought you out simply to inquire if you would enjoy—attending a film." He stuffed the handkerchief back into his pocket with one hand and pushed up his glasses with the other. "A movie, I mean. If that's not acceptable, a theat—a play." He thrust out his hand. "My name is David Steinbach. Your cousin Gertrude informed me of yours."

Norah hesitated before shaking his hand. "You didn't complain to my boss?"

"I most assuredly did not."

Another hesitation. "Are you making fun of me, or is this how geniuses talk?"

"I am not making fun of you." Releasing her hand, he thrust his own back into his pocket. "Who described me as a genius?"

"Aren't you?"

"Frankly, I prefer to be known as Dr. Ketchup." He drew himself up. "If I manage to control my vocabulary, would you agree to accompany me to a movie? Before you reply, let me add that I am a widower with an eight-year-old son. And I am a Jew. If you find any of these facts off-putting in the least, please say so, and I'll respectfully withdraw my invitation."

"Aren't you supposed to be leading a tour?" someone called, drawing Norah's attention to the stage. A man dressed in a turn-of-the-century suit arranged a stack of papers on the lectern. She checked her watch. Any minute now, Joanne or another guide would lead a small army of students into the hall for a lecture on Heinz Company history. The lecturer tapped the stage microphone. "Testing, testing," he intoned between bursts of static.

Norah turned back to David Steinbach. He hadn't the girth or the Hungarian accent, but something about him reminded her of Paul Lukas, who'd played Professor Bhaer to Hepburn's Jo March in *Little Women*. "I'm a thirty-year-old spinster," she said. "I grew up in a coal patch."

"Testing, one—two—"

Static poured from the stage, leaving Norah no choice but to shout. "I only have a high school diploma! And I'm a Catholic!" The lecturer chose that moment to switch off his microphone. *Catholic* thundered like the conclusion of a sermon. Surely her cheeks were now even redder than David Steinbach's. Nearly whispering, she added, "I accept your invitation if you don't find *these* facts off-putting."

They both started when a door at the rear of the hall flew open. Flapping a piece of paper, Trudy ran down the aisle. "She's coming!" she cried. "Your mother! Tomorrow, on the afternoon train!"

Chapter 54: Clare

July 26, 1941
Feast of St. Anne, Mother of the Blessed Virgin Mary

At two o'clock in the morning, Clare dragged the last bucket of dirty water out the kitchen door and across the porch. Tipping it onto the grass, she surveyed the inky alley and the dark shadows of her slumbering neighbors' backyards. What would they be saying over their fences by mid-afternoon? Kamila, whose eager tongue surely quivered in her sleep, had agreed to wait until three, when Clare's train left Uniontown for Pittsburgh, before announcing her departure. Despite her fatigue, Clare smiled. She imagined her friend preaching to a rapt congregation of wide-eyed women at the Company store.

Pffft! If I hadn't pestered Clare till she came to her senses, she'd still be sitting in the cemetery. Let me tell you, some people can't see the truth until it bites them on the nose.

Clare returned to the kitchen. Like the rest of the house, it had been swept and scrubbed from floor to ceiling. Freshly washed and pressed curtains hung in windows she'd scraped free of gritty fly specks, then polished with vinegar-soaked newspapers. Each crumb, coaxed from the pantry's dim corners. Each piece of furniture, dusted. Each plate and pot and teaspoon, scoured and set in its proper place. Her sewing box, tucked out of sight.

Though he'd surely cite countless grievances against her, an unkempt house would not be one of them.

Just before sunrise, she donned her church dress and hat. She removed her grandchildren's photos from the kitchen wall. They went into her handbag, along with the hankie-wrapped paint chips and far more money than she'd need for her journey. After all Trudy had done for her and the girls, it would give her such pleasure to place the bills back in her cousin's palm. All but five dollars, which she would return to Norah. There had been no need to purchase a suitcase.

The sky turned pale pink as she proceeded up a sidewalk she'd never traverse again. When the streetcar arrived, a young woman disembarked. She looked around, her eyes as wide as those of a greenhorn seeing a tipple for the first time. Her gaze settled on Clare. "I'm looking for Norah Sweeney's house. Do you know where it is?"

Clare extended her hand. After a moment's hesitation, the girl clasped it. Her gloves had pretty scalloped edges, a detail Norah would appreciate. "I'm Norah's mother. She doesn't live here—"

"I know," the girl said. "I'm her friend, Carol Ann. She said she'd leave me some dresses. I heard about the big accident, so I didn't want to bother you too soon." She nibbled at her lower lip, smudging a tooth with cherry-red lipstick. "I don't suppose you still have them."

The streetcar driver called, "Hey, missus, I gotta schedule to keep. You getting on or not?"

"I'll catch the next one," Clare told him, and the car rattled away. She pointed down First Street. "Fifth house on the left. See? It has two front doors. Ours is on the right. Norah's bedroom is at the top of the stairs. The dresses are hanging in the closet."

"The door isn't locked? I can just walk right in?"

"That's right. There's nobody home." Clare smiled. "I'm traveling to Pittsburgh today. I'll tell Norah that you came by. Go on, dear. There are four dresses, and they're all yours."

"Oh, thank you so much, Mrs. Sweeney!" Carol Ann threw her arms around Clare, knocking her hat askew. "Could you ask Norah to please write to me?"

Clare assured Carol Ann that she would. Adjusting her hat, she watched Norah's friend cross Main Street. *I'm traveling to Pittsburgh today.* How easily she'd said what had taken her far too long to do.

Norah's pretty friend paused by the gate and looked back. Clare nodded and motioned for her to go inside. A ray of sunlight broke over Carol Ann like a shower of gold. She waved and smiled, bright as an angel, sending Clare on her way.

Clare stepped off the train, dizzied by the surging crowd at Penn Station. Smoke hung over the platform, reminding her of the coke yard in its heyday. Engines rumbled. Iron wheels screeched. She was buffeted on all sides by anonymous elbows and glossy valises. Everywhere she looked, she saw dapper businessmen and women in frocks even finer than the ones Roz had given Norah.

Arching over the cacophony, a voice called her name. Insistent and surprised, joyful and exasperated, it drew her across the platform and through an archway of pinkish-brown stone.

She turned in a slow circle beneath the station's enormous rotunda. At the very top was a circular window, its glass elaborately veined with lead. Its center resembled a magnificent star. Hand pressed to the crown of her hat, she tipped her head back and stared at the window until the clouds dissolved, leaving the star a perfect, brilliant shade of blue.

Again, she was summoned—this time, by a chorus of voices. She noticed a gloved hand thrust above the throng. The hand seemed like a compass point to aim for, showing her the way through this buzzing throng of humanity. She turned toward it, training her ears on the sound of that chorus. *Clara, Clara, Clara.*

The crowd parted just enough, and she glimpsed the trio of women. All with outstretched arms and urgent voices, baptizing her, over and over, with the name she could fearlessly reclaim.

Author's Notes

The mines, coal patches, neighboring towns, and cities mentioned in the novel are authentic—with one exception. The Hive, or Heath, and its inhabitants are products of my imagination, which received considerable assistance from my research of Fayette County's coal and coke industry. (Although I tried to keep the plot as faithful as possible to the chronology of historical events from 1929-1941, I've taken occasional liberties with time, place, and circumstance in service to my narrative.)

The H.C. Frick Coke Company was a dominant, longstanding presence in what was known as the Connellsville Coke Region of southwestern Pennsylvania. The success of company founder Henry Clay Frick led to a highly profitable but contentious partnership with Pittsburgh iron and steel baron Andrew Carnegie. In 1883, Carnegie became the coke company's majority shareholder. In 1889, he named Frick chairman of Carnegie Brothers Steel Company. By 1900, Frick controlled some 40 mines and 15,000 coke ovens (approximately half the ovens in southwestern Pennsylvania), whose products fueled Carnegie's steel mills. The following year, Carnegie sold his company to J.P Morgan and Elbert Gary, brokering the largest American industrial merger to date. The result was United States Steel Corporation, the nation's first billion-dollar steel enterprise. H. C. Frick Coke Company's designation as a U.S. Steel subsidiary, its motto ("Safety the First Consideration"), and the quotation from Abraham Lincoln's address were printed on employee pay envelopes.

The Ku Klux Klan, whose members placed company interests over those of miners, was active in the region during the time the novel takes place.

Baseball was wildly popular in mining communities. Competition for the Frick League trophy was spirited; team standings and game recaps were recorded alongside those of major league ball clubs in local newspapers. While reading transcriptions of Frick miners' oral histories, I learned about the peeled-potato trick. Its originator was not mentioned, so I took the liberty of attributing it to Fin.

King Frick's hump was, indeed, required on miners' wagons and inspired "The Hump is on the Wagon," written by M. P. Kane. Fin sings a portion of this song, whose lyrics are included in *"That Little Red Flag," and 85 Other Pungent Poems, with Reminiscences of the Connellsville Coke Region*, 1918.

Company President Thomas Moses' June 1, 1933, announcement of the employee representation plan is authentic, as well as his July 27th statement to the press that company employees had no interest in United Mine Workers representation. Likewise, United Mine Workers president John L. Lewis and local organizers William Feeney, Philip Murray, and Martin Ryan all existed, along with Sheriff Harry Hackney, Major Lynn G. Abrams, and Pennsylvania Governor Gifford Pinchot. The injuries of Wayne Smell and Charles Riggins are documented in local newspaper accounts, but the altercation involving Jack Kukoc is a fictional composite of various incidents of picket-line violence during the '33 strike. Willie Hunt's lynching is also fictional.

H.C. Frick Coke Company successfully resisted unionization until the United States entered World War II.

Deutschtown, on Pittsburgh's North Side, was once home to a large German immigrant population, with many of its late 19th century homes still standing. (While exploring the area, I chose a restored row house on Lockhart Street as Trudy's residence.) The local German Catholic St. Mary's Church, or St. Marienkirche, was saved from the wrecking ball by the Graf family, deconsecrated, and, with the adjoining Benedictine priory, converted to a banquet hall and boutique hotel. During the Depression, church pastor Fr. Lambert Daller was known for his mediation between parishioners and their creditors. What information I was able to gather about him leads me to believe he would have been sympathetic to Katie's situation. Programs in the church's Lyceum, particularly the annual Passion Play, were highly regarded and well attended. According to a *Pittsburgh Post Gazette* article dated March, 13, 1933, Deutschtown's Workingmen's Savings Bank and Trust

Company was, unlike many financial institutions at that time, open for business and, thus, the most likely issuer of Trudy's cashier's check.

La Femme is a fictional construct; Wright-Metzler's and, of course, H. J. Heinz Company are not. Heinz was an industry trailblazer in employee benefits, providing an on-site roof garden and conservatory, lunch-hour dances, organ and band concerts, and a variety of recreational outings and sports clubs for its workers. Free factory tours, popular with tourists and school groups, began in 1899. The Heinz Quality Control Department, one of the first in the nation, had its beginnings in 1912, when bacteriologist Herbert N. Riley was hired. David Steinbach is Riley's fictional successor.

Lastly, there's Drastovic, whose name and vocation were too wonderful to alter and whose activities required no fictional embellishment. Unlike me, this real-life tale-teller believed that facts should never stand in the way of a good story.

Select Bibliography

I gleaned information from too many books, articles, and oral histories to list in detail here, but certain volumes stand out—*Common Lives of Uncommon Strength: The Women of the Coal and Coke Era of Southwestern Pennsylvania 1880-1970* by Evelyn A. Hovanec (editor), 2001, Patch/Work Voices Publishing; *Patch/Work Voices, The Culture and Lore of a Mining People* by Dennis F. Brestensky, Evelyn A. Hovanec, and Albert N. Skomra, 2003, Patch/Work Voices Publishing; *Coal and Coke in Pennsylvania* by Carmen DeCiccio, 1996, Pennsylvania Historical and Museum Commission; *Cloud by Day, The Story of Coal and Coke and People* by Muriel Earley Sheppard, 1974 (second edition 1994), University of Pittsburgh Press; and *Wealth, Waste, and Alienation, Growth and Decline in the Connellsville Coke Industry* by Kenneth Warren, 2001, University of Pittsburgh Press. Also deserving mention are *Three Slovak Women* by Lisa A. Alzo, 2003, Gateway Press, for wonderful details of a traditional Slovak wedding, and *Hoods and Shirts, The Extreme Right in Pennsylvania, 1925-1950* by Philip Jenkins, 1997, The University of North Carolina Press, which shed light on ethnic and religious conflicts in the mining region.

Acknowledgements

I could not have written this book without the gracious and enthusiastic research assistance of Pam Seighman, former curator of the Coal and Coke Heritage Center at Pennsylvania State University's Fayette campus, and that of Elaine Hunchuck DeFrank, the center's oral historian, and co-founder Dr. Evelyn Hovanec. All offered invaluable information about coal patch life and corrected technical errors in the novel's early drafts. Special thanks to Elaine for directing me to the remains of the Youngstown (Stambaugh) coke ovens, which I eagerly explored. Another tip of the hat to Julie M. Porterfield, Pam's successor, who went the extra mile in locating archival photos related to my subject.

I'm also indebted to Mike Dabrishus, who provided detailed coal company police records while serving as University of Pittsburgh Assistant Librarian for Archives and Special Collections. He also gave me a tour of the area once known as Millionaires' Row, where Clayton, H.C. Frick's Pittsburgh mansion-turned-museum, is located. Additional research assistance came from Art Louderback, Chief Librarian at Senator John Heinz History Center library and archives, which afforded information about Pittsburgh's North Side and Deutschtown during the 1920s-30s. John Graf, owner of The Priory Hotel (formerly St. Marienkirche and adjoining Benedictine priory), unearthed a copy of the church's early history, written by Trudy's real-life pastor Fr. Lambert Daller, and invited me to use the hotel's beautiful parlor for reading and note-taking. Thanks, too, to the staff at Pittsburgh's Carnegie Library Pennsylvania Room and Vicki Leonelli, curator of the Uniontown Library Pennsylvania Room, for her assistance in locating newspaper microfiche reels and, with patience and good humor, showing me (repeatedly) how to operate those cantankerous scanners.

I could not have written Part II without the article "The Western Pennsylvania Coal Strike of 1933" by James Pope, Professor of Law and Sidney Reitman Scholar at Rutgers

University School of Law/Newark. I especially appreciate his willingness to track down and send me a copy of the Frick Company's June 1, 1933, announcement of the employee representation plan.

Vielen Dank to my translation helpers: Susan Sisler, Nico Hülsmann, and Hilary Szczepanski (German), Carla Geiger (Italian), Edward Ulicny (Slovak), and the Croatian Consul General's Chicago office. Sandra Cesario, RNC, PhD answered essential questions about the history of gynecology. My parents Edward and Mildred Ulicny and aunts Sr. Cecilia and the late Sr. Mildred McClain shared reminiscences of coal patch life, especially baseball. Hedgebrook and the Writers' Colony at Dairy Hollow provided lengthy residencies that enabled me to write significant portions of the novel. Copious applause for my husband Adam, who held down the fort while I was away.

Writing Clare's story has deepened my admiration for the many courageous women I spoke with as a volunteer advocate for the Houston Area Women's Center Domestic Violence & Information Referral hotline. I can only hope that their difficult journeys resulted, like Clare's, in liberation.

My sister Mo Ulicny of Peach Tree Studio designed a cover more beautiful than I ever imagined. Every author should be so lucky!

Words are inadequate to thank Lou Turner at High Hill Press for her enthusiastic response to this novel and Lonnie Whitaker, who paved the way. Also invaluable were tireless cheerleaders, encouraging me to keep the faith: Chris Hale, Kevin "Mc" McIlvoy, Richard Russo, Debbie Leo, Peggy Landrum, Jean Springer, Charlene Finn, my writers group (Ann Boutté, Carolyn Dahl, Gretchen Havens, Jan Ruffin, Sally Ridgway, Kellye Sanford, and Carol Williamette), and the contagiously creative members of Women in The Visual and Literary Arts (WIVLA).